Sue MacKay lives with her husband in beautiful Marlborough Sounds, with the water on her doorstep and the birds and the trees at her back door. It is the perfect setting to indulge her passions of entertaining friends by cooking them sumptuous meals, drinking fabulous wine, going for hill walks or kayaking around the bay—and, of course, writing stories.

Born and raised just outside Toronto, Ontario, **Amy Ruttan** fled the big city to settle down with the country boy of her dreams. After the birth of her second child, Amy was lucky enough to realise her lifelong dream of becoming a romance author. When she's not furiously typing away at her computer she's mum to three wonderful children, who use her as a personal taxi and chef.

Discover more at millsandboon.co.uk.

A SINGLE DAD TO RESCUE HER

SUE MacKAY

FALLING FOR THE BILLIONAIRE DOC

AMY RUTTAN

MILLS & BOON

Published in Great Britain 2021
by Mills & Boon, an imprint of HarperCollins*Publishers* Ltd,
1 London Bridge Street, London, SE1 9GF

www.harpercollins.co.uk

HarperCollins*Publishers*
1st Floor, Watermarque Building,
Ringsend Road, Dublin 4, Ireland

ISBN: 978-0-263-29771-3

07/21

MIX
Paper from
responsible sources
FSC™ C007454

This book is produced from independently certified FSC™ paper
to ensure responsible forest management.
For more information visit www.harpercollins.co.uk/green.

Printed and bound in Spain
by CPI, Barcelona

A SINGLE DAD
TO RESCUE HER

SUE MacKAY

MILLS & BOON

PROLOGUE

KAYLA JOHNSON COUGHED out a mouthful of snow and forced her eyes open enough to blink into yet more snow. Her arms were jammed against her sides, preventing her from wiping her face clear. What the hell? This was weird. Frightening. She was immobilised, not sure where she was. Scary. What had happened?

Wake up, Kayla. It's a nightmare.

Except her arms didn't move. This was real.

'Help. I—I'm stuck,' she shouted, except it came out as a croak.

How long had she been out for the count? Was she really awake? Or was this truly a nightmare? Trying to move proved she was awake and this was real. Didn't it? Deep breath, pain in her lungs. 'H-help.'

'Hello? Anybody there?' A booming voice cut through the cracking sound of restless snow.

'H-here.' Waving might catch someone's attention, but she needed her arms free for that. The weight holding her immobile felt enormous and expansive. Her legs couldn't move, and from their direction a trickle of pain was making itself known. More damned snow. Her teeth chattered. She was so, so cold. If she ever got out of here she was moving to an island in the sun.

What the hell happened? Slowly it came to her, one

image at a time. She was skiing. Then a deep rumble like an approaching road train. Her feet going from beneath her. Hurtling down the slope, head over boots, head, boots, tossed about like a pebble on the side of the mountain. An avalanche maybe…? All she knew was that she was stuck.

'I'm over here,' she yelled, putting everything into it and managing a little better than the previous croak. Why couldn't she move? If she didn't get someone's attention soon she would be in big trouble. Panic rose. She was helpless, unable to do a thing. Except keep squawking. 'H-help.'

'Hey, I see you.' A dark shape reached her, covered her with a shadow as he blocked out the little sunlight left, chilling her further even as relief rose.

'Hello,' she croaked. *Get me out of here.*

'I'm Jamie.' He looked over his shoulder and waved. 'Over here, guys.' Thankfully he turned back to her. 'There're teams out looking for people caught in the avalanche. How many were with you?'

She thought about it. 'Two. Women from the club.' So it was an avalanche. With the confirmation came the horror of having been thrown about totally out of control and fearing for her life, swamping Kayla as she stared at the giant of a man kneeling beside her. She tried to hang onto his presence and the sense of reality he brought. She wasn't alone any more. Or was this still a nightmare she had yet to wake up from? Or worse. 'I am alive, right? I mean…' Her voice petered out as she began shaking harder. What was wrong? Why *was* she unable to move? She hadn't broken her back, had she? Panic rose. Her mouth dried, her heart banged erratically.

The man locked a strong gaze on her. 'Yes, you are

well and truly alive. What's your name?' He began scooping snow away with his gloved hands.

My name? Think.

She tried to clear her mind with a shake of her head, and a throb started up.

Think. Got it.

'Kayla Johnson. I'm a paramedic.' Like that was of any use right now. She needed a paramedic helping her, not to be one, because that pain was racing now, taking over, beating the cold aside. 'Something's wrong with my legs.' At least her mind had cleared.

'Easy now, Kayla.' A large gloved hand tapped her shoulder. 'First we've got to get you out of the snow and wrapped in a thermal blanket.'

'Don't move me until you've checked me over.' Once a medical brain, always a medical brain. She didn't think her spine was injured or surely she wouldn't be feeling this pain from her legs? But her rescuer had to be careful until she was certain. 'Who are you?' she asked. What had he said his name was? He looked a little familiar. That deep voice also struck a chord. 'Do we know each other?'

'I'm Jamie Gordon. The local fire chief. I do search and rescue in my spare time.' Other people were now working with him to shift the snow. Her saviour took off his gloves and reached for her first freed hand, wrapping it tightly in his strong, warm fingers. 'Are you visiting Queenstown?'

Was she? 'No. I've moved back permanently.' Of course. She had come home three weeks ago to kick-start her life, to put the debilitating sadness behind her and find some of her old zest for living that had died with her husband.

Doing a great job of that, Kayla. This is going to set you further back.

'Kayla? Are you with me?' A deep, tense sound was like sugar to her ears, warmth to her cold.

Opening her eyes, she stared up at a concerned face. 'I think so. My head's thumping and I feel like I'm coming and going.' She understood why he was making her talk; it would help keep her focused.

Jamie nodded. 'You're doing well. I'll check your vitals shortly but first we need to get you out of this snow and warming up. We're nearly done.' Another squeeze of her hand then he withdrew his touch, put his glove back on.

Leaving her feeling alone despite two other people working to free her.

Come back, Jamie. Hold me.

'There's a doctor waiting at the chairlift building for anyone we find. Also a helicopter on standby.' He hadn't gone anywhere.

Relief again filled her. It was great having a man at her side when she was feeling so out of control. She hadn't had that, or allowed that, since Dylan had died. Dylan? Why think about him now? He'd been gone three years, and she was still trying to get back on her feet and move on, but not like this. Was she going to be all right? 'I'm not joining Dylan, am I?' Was Jamie a figment of her imagination? She tensed, squeezing her muscles to see if she was alive. Pain ripped through her legs up into her abdomen, telling her, yes, she was very much alive. Her head swam. Her eyes seemed to roll backwards. Was she dying?

'Kayla. Stay with me.' A deep voice. Jamie What's-His-Name's voice. Nothing like Dylan's. She *was* alive.

Her eyelids were too heavy to lift.

'Kayla.' Sharp now. 'It's Jamie.' Her hand was being squeezed. 'Your rescuer.'

Her eyes refused to open. But she could hear the man, could hold onto his presence by digging in deep to stay with him.

'Come on, Kayla. You can do this. We've lifted you onto the stretcher and wrapped a thermal blanket around you and are carrying the stretcher to the building where there's shelter and a doctor. We're looking after you, Kayla. You're going to be all right.'

That voice was a lifeline giving her strength. Finally she was staring at him.

Thank you.

The words were tangled in the thumping in her head and the need to hold onto the sight of this amazing man stomping through the snow, holding her hand, sharing his warmth while urging her to stay with him as others carried the stretcher. When had they moved her? Had they been careful? How had she missed all that? Concussion, said her medical brain. She preferred not knowing, chose to keep staring at Jamie Whoever and go with his words, 'You're going to be all right.' Except it wasn't true. The pain in her legs was killing her. What did it mean? Fractures? Bad ones? So bad she—

Stop, Kayla. This isn't doing you any good.

True, but what if she had such serious injuries that there'd be no getting past them? Was this life's way of telling her she had no right to want to kick-start things and begin enjoying life again? Should she crawl back into the dark hole and wait for another year to go by?

'Here we are. Now you'll get warm.' Jamie interrupted her fears, slowed them down. 'Doc, this is Kayla Johnson. We had to dig her out of the snow.' He turned away to fill in the details.

She couldn't hear what he said. His quieter tone wasn't getting through the ringing in her ears that had started the moment she'd been brought inside to the warmth. Frustration took over, and she shoved her arm out of the blanket to bump his hip. 'Tell me what's wrong,' she snapped, cringing when it came out as a whimper.

The big man came into focus as he crouched down beside her. 'I'm not a medic of any kind, but you were feeling pain in your legs and they aren't as straight as they should be.' He pulled a glove off and wrapped those comforting fingers around her hand again. 'It's hardly surprising you might've broken a bone or two, Kayla. From a witness's account of the avalanche you copped the worst of the three women in your group and are very lucky to have survived it.' He squeezed gently.

'Keep talking to me.' He anchored her, helped her believe she was alive. 'Was anyone else caught in the avalanche?' She gabbled so he wouldn't leave her, gripping his hand tight, regaining a sense of reality, along with relief at having made it back from the brink of something too horrible to think about.

'Not that we know.' Jamie stood up, still holding her hand. 'But I have to go out for a final check in case there was someone else on the slope we don't know about.' His chest expanded and he looked hard at her. 'You take care and look after yourself, okay?'

Of course he had to leave her. She'd get through this. She had to, without hanging onto his words and deep voice that held her together. 'I'll do my best. Thank you very much for finding me. Thank the others who helped, too.'

'I will. Now, can I have my hand back?'

His smile struck her deep, made her soft inside, and lifted some hope out of the chill shaking her body. It was the first time she'd felt hope in years. Would there be some good to come out of this latest mess she'd got herself into? History said no, while hope said possibly. She'd hang onto that over the coming days, which she suspected weren't going to be too wonderful. The pain in her legs was excruciating and had nothing to do with cold.

'If you have to,' she gasped through clenched teeth. Slowly unbending her fingers, she let her saviour go. 'Bye, Jamie.'

See you around sometime?

CHAPTER ONE

PARKING OUTSIDE THE Queenstown hospital five days later, Jamie stared at the building as though he'd never seen it before. Which was ridiculous. He'd often been here to follow up on people he'd helped rescue from fires or found with the search and rescue team.

Both his boys had had their share of misadventures that'd brought them to hospital, appendicitis for Ryder and a sprained wrist for Callum, to name a couple. But this was the first time he'd come to see a woman who'd touched him in a way he'd only known once before—the day he'd met the mother of his boys.

Rescuing Kayla had been intense. The pain etched in her face. The fear of dying in her eyes. Her demand to make certain her spine wasn't injured before moving her. His need to make her feel safe. Nothing new for the situation.

But Kayla Johnson's fierce grip on his hand as though she'd needed him to be strong for her and had been afraid to let go in case she lost hold of who she was had reached through the darkness that was his broken heart. Her fear mixed with determination that she would be all right had darkened her gaze, and made him aware of something he'd forgotten. The need to be strong and true to himself, no matter what was thrown at him.

That had brought him to this spot today while his brain was saying he was an idiot. What was to be gained by calling in? He wasn't in the market for a woman to share his life after his heart-wrenching divorce. Leanne had been the love of his life and now that he'd finally got back on his feet he wasn't ever opening up to being hurt like that again.

Whoa. He wasn't attracted to Kayla. Not at all. He couldn't be. There'd been a connection on the mountain, sure, but it didn't mean anything deep and serious. She might've woken him up to himself but that's where it ended. He'd visit as he'd done others and get on with his life.

According to her close friend Mallory—the on-duty pilot who had flown Kayla from the mountain to Dunedin—Kayla had been transferred back from the hospital there to Queenstown yesterday to be nearer her home and family. She'd broken both legs, one of them in two places, and suffered a serious concussion. The head injury explained her floating in and out of consciousness, and some of the odd things she'd said, like, 'am I alive,' and something about Dylan and was she joining him. He hadn't asked about any of that, figuring Mallory would tell him to mind his own business.

Really, he shouldn't be needing to visit a woman he didn't know and couldn't forget. The pain in her eyes, her fear, plus the relief and gratitude that had appeared every time he'd taken her frozen hand in his had got to him. It might've been normal for someone in shock, but that instant connection he'd felt made him wonder who she was other than a skier in need of being saved from those freezing temperatures and the dangers caused by the avalanche.

Rushing to help people kept other worrying thoughts

at bay, like were the boys truly happy now. Except he was about to visit Kayla because he actually wanted to get to know her a little bit more. Hold her hand again? Not likely. That would be going too far. She'd likely kick his butt—if her legs were in good working order, which obviously they weren't. This annoying need blindsided him in the middle of the night when he wasn't sleeping. But there was no denying that he really didn't want to drive away now Kayla was just beyond those brick walls.

So get on with it.

Pushing out of the work truck before he overthought his reasons for being here even more, Jamie headed for the main entrance of the hospital.

There was a small gift shop just inside the door with buckets of colourful flowers arranged seductively at the entrance to tempt people to get their money out. 'I'm such a sucker,' Jamie muttered as he strode along to the general ward, a bunch of blue and yellow irises in one hand. What had taken over his usually straightforward mind? Since when did he take flowers when he visited someone he'd helped rescue? Never. But then no one had drawn him in with eyes like Kayla's beguiling ones. She had appeared a kindred spirit—tough, soft, fierce about what she believed in.

That brought about a flicker of longing for a future he'd long put behind him. Where had she returned to Queenstown from? Why? Was she getting away from something that hadn't been good for her? Dylan? Like he had, was she re-establishing herself after being dealt a bad hand?

Pausing when he saw 'Kayla Johnson' scrawled on a whiteboard attached to the wall, he shook his head. Crazy. He wasn't interested in women other than as colleagues. He'd had his woman, loved her to bits and married her for ever. Then she'd done a number on him by leaving and taking their sons with her. At first Leanne had refused to accept they'd share raising the boys, saying his dangerous work kept him too busy to be able to take good care of them.

Winning the battle that had given him shared custody of Ryder and Callum had come at a cost. He'd never trust a woman to be a part of his life again. Certainly not while his sons were young and vulnerable, and probably even after they'd grown up and left home—perhaps sometime after they turned thirty and could fend for themselves. So why was he standing outside Kayla's room? It wasn't too late to leave.

'Looks like you've got another visitor,' said a woman inside the room, giving him no option but to continue his visit.

Ducking through the doorway, he stopped abruptly. Pale with dark shadows staining her upper cheeks, Kayla looked frail, unlike the fighting woman he'd found on the side of the mountain. Sitting in an awkward position, with long, dull blonde hair lying over her shoulders, she looked so uncomfortable he wanted to pick her up and carry her out into the sun that was trying to banish last night's storm clouds.

'Hello, Kayla. I'm Jamie.' She might not remember him when she'd been suffering from shock and a head knock.

She stared at him. 'I remember that steady gaze. It gave me strength to stay on top of what was happening.' Her words were followed with a tight smile.

'Your concussion can't have been too bad, then.' He'd given her strength? Something moved inside his chest. She was giving him a warmth he hadn't known in years. *Knock it off.*

He couldn't afford to get all cosy warm. Kayla might've been beating around in his head for days, but that's where it ended. Apart from this visit, that was. And the flowers in his hand. Too late to leave them outside the door. 'These are for you,' he said stupidly. Who else would they be for? It wasn't as though he could walk out with them for someone else. He looked around for a vase and saw three bouquets lined up on the window-sill in glass jars.

She gasped. 'They're lovely. You've spoilt me.'

Lady, you've only gone and made me glad I did buy the flowers.

'Any time.' Huh? What was with these dumb comments? Kayla must've unhinged him more than he'd realised. It could be because there'd been a steady stream of call-outs over the last week and he was overtired.

'I'll take those and find something to put them in.' The other woman in the room reached out for the bunch he held, her blue scrubs a giveaway to her role.

'Jamie found me.' Kayla watched him as she explained, a tenseness he didn't understand filling her tired eyes. 'He heard my feeble attempts to yell out and came across to start digging away the snow with his hands.'

'Lucky for you.' The nurse nodded at her patient.

'Very.'

'It was a good result.' The only sort he accepted. The bad ones stayed with him too long, destroying sleep while making him go over and over what he'd done and what more he could have tried, even when there had been no chance whatsoever of saving someone from a horrific event. The worst ones also made him more protective of his boys, while at the same time had him teaching them to be strong and take on obstacles so they could become confident and capable. He had become strong and so would his sons. Strength hadn't stopped life's knocks but it had let him survive them.

'What brings you here?' Kayla slowly put aside the e-book she'd been gripping.

'Thought I'd see how you're coming along.' Like he did with others after a rescue. Wasn't that what he was doing? Not in his book, it wasn't. He didn't usually feel sparks in his blood when he looked at a woman's face, or want to persist in learning more about her. All parts of his body and mind were supposed to be on lockdown around women.

Her eyes widened, obviously not missing his discomfort. 'You were very good to me. I appreciate how you talked so I didn't lose focus too much. I must've blacked out towards the end, though.'

Jamie gave in to the need to get closer and pulled up a chair and sat. 'You did. It was probably for the best as it would've been very painful when we shifted you onto the stretcher once we knew you hadn't injured your back. Your toes kept twitching every time I touched them,' he explained hurriedly when doubt entered her expression. Being a paramedic, she'd know they shouldn't move her without first strapping her to a board if there was any doubt about her injuries. Only problem with that theory was that it wasn't always possible. Certainly not when someone was contorted in a snow hole.

'Surprising they moved at all considering the fractures I received.' She shivered.

'Mallory filled me in on your injuries the next day when we were on a search for two little boys.'

'She told me.' Kayla sounded as though that was the last thing she'd wanted.

'She shouldn't have?'

Kayla shrugged. 'Mallory's convinced me to join S

and R when I'm back on my feet. I did go out once before this happened. I'd like to do more, especially after all the help I received.' She was ignoring his question, then.

'We're always looking for people to sign up, especially anyone with medical knowledge. I heard you've started working on the ambulances.' There'd be no getting away from her. His hands tightened, loosened. Why did that not scare the living daylights out of him? He was used to turning away women who tried to get close but this was different. Kayla had sparked an interest in *him*, not the other way around. He shouldn't have come. Should've dug out last summer's fire prevention plans and studied them in depth, even when he already knew them almost word for word.

But there was no denying there had been something about Kayla's tenacity and that vulnerability on the mountainside that had snared his interest and wasn't letting up. She didn't seem like someone who'd change her mind once she'd committed to something—or someone. His hands tightened on his thighs. Neither had Leanne in the beginning.

Forget that at your peril.

When he'd met Leanne they'd clicked instantly. Both had known what it was like to grow up feeling unloved. Her father had been harsh and demanding, nothing she did was good enough, and her mother had never stood up for her because she hadn't been good enough either. His parents didn't have any time for him or his five siblings. He'd asked his mother why she'd had children if she didn't love them. 'I was careless,' she'd told him. Right then he'd determined never to be like his mother or father, and would find love and give so much back. Yet it had still blown up in his face.

Kayla was talking. 'I started at the ambulance base as

an advanced paramedic three weeks ago.' Despair briefly glittered in her gaze as she stared down the bed. 'The doctors say I'll be out of action for up to four months.' A tight smile crept onto her face. 'I intend to prove them wrong. I'm aiming for three. I mightn't be able to climb mountains or go on long searches by then, but I'll be behind the wheel of the ambulance and helping people in need.'

Like he'd thought—strong. Resilient. And at the moment not happy with him for some inexplicable reason. 'Go, you.' And he'd better go before he got too caught up in trying to figure out what her problem was with him. That message can't have got through to his brain, though, because he asked, 'So what brought you back to Queenstown?'

Her mouth went flat. 'It was time to come home.'

He'd gone and put his size elevens in it. 'You grew up here?' he asked, unable to shut up.

'Yep.' She stared at her hands then looked up at him. 'Mallory, Maisie and I have been best mates from our first term at primary school in town. You probably don't know Maisie. She lives in Tauranga but is thinking of coming home early next year if there's a nursing position in the new children's department when it opens. We've all been away, and now one by one we're returning.'

The resignation in her voice finally stopped him from asking any more. She was hurting. So much for cheering her up. A change of subject was required, but he wasn't turning the conversation onto him. Talking about his divorce was not up for grabs and nothing else came to mind so he stood up. 'I'd better get back to the station.' Yeah, needs must, and he needed to get away before he sank further into that troubled golden gaze. 'It's good you're back in town, if not at home yet. I'll drop by again.'

He would?

Shut up, or you'll come up with something utterly stupid, like you're interested in her.

'I'll keep in touch about S and R, and when you're more mobile we'll get you to a meeting.'

'Got a trailer?'

'You're not feeling sorry for yourself, by any chance?'

'Hell, yes,' she growled. 'I'm not used to being physically stuck like this. I suppose I could take up knitting.'

'Make some mittens to replace the gloves you lost in the avalanche?'

'Get out of here.' Kayla paused, then suddenly reached for his hand, squeezed his fingers gently, sending little wake-up prickles down his spine, reminding him of that connection he'd felt—of why he'd come here in the first place.

He shouldn't have come. Tell that to someone who'd believe him. He liked the little he knew of her, wanted more, which went against the lessons the past had taught him.

He'd been out of contact the day Ryder had been admitted to hospital with appendicitis, which had upset Leanne big time. Sure, he'd been gutted not to be there, but it had been two days of hell. As one of almost one hundred firefighters trying to halt a runaway inferno razing homes and bush like a stack of cards in the wind, he'd been focused and exhausted. They'd also lost one of their firemen in a fireball, which had taken some getting over.

Worse, Leanne had begun saying he wasn't guaranteed to always be there for the boys and they needed constancy in their lives. Within a fortnight she'd packed up and moved to a house she'd rented, leaving him with nothing but memories and pain. And anger.

He hadn't seen it coming, had thought they were still

strong despite the arguments they'd begun having over anything and everything. Showed how trusting he'd been. But wasn't love meant to be like that? You'd think he'd know better after his upbringing, but there was always a knot of hope inside him. Always had been. *Always would be?* He was here, wasn't he? Still unsure of everything.

Kayla said, 'Thanks for dropping by. I wondered if I'd dreamed you'd found me or if it was real.' She stared at their joined hands and colour filled her cheeks. Jerking free, she muttered, 'You do exist.'

So she'd thought about him too. Which, with everything else she'd had to contend with, tightened the connection. He'd ignore that. He was going solo. That wouldn't change because he liked Kayla. 'You were a bit woozy.'

You held onto my hand as though you never wanted to let go.

Tighter than she'd just done but equally disconcerting. Holding Kayla's hand, feeling her slim fingers against his palm, was why he hadn't been able to stop thinking about her. That link he'd felt on the mountain was back as though it refused to break. 'Your medical mind was working, making sure we didn't do any damage to your spine.'

'I wondered about that.'

'A right old nag you were.' He forced a laugh, fighting the need to lean in and kiss her cheek. Definitely time to go. A good talking to was required to remind himself why he no longer had anything to do with women intimately, or in any other way outside his work. 'See you again.' He headed for the door and freedom.

'Maybe when I'm fit and healthy, and not appearing so damned useless,' Kayla said in a low voice.

What? Her mood was about feeling vulnerable? He turned back into the room. 'The last thing you are is useless. There's nothing wrong with your mind or most of your body, and your legs will be catching up as soon as possible.' He didn't add that while she looked wan and tired, her face was lovely and her body, what little he could see of it, was attractive. See what one good gesture got him into? Trouble.

'You don't know me well enough to think that.' Annoyance filled Kayla as she watched Jamie return to sit back down beside her bed. She'd been relieved he was heading away. She'd felt awkward and helpless, which made her squirm. It was so unlike her. She was supposed to be done with feeling sorry for herself. To be scared of falling in love again in case it went horribly wrong was one thing, but she could still live with her head held high and get on with making the most of everything else.

Yet Jamie seeing her like this made her feel vulnerable and that was something she never showed, not even to Maisie or Mallory very often. Did this mean he was reaching her in ways no one had since Dylan? She'd smiled and laughed with all her visitors so far, then along comes Jamie and the cracks in that façade started appearing. She'd clung to him on the mountain and now he'd have the wrong impression of her.

Go away, Jamie. You're worrying me. I am not ready to take chances with any man.

Not taking chances? When had she begun thinking she was even interested in him? She hadn't. She was overemotional at the moment. That was the problem. Not the warmth spiralling out of control in her gut.

Stretching those endless jeans-covered legs she just had to gawp at across the carpet, Jamie said, 'As we dug you out of that snow you weren't giving in to the cold or pain, or the fear gripping you. You're one tough lady.'

When he decided to speak his mind, it seemed there was no stopping him.

'You think?' He didn't have a clue.

Jamie's beaming smile might've once made her smile in return but not these days. Not since her husband had died after falling asleep at the wheel while driving home to be with her through her second miscarriage in five months. It was too much just to let go and relax with a man who tickled her bones. Being incapacitated with nothing to do except watch endless movies on her device or work her way through the stack of books people had brought in made her yearn to do something useful. So much for returning to her home town and picking up what had once been a carefree and happy existence where she'd get amongst it on the mountains or as a paramedic and hopefully—finally—put the past behind her. Instead she'd gone and added to the sense of uselessness that had been a constant companion since losing Dylan.

Toughen up, Kayla. Be the woman Jamie says you are.

'There is something you can do for me.'

His eyes widened, but he didn't look at all perturbed that there might be a difficult request coming.

Her mouth split into a—a smile? She doused it. Back to normal. Smiling at men she didn't know well suggested she was trying to get too friendly, and she wasn't, despite the feeling of wanting Jamie to stay around. 'Find me a new pair of legs so I can get off this blasted bed and do something useful, like drive the ambulance or go searching for some idiots who've ignored weather warnings to go for a short hike and ended up in the bush overnight.'

'So you're not an easy patient?' His smile widened. It suited him, and created a warmth in her that expanded to where there'd been nothing but a chill for years, which was shock enough.

'Not at all.'

Stop smiling at me.

Her plans for coming home did not include falling for a man. She'd lost her husband and baby on the same day. No way would she ever risk facing a loss like that again. Far safer to keep her heart locked down. 'Who does enjoy lying around because they *have* to?' Whenever she did manage to drag herself upright to do some laps of the room on crutches as part of her new exercise routine, the leg with the minor break hurt like stink and the other with all its bits of metal in the form of plates and bolts never played nice, instead impaling her with pain and making her stomach ill and her brow sweat.

'I can't imagine you lazing around for any reason. You're full of suppressed energy, itching to get moving. I bet you'll be running on your crutches by the end of the week.' Now he was laughing softly.

Damn him and his smile. 'Of course I will,' she snapped. This was getting ridiculous. Unfortunately she *did* like him. He kept getting under her skin when she knew she had to avoid that. He showed that even if she was laid up, she was still Kayla—who he didn't even know. She knew she was more than the Kayla she'd become over the last three years, if the way she was reacting to him meant anything.

That blasted smile wouldn't go away. Ignoring the way his mouth curved upwards and laughter filled his eyes wasn't working. Did he know he was winding her up? It was a smile, not a hot, sexy 'touch me let's have fun' hint. Was that the reason he got to her? Because he wanted nothing from her? She was always susceptible to a challenge. Damn it. How to tell him to go without sounding mean?

'Where were you living before returning to Queenstown?' His smile had backed off a little, but remained brilliant enough to light up the room.

Or was that her heart? Couldn't be. It wasn't available. Which was plain out of left field. 'Auckland.' She pressed her lips together at the memory of finally leaving behind the city and all the memories of Dylan that had been in the apartment they'd owned near the waterfront, in the local eateries and on the roads they'd run along side by side. If she told him, he'd leave her in peace. 'My husband died three years ago and I finally decided it was time to leave.'

'I'm sorry to hear that. Was that Dylan?'

Her brow creased. How did he know Dylan's name? 'Yes.'

Jamie nodded. 'You mentioned him on the mountain.'

Kayla closed her eyes as cold filled her. Cold from the snow, from the fear, from— 'I thought I was dying.' Her eyes flew open and she stared directly at Jamie. 'Didn't I?'

'Yes, you did for a moment.'

She'd held his hand and everything fell back into place. Another squirm. He'd been there for her and she'd taken it to heart. He was her rescuer, not a man to get wound up about. She started talking to shut down her disappointment. 'I used to be a competitive skier and looked forward to lots of time on the local ski fields.'

'Then one bit you on the backside.'

'It's been a few years since I've done any serious skiing so I probably shouldn't have gone off the main field.' She couldn't stop watching him, held there by a feeling of hope that came with that smile. Hope that she didn't want to acknowledge. 'When my companions suggested giving the more difficult slope a crack I couldn't resist. It never crossed my mind that there would be an avalanche.

But, then, when does nature send out a memo that it's about to disrupt things?'

Talking too much, Kayla.

'You're quite athletic when your legs aren't letting you down?'

Relax.

He was going with the easy option, not about to grill her about the past. 'I run a lot. Used to hike in the hills when I lived in Queenstown before. I hope to get back to that. I'm an outdoor girl through and through.' There were endless numbers of walking tracks in the district and she couldn't wait to put a pack on her back and get out there. 'You're into rescues so does that mean you like hiking in the hills?' Still talking too much. Dragging her eyes away from that strong face, she drew in oxygen and uncurled her fingers.

'When I get time. I like nothing better than a night in a hut in the middle of nowhere, just me and a cold beer, a steak on the fire, and the birds for company. And the mates I go with, of course.'

They had something in common. Her mood lightened a little. 'So you're not a two-minute-noodle hiker?' Many people took instant food packages to save weight in their packs and time cooking over a fire. She always took meat. 'Nothing like the smoky flavour of steak at the end of a hard grunt getting to the hut.'

'I agree. Sometimes I take my sons overnight to a hut that's easy to get to. They enjoy being out in the bush, until they start thinking about ghosts lurking behind the trees.' Jamie suddenly looked shocked and glanced at his watch before standing up. 'I'd better get going. My boys will be waiting at the school gate if I don't get a move on, and then I'll be in trouble.' For the first time there wasn't a smile to be seen.

He hadn't intended to mention he had children? Was he being dishonest by wanting to hide the fact he wasn't alone? Or was there more to his story? 'How old are your boys?'

'Six and seven.' His gaze was fixed on her. 'They keep me busy.'

No mention of a wife or the boys' mother. 'Are you a solo dad?' If she didn't ask she wouldn't know. Did she need to know? No. Did she want to? Yes. Why? Because he interested her, touched her, in ways she wasn't ready for. She shouldn't have asked, because nothing was happening between them. Especially if he already had a family.

'My ex-wife and I share raising them fortnight about, though that's not fixed in concrete with my hours and Leanne sometimes travelling for her work.' He turned towards the door.

There was more to this story. She felt it in the sudden flattening of his voice, the way he rubbed his thumb over the fingertips of his left hand. She understood his need to keep things to himself. Another thing they had in common. 'Jamie.' She hesitated, waiting for him to look back at her. 'Thanks for calling in. I do appreciate it.' When she was being honest with herself.

'I'll keep in touch and let you know when I'm up and about.' He'd probably only been doing his job as second in command at the rescue unit, but he'd broken the boring moments of her day and for that she was grateful. Though not so grateful for him waking her up in unexpected ways. Finding a man who lit her lights was not meant to happen.

'Take care and get back on those feet ASAP, okay?' His smile was back, not as large or enticing, but it was there. And just as warming—if she allowed it. Why was it getting harder to ignore this sense of finding something that had been missing for a long time? These feelings scared her. She knew too well how it could all go wrong in an instant. But it seemed she couldn't help herself. 'I'll do that.' She even managed a small smile of her own.

'Bye.' He was gone.

Leaving her with a sudden sense that he wouldn't be back to see her again. Leaving her feeling flat, let down, and very, very confused. She bashed her pillow with her fist. What a stuff-up.

CHAPTER TWO

'MALLORY, TAKE ME with you,' Kayla begged her friend. 'I'm going spare, doing nothing.' Two months of sitting around feeling useless had driven her insane.

'It's a training event in the hills. You're on crutches. It won't work for you or anyone else.'

'I can observe.' Sitting on her backside in the hills would be a great change from her couch. No doubt she'd be on her own most of the time but breathing fresh air and listening to the birds was way better than sitting in her lounge, which she was heartily sick of.

Mallory grinned. 'You always were stubborn. I'll check if it's okay with Zac.'

Zac was a cop and head of the local search and rescue teams. He'd visited her a couple of times since she'd returned home from hospital, always cheerful and telling her stories of rescues in an attempt to get her interested in joining. He needn't have tried so hard as she fully intended to, but she enjoyed his company so had let him tell his stories.

An hour later they pulled into the grass parking area where a group of search and rescue members were milling around something on the ground. Something or someone? 'Trouble already?' she mused, reaching for her crutches as Mallory braked.

'I'll go find out.'

'Not without me.' Kayla had her door open and the crutches under her arms to heave herself upright.

'Mallory, bring Kayla over here, will you?' Zac called out. 'Robyn's down.'

Swinging her crutches, Kayla made good time, ignoring the jabs of pain whenever she hit uneven ground. 'What happened?' She looked down at the young woman sprawled on her back.

Jamie looked up from where he crouched beside Robyn and stole the breath from her lungs. Those dark brown eyes had held her attention on the mountain, and then again in the hospital, demanding she stay with him. She'd never forgotten the depth of concern shining out at her. Today his eyes appeared to be smiling. 'Hello, you. Robyn was running over the ground, got her foot caught in a hole and tripped. Her left knee's painful and her leg's at an odd angle.'

Kayla smiled back. 'Hi, Jamie.' Then she looked at Robyn. 'Hello, I'm Kayla, a paramedic.' How was she going to get down to examine her? Face plant, then lie on the ground and push up on her elbows?

Robyn grimaced. 'I'm such an idiot. Wasn't looking where I was going.'

'We've all done that.' Kayla glanced at Jamie, and sucked air. How had she forgotten how he made her feel different? Real, alive, ready to take on anything. Except fall in love. That was too risky.

He was watching her, that unnerving smile knocking her hard. 'Tell me what to do from up there.'

Hold me? Take my hand? A fast tapping started up under her ribs. What was it about this guy? Whatever it was, now was not the time to be distracted so she focused on what was necessary, not desirable. 'First, Robyn, tell us where the pain is.'

'All around my knee.'

'Not your ankle?'

'A little, nothing like my knee though.'

'Jamie, can you take the lower part of that trouser leg off?' The trousers were designed to become shorts whenever the wearer wanted. 'Then roll the top half above the knee.'

'Sorry if I hurt you, Robyn.' Jamie carefully unzipped the lower half and then tug it down to her ankle. 'All right to remove her boot?' His eyes sought Kayla's.

'Since there's little pain, yes, but look for swelling. She might've sprained her ankle.' Kayla stood near Jamie. Watching those large, deft hands untie the laces and begin to slide the boot off, her skin felt as though light air was brushing across it, teasing her, drying her mouth. 'Don't tug or you'll pull the whole leg.'

One eyebrow rose as Jamie glanced up at her. 'Sure.' Then he nodded at Robyn's exposed knee. 'What do you think?'

'It's at an odd angle.' The patella wasn't straight. 'Robyn, Jamie's going to touch your knee and see if he can find anything out of order. Is that all right?'

'It's fine. Have you got any painkillers handy?'

Kayla looked around for her friend. 'Mallory, can you grab some tablets out of my bag?' There were plenty there for when her fractures got too much to cope with, and she knew they were all right to give to this woman.

'Sure.' Mallory was already heading to her car.

'Robyn, did you stand up after you fell?'

'I tried to but my knee gave way under me. It was excruciating.'

'Jamie, can you place your fingers on the kneecap,

like this.' She held her hand out, fingers wide. 'Gently try moving it to the left then the right.' She watched closely. 'It's moving.'

'Very little resistance,' he agreed. 'Dislocated?'

'I think so. Robyn, have you ever put your knee out before?'

'No. Is it serious?'

'You'll need some time on crutches and not overdo it with exercise, but dislocations come right fairly quickly. But it's something you'll have to be careful of for years to come. It's not uncommon in younger people, especially females for some reason.'

'What do we do now?' Jamie asked. 'There's a medical kit in Zac's ute.'

Kayla looked for Zac. 'Can we have the pack? I'm presuming there are crêpe bandages to wrap around the knee so when Robyn's being transferred to a vehicle for the ride back to town it won't swing and cause more pain.'

'Onto it. I'll bring the ute alongside.'

When he had the bandage in hand, Jamie asked Kayla, 'How tight? I'm thinking it has to be firm without causing too much pressure.'

'Exactly. You should be able to slide a finger—' though his were larger than most '—underneath when you've finished and feel it holding in place.'

He stared at his hand and smiled. 'Guess I've got some leeway, then.'

A jolt of pure lust hit Kayla. That hand, that smile. Did it to her every time. Unsettled her. Wobbled her carefully held-together equilibrium. Thank goodness for the crutches keeping her upright. Her head felt light, like it was floating. She'd felt the same on the mountain that day but then it had been caused by concussion. She hadn't taken a hit since then, but it felt like it.

Watching Jamie wind the bandage around Robyn's dislocated knee, she held her breath, absorbed in the confidence he showed, and the gentleness. He was a force to be reckoned with, if she let him. She wouldn't, though. Too risky. Anyway, what if he wanted more kids? Chances were she couldn't have any. Two miscarriages made her think that. Then again, he might think two children were enough and she'd love to have her own if at all possible.

He stood up and locked those eyes on her, reminding her why she was here. 'All done. We make a good team, even if I did do all the work.'

Lifting one crutch, she made to jab him in the backside. She stopped. He might get the wrong idea. His boot was more appropriate. 'You'll keep.' Now, there was a thought. Could she spend time getting to know the man who'd managed to stir her blood with a smile? Not likely. She'd lost too much in her life already and wasn't prepared to risk it happening again. Confusion clouded her thinking. Now what?

'I'll hitch a ride back to town in the ambulance. There's nothing much I can do out here, and I've had a break from my four walls.' Coward. Totally. Or another way of putting it, she was trying to save herself from more drama. Not that Jamie had made any advances, nor did she expect him to. But he gave her such a jolt of longing for all the things she'd persuaded herself weren't for her again that she had to get away.

'You could work alongside Zac, co-ordinating the practise rescue. You won't need to be walking for that. We've still got a man out there, waiting to be "found",' Jamie told her.

Glancing over at Zac, she could see how organised he was, and unlikely to need her hanging off every word. And when the rescue was over everyone would likely go to the pub for a beer, no doubt including Jamie. Looking at him, a longing for family and love again filled her. He had children. Did he want a loving partner too? Was she ready for all that? Would it be enough?

'Kayla?' It had been said like he had when trying to get her attention on the mountain. Wake up, it said. Focus. Concentrate.

'I'll go back with Robyn.' Running away from a jolt to her system? From a man who hadn't encouraged her about anything more personal than working together to help a woman who'd dislocated her knee? 'I'll catch up with everyone later in the pub and hear how the training went down. Hopefully better than it started out.'

'See you then.' Jamie strode away to join the team.

'Like him?' Mallory asked from behind her.

Kayla spun around, and gasped as her legs protested. 'How long were you standing there?'

'Long enough.' Her friend grinned. 'Don't go pointing the bone at me. I only want you to be happy.'

'Just because you're bursting with love for Josue.' Mallory deserved to be happy.

So do I.

But she'd take it slowly, make friends before anything else.

'You okay sitting here?' Kayla asked Robyn as they settled at a table in the pub where the S and R guys were relaxing after what had turned out to be a gruelling hike in the hills, looking for their 'lost' colleague.

'Perfect.' When Zac had turned up at the emergency department he'd offered to drop Kayla at the pub and take Robyn home, but Robyn had insisted on going with her after the doctor had dealt with her dislocated knee.

'I'm loaded with painkillers and can't feel a thing. Guess sparkling water is my drink today.'

'I'll get that,' Jamie said from the other side of the room. 'Kayla, what would you like?'

'A lager, thanks.'

And time sitting yacking with you.

It wouldn't happen, though, as everyone was pulling up chairs and cramming around the table, all talking at once. Kayla sank into the warm vibes coming off the hyped-up group. It was great being a part of the team, feeling she belonged despite not having spent much time with S and R yet.

'Here.' Jamie placed her beer on the table and handed Robyn her water before pulling up a chair between them. 'You stayed with Robyn at the hospital?'

She nodded. 'It was a way of filling in time till you all came out of the bush.' And her empty house had not been tempting. 'Her boyfriend's going to pick her up when he finishes work at six.' Why was her skin tightening? Because Jamie was so close? Because she'd been thinking about him a lot and he was here for real?

'How are you getting home?' He nodded at her crutches. 'You're not up to driving yet surely?'

'Not even I would drive like this.' How would she get home? Her eyes met Mallory's on the other side of the table. 'Mal?'

'Jamie can give you a lift.'

Thanks, friend.

They lived four houses apart. Jamie would see through that in a flash. 'My jersey's in your car.' Why was she protesting when there was a longing to have some one-on-one time with a person not mixed up in her life tripping through her?

Jamie cut that idea down. 'I'm not staying long. I have to pick up the boys from their mother's.'

Of course. His family. Drawing a breath, she turned to him with an attempt at a smile. 'That's fine. I'm not stuck for a ride.'

'Good.' He drained his stubbie and stood. 'I'd better get going.'

She got the message. He didn't want to spend time with her. Hadn't he sat beside her? Bought her a drink? 'You've got the boys for the next fortnight?'

'Yes.'

Okay, so he was making his point. Don't talk, don't get cosy. So why had he been friendly in the first place? 'See you around.' Two could play that game. It was a timely reminder she wasn't looking to hook up with anyone.

'Maybe at the next meeting?' he asked, then looked confused.

'I hope so.' She meant it, despite knowing she shouldn't. He did intrigue her with his no-nonsense attitude and obvious need to look out for his boys. She wasn't only thinking about his build and muscles and cheeky smile. They would make good friends. Didn't have to get seriously close. She could remain safe and steady—if only the fluttering didn't start up whenever he was near.

Jamie strode out to his truck, cursing under his breath that he couldn't stay.

Kayla had a way about her that set him wondering what she'd be like in bed, did she prefer steak or fish, was she moving on from her husband's death? He wanted her and he didn't. He could not have her. It would be too risky. He might fall in love and that must not happen.

Leanne had been his soul mate and she had still walked away, which told him not to trust another woman with his heart or his boys'. They'd grabbed the chance to be happy together yet it hadn't been enough. She couldn't say why she'd begun falling out of love with him, only that the day Ryder had gone to hospital and he'd been unavailable had been the last nail in the coffin.

She seemed very happy with David, something he accepted and wished her well about, but he wasn't ready to take the chance himself. Add in that the boys weren't as comfortable with David now he'd married their mother and he knew he couldn't bring someone else new into their lives.

David didn't get involved with the boys as he had in the early days, almost as if he'd been using them to win Leanne over and now he didn't need to. Callum and Ryder were upset with David's change in attitude towards them, and that made Jamie cross. Another thing to watch out for if he brought a woman into his home.

He'd be broken-hearted for them if that happened. Their insecurities hadn't gone away completely and he wasn't adding to them with anything he chose to do. So he'd got up from the table and walked out of the pub early when all he'd really wanted to do was sit there with Kayla and have a good time. A good move, if a disappointing one.

Kayla wriggled out of the small space in the squashed car, which she'd managed to squeeze her head and shoulders into with difficulty. Another six weeks had dragged past and now she was back at work—and happy. Except for the woman before her. 'We need the Jaws of Life fast. She's unconscious and bleeding.'

'On the way,' a voice she recognised called from the fire truck parked on the other side of the road. A voice that teased her, setting her pulse to 'fast' during nights when her legs were still giving her grief. Jamie Gordon added, 'I got them out just in case.'

Thank goodness for someone using their brain. 'Every second might count on this one,' she informed him and the rest of the fire crew now crowding around the mangled vehicle, which had been driven into a solid tree trunk. At speed, Kayla suspected, given there were no tyre marks on the tarmac and how the bonnet appeared to be hugging the tree.

'Fast and careful.' Jamie sussed out the wreck, indicating where they needed to use the cutting apparatus. 'Is there any other way?'

Kayla stood aside but as close as possible to her patient, and said to her ambulance partner, 'Becca, we need the defib, a collar and the stretcher all ready and waiting the moment she's free.'

'Very soon,' Jamie said over his shoulder without taking his focus off removing the driver's door. A man of few words when necessary.

She liked that. But, then, she liked Jamie, despite having seen very little of him since that moment in the pub when he'd upped and left in a hurry. They'd bumped into each other at the one search and rescue meeting she'd attended since but it had been crowded and busy and not a lot of talking to each other had occurred. She'd known he'd walked away from her with the intention of leaving it at that and he wouldn't be knocking on her door any time soon, and despite the way shock swiped at her when she did see him she'd respected his decision. Whatever his reason, which could even be as simple as he hadn't felt the same connection as she had, it was his to make. Damn it.

Becca placed the defibrillator on the roadside. 'The collar's on the stretcher, which a cop's bringing across.'

'Cool.' It was all hands to the fore, everyone helping where they could. 'The airbag didn't deploy and I'm worried about the woman's ribs as the steering wheel appears to have struck hard and deep. Pneumothorax is a real possibility.'

The sound of screeching metal as the jaws cut through made her shiver and raised goose-bumps on her skin. Stepping forward, she leaned in through the gap the removal of the door had created and held back an oath. 'She wasn't wearing a seat belt.'

'We need to cut the side panel and back door away so you can get her out without too much stress,' Jamie said as he lifted the jaws and began tackling the car again. 'Stand away, Kayla.'

Her teeth were grinding. He was right. If the door frame sprang free as it was cut she didn't want to be in the firing line, but the woman needed her. Fast. Especially if her lungs were punctured. From the little she could see, the woman's breathing was rapid and shallow, backing her suspicion of punctured lungs.

Come on, guys, this is urgent.

Ping. Bang. Screech.

The door frame and back door were cut through, and one of the firemen was hauling them away.

Kayla leapt forward. Pushing in, ignoring her jersey catching on sharp metal, she reached for the woman's arm, which had been flung sideways. The pulse was light but rapid. Too fast, like her breathing. 'Hello? Can you hear me?'

Nothing.

'I'm Kayla. A paramedic. We're going to get you out of here.'

Nothing.

A deep wound on the woman's left temple bled profusely. Kayla drew a breath, began to check the ribs. 'We need to remove the steering wheel, Jamie.'

'Ready when you give us the say-so.'

There was little Kayla could do. When the pressure came off the ribcage, bleeding would start and then she'd be busy. 'Becca, pads I can apply immediately.'

'Here.'

'We'll put on the neck collar before moving her.'

'I've got it ready.'

'Right, let's do this.'

In a short time the firemen had cut through the steering column and were carefully removing the wheel. Kayla hovered with the pads, applying them with pressure the moment there was space to work, all the time watching the woman's breathing, begging her to inhale every time her lungs let air out. 'Don't stop now.'

Becca crouched on the other side of their patient and applied the collar.

'Done. Now we need someone to take her shoulders, you, Becca, take that side. I'll be in here, getting her legs out. How close is the stretcher?'

'Right here,' Jamie answered. 'I'll take her head and shoulders.'

'We need to go fast but carefully. There's a lot of bleeding.' Too much. Kayla checked that the woman's legs were free of the tangled metal. 'On the count. One, two, three.' She strained to lift the woman's dead weight in her stretched arms, gritting her teeth and using all her strength as she helped the others, and the woman was soon out and being lowered onto the stretcher with care. 'Good work, everyone.'

Jamie's hand touched her shoulder, squeezed and lifted away again.

Kayla blinked. He understood how important it was

to her to save this woman. Because it was what she did, who she had been ever since she was a kid and had seen Zac save Maisie after a bee attack that had brought on a severe allergic reaction. That had stuck with her, made her aware how easily people got into trouble, and she always wanted to be the person helping them. Another point in Jamie's favour. They might start adding up to a high number if she wasn't careful.

Tearing the ripped T-shirt wide open, Kayla ran her fingers over the ribcage and tapped. She nodded. 'Hollow sound, indicating a punctured lung. Ribs moving as though fractured, and the gasping, shallow breathing all point to torn lungs. Regardless of other injuries, we need to get straight to the emergency department.'

'Right.' Becca had the heart monitor pads on their patient's chest. 'GCS is two. No reaction to touch, sound or lifting her eyelids.'

'Understandable. There's a lot of trauma. Still no response to sound, movement or the pain.' Kayla noted the odd angle of one arm and deep wounds on both legs, and a memory made her shiver. That pain would be intense. 'Load and go.' No time for anything else when the patient couldn't hold air in her lungs. That took priority over everything else.

A continuous sound emitted from the monitor. A flat line ran along the bottom of the screen. 'Cardiac arrest.' Just what the woman didn't need. Kayla immediately began compressions, not liking what she could feel under her clenched hands.

Becca grabbed the electric pads. 'Here.'

Slapping them in place, Kayla glanced around. 'Stand back, everyone.' She pressed the power knob. Please, please, please.

The woman's body convulsed. The monitor began beeping, the line lifting.

Relief flooded Kayla. 'Watch her head, Becca. Tip it back a little to make breathing easier.'

'Want a hand?' Jamie was beside her.

'We need her on board now. I'll do a full assessment on the way to hospital.'

I am not losing this woman.

Her mantra wasn't always successful, yet she always repeated it in serious situations.

'You need someone to go with you? I can't do much but read the monitor or note down facts as you find them. The guys don't need me here to finish up with the wreckage.' He took one end of the stretcher and moved towards the back of the ambulance with her on the other end and Becca holding the woman's head.

Having Jamie on the short but worrying trip would be a bonus. He always appeared calm. He didn't walk away when people needed him. She wouldn't think about that day at the pub because she hadn't *needed* his company then. But now she might. She didn't know how it was going to go with this patient so an extra pair of hands was a good idea. 'That'd be great,' she replied as she climbed into the ambulance and locked the stretcher wheels in place.

Becca stepped aside for Jamie, then pushed through to the front as someone closed them all in.

'Top speed, Becca,' Kayla instructed. 'Call ED, inform them we have a suspected pneumothorax and other serious injuries.' The medical staff would be geared up, ready to do everything required to save the woman's life.

With lights flashing and the siren shrieking, the ambulance pulled away.

Kayla checked her patient's breathing. 'Still rapid,

short intakes. Lips blue. BP please, Jamie.' She didn't look up as she began intubating her.

As he held a bandage to the woman's head he read the monitor screen. 'Heartbeat's sporadic.'

She glanced up. Swore. 'Bleeding out.' Other than the head wound, she hadn't found an excessive amount of external blood loss but combined with what might be happening in the lung cavity it would all be adding up. 'There could be other internal traumas. The steering wheel made a huge impact and was wide enough to reach her abdomen.' The liver or spleen might've been ruptured. Who knew? She didn't have time to find out. With a final push the tube slipped into place and she turned the oxygen on. 'Now for some fluid.'

'What do you need?' Jamie already had the medical pack at hand.

'Sodium chloride, needle and tube. Everything's in the top left pocket.'

The monitor beeping stopped, replaced by a monotone. Kayla yelled, 'Becca, pull over. We've lost her.' She placed the electric pads on the exposed chest in front of her, jerking sideways as the ambulance lurched off the road and braked.

Jamie grabbed Kayla's arm, held her for a moment while she got her balance. 'You right?' His concerned gaze was fixed on her.

She nodded, watching the monitor and holding her hand over the button that'd give a jolt of current to the woman's lifeless body. 'Stand clear.'

Don't you dare die on me.

Jolt.

Jerk.

The monotone continued. No, no, no.

Her heart in her throat, Kayla said again, 'Stand back.'

Jolt.

Jerk.

Beep, beep, beep.

Phew.

Air rushed across Kayla's lips as she removed the pads. 'Go, Becca.'

Immediately the ambulance was bouncing onto the road and picking up speed.

Lifting the woman's eyelids, Kayla found no response. They weren't out of the mud yet. 'Come on, lady, don't you dare let us down. Hang in there. What's your name?' Not knowing felt impersonal, considering the circumstances.

'The police are trying to find out. They say the registered owner of the car is a male, but they weren't having any luck getting in touch,' Jamie filled her in. 'There didn't appear to be a wallet and cards, or a phone.'

'Maybe she's a tourist.' This was the most popular tourist destination in the country. 'She looks to be in her twenties, though it isn't always easy to tell in these situations.'

'Here.' Jamie handed her the sodium chloride and needle.

Wiping the back of the woman's hand with sanitiser, she tapped the flat vein hard to make inserting the needle easier, slipped it in and attached the tube with the fluid and taped it in place.

'As easy as that.' Jamie smiled. 'You're good.'

A sense of pride filled her. 'I hope so. I've worked hard to be the best.'

'If I ever get into trouble I'd like you to be there to help me.'

As if someone like Jamie would need her, but then again no one knew what was waiting around the corner.

This woman hadn't known she was heading for a tree as she drove. 'Let's hope the need never arises.' She couldn't imagine a man with Jamie's build and strength being laid out, unaware of what was going on around him.

'Just saying.'

Say it as often as you like.

She cut away the woman's shorts to expose severe bruising on both thighs. 'Those'll be from where the bonnet pushed down on her.' Had her femurs been fractured in the impact? Pain nudged Kayla from her own legs. Shoving it away, she looked at the monitor. No change, which was on the side of good but not good enough. They couldn't get to the ED quickly enough.

The ambulance slowed and Becca began backing into the hospital's ambulance bay. 'After we unload I'll take the ambulance next door to the station to clean up and restock while you do what's necessary this end, Kayla.'

'Okay.'

'There's a crowd waiting for us.' The words were barely out of Becca's mouth when the back doors were being opened and helping hands were reaching for the stretcher.

Jamie took the top end to move the stretcher out and then with Becca and two nurses rushed the woman inside.

Kayla followed, filling in Sadie, the doctor on duty, with all the details, and what she thought were the major injuries. 'Her breathing's shallow and rapid, there's a soft area in the ribs on the right and a blue tinge on her lips and face. She's had two cardiac arrests and there's bleeding from wounds and a serious head wound.'

'You focused on her lungs and heart, I take it?'

'Yes.' The life-threatening problems, though who knew about the head injury? It wasn't something she could've dealt with anyway. That required a neurosurgeon, someone not on hand here in Queenstown, so she would have to be sent elsewhere.

'I've given the life flight helicopter lot the heads up that we'll probably need them before the night's out. It depends how quickly we can stabilise the lung problem,' Sadie told her.

Sadie had gone with the diagnosis she'd had Becca call through and believed their patient would be going to a larger hospital further away, which one depending on urgency and theatre requirements. Once again pride filled her. 'That sounds good. Oh, we don't know who she is. The police are onto it, and hopefully will have an answer before you send her off.'

'Great.' Sadie was already focused on their patient and that information seemed to barely register.

Kayla repeated it to a nurse, and then, knowing there was nothing else she could do, headed for the door out into the ambulance bay. She had done her damnedest for the woman and hoped it was enough. But she was in a very bad way and there was no knowing how it would turn out. Now she'd handed over, Kayla felt knackered and her hands were shaking, while her feet were beginning to drag as she walked down the ramp out onto the footpath. Drawing in a lungful of summer night air, she was glad to be alive. A normal feeling after a serious case, she sometimes wondered if she was being selfish or realistic.

'You all right?' A familiar deep voice came from the other side of the drive where Jamie stood, leaning against the hospital wall, his ankles crossed and his hands in his pockets.

'No.' Without hesitation, Kayla changed direction and crossed over, walking right up to him and into the arms suddenly reaching for her, wrapping around her waist to tuck her against his wide chest. She didn't question herself, only knew that she wanted to be close to someone who understood what she'd just gone through in trying to save that woman. Jamie did understand, would've been through many similar traumas as a fireman and a member of the search and rescue squad. 'It was awful.' Calm throughout a trauma situation, she always got wobbly as the adrenalin faded.

'That woman was lucky you were on duty.'

'She's not out of trouble by a long way.' Kayla was glad there were far more qualified people now working on the patient. Under her cheek the fabric of Jamie's shirt was like a comfort blanket; warm and soft. Relief at bringing the woman in still alive washed over her.

'You saved her life—twice. Be kind to yourself.'

'It's hard. I know from when Dylan died what it's like to get that knock on the front door from the police.' It was why she worked so hard to keep up to date on procedures.

Jamie's arms tightened around her. 'That's a bitch.'

Shoving aside her pain, she said quietly, 'I wish we'd had a name for her. It felt impersonal when what I was doing was very personal.' There were no restrictions when it came to saving a person's life but sometimes it still felt as though she was being intrusive.

'Know what you mean.' Jamie's hand was spread across her back, his palm and fingers recognisable, more warmth soaking into her.

She snuggled in closer and stood there, breathing in his scent, soaking up his heat, and just plain breathing. She needed this. She shouldn't be standing here in Jamie's arms, but she was, and liking the strength he lent her. It was as though she was allowed a history and did not have to explain it all in depth. He made her feel, briefly, like she belonged. Yet that had to be blatantly untrue. She put it down to being lonely in the hours she wasn't working.

Coming home hadn't worked out how she'd thought it would. Mallory had Josue, and Maisie still wasn't here. She and Jamie got along whenever they bumped into each other, but neither of them had sought out the other specifically to have time together. A sigh escaped. Just a couple more minutes and then she'd be on her way.

Jamie leaned back to look down at her. 'Kayla? You sure you're okay?'

She looked up into his eyes, which were as focused on her as they'd been on the patient a little while ago, deep and caring. 'Yes, I am.' But she didn't want to leave this safety, this comfort, this place. This man.

Big pools of brown goodness locked on her, coming ever closer, until his mouth was on her cheek, a light kiss on one, then the other.

Her feet were lifting her up closer to his warmth, his understanding. When Jamie's lips brushed her mouth she sighed. And brushed back, banishing more of that loneliness. Obliterating the feeling she'd had since the avalanche. It had taken over her determination to start again, made her feel that she was on the path to nowhere. It had slowed her down and dragged her back into the pool of sadness and worry clouding her future.

Standing this close to Jamie made her yearn for fun and happiness—with someone else, someone new. With him. Jamie. He made her long to kiss him and to be kissed. Her heels slammed down on the pavement. Her body tensed. This was all wrong. It could not happen.

Jamie's firm hands took her shoulders, held her away just enough to break the connection, keeping her upright while her head spun. 'We need to get back to our respective stations. We're on duty.' He stared at her as though boring a message into her.

'You're right.' She didn't get what the message was, other than she needed to move away, head back to work. But why, when she might've found what had been missing for so long? Why not grab Jamie's hand and run away to a place where no explanations were needed, where they could get to know each other, to explore this sudden longing pulsing through her? As much as he clearly didn't, she also didn't want that. Getting hurt again wasn't an option. Locking her eyes on his, she dug deep for air. Why wasn't she feeling relieved that there was a gap between them? A physical *and* a mental one.

'I am.' His smile was soft, gentle and gave her hope that he might've found something he'd also been missing.

'See you around?' She hadn't meant to ask.

The smile slipped off his lips. 'So far we've mostly only met at accident scenes.'

'We can change that.' Where had this sudden desire to spend time with him come from? Hadn't she started backing off from kissing him at the same moment he'd held her away? She wasn't getting into a relationship, be it a fling or a one-night stand, or the whole caboodle. Jamie did make her feel more like the old confident, happy Kayla when he was near. He drove away the sadness she'd carried for too long. She was beginning to think there might be a chance at a future of some sort. But it was too soon, if it happened at all.

'Kayla,' Jamie interrupted. 'I'm sorry. I can't follow up on more than as a colleague. Not saying you don't push my buttons. I'm saying I'm not in the market for a partner. I'm sorry. I shouldn't have held you like that.'

No, you shouldn't have. Then I'd be striding back to the station, totally focused on what's important.

Then his words sank in. He'd made a mistake, and was about to walk away. That hurt when it shouldn't. It had already been obvious he wanted no part of a relationship when he hadn't visited her again in hospital, or phoned through the months of her rehabilitation.

Whenever they did come across each other, she was jolted alive with one glance. Obviously the same didn't go for Jamie. Which made it easier to keep to her decision of not getting involved. Didn't it? She was tough so why not get to know him as a friend? 'You're rushing things. I don't want a relationship either. But we can have a drink together some time.'

He stared at her for a long moment then seemed to make up his mind. 'That sounds good. Now I need to get back to work. Let's hope we don't have any more call-outs tonight like the last one.' He was stepping away, turning towards the fire station a kilometre down the road.

Kayla watched him walking off, knowing he would not be rushing to phone and suggest meeting up somewhere. She should be glad. She wasn't getting caught up in a relationship again. She'd had her chance, the love of her life. It would be greedy to expect a second shot at a happily-ever-after marriage. As for a baby—forget it. Two miscarriages made her think she wasn't meant to be a mother. The thought of another miscarriage also made her feel ill. They took their toll, left her bereft and feeling useless.

But watching those long legs eat up the distance, there was no denying she wanted to spend more time with Jamie. Even as a friend.

Jamie strode away, feeling a heel for wanting to kiss Kayla when she was upset over her patient. He'd let her down. Hell, he'd let himself down. He should've been strong, ignored the need ripping into him as he'd watched her coming out of the emergency department, her shoulders slumped, her body oozing fatigue. It had been hard to keep his distance. She'd got to him more than he'd realised. There were the few memories of talking with her, holding her hand on the mountain, seeing her vulnerability in hospital, her medical confidence.

Tonight she'd been amazing. That woman owed Kayla her life. Those memories rubbed salt into the undeniable fact that he couldn't forget her, and it made him wonder if he was gutless for not taking a chance on a second relationship. Then he'd think of Callum and Ryder and know he was doing the right thing.

He'd kissed Kayla Johnson.

Holding her, breathing in her scent, feeling that soft body against his had turned him on. More difficult to ignore was the need she brought up in him for love. To have a special person in his life—someone to share the ups and downs, laughter and tears, someone to raise his kids with. A fierce need to run back and swing her up into his arms and kiss her senseless while carrying her away to some place where no one or anything could interrupt gripped him. No car accidents, no kids, nothing.

Passion had been missing in his life for so long he'd thought it was gone, but Kayla had woken him up. There was a bounce in his step that'd been missing. And it was all because of Kayla.

She was something else. From the moment he'd found her buried in the snow he'd felt a connection. Nothing large or all-consuming, more like an irritant, always scratching whenever he heard her voice or saw her with a patient. Not often. When their paths crossed he'd deliberately kept his fireman's hat or S and R cap on to remind her—and him—of their places because she got him wound up and starting to question his need to remain single while Dylan and Callum were still young. What the hat hadn't done was quieten the sense she brought with her of gaining something special.

He had to move on from temptation. The boys were finally settled into a smooth routine, having taken a long time to trust their parents to be there for them no matter what was going on between him and Leanne. How would he ever trust a woman to be there for ever? If Leanne could change her mind when they'd found in each other what they'd been searching for all their lives, why would another woman be any different? But Kayla set him alight with a need he couldn't deny. Need he wasn't going to fulfil. He wasn't thinking love stakes here. He had to stay strong and steady, and stick by his guns. He was single and staying that way. He mightn't like it, but that was how it was.

So there, Kayla.

So there, Jamie.

But he'd kissed her. What about a fling? He shook his head at that. A fling with Kayla would not be enough. He knew it in his bones. It went back to that connection the first time he'd held her hand, and knew it would be strong if he ever followed up on it. It might seem ridiculous, but he believed it.

'You need a change of clothes, man.' Ash stood in the doorway of the fire station.

His head shot up and he looked at his friend. 'Didn't know I was here already.'

'Yeah, you looked like you were doing a spot of thinking. What's got you in a twist?'

Nosy bugger. 'Life.'

'Profound.' Ash laughed. 'I'm picking it's either that

horrendous car accident I've heard about from the crew or the paramedic doing her utmost to save the woman's life.'

Like he'd thought, nosy bugger. 'Put the billy on, will you? Tea would be good about now. I'll get out of this gear.' Now that he was in the light he could see the blood smears on his jacket and trousers. 'It was a messy scene.'

'Apparently.' Ash was no longer laughing or even smiling. 'The cops called. The woman's from Germany. She had a fight with her Kiwi boyfriend and drove off in a rage.'

'That never works out well.' He'd seen too many accidents caused by upset drivers. It was why he was so skilled with the Jaws of Life and why it hadn't taken long to release the woman. Sometimes he wondered if he was a fireman or a vehicle dismantler.

He headed for a shower, the need to feel completely clean, to wash away the sights and debris from the accident taking over. There'd be no washing away the memory of Kayla in his arms, her back under his hand, her cheek against his chest, her hands on his waist.

No, it was going to take a whiteout to delete those images. But he had to try.

CHAPTER THREE

'YOU HAVEN'T SAID how your holiday in Rarotonga went,' Kayla said to Becca as they drove towards a dangerous fire where they were required on standby. Jamie had better not be there. Jamie and danger in one thought got her heart beating fast.

'It was great, swimming, eating and drinking. The perfect relaxation after a hectic year. I'd recommend Raro to anyone.'

Kayla laughed. 'I'm happy as a pig in muck, working. I missed this while I was out of action.'

'You need a life, girl.'

I know. The one she had was all right, though the excitement came at a cost. Jamie had been out of sight but not out of mind since that night a few weeks back when he'd held her in his arms while the tension from saving the German woman had slipped away. According to Mallory, he'd been spending more time with his kids over the school holidays. He attended call-outs from home when he was rostered on. It was great how the fire department made it work for him. She'd phoned twice since Christmas but he'd been busy so she'd stayed away, sensing she was somehow intruding on his family life.

'It's good being behind the wheel of this beast. What more do I need?' Kayla nodded at Becca.

'If I have to answer that then you've got a problem.'

'True.' After all those months laid up with broken legs, work made her feel useful and needed, and helped the loneliness. 'Thank you,' she called as a car in front pulled abruptly to the side of the road to let her past. The flashing lights had done their job. 'I hope nobody gets caught in this burning building we're headed for.' She had to voice her worry in the hope it stopped.

'It's an abandoned building beyond the airport, which used to be a hay and implement shed.'

'The smoke must be playing havoc with flights. It's blowing in the direction of the runway.' Billowing black clouds beyond Frankton were unmistakable, enticing nosey townies to drive in the same direction as Kayla, and as fast—legal for her, not so for them. 'Hope there's a police checkpoint before we get to the scene. This lot aren't welcome.'

'I heard the guys talking on the scanner while we were at base. Two squad cars should be there.'

'So the fire crew must want us because they're concerned one of their own might get hurt.' Kayla didn't mind that. It was better than sitting in the station far away, waiting for a call that might not come but if it did it meant one of their own was in trouble. Any of the firefighters getting injured did not bear thinking about.

Was Jamie on duty today? It would be great to see him. She just couldn't seem to get past him. Being held in his arms had made him so much harder to ignore. The way he understood her concerns, his gentleness when he was so big and tough. Lots of things about Jamie had her thinking about him way too often. 'I hope it's not a more dangerous scene than usual.'

Where had this negativity come from? Next she'd have all the fire crew in the back of the ambulance on the way to hospital just to get checked out for the hell of it. It was rare any of them got caught out at a fire. The safety precautions were intense, and from what she'd heard common sense was the first requisite for joining the service under Jamie's watch. No 'he man' antics allowed. Only men and women with his attitude need apply. Strong, focused on what they did, and calm in tense situations.

Yeah, Kayla sighed. Jamie was all of those and more. The times she'd spent with him had had nothing to do with fire—except for the heat he created in her. When he'd retrieved her in her half-buried state with severe injuries, he'd looked after her, made her feel safe, and had given his hand for her to cling to. He was something else. Something she was supposed to ignore, not waste time thinking about. Then they'd kissed when he'd held her, and forget trying to pretend he hadn't pressed her buttons. Impossible.

Becca diverted her with, 'How're your legs doing these days?'

'They're good.' Still hurt like stink at times, but that was to be expected, especially the right one with all the extra steel and nuts and bolts it now contained. 'I'm walking about six k a day, and should be fit enough to go on mountain rescues soon.' The day she'd gone on a rescue before the accident she'd loved being out with the other searchers, doing something exciting and useful. Attending the meeting last month had been a break in the routine of nights at home and catching up with the people she knew through work and from when she'd lived here previously. Especially Jamie. Every time she saw him her spirits lifted, despite the way he remained friendly yet distant.

'Gees, Kayla, don't take it too easy, will you?' Becca was shaking her head. 'We're glad you're back on board the ambulance. We don't need you having more time off due to overdoing the fitness regime.'

'I like to be good to go all the time.' Her head space also needed to be filled with work, medical problems, saving people, being busy. It dispelled some of the loneliness. Those months when she could hardly get around had driven her bonkers, the first weeks when she couldn't do anything and had spent too many hours thinking about the past had made her gloomy. Now she was finally crawling out of that hole of grief brought on by losing Dylan and the baby. At last she believed she'd done the right thing to come back to family and friends and a job she loved despite having been wiped out by an avalanche.

'You push yourself too hard.'

'You reckon?' Becca never hesitated over saying what she thought, and Kayla appreciated that after years of people tiptoeing around her after Dylan had died.

Their marriage had been wonderful. She'd felt loved and special and happy past measure. It had been beyond all her expectations and had tamed her rebellious streak while allowing room to be her own person at the same time. Life without Dylan had been empty. Now she was working at finding a balance. On her own. It was too risky to try for love. The thought of going through all that pain again terrified her.

Growing up, her mother had always expected her to be compliant while her brother, Dean, being a boy, had been allowed to do whatever he'd liked. Kayla had resented that and had gone out of her way to prove she was just as capable as he was, and nothing and nobody could stop her having fun. That attitude had got her into trouble at times but it had also made her strong and focused, which had helped to make her a champion skier.

Yet that strength had disappeared in an instant the night Dylan had died, replaced by despair.

Dylan had been busy with night shifts at the hospital and studying for exams, and she hadn't seen much of him for a few weeks. Then she had begun miscarrying for the second time and he'd dropped everything to rush home to be with her. Except he'd never made it, falling asleep driving on the motorway. His car had crossed two lanes and slammed into the barriers, spun around and been hit by a transporter. He'd never had a chance.

Stop it. Why turn all glum now?

Becca hadn't finished. 'Just go easy, all right?' Then she laughed. 'I'm wasting my breath so if you want a walking partner any time, give me a call. I like getting out of the house and taking in the fresh air. It's my thinking time.'

Kayla shrugged. 'Thinking's the last thing I need.' Do too much of that and Jamie slipped into her head space. Since she'd returned to work he should've been fading from her busy mind. Instead he was there more often.

Becca leaned closer to the windscreen. 'That's one hell of a fire.'

Kayla's heart pumped harder. 'Those firefighters had better not go in where it's too dangerous.' Except they'd do exactly that if they thought someone was inside. The whole idea of going close to an out-of-control fire, let alone inside a burning building, made her break out in a sweat. Each to their own, and fire wasn't hers.

Give her a head-on crash victim any day. They broke her heart and pushed her abilities to save a life, but they did not drag out fear of being devoured by heat and pain. It was one of those phobias that came without reason and had been with her since she was a kid. Her dad used to be very careful, sometimes to the point of paranoia, about their log burner, but that shouldn't have caused this aversion. Maisie reckoned she'd been burned in a previous life, which only made her laugh and had probably been the whole idea behind saying that.

The police had set up a barrier on the corner of the road they were headed for and were already waving her forward.

'Thanks, guys,' Kayla called through her open window, and received friendly smiles in return.

'That one's hot.' Becca twisted to look back the way they'd come. 'Haven't seen him around here before.'

'He's still in diapers.' Kayla laughed. If he was hot, she was so out of date she might as well be old. But it didn't matter, she wasn't looking. 'Here we are.' Backing onto the verge well out of the way, she stopped the engine and undid her safety belt. 'I guess opening up the back's not a good idea with all that smoke.' She leaned forward, forearms crossed on the steering wheel. 'Now we watch and wait.'

Firemen were spread out, their hoses pumping water onto the fire engulfing the massive shed. One member loomed above the rest, wide shoulders in heavy fireproof yellow gear enhancing the picture. Jamie. His face was invisible behind breathing apparatus, but his defined movements spoke of control and power.

He'd dwarfed her hospital room, and out here where the spreading fire and billowing smoke made others appear smaller, he seemed taller, broader than ever. Must be the protective clothing. He was a big man but not huge. He'd been wearing jeans and a dark T-shirt under a thick jacket when he'd visited, clothes that had accentuated his virility.

She sucked air through her gritted teeth. Why remember that four months later? Like it was important?

It wasn't, never had been, and wouldn't be. Yet she was thinking of what he'd been wearing that day and how much space he'd taken up. She tapped her forehead. The doctors had never mentioned that her concussion could suddenly return to wreak havoc with her mind, but something was causing these images to fill her head. That near kiss.

Even weeks later, just remembering it sent heat throughout her body. Jamie hadn't phoned, despite saying he'd be in touch. She obviously hadn't affected him as he had her.

So she could forget noticing how solid he was and get on with why she was here—hopefully to wait out the fire and go back to town without any patients.

'What are they doing?' Becca asked.

'Are they going in?' Kayla's mouth dried. 'This doesn't look good.' She took a big gulp from her water bottle. 'Have they heard something? Surely it's a bit late for someone to be yelling out?' As if they'd hear anything above the roar of flames. She leaned further forward but the scene unfolding at the burning building didn't get any better. 'I'm counting three going in.' Including one large frame. 'That's Jamie on the left.' He shouldn't be putting himself in danger if he had kids to go home to. None of the crew should. Their families came first.

'I think the short one's Kate. No idea who the third person is.'

'They'd better be careful.' She knew Kate and her husband from when she'd lived here before. 'Sometimes it was easier living in Auckland. I hardly knew a soul.' Unable to watch any more, Kayla slipped out of her seat and squeezed through to the back to go over the equipment, even knowing everything was topped up and whatever she might need if they got a patient would be easy to lay hands on. 'Please, please, please, be safe, everyone,' she murmured. 'Jamie, that means you, too.' *Especially you.*

'Trouble. The overhead beams are falling outwards,' Becca called back to her.

So much for pleading for nothing to go wrong. A lot of yelling was happening. She shoved through to the front and stared at the horrific scene, her heart pounding. 'The framework's landed where Jamie and Kate were standing.'

Please, please, please, come out, Jamie, Kate and whoever.

'There, someone's at the edge of the fire.'

Unable to sit still, Kayla shoved her door open and dropped to the ground, grabbing the medical kit before running closer but not so close as to be in danger. She had to know if anyone was injured, had to be as near as possible without getting in the way in case her skills were required urgently. She had to know Jamie was safe.

Why Jamie and not the others? Of course she wanted to know if everyone else was safe. But she *needed* to know about Jamie. Kayla stumbled, righted herself, carried on, ignoring the questions popping up in her head. Jamie was one of the crew. No, he was more. He'd seen her weak and vulnerable. It was hard to forget that.

'Kayla.' Ash waved at her. She now realised he was the other firefighter who had gone in with Jamie and Kate. 'Over here. Jamie's taken a blow. Those beams came down as we were about to go around the other side. Got Jamie fair and square.'

She swerved in Ash's direction, shocked to see a firefighter on the ground at his feet, even when she'd half expected it. A big firefighter gasping for air, his face mask pushed aside, his chest rising and falling as he struggled to breathe. Smoke inhalation. Her knees weakened. Deep breath, straighten up, get on with the job; forget who this was other than a patient. A man she knew got no more help than anyone else because she gave her all, and then some, every time her skills were required. Turning, she yelled, 'Becca, bring the oxygen.'

'I'll help her with anything you need,' Kate, the other firefighter who'd been with Jamie, said.

'Thanks.' Dropping to her knees beside Jamie, ignoring the shaft of pain in her right leg, she said to Ash, 'Get on the other side and help me sit him up. He's got to breathe.' This was a role reversal, her turn to help Jamie, to do all she could for him and make him safe.

'The mask was knocked off when he hit the ground,' Ash told her.

'Jamie, it's Kayla. Did you inhale smoke?'

'A little,' he gasped.

A little was more than enough. 'We need to get your helmet off. I'll be careful but it might hurt. I don't know what we're going to find under there.'

'Do it.'

With Ash's help they eased the helmet away. When Jamie groaned, Kayla's stomach tightened. He must be in agony to make that sound. 'Sorry. I'll get you onto oxygen shortly. That'll help. Ash says you took a hit.' She began to feel his skull for indentations or soft spots.

Cough, gasp, cough.

Jamie nodded slowly.

'Back?'

Nod. Cough.

'Head?'

Cough, nod.

Jamie dropped back. If not for them holding him up, he'd have hit the back of his head on the ground.

'Careful. Here's the oxygen. I'm going to keep you

upright until we've got you attached, then we'll lay you down on your side so I can examine your back. Okay, Jamie?'

You'd better be.

'Yeah.' *Cough.*

'A nod does fine. Save your breath.' Her mouth lifted into a smile of its own accord. Then she saw blood running down the back of his neck from his head and she deflated. 'Becca, get the oxygen happening.'

With her latex-covered hands, Kayla continued checking his skull. 'You've got a cut behind your ear that's bleeding but I can't find any bone damage.' It was the best she could hope for without an MRI scanner on hand and it wasn't her place to order a scan.

Jamie flopped left, then right. The moment the gas was flowing into his throat, they lowered him full length on the grass. He tugged the mouthpiece aside. 'Why do I feel woozy?' *Cough.* 'Like I'm going to faint any minute?'

Placing her hand on the mouthpiece to press it back in place, she asked, 'Did the beam hit you on the head?'

'A glancing blow.'

Really? When something solid had hit him? 'You're possibly concussed. I'm going to examine your back.'

His chest was easing, the oxygen helping so that his breathing wasn't such hard work. Jamie tapped his left shoulder, tried to lift his arm and winced. 'Here.'

'Your shoulder copped it? Are you hurting anywhere else? Lift a finger if yes.'

'No,' he answered. Not very good at following instructions, then.

'Save your breath,' she growled lightly. 'I have to see if there're any obvious injuries elsewhere on your body.' Body. As in Jamie Gordon's body.

Hey, this is a patient. Not a man to get in a fix about.

She wasn't.

Tell that to someone who'll believe you.

'Then we're taking you to hospital.'

No nod this time. Instead he glared at her and took a deep suck of oxygen.

Kayla held up her hand. 'Don't talk.' She might've laughed if she wasn't worried about his condition.

He continued glaring.

'I get the message. You don't want to go, but I'm in charge here. That head wound needs stitches, and you need to be seen by a doctor.' There were some well-honed muscles under her hand as she examined his chest. She pulled away, growled to cover her embarrassment, 'Take a long slow breath.'

Jamie winced when he did as told.

'Pain in your chest?'

He nodded.

'Did you hurt your ribs when you fell?'

His eyes darkened as he gave that thought. 'Don't know.' Then his gaze closed over and his head dropped forward.

Kayla felt certain Jamie was concussed. The left shoulder was slightly out of line, suggesting possible dislocation. Her teeth ground together at the thought of having that put back in place. It wouldn't be a picnic, even for a tough man like Jamie. Heavy sedation would be required, and the sooner she got him to hospital where a doctor could perform the procedure the better. Too long a delay and he might need surgery. 'Becca, how's that pulse?'

'Strong.' The other woman nodded. 'Heart's good.'

No surprise there. Jamie was one tough guy, but having a beam hit him, even a glancing blow, was no easy thing. Reaching for his hand, she gave it a gentle squeeze. 'You're doing great, Jamie.' The relief was immense. She never wanted a patient to suffer, but this one... Even a scratch was too much.

'I'm doing great,' Jamie repeated under his erratic breath. 'Tell that to someone who believes you, Kayla. I've got a raging headache, pain in my shoulder like I've never known, and nothing looks very clear right now.' A freaking beam had wiped him out, and he was doing fine? Had to be something good in there, but he wasn't getting it. He felt like hell. Except for Kayla's hand wrapped around his. Being held like that softened his heart.

'Yeah, you are.' She'd leaned closer, like it was only the two of them in this conversation. 'Hang in there. I'll give you a shot to take the edge off the pain before we put you on the stretcher.'

'I hate admitting this, but bring it on.'

'I won't tell a soul.'

Her smile rolled through him, touching him softly, gentle and understanding. Right now he didn't care that he wasn't interested in getting close to a woman. It wouldn't hurt to bottle her smile so he could take it out during the night ahead and feel a little less uncomfortable and alone. He was surrounded by people intent on helping him, and he felt lonely—except for Kayla. Something was definitely not right, but he didn't have the energy to work through the idea, so he went with it.

'I'll get the stretcher,' Becca said, stepping away.

They weren't alone, despite Kayla making him feel like they were. He watched her dig into the kit and bring out a needle and bottle, saw her draw up a dose and waited for the prick as she injected him. 'You're good at this.' Anything to distract his banging head and maybe earn another smile. He must be in trouble if he was trying to win smiles from the paramedic.

'Had plenty of practice.' There. Another smile.

A man could get to like those. Except he wasn't supposed to be looking for them. Today he could be a bit lax. He was injured and hurting and therefore entitled to some tenderness as long as she didn't think he was a soft touch. 'I bet.' He glanced away from her endearing face, looked beyond to the destruction behind them for distraction. 'What about Kate and Ash? Did they get out without injury?' How selfish could he get? He'd been thinking only about himself. What sort of leader did that make him? Not a good one.

'Relax. They brought you out and, no, they didn't get hit by the beam. Neither did they inhale smoke.'

'They brought me out?' His head was in a bad way if he hadn't realised that. In fact, he couldn't remember being carried out at all. 'My memory's not flash,' he admitted grudgingly. Best to be honest with the medic even when it was Kayla. He didn't want anything worse happening all because he'd been reticent over letting her see he wasn't always strong. It was more important that he get home to the boys than to lie around in a hospital bed so the sooner they were through checking him over the better. 'Is that because of concussion?'

'Possibly.' Kayla nodded. 'But only the doctors can confirm it.'

'Your highly qualified medical opinion is?'

She took a moment to answer, then shrugged and smiled. 'That you've had a hard whack on the head and you're more than likely concussed. That'll mean time off until your mental faculties are up to scratch.'

'Bet that's not a medical phrase found in the textbooks.' How could he be talking like this when his memory was on the blink and he felt as though he was on another planet?

'I'm currently rewriting those.' There was a definite twinkle in the golden eyes watching him. Looking for his reactions to his injuries?

Bet she was. From what he'd seen, she never relaxed on a job. The smoke tasted gross as the air whooshed out of his tight lungs in a wave of relief. He was in good hands. And liking it. He gasped, coughed, then pain struck his chest and shoulder as his muscles tightened. So much for relaxing. It wasn't good for him.

'Careful, Jamie. Your lungs are super sensitive at the moment.'

He closed his eyes, blotting out the sight of a lovely, caring face. But her concern for him got past his eyelids and into his mind, settling in as though it intended to stay for as long as he needed her there. 'I don't need a woman at my side. Not now, not ever.'

'Only till we get you to the emergency department.'

Jamie groaned. He'd said that out loud? She'd think he was ungrateful and trying to shove her away. Wasn't he? Not now he wasn't. Fingers crossed, she'd blame it on the concussion and think he was hallucinating. More fingers crossed that he did have a concussion. Had to blame something for his random mutterings. What he'd said was true, but that didn't mean saying it out loud for everyone to hear. He wasn't that crazy. His head was getting foggy. Foggier. His body felt as though it was bobbing on water. 'Kayla? Where am I?' What was happening?

'It's all right. I'm here.' Her hand touched his. 'You're in shock, and about to be loaded into the ambulance and taken to hospital. I'll be watching you all the way.' She sounded so comforting. Her voice was soft and smooth, not worried something terrible might be happening to him.

He clung to that. Believed her. Trusted her not to tell lies, not to let him down.

He what? Trusted this woman? Something was wrong here. But then he'd had a beam bang his skull. Give it time and everything would be back to normal. Wouldn't it? Something else was nagging at the back of his mind. Something he needed to be doing. Like what? Putting out a fire was beyond him. 'Ash?' he croaked.

'He's gone back to the fire,' Kayla told him. 'Looks like he's taken charge.'

It's what he was trained for. 'Good.'

'Right, let's do this.'

'Do what?' Jamie tugged his eyes open and looked around, saw a trolley coming his way.

'Get you onto the trolley,' Kayla answered.

He shook his head, immediately regretted the movement. 'I can walk,' he muttered.

'You're light-headed, attached to oxygen and a heart monitor. You'll go by trolley.'

'Yes, ma'am.' Kayla was no pushover. He'd been put in his place and given in too easily. Be warned, he thought. This woman was one tough cookie. She was also knowledgeable. His head was pounding fit to bust, and he couldn't see himself carrying his helmet let alone even one piece of the equipment she'd mentioned. So much for being in charge on this job. It seemed he'd handed himself over to Kayla, and she was going against his wishes. Typical woman, and why he stayed clear of them these days. Except she wasn't that bad. Not from what he'd seen so far, but he barely knew her. Neither did he intend to other than working together occasionally in the future.

'Glad you understand,' she retorted.

If not for the slight uplift at the corner of her mouth he'd have believed she was being grumpy with him.

'Guys, help me up onto my feet,' he said to the two cops standing by.

Kayla spun around. 'You are not walking to the ambulance.'

'No, ma'am. But I am standing to sit on the stretcher trolley and save everyone's back trying to lift it from the ground with me on board.' It was the most he'd said since this mess had happened and he ran out of breath on the last words and had to gasp hard at the oxygen mouthpiece while ignoring the glint of 'told you so' in Kayla's eyes.

She was at his side, holding the oxygen tank, making sure he had the mouthpiece in place. 'Slowly, don't gulp or you'll start coughing.' She leaned closer and said quietly enough for no one else to hear, 'Don't ever call me ma'am again.'

Or what? There wasn't enough air in his lungs to talk. Damn it. Even feeling like he'd been run over by the fire truck instead of having ridden in it, there was a certain element of enjoyment tickling him on the inside at this silly game of words with Kayla. For a moment she made him forget the pain enough to think clearly, or clearer than he had been. Or that might be because of the jab she'd given him. For whatever reason, she was good at her job and he was grateful it was her who'd been called out. Speaking of which, 'How's the fire going?'

'It's looking more under control than it was twenty minutes ago,' a cop replied. 'Let's get you upright. Tobin and I will take an arm each and haul you up.'

'Won't be easy.' Tobin grinned. 'He's not exactly a nipper.'

Jamie held his breath, tried to ignore the stabbing pain, and gasped as the world spun. He was about to land exactly where he'd been dragged up from.

'Easy. Breathe slowly.' Kayla was right in front of

him, hand on his arm, eyes watching his every twitch and blink and breath. Calming him. 'That's it. Becca, trolley,' she said over her shoulder.

Slowly the world settled and he didn't feel as though he was about to go face first into the lovely woman before him. He'd flatten her. She might be tall, and strong, but he was taller and far more muscular. The guys manoeuvred him onto the trolley, and he focused on ignoring the pain. Impossible. He was better off looking at Kayla.

'Instead of pushing Jamie across to the ambulance, back the ambulance up to the trolley,' Kayla told Becca. 'That's rough ground to be getting the wheels over and I don't want to damage the trolley.'

Yeah, he knew he was heavy, especially with boots on and all the attached medical gear. 'You'll keep,' he sighed, closing his eyes as his sight blurred. He was getting more tired by the minute, unable to focus on any one thing. His eyes shot open. He looked straight at Kayla. 'Concussion makes you feel woozy, right?' A head injury was the last thing he needed. Then Leanne would be swooping to take the boys away for an untold time. No, she wouldn't. Everything regarding the boys and custody had been resolved.

Remember?

Remembering anything was difficult. Except Kayla and her smiles.

'It can. So can stress.'

Thanks for nothing. 'It has to be that.' Otherwise… Otherwise he mightn't be able to look after the boys for a while. That could never happen. He would not relinquish time with them. It had been a battle to win shared custody, but he and Leanne had finally come to an arrangement and everyone had calmed down to the point the boys could now plan time with their mates and know where they were living from week to week. If he had medical problems that might go down the creek temporarily and he couldn't bear to think of not having Callum and Ryder at home where he could look out for them. He knew Leanne didn't have lots of spare time these days as she was busy working for her new husband.

She always makes time for Ryder and Callum.

True.

Kayla gave him a long, hard look. 'The sooner we get you to hospital the sooner you might have the answers you're looking for.' Understanding underlined that look. She might not know what was bothering him, but she knew something was.

'Come on, mate.' Tobin was on the other side of the stretcher. 'You need help.'

He lay back and let everyone get on with their job of loading him into the ambulance. All he wanted was to fall asleep and wake up feeling normal. 'Fine,' he muttered, and held his breath until the stretcher stopped moving and was locked into place. 'Tell Ash to keep me posted, Tobin.'

'Will do.'

'Not today he won't,' Kayla said as she closed the back of the ambulance. 'I'm going to check your readings again.' She stood beside him, looking at the monitor behind his head. 'Your heart rate's fine.'

'I'd have thought it was going crazy with everything that's happened.' With her standing so close. And the way she thought she could tell him what to do. Any minute now she was going to tell him—

'Don't think so much.'

Exactly. He stared up at the lovely face above him. She'd be wonderful to wake up to every morning. 'Ahh!'

'Jamie? What happened?' Instant worry filled her eyes

and she began looking over his body, which stretched beyond the end of the stretcher.

'Nothing,' he snapped. Hadn't he learned anything over the past few years? A pretty face meant nothing when it came to knowing a person, to understanding what went on behind those enticing looks. Nothing at all.

'Jamie?' Her voice was lower, softer as she watched him and reached for his hand.

'I'm okay,' he answered less abruptly. 'Honest.'

Apart from letting my guard down.

How could he do that? There was more than his heart at stake when he started thinking a woman was lovely. The boys could get hurt again, and he'd sworn that was not happening. Ever. Yet he'd tried to convince Kayla he had no problems by saying, 'Honest'. Convince Kayla or himself? Another unanswerable question to deal with. Or ignore. Or deny.

'You're sure? It's important I know any little problem.'

Not this one you don't. I just had a moment of forgetfulness.

Now he knew how easily he could get sidetracked he'd be more vigilant. Tomorrow he'd be up and about, getting on with life as though nothing had happened. He had to be. The boys were with him this week and they weren't going back to their mother even for a few days because he'd taken a knock on the skull.

CHAPTER FOUR

BECCA DROVE SINCE Kayla was far more qualified to deal with Jamie's condition. Not that Kayla would move aside for someone else to look after Jamie until they reached the emergency department. She wanted to be there for him, to reassure him if he became bewildered or the pain increased or if he got upset at being in this situation. Like he'd been there for her after the avalanche, a lifeline to cling to while wondering if she was alive.

It still felt as though that connection ran between them, not to be severed until he was pronounced fit and healthy. Then he wouldn't need her and everything would return to normal for both of them.

Except she was still creating her new normal by working long hours and taking part in search and rescue. Her new life included wanting to spend time hanging out with a hot man who seemed to see right through her whenever she let her guard down.

The ambulance had never felt as claustrophobic, not even when she'd had two patients in there at one time. Studying the semi-conscious man on the stretcher, Kayla's heart fluttered. He was large, but so had been the guy she and Becca had taken to Invercargill by road on Monday, and she hadn't noticed anything different then. It was Jamie getting to her, making her look beyond where she thought she was with settling down, had her wondering if she should grab him with both hands to see where it led, or to remember Dylan and the ensuing pain when she'd lost him and the last chance of a family. The more she saw of Jamie the easier looking forward, not back, became.

Jamie groaned as he moved his shoulder.

'Try to stay still.'

He didn't open his eyes. Had he heard her?

Watching him made her feel slightly breathless, as though she'd fallen asleep and woken up in a different place with the same patient. It was like she wasn't back to full speed, as though her mind hadn't kept up with her legs on the road back to normal.

'Kayla?'

'Yes, Jamie?'

'I am in an ambulance, right?'

Long-forgotten words hit her. 'I am alive, right?' Jamie had been quick to reassure her then. Reaching for his wrist on the pretext of taking his pulse, she nodded. 'You sure are, only minutes from hospital.' Under her fingers his pulse was strong, and she automatically found herself counting while focusing on the timer to keep from diving into those deep brown eyes now watching her. Melted chocolate came to mind. Soft, creamy and delicious. Except she'd never seen anything creamy about Jamie Gordon. Delicious maybe. Snatching her hand away, she wrote the result in the notes. Normal despite the shock showing in his eyes and speech.

'I don't feel flash.'

Glancing at the heart monitor, Kayla smiled. Technically his heart was fine, but the knock he'd taken might've cracked some ribs, along with the damage to his shoulder and likely concussion. Throw in shock catching up and no wonder he felt bad. Glancing out the window, she saw the hospital coming into view. 'In case you're wanting better service, the emergency department's got way more gadgets to hook you up to, and doctors and nurses and proper beds.'

'In other words, stop moaning.' Jamie gave her a tired smile.

'No, in other words, you *are* doing well and shortly Josue will be giving you all the attention you need.'

'You've been doing that since I was hauled out of the blaze.' He stretched a hand out to tap her arm. 'Thanks.'

'You're welcome, but I'd prefer you didn't get into trouble again.' The strange thing about being an advanced paramedic was that while she loved the work, helping, saving people, she hated it that people had to get hurt for her to use her skills. She continued watching Jamie—how could she not?—looking for any signs of an injury she might not have picked up on, while knowing she had all the bases covered. Even strong men got knocked off their feet and took a bit to get back up and running.

The feeling of wanting to be there for him beyond the door to the emergency department had her looking over her shoulder to see where that had come from. That invisible cord between them tightening? All she saw was the familiar interior of the ambulance, no signs saying she might be getting off track. Good. Everything was normal. Back to watching Jamie. Enjoying the picture before her. Maybe not so normal.

When he closed his eyes he appeared relaxed, but that was probably the painkiller making him drowsy. What would it be like to run her fingers over his square chin covered with dark stubble? Tingling started in her fingertips. Thick black hair was plastered to his forehead. A working man with no frills. Who did he go home to at the end of the day? He'd never mentioned anyone, but why would he? 'Is there someone you want called and told about what's happened?' she asked quietly. They hadn't spoken properly in a while— Did he have a new partner? Her chest tightened.

His eyes snapped open. 'I'll sort it when I've seen Josue.'

Something not right at home? 'You'll probably have to spend a few hours in hospital while they monitor you.' Might as well give him the heads up so he could figure out if he needed to contact anyone. 'They may even want you to stay overnight.'

'Not happening.'

She wasn't getting into an argument. It wasn't her place. A stubborn tilt to his chin suggested he wouldn't take any notice of anything she said anyway. She still wanted to reassure him. 'Everyone will do their best for you. You know how the system works.' He'd also been part of enough rescues to know the people who worked at the small hospital. 'Wait and see what Josue says before getting wound up.'

'And you?'

'And me what?'

'Will you hang around to make sure I'm all right?'

She stared at him. What did he want from her? More than a paramedic? A friend? 'I'm still on duty for…' she glanced at her watch '…another three hours.'

'You might bring someone else into ED.'

He wanted her to look in on him? 'Then I'll come by and annoy you some.'

Becca was backing into the ambulance bay.

'We're here.' Kayla stood up to open the door, feeling a little shaky, not understanding what was behind his request.

Jamie reached for her hand. 'Thanks for everything.'
Worry filled his face, and something else she couldn't read.

'What's up?' She could ask. He was more than a patient. Like her, he was part of the emergency services,
and they all looked out for each other. They didn't all
look at each other with such depth and confusion, though.

His eyes were fixed on her, dark chocolate this time.
'I'm not in control. I hate it.'

'Believe me, I see that all the time. You'll be back
on your feet soon enough and everything will return to
normal.' It hadn't worked like that for her. She'd spent
months frustrated about having little control over her
legs and therefore her mind because it wasn't getting
distracted with work or other people's needs.

The door opened before she could think of anything
encouraging to say. So much for being focused on her
patient's needs. This particular one was tipping her sideways in ways none had before. Since when did any male
upset her focus? She lived a solitary life, and her goals
were simple. Be fit and healthy and help others. Enjoying herself came into that, but dating and having another
relationship didn't. Losing Dylan had been too hard.

'Jamie, what have you done to yourself, *mon ami*?'
Josue was striding towards them.

'I had a fight with a beam.'

'Came off second best by the looks. Kayla, fill me in.'

After running through the notes, she handed them
over and crossed to Jamie, who'd been shifted onto a bed.
'I've got to go.' She didn't want to. 'Another call.' Which
was good or she might've stayed to keep him company;
the ambulance in the bay, the radio on hand. It wasn't
unusual for the ambulance crews here to do that with a
patient they knew with their base close by, but this need
to hang around with Jamie was different. For someone

she'd only ever seen as upright and positive, in command not only of his crews but himself, he looked so forlorn her heart melted. Was he all for show? Did loneliness lie underneath that tough exterior? Another thing they had in common?

'I'll catch up when we bring our next patient in. Okay?'

'Thanks.'

Jamie watched Kayla walk away, already focused on her next job. Her right leg dragged a little, making her limp more pronounced. A couple of times when kneeling beside him on the ground she'd winced like it still hurt. He shouldn't have encouraged her to check up on him later. They weren't becoming best buddies. Or anything else. He'd been trying to stay away from her as much as possible because of how she wound him up with longing. Yet he'd almost begged her to see him if she was in the ED.

At the last S and R meeting before Christmas he'd overheard her telling Zac it must've taken someone with an engineering degree to put together all the metal she was carrying now. The way she'd described it he'd pictured welding gear and metal cutters and had laughed. Which apparently had been her point, because Zac had laughed too. But today not once had she faltered or given in to the pain.

She'd been there for her patient, focused entirely on *him* and finding out what his injuries were, on helping him through *his* pain and getting him to hospital. Doing her job more than well. Putting her own problems aside. Holding his hand when he'd been losing focus. That soft, warm hand did wonders to his beleaguered mind.

She'd gone up a long way in his estimation, and she'd been fairly high up already for her competence with the German woman who was now on a long but steady path to recovery. Nor had he forgotten the quiet way Kayla had dealt with her injuries and fears when she'd been airlifted off the mountain after the avalanche. Yes, she was one strong woman.

It was hard to describe this wonder he felt around Kayla. It had started at the avalanche rescue and had stuck with him ever since. She brought sunshine into his world even when he wasn't aware of needing it. His life had been cruising along in a bit of a rut since Leanne had given him some space to get on with raising the boys, but the sense of having something to look forward to whenever Kayla was around wouldn't quieten.

As though he might be able to take another look at his world and chance a crack at a future he hadn't imagined in a long time. 'Might' being the word. It wasn't going to happen. His sons came first, first and only first. Never again were they going to be pulled in all directions as the adults in their lives fought their battles. Hence staying away from Kayla as often as possible. It hadn't been easy, but necessary. He didn't need the distraction of worrying about her getting between him and the boys if they fell out. But— But a lot of things.

'I'll check that head wound, then your shoulder and chest.' Josue stood above him, about to poke at his pain-racked body.

The drug Kayla had given him was wearing a little thin, but he'd been moved around a few times since she'd jabbed him so the pain level might've increased. Or he was a big wuss.

He was grateful Josue had cut through the meanderings of his brain and shoved Kayla aside. He wasn't meant to be thinking about a woman and his future in one sentence. 'Let's get it over with. I've got to collect my boys.'

'Slow down, *mon ami*. You won't be driving anywhere collecting anybody today.'

Everyone around here was beginning to learn a few words of French now that Josue was a permanent fixture in their midst, but Jamie hadn't learned the words for what he wanted to say so he went for something less expressive. 'You don't understand. I have to be home for Callum and Ryder.' All hell might break loose. It definitely would've once, maybe not now. Leanne had calmed down a lot and they were now getting on a lot better when it came to the boys, but he still held his breath whenever something out of the ordinary occurred. Old lessons weren't easy to forget.

'First things first,' Josue said, snapping on gloves.

Good idea. The sooner he got the all clear the sooner he'd be heading home. His neighbour and good friend, Christine, would pick the boys up from the summer school where they were learning outdoor skills, but he'd given his word he wouldn't be late tonight as she and Jack were going out for dinner for her birthday with their family. Damn, he'd forgotten to tell the boys where their gift for her was. He was slipping. Forgetfulness didn't used to be one of his problems. 'Is forgetfulness a known disorder? And, no, I haven't got dementia.'

'Concussion can make you forgetful for a while.'

He'd forgotten the present before he'd been hit over the head. Jamie gasped as Josue's finger found a tender spot on the back of his skull.

'Sorry, it might hurt as I assess your injuries. I'll try not to cause too much discomfort.'

'Do what you have to.' Jamie lay still, closed his eyes and tried to conjure up something a little more enjoyable than prodding fingers and damaged bones. Kayla slipped in behind his eyelids. That pert mouth when she'd been cross was wearing a soft smile. A smile that he could re-call in a flash. It lightened her face and put sparkles in her eyes and sucked him in like a puppy to food.

Except he wasn't as soft and soppy as a puppy. He wasn't anywhere near as trusting either. Just because those glowing eyes snagged his attention more often than he cared to admit, it didn't mean he was letting her in. There was a steel grill over his heart that would take more than a blow torch to cut through.

If he ever felt he was faltering because Kayla might be moving past his shield then he only had to remember Ryder clinging to his leg and crying that he didn't want to leave and go with Mummy when he'd been prom-ised a week with his dad. That day was etched in his mind. Leanne stamping her feet and hustling the kids into her top-of-the-range, brand-new wagon, yelling at him that he had no right to promise the boys anything. They were crying because they couldn't be there for their dad's birthday.

It had been a horror of an afternoon, and he'd finally backed off because the boys had started getting hysteri-cal. The only way to calm them had been to explain he'd see them in a few days and then they'd have a party, just the three of them. It had been a turning point, though. Since then he and Leanne had worked together for their sons' sakes, and he had the boys two out of every four weeks. It worked for him.

'A nurse will give you more painkillers shortly.' Poke, prod. 'I'm sending you for X-rays. I don't think your skull's fractured, but better to be certain. I suspect some fractured ribs. Your shoulder's badly bruised and might've pulled in the socket so won't move easily for a few days but it's not dislocated.'

'Thanks, Josue. Nothing sounds too bad considering the size of that beam.'

'You might've got off lightly, but no holding fire hoses for a week. No driving until you get the all clear about the concussion.'

'In other words, get a bank teller's job.'

'Or sit at your desk, issuing orders to your staff.' Josue laughed. 'It won't hurt to take a few days off. When was your last break? In the time I've been in Queenstown I've only ever seen you in work attire, on rescues, or at S and R meetings.'

'I took time off over the school holidays.' No denying Josue had a point, though. He did put in a lot of hours at the fire department or with the S and R crowd, practising or doing real jobs when he could, banking time so that when the boys were with him he could step away and let someone else pick up his role temporarily. He hated handing over control but it wasn't as hard as not being with Ryder and Callum. Balance. That's what was missing in his life, and he probably wouldn't find it for a long time to come. Most likely when the kids were adults and able to fend for themselves, and even then he'd be keeping an eye on them.

They were little rascals; adorable and trouble, fun and heartaches. Like most children, from what his mates said about their kids. One day they had him wanting to pull his hair out, the next making him curl up all soft with love as they watched their favourite programme with him. Being a dad was the best thing to ever happen to him, and watch out anyone who got in the way of that, as Leanne had found out when she'd tried to gain full custody. It had taken a while, but he'd finally come to realise she'd had exactly the same fear of losing Callum and Ryder. After that it had all become easier to sort out the divorce details.

A yawn pushed up and out. His body ached with weariness and stabbed with pain. The drug Kayla had given him was definitely wearing off. Kayla. Once again she was in his head. Had she even left? After all this time living alone, why did this particular woman take over his thinking so easily? Why was he thinking about her at all?

She was a head turner. His head was always moving when she was near. He had to see her, get his fill of that open, friendly face, to see her beautiful eyes and those full lips. Hearing her talk in her southern lilt stirred him, as did her light laughter, which didn't come often enough. Though she had laughed on the way in here. Paramedic reassuring her patient, or had she been so relaxed with him that she'd been a friend as well?

'I'm giving you an injection before taking you to Radiology.'

Where had Damian come from? 'How long have I been here?' he asked the nurse.

'About thirty minutes. You haven't asked for anyone to be notified you're here. Can I get that sorted while you're having your X-rays?'

He shook his head and immediately regretted it. 'No.'

'You sure?'

Which bit of no didn't he understand? 'Yes.' His head was floating again. Was this normal for concussion? Where was Kayla? She'd know. She'd probably already told him but his memory failed him. As long as he got past this concussion sooner rather than later because he had to get out of here before six o'clock. 'What's the time?'

'Three thirty.'

He yielded to the drowsiness engulfing him. He still had plenty of time to get home to the boys.

Kayla stepped into the ED and looked around for Jamie. She should've gone straight home after finishing her shift but, hey, she was here now. Nothing to do with the fact that Jamie had been front of mind whenever she hadn't been with a patient.

When she and Becca had brought John Baxter in, Jamie had been having X-rays and Josue was busy, so she hadn't learned anything more about his condition. There was no way she could head home without seeing if there was anything Jamie needed, though she fully expected someone to be here for him by now. He did have a family, right? It wasn't her role, but there'd been that moment in the ambulance when he'd looked as though he'd been about to ask something of her, as if he didn't have anyone else to ask. She was probably making it all up because of some warped sense of wanting to get closer to him.

Best get out of here. Go home and unwind. Kayla turned for the exit.

'You here to see Jamie?' Josue asked from behind her.

Turning slowly, she looked at Mallory's fiancé, and kept her mouth shut.

'He's in cubicle three. On his own.' Josue's smile was gentle, as though he understood she didn't want to be here when there was little that could keep her away.

'How is he?'

'Very lucky there wasn't more damage. Go see him. I'll be along in a few minutes. There're some things I need to talk to him about and I'd like you there.' He headed away.

She called after him, 'Jamie might not be happy with

that.' What said she was? Josue seemed to expect her to hang around like she had a role in Jamie's life, which couldn't be further from the truth. But Josue knew that so what did he want to raise with Jamie in her presence? It didn't add up. So, was she leaving, then? Going home? She couldn't. Not until she'd seen Jamie. She just had to. No reason.

You sure about that, Kayla?

Most definitely.

A wave of sadness touched her. To have another relationship with a loving man would be wonderful, but highly unlikely. Some people didn't get one go at it. Why would she get a second chance? She was afraid to try again, remember? Even more now she'd met this sexy man. She wouldn't want to hurt him. Or herself.

Josue continued walking away.

Kayla rubbed her right thigh, easing the aches that had throbbed most of the afternoon. Physical pain she could handle, heartache she could not. She'd learned that lesson.

So go home.

She limped into cubicle three.

Jamie took up most of the bed, his eyes closed, his cheeks white, a bandage wound around his head, another around his shoulder, and large bruises coloured most of his exposed upper body where the sheet had been pushed aside. Jamie in his sleep? The concussion, drugs and shock were taking their toll but his underlying strength came through in his steady breathing and his relaxed hands. He'd do fine.

Kayla fought not to reach out and slip her hand into one of his. Her slim fingers would be warm against his, her palm smooth against his rougher skin, but it was the trust in his face, the gentleness on his lips, the strength in his jawline that were drawing her in. As though he had room in his world for someone else. Quite the opposite of the worry she'd witnessed in his face earlier when she'd asked if there was someone she could call for him. What would he say if she climbed onto the bed and stretched alongside him, draped her arm over his waist and held on?

She had to get away. This was all wrong.

Spinning around, she bumped the chair, making a racket loud enough to wake the dead.

'Kayla?' Jamie's voice was deeper than usual, filled with sleep, and well and truly alive.

She could still run. But she didn't do running. 'Hi. Thought I'd see how you're getting on, but you're not much fun, sleeping the afternoon away.'

'What time is it?' He licked his lips as though they were dry.

'It's just after six. Do you want a drink of water?'

'It's what?' He shoved upright, groaned and clutched his head.

'Careful.' Kayla reached for him, held him steady.

'I've got to get out of here. I have to get home for my boys.' He began shuffling his legs off the bed.

'Whoa. Josue's coming to talk to you first.'

'There isn't time.'

'Jamie.' She tapped him. 'Stop this. You've been in an accident. You can't just up and walk out of hospital. Is there someone else who can look after the boys?' She had to get away from the unusual sensations he created in her, but first she'd help him out of his predicament.

'No. Christine's going out.'

So there was another woman in his life. Gulp. 'Does she know you're in here?'

'Yes, but I told her I'd be back by six so she wouldn't miss any of her celebration.'

Christine was going out celebrating something when Jamie was in hospital? Okay, now she was confused.

A shadow fell over the bed. Josue had joined them. 'Lie down, Jamie. I overheard you telling Kayla you're going home. Sorry, but that's not happening when there's no one to keep an eye on you throughout the night.'

'To hell with keeping an eye on me. It's my boys who need looking after, and there's only one person doing that. Me.'

'You think it's all right for a six-year-old and a seven-year-old to take care of their *père* when he's not in good shape?' Josue asked.

'What else am I supposed to do?' Jamie demanded. 'You're saying I can't go home under any circumstances?'

Josue glanced at Kayla.

So did Jamie.

'After receiving a concussion it's important someone's on hand in case you black out or have a fall.' The words were out of her mouth without any thought of where this was headed.

'What are you doing tonight, Kayla?' Josue asked. 'Would you be prepared to spend the night at Jamie's house?'

'You can't ask her that. Take no notice of him, Kayla. I'll ring Ash or someone else from work.' His voice trailed off and he stared at her as though he hadn't meant a single word.

'You sure Christine—' whoever the heck she was '—can't change her plans for the night?'

'Not when she already gives up so much for Callum and Ryder. It's her birthday.'

Wasn't Jamie more important?

He was watching her. A big 'O' appeared on his

mouth. 'She and her husband are neighbours and take care of my lads whenever I can't be there.'

A knot loosened in her chest. Did she want to help Jamie out? Going back to his house and spending the night, keeping an eye on him and his sons, went against all the arguments she'd put up about staying away from involvement of any kind. She was already at odds with herself about Jamie, wanting to get a little closer and terrified of messing it up. Kayla looked from Josue to Jamie, then at her boots.

'Nothing you can't handle, Kayla,' Josue said.

Yes, there was, but she wasn't saying it out loud. 'What are Jamie's injuries?'

'Three cracked ribs, mild smoke inhalation, shoulder bruising, a large cut on his head and mild concussion. It's the last one that I want someone to oversee tonight and as Jamie needs to go home, you're a great option.'

Thanks.

What other options were there? Jamie wasn't rushing to say. What else did she have planned for the night? Not watching movies or serials, for sure. She'd had enough of them. After all Jamie had done for her when he'd rescued her, she didn't want him thinking she wouldn't do the same, despite the warning bells ringing in her head. She went back to appraising Jamie, who had a look of will-she-won't-she in that usually steady gaze. 'I'll take you home.' She stared at him. 'And spend the night at your house.'

The right corner of his mouth lifted in an ironic curve. 'You're sure?'

No. I'm stepping outside my comfort zone.

Being chaperoned by two young boys should mean not a minute alone with their father. Was that a good thing? Showed the mess she was in if she didn't know the answer to that. 'Absolutely. I'll just collect some gear from my locker at the station.' She turned for the exit, glad to be getting away for a few minutes. Fresh air might help settle her mind. 'Unless I get called out as an extra at a major incident,' she added less crisply over her shoulder. A six-car pile-up in the middle of town would certainly be a distraction. Guilt squeezed, taking the air out of her lungs. She'd never forgive herself if there was even a car versus rubbish bin with no injuries now.

Her comment was rewarded with a low, rough laugh, which didn't help her guilt.

Jamie shouldn't be laughing. He was lying on a hospital bed with his shoulder bound tight and a head filled with stitches and drugs to alleviate pain. Only since Josue had declared there were no other serious injuries had the worry begun to quieten in her chest. If Jamie had been hard to ignore before, now it was impossible.

CHAPTER FIVE

JAMIE WRIGGLED HIS BUTT, trying to get comfortable. It wasn't working. His head pounded and other parts of his body were having a grizzle. His bed would be far more comfortable but he'd insisted on the couch so he'd be around while the boys got used to Kayla.

'Ryder, Callum, over here,' he called. So far they hadn't said anything about the bandage around his head or the fact he was laid up. They'd just looked at him with their heads to one side and then at each other and had gone out to the family room, but he recognised the denial in their faces. They'd had to deal with so much in their short lives. They returned to stand staring at him, still not saying a word, which said it all. He longed to hug them, but they'd remain remote until they knew everything was going to be all right. 'Boys, this is Kayla. She's staying the night to keep an eye on me. I've banged my head and hurt my shoulder.'

'How?' Ryder asked.

'At work.' The less they knew the better. He didn't want them stressing every time he walked out the door to go on duty. Since that hideous fire, they'd often heard their mother complaining about how dangerous his job was. 'Nothing serious.'

'What were you doing?' Ryder always asked the questions. When Callum wanted to know something tricky he'd get Ryder to do the interrogation. And, man, could Ryder be persistent.

So could he. 'Listen up, both of you. Remember your manners. Say hello to Kayla.'

'Hi, guys.' Kayla was sitting on the armrest at the end of the couch, looking relaxed except for her fingers rubbing her thighs. There wasn't a wedding ring, but it could be on the gold chain that fell between her breasts, or she might've put it away for good. She was widowed, and there'd been no mention of a child. Didn't she like kids? Or was she just nervous? Kayla?

Try another one, Jamie.

'Hello, Kayla. I'm Ryder.'

'I'm Callum. Are you really looking after Dad?'

Jamie blinked. He looked at Kayla, but she wouldn't understand how unusual that was. Callum was shy around strangers. Seemed Kayla might be an exception. Was that good? His boys were vulnerable, wanted to be loved, then when David had withdrawn from spending time with them they'd become even more cautious. Kayla was only here for the night to keep an eye on him. For them to think she might become a long-term part of his life would be upsetting.

Kayla smiled. 'I work on the ambulance so I know how to look after your dad. When a person gets a bang on his head, it's best someone stays with them for a few hours. Is that all right with you both?'

'Yeah.'

Ryder's eyes lit up. 'Can we have takeaway for dinner?'

'What's your favourite?' Kayla asked before Jamie could.

'Chicken nuggets and chips,' Ryder was quick to reply.

'Hot dogs and chips.' Callum was right behind him.

'Then guess what you're having?' She turned to Jamie and winked. 'No, I'm not trying to score points. Not being the world's best cook, I'm thinking about their stomachs. Anyway, I'm too tired to go digging around your pantry.'

He was getting nervous about how well this was going. Ryder and Callum obviously liked Kayla. What did that mean for their future? 'You could heat up the casserole I prepared last night.' Though right this minute takeaways sounded a good idea even to him. He rarely bought them, and tonight, give him half an hour and he'd be beyond eating anything. All he wanted was to sleep and then wake up ready to get moving.

'No, I'm having chicken nuggets.' Ryder punched the air.

Callum copied the gesture. 'No, I'm having a hot dog.'

Kayla shrugged. 'We'd better keep Dad happy. He's the invalid here. What do you think, Jamie? How about a treat tonight?'

'What's an invalid?'

'Someone useless, lying on a couch while his kids get to choose what they want for dinner.' It took effort to wink at them. 'Go on. Order in something to keep them quiet,' he told Kayla. 'And something for yourself. I'll have a beef burger.' It would probably still be in its box tomorrow morning, but he'd try to get some sustenance on board before he crashed. 'My card's here.'

She leaned towards him, laughter in her voice. 'Behind that gruff exterior lies a softie.'

A warm softie at the moment. Despite the aches and pain forcing everything out of his head, he was comfortable having Kayla in his house and around his boys. They weren't bothered by her presence at all, which was unprecedented. They usually got wound up whenever anyone other than Christine or Jack came over. Progress? Or Kayla's genuine caring nature? 'Don't tell anyone.'

'I won't. What time do these guys go to bed?'

'Nine o'clock.' Callum this time.

Jamie locked one eye on him. 'Really?'

'Um, no.'

'Seven thirty,' he told Kayla, who was holding back a laugh.

'Just after you, then,' she murmured, and stood up. 'Right, boys, I'm phoning out for dinner. Definitely nuggets and hot dogs?'

'Yes,' they shouted, and followed her to the kitchen.

Jamie sank deeper into the couch, closing his eyes but not his ears. The boys were happy, not a hint of wariness around Kayla. That had to be good. Or not, since she wasn't becoming a part of their life. Why not? She was another person not connected to the past they could say hi to if they bumped into her in town. Someone new.

Who are you trying to convince here, Jamie? Why are you trying to persuade yourself Kayla could slot in with the boys when the only way they'd have anything to do with her is if you do?

Did he want that? She was the only woman since Leanne who'd made him feel there might be a reason to start looking forward. Careful. None of this meant he could take notice of how she had his blood heating and a fierce longing stirring where nothing had stirred for ages. At the end of the day he had to protect the kids from any harm whatsoever, and that meant putting them before his own needs. She could as easily upset them as not. Too early to know what she might do.

'Are you dad's girlfriend?' Ryder asked.

Jamie tried to leap up and stride into the kitchen to demand Kayla leave right now, but his body wouldn't play the game. He was stuck in a position that would take some leverage to get out of. Time for a new couch that didn't sag in the middle.

'Me?' Kayla squeaked. 'No.'

Did she have to make it sound as though that was the last thing she wanted? It was a small hit to his ego. Shouldn't have been, but was.

'Dad doesn't have a girlfriend,' Callum said.

Thanks, guys. You're supposed to be on my side here. Keep the family secrets in the family.

Not that there was anything secretive about not having a woman in his life. Everyone who knew anything in this town knew about his divorce.

'Don't you like Dad?' Ryder to the fore. 'He's cool.'

'Ryder,' Jamie bellowed. 'Stop it right now.'

Kayla carried on like he hadn't said a word. 'I've been on a rescue with your dad. He rescued me off a mountain once, so he's really cool. Now, Ryder, you grab the salt and pepper.'

So I'm cool?

Or else Kayla was taking the easy route through the grilling. Jamie's ears strained for more.

'Do you like him?' Persistent Ryder was not taking a jot of notice of him.

'Of course I do.'

'Where do you live?'

'Ryder.' Give that kid a bone and he'll make short work of it every time.

Kayla was handling the questions with ease. 'Up on the hill behind the school. I can see the mountains in the distance.'

'Can we visit some time?'

Kayla laughed. 'Are you always this inquisitive?'

'Yes,' Ryder answered. 'You didn't answer. Can we come to your house?'

'Only if your father agrees. Now, where's the sauce?'

You're not going to sidetrack them that easily. They're taking no notice of me so you might as well settle in for the long haul.

The little blighters seemed to like her. Good or bad? Of course it was good as long as they didn't get too connected. When they accepted someone they tended to leap in and not look sideways. It didn't happen often, so far only with Christine and Jack, and Zac who came round for a beer occasionally.

But those three people were open and friendly, honest and genuine, didn't knock their trust sideways, as David had. Obviously Ryder and Callum thought Kayla appeared reliable, but he knew from experience that people changed when things weren't going their way. He swore through the pounding in his head, now added to by the woman here to keep an eye on him. He needed more painkillers and something to make this exhaustion drag him under so he couldn't think any more. Then he *did* trust Kayla with his boys? Good question.

'I've got the sauce,' Ryder said. 'Do you have kids?'

'No, I haven't.'

'Why not?'

'Ryder, that's enough,' Jamie called out. Maybe he shouldn't trust the boys not to cause trouble. Who knew what the next question would be, and although he wanted to learn more about Kayla, he'd find out directly. He would? He coughed, tasted smoke. Or imagined he did. A bitter flavour filled his mouth. He would not get to know Kayla that well. He couldn't afford risking getting close and then having to deal with the ructions that'd follow if it went belly up. And what was to say it wouldn't?

What said it would? This was ridiculous. Kayla intrigued him when he wasn't looking for a relationship. Here he was wondering what might happen if knowing Kayla got out of control. He needed another bang on the head to clear his mind.

'Can we have a fizzy drink?'

'Do you usually have one before dinner?' Kayla replied.

'Dad says we have to have water at night.'

'Then water it is. Did you have fun at summer school today?'

'Yes.' The boys talked on top of each other, keen to tell her everything.

Well done, Kayla. Diversion in place.

Jamie relaxed further. Whether it was good the boys were totally comfortable with her or not, tonight it made everything simpler. He didn't have the energy to make them dinner, or oversee their showers before bed. That beam had done a number on his body and everything was catching up. He'd leave worrying about how Kayla was fitting in with his family too quickly, too well, till tomorrow.

Tomorrow. She'd be heading out the door to go to work. Out of their lives other than whenever they met through work or rescues. Wouldn't she? Or was she done for the week? Four days on, four off. Wasn't that how it went with the ambulance staff? The pounding in his head made it hard to recall details he knew as well as the scar on his hand from once pulling a dog out of a flaming laundry. Another fire, another memento. Another fib to the boys to hide the danger of his job.

A long yawn dragged in air and forced it out again. Dang but he was shattered.

* * *

'Here's your dinner.' Kayla spoke quietly in case Jamie had nodded off. Sleep was better for him than a burger.

His answer was deep, slow breathing. Good. She'd have to wake him soon so he'd go to his room and into bed. His body fully stretched out on a mattress would be easier on those bruises than having his legs hang over the end of the couch and his shoulder digging into a lumpy cushion. The drawn look marking his face had gone. She knew it would return when he woke, but for now his body was resting.

It was strange to be nursing Jamie, if that's what she could call this. Very used to giving urgent attention to people who'd had an accident or medical event, she wasn't used to caring for someone after the doctors had finished with them and didn't know much more than taking note of pain levels and watching for symptoms suggesting the concussion was worse than initially diagnosed. A nurse she was not. But Josue believed she was capable, and she was. Even stranger was how happy she felt. She wanted to make sure Jamie would be all right, that nothing untoward happened during the night. This wasn't about a patient, it was about Jamie, and how he'd held her hand, given her courage and strength when she'd been floundering.

She should be running for the hills, hiding until this new sense of wanting to be with a man disappeared. Dylan had been the love of her life, and he was gone. The emptiness that had followed had dragged her down, turned her life into dark solitude, a place that now she was out of she never wanted to return to.

'Dad, why aren't you eating your burger?' Ryder asked from the other room.

Kayla headed for the other room, her finger to her lips. 'Shh, Dad's sleeping and that's good.'

'Are you staying all night?'

'Yes, I am.'

'You'll have to sleep on the couch. There aren't any other beds.' Ryder was grinning like a cheeky monkey.

'That's okay. My legs aren't so long they'll hang over the end like your father's.' Not quite anyway. Kayla grinned back. She'd curl up on the couch, though those cushions didn't look very comfortable. Might be better to lay them on the floor and stretch out to soften the aches she got in her legs after a day at work. 'Do you have a shower at night?'

The boys looked at each other. 'No-o.'

'Guess what? You are tonight. Let's do it before Dad wakes up and then you can surprise him.'

And me, if you take any notice of what I say.

'Okay.' They headed in the direction of the bathroom, leaving Kayla shaking her head.

Were they really doing as she'd asked?

Squeals came from the bathroom, followed by shouts. Guess they were.

Kayla walked across to see if Jamie was still asleep.

'You have them wrapped around your little finger,' he said in a sleepy voice that made her feel as though a light scarf had caressed her skin and teased her with longing.

'They're probably outside the shower in their clothes, pretending to be washing.'

'Anything's possible with those two.' The love on Jamie's face told her all she needed to know about this dad. He'd do whatever it took to keep them happy and safe.

But he was also unbending when it came to rules. She'd seen him leading a search team with authority but not overdoing the I'm-in-charge part of his job. He led from the front.

'What woke you?'

'You insisting they have a shower.' His smile was slow and kept ramping up her need for him. 'You seem to understand kids. You told the boys you haven't got any.'

'No, I haven't.'

Come on, explain. It's part of getting to know each other.

'Dylan and I were trying. I had two miscarriages.' She nipped her bottom lip. 'The second one on the day Dylan crashed his car and died. He was on his way home to me.'

Jamie reached for her hands, clasped them, squeezed gently. 'Oh, Kayla.'

'Yeah,' she sighed. She liked the way he didn't try to say the right thing when there weren't any words to help. Time had diminished the pain, hugs from close friends had helped, but nothing she'd been told had gone towards her recovery. Sitting there, Jamie once more holding her hand, was enough. Then she went and spoiled it. 'I missed him so much, and it's taken for ever to start moving forward. I'll probably never have a family now.'

'You'd like children?'

'Yes. Absolutely. I was so excited both times I learned I was pregnant. Losing them was hard. I don't know if I could go through that again. Or if I can even carry a baby to full term.'

'Other women have multiple miscarriages and still go on to have their own children. It can happen for you.'

Her hand was being squeezed tighter. She held on, savouring the moment, glad she had told him. 'It's the heartbreak that's the hardest to deal with. And losing Dylan and a baby at the same time was agony. Another miscarriage would bring all that back and I don't think I could get through it again.'

'That I can understand. But you're a strong lady, Kayla. Don't ever forget that.'

Oh, wow. He said the most wonderful things. She'd just spilled her soul, and he was understanding. She doubted he'd forget this conversation by the time he woke up in the morning, concussion or not. Finally, after a few minutes, she straightened her back and asked, 'Are you hungry? Your burger will only be lukewarm, but I can get you something else if you'd like.'

Moving his head slowly from side to side, Jamie winced. 'I'll try the burger. I'm not ravenous but a couple of bites might shut my stomach up.'

'Thought I heard a noise.' She helped him sit up and went to get his meal. 'I take it I'm sleeping on the couch.'

Jamie's shoulders slumped. 'I didn't give that a thought. The boys can top and tail so you can have a bed.'

'No way. They need to sleep properly if they're going to summer school tomorrow. I'll be fine sprawled out in here.' Until the bones started complaining.

'Are you sure? It's hardly fair when you've gone out of your way to help me.'

She had, hadn't she? How cool was that? Helping people was her go-to place all the time. It was something she enjoyed and got a buzz from. Falling for a man wasn't like that. Jamie waking her up in ways she'd never believed possible again was very different, exciting and scary all in one, but she'd get through the night and go to work no worse off. She had to. 'Stop talking and eat. I'll cope.'

Jamie managed half the burger before putting it aside and clambering awkwardly to his feet. 'I'm going to bed.'

Kayla stood beside him. 'Your head spinning?'

'A little, but don't think you can catch me if I trip.'

'You reckon?' She laughed, feeling right at home with him. Same as it had been with Dylan right from the beginning. A sense of being with her other half, of becoming whole. She swore.

'Careful. There're kids within hearing.' He was serious.

'Sorry. I wasn't thinking.' She'd been out of line but it had been an instant reaction to that preposterous thought. Jamie was nothing like Dylan. In any way, shape or form. Other than his gentleness, love for his family, strength and determination. Nothing like Dylan at all. Nothing. Trying too hard to convince herself?

Not looking good, Kayla.

'What rocked your boat?' They'd reached his bedroom door.

'Nothing important.' Glancing at Jamie, she instantly knew he saw through her denial. 'Nothing I care to talk about,' she added to shut down ideas he might have of pushing for answers. There'd been enough talking tonight. 'I'll pull your bedcovers back and leave you to get undressed.' Heat filled her cheeks at the thought of helping Jamie out of his clothes. 'You won't need a hand, will you?'

Grow a backbone, Kayla. How many semi-naked patients have you worked with? Why would this man be any different?

Because he was Jamie, and like it or not he was winding her up something shocking. Shocking in that no man had done this to her for years, hadn't created any kind of reaction that had gone beyond friendship. These feelings were more than friendly. Unheard of, in her book.

He took a long, measured look at her, as though trying to read her, to see what made her tick. Or trying to fathom what she'd meant. What could be plainer than she wasn't interested in undressing him for bed? Then he gave an abrupt shake of his head and winced. 'I'll manage.'

Perfect answer. 'Good. Want a hot drink to down more painkillers?' Paramedic to the fore, not the blithering female who hadn't had anything do with a male in an intimate way in so long her body had probably forgotten the moves, let alone the emotions.

'Tea would be good.'

'How do you take it?' They were being distant. Probably the best way to go. Except she did like him, and wanted them to get along. She wasn't only thinking about how he made her blood race or her fingertips tingle. He was a great guy and she didn't intend walking out of here tomorrow and not have anything more to do with him outside work or S and R. She wanted to become friends. That was one word for these foreign emotions swirling through her. Friendship was safe. Didn't cause as much pain if it went wrong. But it could. Her heart was involved with Maisie and Mallory.

'White and one.' Jamie stood, hands on hips, waiting for her to disappear so he could get his gear off.

She'd laugh if it wasn't so damned ridiculous how her gut got in a twist over something so ordinary. Except nothing about a hot man taking his clothes off in front of her would be ordinary. It would be exciting and fun and—

Stop right there. If you can't be sensible, at least pretend to be.

'I'll see what the boys are up to.' Sensible enough? She sighed. More like boring. Not that Jamie's kids were boring. They were adorable, and Ryder was the spitting image of his dad. The same thick black hair and piercing brown eyes, and his mouth did that cheeky twist at the corners when he was being smart. Callum must have his mother's looks as he was blond with blue eyes, but that cheeky glint in his shy gaze instantly reminded her of Jamie. Not the shy, but the cheeky.

'Don't let them talk you into being allowed to stay up an extra half-hour. They'll try every trick in the book,' Jamie warned.

'Onto them.' She headed for the lounge where a programme was blaring on the TV screen. 'Okay, guys. Ten minutes before you have to be in bed.'

'The programme won't be finished,' Ryder muttered.

'Then you can record it.' Fingers crossed he was allowed to. 'Your dad wants to say goodnight. Don't bounce on the bed or jump on top of him. He's very sore.' She was sure these two would be exuberant if allowed to be.

'Is Dad going to be all right?' Callum asked, staring at the floor.

'Yes, he is.' Sitting on the couch armrest, she explained. 'He's got lots of bruises on his arms and shoulders, and his head. He needs time for them to get better and stop hurting. But don't worry, he's strong. He'll soon be playing games with you again.' There was a football and three bikes on the front porch, suggesting he got involved with these guys as much as possible.

'Will he take us out on the boat?'

'You'll have to ask him.' She wasn't getting caught up in saying things Jamie might not want to partake in. 'He knows his work schedule. I don't.' How did he manage the erratic hours of his work and the sudden, unexpected calls for S and R with these two to take care of? Christine obviously had a lot to do with them, but surely not every day of the week?

There was more to him than what she knew so far. At S and R he was always totally focused on the job at hand, and nothing else seemed to bother him, but who knew? He might be a master at covering up his worries. Or he might compartmentalise everything, dealing with the immediate problems and leaving everything else till later.

Ryder waved the remote in the direction of the TV and increased the volume.

Checking her watch, Kayla shook her head. 'Sorry, kiddo, it's time to turn that off.'

'But I want to watch it.' A pout shaped Ryder's mouth.

'Let's record it and go say goodnight.' Then she'd make the tea.

Moments later the only sound she could hear was giggling coming from Jamie's bedroom. A lovely sound that clenched her heart, reminding her of what she was missing out on.

CHAPTER SIX

'YOU'VE PASSED MUSTER with my boys,' Jamie said. Their reactions to Kayla were heart-warming, and surprising. He hadn't believed they'd be so trusting so fast after David. Maybe they weren't as jaded as their old man.

'They're easy to get along with.' Kayla stood with her mug in hand, appearing to be sussing him out.

Medically or otherwise? Surely she didn't think of him as just a patient? After talking about her longing for children? Would her emotions make his boys vulnerable? He didn't believe so but he still had to put them first in case he was completely wrong about Kayla. 'They usually ease into being friendly.' He'd only felt that way twice, with Leanne and now Kayla. It was still hard to believe that the strong and wonderful love he'd had with Leanne could go belly up so fast. He couldn't have loved her more. His heart had been completely invested in their love and marriage, so her leaving had crushed him. He hadn't known then how big a fright she'd got when she'd thought it was him who'd been killed in the fire he'd been attending, and if he had, she'd still have left because she was over him.

Caution was his go-to place now. Even if he could shrug aside the hurt of the past and find a woman he might—a very big might—fall in love with, he had to remember it wasn't on his agenda until Ryder and Callum didn't need him for every step they took.

'Why are they cagey about strangers?' Kayla sat down on the end of the bed. 'I'd have thought Ryder was always outgoing. He's such a chatty little guy.'

Sometimes he just had to give up on holding out and move on as fast as possible. This was one of those moments because he didn't want Kayla thinking he was being aloof. Not when she'd given up her night to be here for them. 'When their mother and I split, things got nasty for a while and sadly they were in the middle of the battle. Ever since then they've been wary around people they don't know. Except you.' Despite his worries he liked that she'd been accepted so readily. It felt as though he'd passed one hurdle on this new road he found himself on.

'It's been hard for you all.'

Her tone was non-judgemental but still he felt the need to defend himself. 'I fought hard to be in their lives, to have a solid footing in their day-to-day goings-on. I like being the father who takes his sons to the ski field or on a holiday or spoils them by occasionally buying the toys they ask for. I want to be there for the arguments over what I make for dinner, for the days they're unwell, and the football games and parent-teacher meetings.'

That's enough. If Kayla doesn't get the idea then she's never going to.

'A true dad.' A smile lifted her mouth, and sent warmth throughout his battered body.

That was the nicest thing he'd heard for a long time. She hadn't stopped to think about it either. He sipped his tea to hide the emotions rolling through him. Something about Kayla made him open up a little. He'd never spoken about Leanne and their battle to anyone. If one of the men at work or S and R asked about being a solo father, he shrugged the questions aside with, 'I love my sons.' It was the reason he'd fought so hard for his right to be an involved parent. That, and taking his responsibility seriously. 'I do my best.'

His parents hadn't been a shining example of how a loving family worked. It had been every kid for themself and there'd been six of them in total. He and none of his brothers and sisters were close. As the youngest he'd tried hard to be loved by any of them, but it hadn't happened so he'd learned to hold himself tight and get on with things until he was old enough to get away and create a life of his own. One that had to include love and happiness. He'd found it with Leanne.

He'd also lost it with Leanne. But he had two sons he adored and would fight to the end of the world and back to be there for them. He lived how he wanted, not how he was raised—caring and supportive of others, and especially of his boys. 'Ryder and Callum are my world.' Just to emphasise the point.

'I can see that.' Her smile was soft and genuine.

A new ache started behind his ribs. One that any amount of painkiller tablets was unlikely to dull. Kayla was definitely getting to him, stirring a need for someone special to share his life with. Subject change required. 'Why did you choose to come back here? Family? Friends?'

Her smile dimmed as her gaze dropped from his face to the mug she held in both hands. 'After Dylan died I continued living in our apartment for nearly three years, believing my life was over. No man I loved, no children of my own. Then one day I realised if I didn't get out I'd be there till someone came looking for me and found a fossil sitting in the chair by the window.'

Sadness touched him. Obviously Kayla still hurt.

If only his body could move easily and he had more than boxers on, he'd be out of the bed and hugging that sadness away. Instead he gave her a heartfelt smile. 'Do you think you made the right move?'

She nodded. 'I grew up here, and rushed away as soon as I was old enough to support myself in the big city up north. It wasn't that I didn't like Queenstown, it was just that there seemed to be so much more to do out in the wider world that my parents didn't need to know about. They were quite possessive of me, growing up.'

'And was there?'

Kayla drained her mug, then nodded. 'Definitely. I found everything I was looking for. Fun, excitement, a career I put a lot into, and then there was Dylan. Yes, Auckland was good to me. And then it wasn't.' She stood up. 'How's your head? Still pounding like a bongo drum?'

End of conversation. He understood. 'More like a pair of them. When's my next dose of pain relief?'

Glancing at her watch, she smiled again. 'Not for a couple of hours but I can give you something lighter to be going on with.'

He watched her step out of the room. Confident without putting it out there too much. The type of woman he preferred. He sank back into the pillows, groaning as pain throbbed and his head filled with images of having fun with Kayla. The next groan was louder.

'Here, get these into you.' A slim hand appeared in his vision with two white tablets in her palm. The other hand held a glass of water.

Those pills weren't going to make the slightest bit of difference to what was ailing him. Kayla would not vanish as they dissolved in his gut. Her smile and soft voice would remain inside his head, teasing him, pestering him with her genuine concern and care. 'Thanks,' he muttered.

'Have you ever worried about the dangers of your job?'

He had to stare at her for a moment to make sure Leanne hadn't turned up. 'No,' he snapped. 'I have not.'

Those beautiful eyes filled with remorse. 'Steady. I didn't mean to upset you. Nor was I being critical of what you do.'

Then why ask? 'I'm probably less at risk than Joe Blogs driving to work on the main road. I trained to be prepared for when mistakes happen.' He paused.

Want to rethink that?

'Okay, things can and obviously do go wrong, but I don't spend my time worrying about it. I won't give up my work because of today.'

Kayla swallowed and said quietly, 'I've obviously hit a nerve. I wasn't looking for trouble or suggesting anything such as you shouldn't do your work because of the boys. Life's full of obstacles and there's no avoiding all of them.'

It was good to know she wasn't accusing him of not thinking about his boys when he went to a fire. But then why would she? 'I guess I'm the one who should apologise.' Old habits didn't die fast. 'Sorry.'

Her smile was brief. 'No problem.'

He'd hurt her with his reaction. Seemed he could still get annoyed over things Leanne had belted him with too often. 'There was a fire in the hills and along the lake edge. One of our firemen was caught in a fireball and died. That same day Ryder had appendicitis. Leanne tried to get hold of me but I was out of reach. When she heard about the death she thought the worst.'

Kayla nodded. 'Understandable.'

'It flicked something in her. She was afraid it could

happen to me and she didn't want the boys to suffer. That's when she packed up and left, taking Ryder and Callum to have a life where they weren't worrying about whether I came home or not.' His mouth tasted bitter.

'She told them what happened?'

'I'm not sure. The guy who died had kids at the same kindergarten so of course they heard. I didn't figure how much they'd understand. They were so young.'

'I can see why they were edgy when you came home with a bandage around your head.'

His sigh was full of despair. 'Me, too. But once you talked to them, they came right. Maybe honesty pays off, even about something like this.'

'No gory details.' Kayla smiled.

'Not a one.' He returned the smile around a yawn.

'Sleep time for you.'

She was right. If only he didn't have to be there alone.

Kayla stepped quietly into Jamie's room and paused, listening to deep breathing. He was either asleep or pretending to be. She'd leave him be. Groping around in the dim light from the hall for his wrist to check his BP wasn't going to achieve much except an annoyance factor.

'You all right?' Jamie grunted.

'I'm fine. I came in to check up on *you.*'

'You can't sleep?'

Tell him yes, save him worrying about something he had no answer for. 'No.'

There was movement in the bed. He was shoving to one side, leaving the other half empty. 'Get in. It's a damned sight more comfortable than the couch. I won't touch you, I promise.'

Did he have to sound so certain? Like she didn't ring

his bells even a tiny bit? 'I'll stick to the couch. You need your sleep.'

If you say I won't affect that then I'm going to curl up in a little ball and pretend I'm the most wanted woman in the country and deny the hurt you inflicted.

'You snore?' Was that a hint of laughter?

'Not that I've heard.'

'I'll be the judge. Get in. We can put pillows between us if that'll make you feel more comfortable. They're in the wardrobe.'

'Jamie, is your head throbbing? Your vision blurry?'

'Yes, to both. So I can't see you and I have no strength to do more than go back to sleep. Seriously, how do you think I feel knowing you can't sleep and that your legs are probably aching badly all because of me?'

'You have such a beguiling way with words.' That mattress was so tempting, no matter that Jamie was taking up two thirds of it.

'Take your trousers off. They won't be comfortable for sleeping.'

Another putdown. Take her trousers off for comfort, not because he wanted to see her shapely legs. She laughed. 'Charm isn't your thing, then.'

'Am I getting through to you?'

Yes, damn it. She went to turn off the hall light, returned to sit on the edge of the bed, her heart fluttering as if she might be making a mistake. Or was it because she felt happy, even excited? Why excited when Jamie was beyond doing anything more than sleep? Because he'd be close, if unattainable. The memory of being held in his arms was blinking like emergency lights. Appropriate considering she might be in trouble here. Except the cure was simple. Return to that uncomfortable couch, aching legs and all.

Shucking out of her trousers instantly cooled her overheated skin. If only it cooled all her body. Grabbing a handful of sheet she lifted it, slid underneath and pulled it up to her chin.

Straight away her legs felt better, though still tense, as was the rest of her for fear she'd move and bump into Jamie, who, despite moving to make room for her, was sprawled in all directions.

'Goodnight, Kayla.' His voice was thick with sleep as his breathing deepened, slowed.

''Night, Jamie.' She waited and waited, and then heard a small snore and smiled. 'Go, you.' Oh, to fall asleep so easily. She should. The last few days had been busy with a spate of older people having falls, and there'd been the death of a paraglider after getting caught in a downdraught that had dropped him on rocks on the Shotover River. She'd longed for one of Jamie's hugs that day but hadn't had the guts to call and say what had happened and how she needed him.

Closing her eyes tight, she breathed deeply for calm. Close enough to Jamie that she only had to move her arm a few centimetres and she'd be touching his muscular body. Get out of here. Right now. Before she fell asleep and snuggled into him. She might hurt him. His bruising wouldn't take much of a knock to ache like hell.

Excuses, excuses. You're afraid of touching him in case you can't find it in you to move away again.

Kayla's eyes shot open. Really? She stared into the darkness above them. They hadn't even kissed. Not once. Near, but not near enough. She wanted to kiss him. Really kiss him, long and deep, find the man behind the smile. But that didn't mean she cared more than a little about him. She might yearn to press her length against his hard body and absorb his warmth and strength and kindness, wipe away the sense of being too alone, but she could not give in. She mustn't.

Why did Jamie make her feel this way? Why not any of the other good-looking, friendly men she met as she went about her work? Tipping her head sideways, she tried to see him in the dark. Impossible, so she relied on memory, which showed how gorgeous he was and why she felt soft and gooey on the inside, hot and tight on the outside. Jamie did this to her. No other man. And here she was, lying right beside him in his bed. 'Why am I here?' she demanded of the darkness.

'Kayla? That you?' croaked Jamie.

'Yes.'

Glad I came tonight.

It felt like home, comfortable with this little family. Family. She tensed.

If only.

'You all right?'

'I'm fine, and looking after you, not the other way around.'

'We seem to have a knack of getting knocked over and the other one appearing to do something about it.' Jamie was starting to wake up properly. Not good when he needed to rest and sleep.

'We're quits. One accident each.'

A yawn filled the air.

'Go back to sleep, Jamie. It's the best cure for what ails you.'

'I don't think so.'

'Need more painkillers?'

'No.'

What was the problem then? 'Jamie?'

'Shh. You talk too much, woman,' he quipped.

She talked too much? Hadn't he said he couldn't sleep?

No, Kayla, he said he didn't think painkillers would help what was bothering him.

Oh. Had she got that right? Was having her in his bed disturbing him? She couldn't help smiling. She wasn't suffering on her own. Or she was because she'd got it all wrong. Wouldn't be the first time, and most likely not the last. Rolling over to face away from him, she muttered, 'Sleep tight,' and closed her eyes. She'd fake sleep until hopefully it happened. If it didn't then she'd be a grump all day tomorrow.

Jamie woke muscle by muscle, desperate to breathe slowly and not to over-activate the dull throbbing going on in his head and shoulder. It had been a long night, pain interspersed with sleep, tablets swallowed with water, and that tantalisingly warm body curled up beside him. Kayla did a number on him even as she slept.

Sometime during his last snooze she'd backed up against him. Whether she'd been aware or not, he hadn't moved away. Instead at some stage he must've draped his arm around her waist and tucked her even closer because there was a new warmth on his skin from his ankles to his neck where she touched him. Her hair was splayed on the pillow between them, and her chest was rising and falling softly.

Hopefully she wouldn't attack him when she woke, believing he'd done this on purpose. He should back away, withdraw while she slept. It would be safer. And impossible. Being so close to another person chipped away at the loneliness he'd carried since Leanne had left. It gave him hope. For someone to care about and who might do the same back. But what if it was thrown back in his face when the going got tough? That'd hurt too bloody much.

Was this why his parents had never been loving towards him and his siblings? They were afraid of losing their love? Of having it tossed aside like it didn't matter? Hadn't they realised how loved they were by all of their children anyway?

Kayla's background sounded loving. She spoke adoringly of her family, and there was only love in her face when she mentioned her late husband. Did she want to love again?

Jamie jerked, gasped. What was he thinking?

'Hello? What happened?' Kayla murmured beside him. Then she stilled. 'Jamie?' she whispered.

'Morning, sleepyhead.'

'How long have you been awake?' she asked, caution in her words and her body tensing.

'All night,' he teased, then realised he'd probably upped the tension. 'Ten minutes max.'

She began to roll away, and he retracted his arm instantly. 'We were like this when I woke, and I didn't want to disturb you.'

I was enjoying myself, making the most of having you close. It was magic.

Swinging her legs over the side of the bed, she sat up, scrubbed her face with her knuckles. 'How're you feeling?'

Hot. Tight. Needing you.

'Achy and ready to stretch the body.'

'I'll put the kettle on. What time do the boys get up?'

Jamie sat up fast, groaned as pain lanced his chest and shoulder. The boys. He'd forgotten them. What if they'd walked in here while Kayla had been lying in his bed, snuggled up to him? 'Seven, when I usually have to shake them awake.' What was the time? He tried to twist around to pick up his phone and more pain stabbed his shoulder.

Kayla was pulling her trousers on at the same time

as tapping her phone on the bedside table. 'Slow down, Jamie. It's just gone six. I'll go out to the kitchen and they'll be none the wiser.'

'I hope.'

Kayla's face dipped, and her mouth tightened. 'Right.'

She hadn't liked what he'd said. He couldn't blame her, but she didn't know how much he protected his boys from getting caught up in things that would upset them. 'They're smarter than you think.'

'Tea?'

He nodded. 'I didn't mean to insult you. They're still not happy their mum doesn't live with me and if they saw you in my bed they might get the wrong idea and think you're replacing her.'

She ran her fingers through her hair, tangling with the knots that had formed overnight. 'That's sad. For all of you.'

She was right. 'It's a work in progress. For me too,' he admitted. Kayla brought things out of him that he hadn't even admitted to himself, let alone anyone else. 'Be happy they accepted you so easily.' Hopefully it boded well for the future, and the day would come when he could have a woman—this woman—in his life, not necessarily in his house or family but there to have some fun with. 'I'm not in a hurry to get hooked up again. Too much to get my head around. And my trust levels barely touch the scale.'

Her eyes darkened. 'I understand how you feel. It's not been easy putting Dylan's death behind me. I'm not sure if I'm even meant to. Sometimes I wonder if people would think I'm selfish to want to be happy again when Dylan has no chance. It makes me cautious.'

'To hell with what other people think. Some will be like that, but most, especially your family and friends, wouldn't wish a life of unhappiness on you.' Yet here he was doing the same thing to himself. 'Stay for breakfast.'

Kayla stared at him for a long moment, then suddenly laughed. 'My first date in years and I wasn't even asked, just told to stay for breakfast. I like it. Except I have to get to work.'

That unexpected laugh dived right into him, lifting his spirits in a way he hadn't known for so long. 'That's a shame.' He slowly stood up.

Her eyes dropped to his chest, then lower to his boxers. The laughter died. 'I'll head to the kitchen.'

He hadn't thought when he'd stood up. That's how relaxed he was with her. 'I'll join you in a moment.'

'Go easy. It hasn't been twenty-four hours since you had a fight with that beam.'

'Yeah, but I won. It's probably ash by now, whereas I'm slower than normal but otherwise doing okay.'

Kayla shook her head at him. 'You're nuts.'

'I know.' He enjoyed this light-hearted banter. It was something else that had been missing for a long time. Maybe he did need to get out and start mixing and mingling with the opposite sex, then he'd be more relaxed, which had to be a good thing for them all.

Slow down. One night with Kayla in your bed not having the ultimate fun and you're thinking about getting amongst it?

'Why not?' It was the only answer he could come up with.

She popped back around the door. 'Who's driving the kids to school?'

'The neighbours,' he said, his breath stalling in his lungs. She was beautiful with her mussed-up hair and sleepy eyes. 'I'm glad you were here last night. I would've been worrying without someone to keep an eye on things. Thank you.'

Those golden eyes were fixed on him, her lips slightly apart. Her breasts were rising and falling too fast. 'Any time,' she whispered.

He stepped closer, brushed the back of his hand over her cheek. 'I might take you up on that.'

'I should go.' She didn't move an inch.

'I know.' Placing his hands on her shoulders, he gazed into her eyes, falling deeper into her hold over him. He didn't want her to leave. Not at all. But she had to. Suddenly he couldn't imagine her not being around to talk to or share a coffee with. 'Kayla?'

'Jamie?'

He had to kiss her. Had to. His lips touched hers, brushing across them to the corner, and returning to cover them completely. Her mouth opened under his in invitation and he was lost. Sunk in a softness that absorbed him, overwhelmed him, took charge of him. Wrapping his arms around her, he held her against his hungry body, felt her curves against his tight muscles as he tasted her mouth.

Kayla pulled back in his arms to lock her eyes with his. The tip of her tongue slid along her lip.

Hell, he wanted to kiss her some more. His whole body was responding to that tongue. But she'd lifted her mouth away from his. 'Kayla? I know I said I'm not leaping into anything, but I've been wanting to kiss you for so long.'

Her smile was slow and sexy. Then she was pressing hard against him, holding him tight around his waist, kissing him like she wanted to give herself. It couldn't get any better.

Bang. 'Callum, give me that book back.'

Jamie froze.

Kayla jerked out of his arms, stepped away, smoothing her hands down her clothes. Shock registering in her eyes, she murmured, 'Thought you said you had to shake them awake.'

'I usually do.' He puffed out the breath that had got caught in his throat.

''It's mine, Callum.'

The boys' bedroom door swung open and two little bodies hurtled down the hall towards them.

'I'll make that tea and leave you to it,' Kayla muttered.

'Hey, Dad, Callum's got my book.'

'Watch out,' Kayla warned from the doorway. 'Your dad's hurt, remember?'

Ryder slid to a stop before him. 'You still sore, Dad?'

'A bit. Why are you arguing?'

Ryder shrugged. 'Don't know.'

'Yes, you do,' Callum shouted. 'You took my book.'

'So what? Where's Kayla, Dad?' Ryder headed to the kitchen. 'Kayla, can you come to my birthday party at the weekend?'

Where the hell had that come from? This needed to be dealt with immediately. In the kitchen Kayla looked stunned. Would she say yes and make Ryder happy, or no and quieten his concerns? Or would she delay answering until she'd talked to him?

She glanced at Jamie, worry darkening her face. Looked at his son, waiting with something like resignation in his eyes, and smiled. 'Thanks for asking me. I'd love to come.'

'Cool.' Ryder's shout ricocheted around the room. 'You hear that, Dad?'

'I did.' He didn't know whether to be pleased or annoyed. This was raising the bar higher than ever,

'How old will you be?' Kayla asked.

'Eight.' Ryder was already racing back to his bedroom. 'The party's at the skating park. We're taking our skateboards. You can have a turn on mine, Kayla.'

'No, thanks. I've already broken my legs once. I don't plan on doing that again.'

'Chicken,' Jamie muttered, uncertain about this. He should be pleased she hadn't turned Ryder down.

Then be pleased.

'Thanks for not disappointing him.'

Finally she relaxed. 'That doesn't sound like me.'

'I agree. You don't let people down, do you?'

'Not if I can help it. But is it all right if I come? What about the boys' mother? Will she be there? I don't want to cause problems or give her the wrong idea.'

Jamie bit back a retort. Leanne would be there, but if she made any comments about Kayla she'd have him to deal with. She had a new husband so he doubted she'd react badly to him turning up with a woman, but he'd been wrong before. 'Leanne will be fine.' One way or another, he'd make certain of it.

'Then I'll look forward to the party.' Kayla stretched up on her toes and she brushed her lips over his. 'And to seeing you again.' Then her cheeks turned bright red and she stepped back. 'So much for being cautious.'

'Yeah.' One kiss and everything had changed. One damned kiss and he wanted more. Maybe not the whole deal, but more kisses and holding that sexy body, and getting to know her so much better.

Too soon, too fast.

This wasn't how the future was supposed to go. Not yet. But no denying he wanted more of Kayla. 'I'll see you Saturday.' He had to accept she'd be at Ryder's party, and that he was already looking forward to more time with her. As long as he could squash the idea she might let him down in the future and believe that his boys would be safe with her. So much for waiting a while before getting involved even a little. Right now he felt as though he was standing on a precipice and he could go either way.

CHAPTER SEVEN

'COME ON, KAYLA, you have to take a turn on my skateboard. It's my birthday.' Ryder stood in front of her, hands on his hips, wearing a cheeky smile that got her right in the chest—just where his father's smiles hit her.

The little ratbag. How did he know she didn't dodge challenges? Right now she was hyped up and ready to take one on, both for the hell of it and to quieten her nerves with Jamie's ex about to turn up. 'I'll give it a go.'

'You don't have to do this, Kayla.' Jamie joined them, worry reflecting out at him. 'Think about those fractures you sustained last year.'

Too right she was thinking about them. But she was a dab hand on skis and snowboards so balance was on her side. She squeezed his arm. 'I'll be fine.' Or sensible. Another challenge going on right there.

'Out of the way, guys. Kayla's having a turn and she might crash.' Ryder was running at his friends, shooing them back.

'I'm not that decrepit.' She laughed.

'Don't do it. You haven't had birthday cake yet.' Jamie sounded light-hearted but his hands were clenched.

'Watch this.'

Please, please, please, get it right.

She placed one foot on the board and pushed off

with the other, kept her balance as the board moved forward slowly.

'Too slow.' Ryder walked beside her. 'You've got to go faster or you'll crash.'

'Okay.' Same as snowboarding. Except landing on concrete would be inflexible. This wasn't her wisest move in a while but, hey, wise was highly overrated. Pushing harder, she was off, balancing better as she tucked her left foot behind the right one. Leaning to the side, the board began turning. Just like snowboarding.

'Cool.' Ryder was still with her. 'Do a jump.'

'Nope.' That was one challenge she wasn't ready for. She managed a sharp turn, wobbled, then pushed with her foot and headed back to where she'd started. Straightening the board by angling her body, she aimed for the grass strip and jumped off, holding her hand up to high five the air. 'How's that?'

Jamie shook his head. 'I'm impressed.'

'That easily?'

'I'm hoping the boys don't challenge you to anything else. You won't be able to turn them down. Weren't you worried about falling off?'

'Worry and it happens.' Something she'd learned on the ski slopes as a five-year-old. Strange how she couldn't react the same about a new relationship. Since leaving Jamie's house the other morning, she'd spent most of her time thinking about needing to get to know him even better. His kiss was something else, and waking up to find herself wrapped against his body beyond awesome. The sense of belonging had remained ever since. She'd dropped in to see how he was and had had a coffee with him the next day. It had felt right, and Jamie had been relaxed about her being there when the boys had come home. She was starting to let go of her worries over a new relationship.

'Hello, who are you?' A woman stood in front of her, dressed in classy trousers and a sleeveless top. 'I'm Leanne, Ryder and Callum's mother.'

Jamie stepped closer to Kayla. 'Hi, Leanne. This is a friend of mine, Kayla Johnson.'

'Hello, Leanne, nice to meet you.'

'I wasn't expecting you.' Leanne was sizing her up with a shrewd look in her eyes.

Glad she'd worn her new white three-quarter-length pants and snazzy red shirt, Kayla smiled.

'I invited her, Mum.' Ryder appeared between his parents, a frown on his brow.

'You didn't mention it to me,' Leanne snapped.

This could go either way, so Kayla intervened, 'Probably because I had to check my roster to see if I was working.' A little lie, and shouldn't have been said in front of Ryder, but he wasn't getting into trouble on her account.

Leanne studied her for a moment longer, then glanced at Jamie. 'I see.' Then she walked across to a group of mothers watching their kids skating.

See what? Kayla wondered. Jamie's ex didn't know he'd kissed her, made her warm and happy.

I'm not wearing a sign on my forehead.

But there was one in her chest, expanding even as they stood here. She liked this woman's ex-husband enough to want to become a part of his life. They'd connected instantly, and got on whenever they were together, which was never often enough. More than that, she felt as though she'd found her match in Jamie. Enough to want to have more. Nothing full time and permanent, but to be able to do things together would be wonderful.

'You want to try my board?' Callum asked quietly from behind her.

She wasn't letting either of these boys down. 'Sure. Shall I do the same loop or try something different?'

Don't suggest a jump or this time I might have to accept the challenge.

'What you did on Ryder's is okay.' A nervous smile appeared on Callum's face.

Kayla held out her hand for the board. 'Come on, then. Watch this.' She glanced at Jamie, and winked before mouthing, 'No jumps, promise.'

He grinned, surprising her. 'We'll see.' Then he called across to Leanne, 'How's David? I thought he'd be here.'

'He's coming shortly. He's got a problem to sort out with work first.'

'Good. Ryder was hoping he'd turn up.'

It was the weekend. Shouldn't David be here with his wife's kids instead of working? Kayla shrugged. Not her problem, though she knew where she'd be if she was in the same position. 'Okay, Callum, let's do this. Why don't you borrow another board and ride with me?'

Ten minutes later she rolled up to Jamie and stepped off the board. 'Your turn.'

'Concussion, remember? And a badly bruised shoulder.' He'd had the all-clear for his concussion but his shoulder was still stiff and sore.

She laughed. 'Wimp.'

'And proud of it.'

'Then I'd better do another lap.' It was fun zooming around.

'Thanks for letting Ryder off the hook.'

On the other side of the dome Leanne was watching them. 'I know I fibbed, but I didn't want him getting into trouble over me.'

'I think Ryder understands. Anyway, I'm fine about it. The last thing we need is him being scolded in front of his friends.' Jamie had his hands in his pockets as he stood watching the kids charging all over the skating dome. 'They're carefree and happy. It's all I want for them.'

'What about for you?' The question was out before she'd thought it through. 'Sorry, I take that back. None of my business.' Except it could be now that they were getting a little more involved. The other morning Jamie had kissed her like it mattered. She waited for his answer, but after a moment of tense silence she shook her head and made to move away. He wasn't sharing anything at this stage.

Jamie caught her elbow, pulled her against his side. 'There's a big gap between what I'd like and what I'm prepared to give up to get it.'

Still none the wiser, Kayla waited, making the most of her side pressed against his, the warmth between them, the strength she could feel that was inherently Jamie. This could be the beginning of a big let-down, but she was willing to give it a try. Ready to take the knocks on the chin and see if she was lucky enough to have a second chance at love. Falling for Jamie might happen, or it might not. Only one way to find out.

'Ryder and Callum come first,' he said.

'That shows in everything you do.'

His hand tightened on her waist. 'There was another woman about a year back who wanted a relationship with me. I liked her, but wasn't interested in more than friendship.' He paused. 'She overdid it, trying to get onside with the boys as a way to me.'

'They saw through her?'

Jamie nodded. 'They're not silly. Or they learned their lesson from how David treated them.'

Where was he going with this? She was here because Ryder invited her. Surely he understood that? 'What are you trying to say?'

'Want to come round for a meal one night next week?'

That'd been a long-winded way of inviting her. He was probably as nervous about a relationship as she was. 'I'd love to.'

'Great.' His arm slipped away and he wandered over to begin organising the barbecue to feed hungry kids and their parents, a smile lifting the corners of his mouth and a swing in his stride she hadn't seen before.

Christine joined her. 'I see you two are getting on like a house on fire. Though that's probably not appropriate, considering the work Jamie does.'

'You know what? I think we might be.' Kayla chuckled, glad someone was okay with it. 'But don't tell him I agreed.'

'How's that shoulder?' Kayla asked as Jamie handed her a glass of Merlot.

'Coming along well. I've been warned it'll take weeks to settle completely.' The bloody thing ached most nights and gave him grief whenever he lifted heavy objects like the rubbish bin. Not that he'd ask anyone to put it out for him. He sat down beside Kayla on the outdoor lounger and sipped his beer. 'Since Josue's given my concussion the all-clear I'm going on a small hike at summer school with the kids tomorrow. The instructors are all for parents tagging along and it's more time with Callum and Ryder for me.'

'Were your parents so hands on when you were growing up?'

'Nah.' Guess getting close to Kayla meant sharing some of who he was, and for once it didn't seem so bad.

'They didn't get involved in anything we did. I'm one of six and it was made clear we had to look out for ourselves.' It had been a harsh upbringing and one he was adamant his boys would never know. 'I grew up tough and independent, but every kid needs to know they're loved by their family.'

He stared at the beer bottle in his hand. Why did he feel so comfortable around her and not other people he spent time with? Could be her strength, or her easy acceptance of him. Or simply that he liked her heaps.

'Were you and your siblings close?'

He wouldn't look at her in case there was pity in her face, though her voice sounded devoid of it. 'Not really. It wasn't encouraged. I was the youngest and by the time I was getting around they'd all learned to stand alone. I swore I'd never be like that.' But it had taken Leanne to show him that love was real, even possible, and he'd grabbed it with everything he'd had.

Sometimes he'd wondered if he'd gone too hard and that's why they'd fallen apart, but she'd told him she'd just fallen out of love when she'd got in such a panic about what would happen if he didn't come home from work one day. He'd once had a lot of questions about that, but gradually he'd come to accept that if she didn't love him any more there was no point longing for what wasn't to be.

Kayla's hand was on his, squeezing lightly. 'You're very involved and loving with your boys. They're happy with you.'

A lump formed in his throat. 'Y-yeah.' Time to change the subject. He swallowed some beer. 'You always sound happy about your family.'

Another squeeze and her hand was gone. 'Our parents are great, though Dean—that's my brother—got away with a lot more than me because he was a boy.'

'That's why you accept challenges?'

Her laughter tinkled in the night air. 'Absolutely. I drove Mum crazy with some of the antics I got up to, proving I was clever as any boy.'

'I'd better keep you away from my two. Who knows what you'll teach them?'

'Come on. You don't want them to be wusses.'

'Not at all.' He laughed. He did a bit more of that whenever Kayla was around just because it seemed life was easier and more relaxed. Next weekend he'd be at the wedding where Kayla was bridesmaid. 'Josue's pumped about the wedding.'

'Best thing to happen to Mallory. She deserves someone special in her life.'

Don't we all?

Where had that come from?

Kayla's smile was lopsided, like it was exciting but also sad, no doubt a little unhappy for herself having lost her husband. 'It's going to be awesome.'

Jamie reached for her hand, held it, rubbing a finger back and forth over her palm. 'You're not skating down the aisle behind her by any chance?'

She grinned, sending shafts of heat through him. 'I couldn't find skates to match my dress.'

Putting his bottle aside, he removed the wine glass from her other hand. Tugging gently, he pulled her close and wound his arms around her. 'I've been wanting to do this from the moment you walked in the front door.' If not for two nosey little blighters he might have. Her mouth was soft under his, her lips opening with his. She tasted delicious. Behind his ribs his heart bumped along rapidly, caught up in the thrill that was Kayla. He couldn't help himself, he had to keep kissing her, deepening it so their tongues were entwined, and his body was reacting like there was no tomorrow.

But there was, so he'd only go so far. His boys were tucked up in bed, hopefully sound asleep. He still didn't know how far he wanted to take this. Kayla pressed a lot of buttons within him, but enough to be thinking there might be more than a bit of fun? Dangerous as hell. He wasn't ready for any risks.

She pulled back and gazed into his eyes. 'Jamie, I'd better get going.'

Disappointment warred with relief. When he was kissing her he didn't want to stop. But she was being sensible. 'Right.'

She brushed her lips over his. 'I want to take my time. I'm not sure I can be lucky a second time, and I don't want to hurt anyone while I find out.' Looking out for herself, by the sound of it.

Jamie nodded. 'I understand.' His arms fell away as she stood up. 'Kayla, I like you. A lot. I won't countenance the boys being hurt either, which in my book means staying away from a relationship for the next few years.'

She nodded. 'But?'

He rammed his fingers through his hair. 'But I also don't want to be alone for ever.' Damn it. 'Let's see where this goes.'

'I can go along with that.' Those soft, warm lips split into a wide smile, tightening his groin and making him want to throw caution to the wind.

But he wouldn't. There was too much at stake. For both of them.

Kayla was winning Jamie over, softening his stance on not getting romantically involved, though not far enough that he was prepared to dive right in. They were at Mallory and Josue's wedding. The formalities were over, and everyone was talking and drinking, and having a good time.

The band struck up a rousing tune and he scanned the guests, looking for Kayla. She wasn't hard to find, standing tall beside petite Maisie, that thick blonde hair piled on top of her head, her carefully made-up face so tantalising. She was gorgeous. All he wanted. Which was not good for his determination to remain single. Determination that was falling away the longer he knew Kayla. He'd admitted as much the other night as they'd sat on his deck after dinner.

Wandering past the guests standing with glasses of champagne as they watched the bride and groom take their first dance as a married couple, he was focused on the woman changing his life. He hadn't taken his eyes off her from the moment she and Maisie had begun walking up the aisle, leading their friend to Josue. The cream bridesmaid gown accentuated her curves and those seriously high heels made her long legs go on for ever. Her continuous smile set his stomach tripping like a community of butterflies lived in there.

Basically, he'd given in to the hope and expectation, the wonder and happiness Kayla caused. Emotions he'd thought he'd never know again. He'd held out for months but couldn't any longer. He wanted her in all ways. The other night when she'd come round to join the family dinner, it had been a normal, rowdy few hours with the boys constantly in their midst and she'd accepted it. For him, it had been the tipping point. He hadn't slept much that night, too busy thinking about how he wanted to hold Kayla and make love to her, wishing he hadn't agreed when she'd said they should take things slowly. She took his breath away. 'Would you like to dance?'

Her hand slipped into his. 'I'd love to.'

Tamping down the urge to sweep her into his arms and rush out to the garden to find a quiet corner where he could kiss her again and again, he led her onto the dance floor and began moving in time to the music.

Kayla clasped her hands at the back of his neck, pushing her breasts against his chest. Her hips swayed, cruising across his, sending thrills of hot lust zipping to every corner of his hungry body. 'This is how to dance,' she whispered.

There'd never be any other kind again. He breathed in roses, and adventure. When his hands slid around her waist heat came through the silky fabric of her dress, and excitement tingled in his fingers. Why had he held out on getting together with her? *How* had he?

'Hello?' She was watching him, that smile in her eyes luring him in, teasing, happy.

'Hi.' He leaned closer, his lips touching hers, his feet moving with the music, his body moving with Kayla's. Her breasts were tender against the hardness of his chest, her hands soft as they tapped a rhythm against his neck. 'Kayla.' Her name slid across his mouth into hers, long and low and filled with the need clawing through every cell of his body.

'We'd better slow down,' she murmured, that hot breath lifting the hairs on his arms. 'We're surrounded and unable to leave until after the bride and groom.'

'Damn it,' he muttered. 'I hate that you're right.' Keep this up and it could get awkward. More awkward. Reluctantly he removed his hands from her waist.

Kayla reached for his hands and began moving to the music again. 'We've got this.'

I don't think so.

But as they continued dancing, altering their moves to the different songs, he conceded she was right. They could dance and not get too carried away. Barely, but enough not to make a spectacle of themselves.

Maisie and Zac joined them, Zac dancing like he had nothing else on his mind except impressing Maisie, who was doing her damnedest to pretend she didn't notice and wasn't interested.

Josue and Mallory finally prepared to leave, doing the rounds of their friends and family, taking for ever. 'I thought they'd never go,' he muttered.

Kayla hugged Mallory, wiping her hand over her face and sniffing. 'I'm so happy for you both.'

Jamie's heart twisted and he stepped closer, reached for her hand and squeezed lightly. He held his other out to shake Josue's. 'Congratulations again.' He'd never seen a guy quite so happy as the Frenchman looked. A stab of something like envy caught him. He'd once had that, and he definitely wanted it again. He did. If he could make it work for himself and his kids. Other people in the same situation managed. Why not him? Had he turned into a wimp over the break-up of his marriage?

Mallory glanced at his hand holding Kayla's and then back at him. 'Glad you came.' She leaned in for a hug. 'Look after my friend.'

Or she'd kill him? He hugged her back. 'I'll do my best.'

'Then there's no problem.' Mallory stepped back and looked at Josue with love. 'Let's get out of here.'

'*Oui.* The sooner the better.'

Kayla laughed. 'Have a great honeymoon. I'll try not to spoil Shade while you're away.'

'Does that mean you'll take the dog on a search if

the need arises?' Jamie asked as they cheered Josue and Mallory off.

'Shade could show me a trick or two, being more used to searches than I am.' Kayla suppressed a yawn. 'What a day. Mallory deserves to be happy. And now I'm shattered.'

'I'll give you a lift home.' Kayla did look exhausted. Guess that meant what had started while they'd been dancing was over. He couldn't deny the disappointment filling him. He wanted her. No question. But if it wasn't happening then he'd get over it.

'You coming in?'

Please, please, please.

Kayla's heart was pounding in her throat. On the dance floor Jamie had been hot and coming on to her, and there was no way she could deny the need he'd created. What if he drove away? Left her on the front doorstep with a wave? She'd feel stupid. And sad.

'Yes.'

Yes? Yes.

'Then what are we sitting out here for?' She pushed the car door open, not waiting for him to come around. Nervous energy swept through her. She wanted to make love with Jamie. But it had been a long time and there'd been no one since Dylan. She might not be any good.

'Relax. I'm not rushing you.' He took her hand as he had the day of the avalanche. A strong, caring and supportive hold. 'We've got all night.' Then he laughed. 'That's if you don't turn me on as fast as you did on the dance floor.'

Was he nervous too? Not Jamie. He exuded confidence. Though there were moments when she'd see doubt in his gaze and wonder what caused it. How much had his marriage break-up altered who Jamie had been? She hadn't known him then, but it was hard to imagine him as anything other than the strong man before her. 'I'll put on some music.'

In the next moment she was being swung up into those arms that she'd seen haul fire hoses and operate the Jaws of Life as easily as carrying a loaf of bread, and Jamie's mouth was on hers. Kissing her like there was no tomorrow, and no time like the present. Kissing her so she forgot everything but the arms holding her and the expansive chest against her breasts. Jamie. One in a million. Had she got lucky a second time?

You're rushing ahead of things.

They were kissing, going to make love. Didn't mean they were in a relationship of any permanency. No, but she was going to grab everything and see where it led.

He tugged his mouth away. 'Key?'

'What?'

'I'm not making love to you on the doorstep.'

Shame...

Hussy.

Why not? She wanted this man. 'In the meter box.' Easier to get at than foraging in her bag, which was still in Jamie's car. She'd never shifted the key after Josue had discovered Mallory's hidden in the same spot by mistake and let himself into the wrong house. That debacle had led to today's wedding. Would hers lead to something equally exciting and wonderful?

Jamie crossed to the box, and still in his arms she retrieved the key and let them inside, nudging the door shut with her foot. 'Straight ahead.' Music would re-create that hot, sensational atmosphere between them with some moves. Not that they needed any help. First she leaned in and kissed him. Long, hard and breath-taking.

Without breaking the kiss, Jamie stood her up against him, tightened his arms around her, and spun her world out of control.

Walking backwards to the music system, her mouth still under his, she fingered the buttons and pressed the middle one. Anyone would think she'd planned this, she mused as soft, sensual music filled the air. But when she'd left home early that morning to join Mallory and Maisie to get their hair and make-up done, she hadn't imagined Jamie coming home with her tonight. 'Care to dance?' she whispered, slipping her hands behind his head.

Placing his hands on her hips, he drew her up to his length, and moved in time, taking them round the room, his steady gaze on her face, watching her every expression, seeing her smile. This was magic. The two of them close and getting closer. Sending quivers up and down her skin. Heating her blood. Turning her muscles into a molten blob of need. She found his mouth, and groaned as she tasted his wet heat.

Jamie's hands were in her hair, removing the clips, letting it free from the bob to swing across her back, his fingers combing it to the ends. Then he took her head between his hands and concentrated on returning her kiss, holding her at the perfect angle to get the best access. All the while, her hips moved in time to the music, up against him, against his manhood, turning it hard and long.

'Kayla,' he murmured in a deep, sexy whisper against her cheek. 'I want you. I need you.'

Her ribs were going to burst open under the thumping going on behind them. This wonderful man wanted her. Her, when she had felt so alone. Her, when there were other women less likely to hurt him out there. 'I want you, too.'

Their feet still moved in time with each other and the

music. Their bodies absorbed each other's heat. Their mouths devoured each other, and Kayla's head was floating on the exotic sensations filling her. Hot, gentle, tough, wonderful, demanding. Her knees buckled, tipped her further up against him. He was her strength, her weakness. Without Jamie she'd be a useless heap on the floor. Her hands found his buckle and undid it, pulling his shirt free and pushing under to touch the warm skin beneath. To feel the muscles that tightened at her touch. His trousers slid down to his feet when she pushed at them.

He stepped out of them and kicked them aside. Reaching for her hips to draw her close.

She pulled back enough to look into his eyes. He was so close, beautiful to touch, to gaze at. To want. 'Jamie.' There was nothing more she could say. 'Jamie' summed up her longing. She reached for his hand and held it tight, as she had that day on the mountain. 'Please.' Please, please.

'How can I resist?' Jamie's smile grew wider as his hand tracked down her cheek, over her neck and reached her cleavage.

Her eyes closed as she tipped her head back.

'How do we get you out of this dress?'

Blink. 'Easy.' The off-the-shoulder netting hid the zip. Leaning forward, she scooped the netting up and sighed with relief as Jamie's fingers unzipped her dress, skimming over her feverish skin. Shaking her way out of the soft fabric, she reached for him. Slid her hands over those tight abs and down to the tightest, hardest part of his body. She held him, felt his strong pulse against her palm, and groaned with delight.

He swept her into his arms and walked to the couch. 'Don't stop,' he growled as he found her spot. Then, 'Yes, you'd better stop. Now,' he growled. 'Oh, Kayla, seriously. Stop. We're doing this together. No, I mean you first.' His finger was moving on her, fast, slow, fast.

Her hand was following his moves. Yes, they were together. She was so close.

'Whoa.' Jamie's head shot upwards. 'Stop. Protection.' He rummaged in his jacket pocket, removed a foil packet.

She could've laughed if she wasn't so near to exploding. He hadn't taken his jacket off. Shoving at it, she forced it off his shoulders, down his arms so he could shrug out of it without taking his intense eyes off her. They were smouldering with lust. And something else hovered. A depth of his feelings for her, for this moment. It gave her something to hold onto. 'Give me that.' Taking the condom, she began sliding it on, slowly, slowly, until he growled.

'Just do it, Kayla. I can't hold out much longer.'

Slowly, slowly, she teased with her hand.

He took over, placing his hand over hers and pushing down so he was encased before touching her again, hard and fast, and they were together, a rhythm of their own that became ever faster and then Jamie was inside her and she was shuddering and crying and falling into a deep hole of heat and stars. So magical she knew she'd never be the same again.

CHAPTER EIGHT

'KAYLA, IT'S ZAC. We've got a search going down and we need a medic. You available right now?'

'Absolutely. Fill me in.' Kayla headed for the laundry and her boots.

'Two people missing after a kayak was hit by a jet-ski on Lake Wakatipu. We're taking the police launch out.'

'I'll meet you at the jetty. You want Jamie too?'

'He's with you?' Zac didn't sound surprised.

Had they been that obvious last night at the wedding? Probably.

'What's going on?' Jamie asked, right behind her. 'We got a job?'

'Missing kayakers on Lake Wakatipu,' she answered, handing the phone over.

'Zac? I'm available.' As he listened he looked down at his clothes and grimaced. 'I'll change while you drive,' he said in an aside to her.

Great, now Zac would get the picture if he'd been in any doubt. 'Let's go.'

'Yes, bossy pants.'

'Nothing wrong with my pants.'

'I like what's in them best.' They raced out to his car, and he pinged the locks to grab a bag out of the boot before tossing her the keys.

She gunned the motor and headed away before he'd got his door shut. 'Zac didn't say how long these people have been missing.'

'Can't have been too long if the accident was reported immediately. Surely they won't be hard to find.' His trousers disappeared over the seat and those long legs were briefly visible, taking up all the space in the front.

Kayla grinned. Her legs had felt dainty lying between Jamie's when she'd woken that morning. 'Let's hope they've made shore.' Trying to ignore the undressing going on, or at least have some capacity for concentrating on what was important as she drove, she ran through a list of things to do when they found these people. Not *if*. That wasn't allowed to enter her thinking.

Zac had the motor idling as she and Jamie climbed aboard the boat. 'We've got everyone possible out looking for these people.'

'You wearing your police or your S and R cap?' Jamie asked Zac, already scanning the surface they were motoring through.

'Both. There are half a dozen boats out searching with locals, cops and Search and Rescue members on board, some on shore as well. I waited as we might need a medic. It seems whoever was riding the jet-ski has done a runner. There's no way he or she could've hit the kayak and not known.'

'I can't believe anyone would do that. What if someone's sustained serious injuries?' Bracing against the thumping of the aluminium boat, Kayla pulled the first aid pack out of the cupboard to check through the contents. Doing this kept her calm and ready for anything. When they were in position she'd join those on deck looking for any sign of life.

Reports came through intermittently on the radio. No

sightings so far, and the frustration was mounting in everyone involved in the search. Kayla stepped out into the chilly breeze and picked up a pair of binoculars to start studying the choppy water, the trick being to look for a movement or shape that was out of the ordinary, not to over-search everything in the viewfinder. It was a slow, methodical job, and kept them all busy until they reached the spot where the kayak had been found, and proceeded along the lake's edge.

Zac explained, 'If you have to go ashore, Kayla, Jamie will go with you.'

'When you take over as Chief of Operations you rub it in, don't you?' Jamie laughed, searching the water and the lake edge.

The radio crackled. 'We've got someone. On land. Male. Unconscious.'

'Co-ordinates?' Zac listened. 'We're almost on top of you.'

Kayla took the handpiece. 'Is he breathing?'

'Yes. Very shallow.'

'Have you laid him on his back?'

'Yes.'

'Tilt his head back to allow more air into his lungs. Keep a watch on his breathing—it can stop quickly.'

'He's not responding to stimulus.'

Not good. 'Try CPR for one minute. I'll be there ASAP.'

'What do you want me to do when we get there?' Jamie had already got the medical pack over his shoulder.

'I'll take over CPR if required. First I want to get water out of his lungs. I'm presuming he swallowed some or he'd be breathing properly.' She added, 'We'll need the rescue chopper, Zac.'

'Onto it.'

It felt like for ever, though it took only a couple of minutes to get to shore and clamber off the boat where one team member was waiting. 'Right here.' The woman indicated a large rock formation. 'I'd say he crawled away from the water before losing consciousness.'

Kayla dropped to her knees beside the lifeless-looking man and reached for his wrist, huffing in relief when she felt a light pulse. Better than nothing. 'You can stop the CPR, Simon, while I check for injuries.'

'Thank goodness. That CPR's no walk in the park.'

Jamie nodded. 'I agree. I can lift a power pole off a person in the heat of the moment but ask me to pump someone's chest for twenty minutes and I'm buggered at the end.'

'You wouldn't give up though,' Kayla said as she felt the man's chest, arms and then legs.

'True. We'll take over while you two get back to searching,' Jamie said to the others who'd been working with the man. He definitely had his second in command cap on.

'Roll our man towards you, Jamie. I need access to his back to listen to his lungs.'

As soon as Jamie had him on his side the guy coughed and water spewed out. 'How could he breathe with that in his lungs?'

'I never understand how lucky some people get. Not that he's out of trouble yet. But I can't find any other injuries, which is good. We need to keep him breathing and wait for the chopper.' Kayla reached for the man's wrist. 'Pulse still weak. Tilt his head back again, Jamie. I'll do some compressions and then we'll roll him on to his side again to see if there's more water in his lungs.'

Overhead the sound of rotors beating up the sky was getting louder, filling Kayla with relief. Never too soon for help to arrive. 'That was quick.' They must've been hovering in the air already, expecting urgency to be the main factor with anyone the rescuers found.

Becca was lowered to the ground and sent the hook back up for the stretcher. 'Hi, there. What've we got?'

Kayla filled her in on the scant details. 'Let's hope we find the second person in as good nick.' In other words, alive.

'You staying out here?' Becca asked.

'Yep, I might be needed when the second person's found.'

Jamie packed up the pack and slung it back over his shoulder.

'I saw that,' she growled.

'What?' he asked with false nonchalance.

'Stop being a bloke. That shoulder still hurts so I'll carry the pack.' She reached to take it off him, but Jamie stepped back. 'Or use the other one.'

'I'm fine. Anyway, I *am* a bloke. Or hadn't you noticed?' There was a cheeky gleam in his gaze.

'No comment.' She laughed. She'd noticed all right. More than once during the night. At the moment his height shrank hers while his shoulders blocked the wind coming from the lake, and his 'help anyone who needed it' attitude won her over every time.

Of course he put his kids before others, but he did the same for anyone needing help. Look how he'd had her back on the day the mountain had done its number on her. He'd held her hand and encouraged her to hang in there when she couldn't always focus on where she was. He'd made sure she was safe until the chopper had flown her off the mountain, and then he'd visited her in hospital. Yeah, this man had what it took.

A keeper.

Like Dylan. Gulp. Why did *he* have to pop into her head right after a night of over-the-top lovemaking that had caused her to feel as though she belonged with Jamie? Because she *was* more than comfortable with him. Could be she'd begun to let go of the past and by popping into her mind Dylan was reminding her of what had been? Their relationship had been wonderful, but it was gone. Though not entirely. She'd never forget Dylan and their special moments, no matter what came her way from now on.

Leaping onto the boat when Zac brought it alongside, Kayla reached for the binoculars, ready to focus again on what they'd come for from the moment they pulled away from the shore. She had to stop thinking about Dylan. It wasn't fair on herself or any man she became close to. And it would never be right to compare him and Jamie. But there were certain attributes she looked for in a man, and they both had them. Caring about other people was right up there.

'Take a pew.' Jamie gently pressed her down onto the steel seat at the back of the boat. 'Give those legs a rest.'

Now that she'd stopped working with her patient she was beginning to feel an ache niggling in her right leg, which might have something to do with last night's work-out. She grinned. Nothing to do with her injuries; they were months old and it was past time for them to get in the way of anything she did. 'Okay.'

'What? No argument?' One bushy eyebrow lifted in her direction.

'Saving it for something important.' He was too ob-servant. She put the binoculars to her eyes to keep Jamie from reading her mind and seeing how relaxed he made her feel, how hopeful for the future she was becoming. So much for never looking at another man or thinking she might not be able to get close to one again. He was knocking that idea down piece by piece. It was early days. He was special, but they were still getting to know each other. From her experience with Dylan, and watching Mallory fall for Josue, she knew true love was often an instant connection that only improved with time.

But she needed to get to know Jamie better before she threw in the idea of children and her worry about not being able to have any. She'd mentioned it to him before, but not in the context of their relationship.

'Zac, slow down,' Jamie called. 'Over there, just beyond those willow trees.'

'Where?' Kayla was up, looking across the expanse of water to the lake edge.

'See. Blue amongst the bushes.'

'Why don't people wear a colour that stands out?'

'He or she looks lost, dazed.' Jamie reached for the pack. 'Ready, medic?' His smile went straight to her gut.

'Absolutely.' She focused on the person they were getting closer to. 'There's profuse bleeding on the side of the head. It's a woman.' The figure dressed in a wet body-hugging sweatshirt and sports trousers was definitely female. 'Hello? Can you hear me?' she shouted over the idling motor.

No acknowledgement flared in the dull eyes looking around as though unsure why she was where she was.

Zac brought the boat close and Jamie grabbed a branch on the willow so the engine could be turned off.

Kayla slipped into the ankle-deep, freezing water and moved towards their second victim. 'Hello? I'm Kayla. A paramedic. This is Jamie, a rescuer.'

No response.

Reaching the woman, she went to take an arm and stopped. It hung at an odd angle. 'Broken below the elbow.'

Jamie took the other arm gently to lead the woman across to a fallen tree trunk a metre away. 'She flinched when she sat.'

'Could be severe bruising on her legs or buttocks.' Had she been hit by the jet-ski or the kayak as she'd been tossed out? The head wound suggested something had hit her hard. The woman had been walking so hopefully that meant her spine wasn't injured. 'I'm going to check her vitals, and then I think the best plan is get her on the boat so Zac can take us back to town.'

'You don't want another chopper?'

Kayla was looking at the head wound, and not liking what she saw. 'She needs a doctor urgently and by the time another helicopter gets to us we'll almost be back to town.' As they'd found the second person there was no reason to stay out here any longer. 'Unless there's one already in the air?'

Jamie shook his head. 'Not from what I heard.' He was holding the woman upright as she swayed on the log. 'We need the stretcher. She can't go into the water on her feet. Can you hold her while I get it?' He looked over to the boat. 'Forget that. Zac's bringing it.'

That's where a good team worked well. 'Pulse is rapid. Her breathing's erratic.'

Kayla talked to the woman while she examined what she could see. 'I've got you. Jamie and Zac will place you on a stretcher.' It was an old habit to talk to a patient even if they couldn't hear her. She liked to think either her words or the caring tone of her voice got through in some way. 'We'll get you in the boat and take you to hospital.'

'Zac, can you put the stretcher on the ground so Jamie and I can lift her onto it?'

'Sure can.'

'Jamie, on the count.'

Blink. The woman was staring at her as they lowered her.

'Hello. I'm Kayla, a paramedic.'

'Where am I?'

'By the lake,' she answered.

'What happened?'

As Kayla placed the woman's broken arm over her belly, she told her, 'You were kayaking and thrown into the lake by a passing jet-ski. Do you remember that?'

'No.'

'What's your name?'

'Lucy Moran.'

Good start. 'Right, Lucy. Is there pain in either of your legs?'

The woman's brows met. 'Not really.' She moved her feet. 'One foot doesn't move properly.'

'Wriggle your toes,' Kayla ordered. 'Tell me if you feel anything.' She couldn't see movement because of the woman's aqua shoes. Those would be removed once aboard the boat.

'Everything feels normal,' Lucy replied.

'What about your head? Any pain? Don't shake it,' Kayla cautioned.

'Big headache. That's all,' Lucy said, keeping very still.

Yet she didn't remember what had happened. 'Did you hear us talking when we arrived? Feel me touching your wrist? Before you opened your eyes?' Kayla added for clarity.

'I'm not sure. I don't think so.'

Then her eyes widened. 'Where's Avery? My boyfriend.' Tension began tightening Lucy's body. 'Is he all right?'

Under Kayla's fingers Lucy's pulse was increasing. 'That who you were kayaking with?'

Lucy was thinking, her brows knitted together again. 'What happened?'

'You tell me,' Kayla answered, needing to find out if there was a head injury at play. Lucy might've hit the water hard head-first. Apparently it was a sit-on kayak so the occupants hadn't been stuck underwater, trying to get free.

'I'm thinking. Yes, Avery and I hired a kayak yesterday to go camping on the other side of the lake.'

When she went quiet again, Kayla made up her mind. 'Let's go. I can't find any other injuries apart from that head wound and the fractured arm.' But the head wound worried her. Odd how Lucy had gone from dazed to aware so quickly, and was now rapidly fading again.

'Not good?' Jamie asked quietly.

She shook her head. 'I'm worried.'

The moment Lucy was loaded on board Zac had the motor running and Jamie untied the rope holding the boat in place. 'Let's go,' he said, then knelt down opposite Kayla. 'What can I do to help?'

'Try getting Lucy to talk while I deal with that head wound. I don't like her going under.' She called to Zac. 'Give the ambulance station a buzz, will you? Tell them Lucy's GCS is thirteen.' She began cleaning the wound, taking care not to cause pain.

'You feel anything where Kayla's touching your head, Lucy?' Jamie asked.

She blinked. 'What?'

Jamie frowned. 'I'm taking your shoes off, Lucy.'

Blink.

'Wriggle your toes, Lucy.'

'No problems there,' Kayla noted as Lucy responded.

Maybe it was shock causing her to wander in and out of full consciousness.

'See what you can find out about the accident,' Zac suggested.

Jamie nodded. 'What time did you set out this morning?'

Kayla found the cardboard splint in the medical pack and slid it under Lucy's arm, careful not to jar it.

'About seven.'

'So you do remember Avery being with you?'

'Did I forget?'

Jamie glanced up at Kayla, a question in his eyes.

'Keep questioning,' she mouthed. Whatever had inflicted the head wound might've hit hard and caused temporary brain impairment, though it was unusual that Lucy could remember most things other than this morning, and now that seemed to be returning. The sooner she was in hospital with the doctors the better.

Lucy's ankles felt normal. No swelling or bones out of place, no reaction to suggest pain. Her knees were the same. She could be wrapped in a thermal blanket without hurting her further.

'Are you a skilled kayaker?' Jamie asked.

'Only done it twice.'

'Do you remember how you got thrown out of the kayak?'

Lucy stared at Jamie. 'Where's Avery?'

He looked at Kayla.

She took over. 'If that was Avery we found lying beside the lake, then he's on his way to hospital, just as you are.'

She waited to be asked if he was all right, but the question didn't come. Lucy was staring over Jamie's shoulder at who knew what. Her pulse hadn't altered, nor had her breathing. 'Can you follow my finger with your eyes, Lucy?'

Lucy looked at her. Said nothing. Did nothing.

'Lucy.' Jamie spoke sharply. 'Can you see my finger?'

'Yes.'

'Follow it with your eyes.' Still a strict voice.

It worked.

Kayla nodded. 'Good.' Smiling, she noted down her observations for whoever met them with the ambulance at the wharf. Jamie was good. But, then, he'd spent years working in the fire service and would've worked with his share of injured people. She also liked how he read her well when she needed something done with a patient.

She liked Jamie. Full stop. Liked? More than liked. Cared about him, for him. Cared as in coming close to loving him. Yeah, life was heating up and there wasn't a fire anywhere in sight. Just the man beside her who flipped all her switches.

'I think we deserve brunch.' Jamie sighed as they stood on the wharf in town. 'Don't know about you but I'm starving.'

'The wedding dinner was a long time ago,' Kayla agreed with a cheeky smirk.

'We've been busy ever since.' He laughed. Hell, he felt good. A night like he hadn't known in years. Kayla was as sexy as sexy could get. They'd made love and settled into cuddling the night away, only to wind each other up to the point they had been exploding with need again. Oh, yeah, it had been a night and a half. Hopefully there'd be more on the horizon. Nah, closer than that. Tonight maybe. This afternoon? 'Come on. My shout.'

He took Kayla's hand and marched her along the narrow streets to a stone-walled pub hidden away from the tourists that served the best brunches in town. 'Are you catching up with Maisie today?' Just in case he was getting carried away with ideas on how to spend the day.

'No. She was on the first flight out this morning back to Tauranga via Wellington. She's on duty tonight.'

His heart soared.

Thanks, Maisie.

'When's she moving home?'

'In four weeks.' An elbow tapped his ribs. 'So we've got the rest of the day to ourselves.' There was a lot of teasing going on in those golden eyes.

Teasing he liked and would follow up on. Starting now. 'Champagne brunch? To keep the mood going.'

'Why not?' She grinned. 'Not that my mood's slipping. Not even those two people being thrown off their kayak and left to fend for themselves can dampen my spirits. My best friend married her soul mate yesterday and I had a night to remember.'

'We don't have to stop at one night.'

She squeezed his hand. 'I wasn't intending to.'

Her words didn't frighten him off. Life was looking up. Fast. Talk about suddenly rushing things, but he didn't want to stop, or slow down and think everything through—even if he could, which was doubtful. His body hummed tiredly with satisfaction and plain old happiness. If this was fast then he was up to running with it and seeing where it took them. 'Did I mention the boys are with their mother for two weeks?'

'About four times.'

'That all?'

'So this your way of filling in the hours till they get home?'

He knew a serious question when he heard one, even when it was hidden in smiles and laughter. 'I always miss the little blighters when they're away. I usually end up working extra hours at the fire station for the hell of it.'

'You need a life. Like I do. I'm all about work and avoiding the quiet times at home.' Now the smile was less intense.

But still knocking his socks off. Talking of which, 'Our boots are soaked from the lake.'

'We'll remove them at the door.' It seemed nothing could upset Kayla this morning.

Was he responsible for her happy mood? His chest expanded. That had to be positive. It meant they were in this together, having fun and enjoying each other's company. He felt valued, like Kayla wanted him for himself and not as a father or fireman. They'd turned a corner. 'Here we are.'

As they settled at a table with menus, Kayla asked, 'Are the boys okay with going backwards and forwards between you and Leanne?'

'They seem to be. At first they didn't trust it, thought we'd start fighting over who did what and where again, but they've come to accept we've reached an agreement and intend to stick to it. I was slower coming to terms with the arrangement.' Especially once David had married Leanne and stopped being so interested in Ryder and Callum, as if he'd used them to win over their mother.

'It must be hard—for all of you. I know how difficult it's been after losing Dylan, and there were no negotiations about anything to deal with, especially children.' She locked her gaze on him. There was no judgement in her voice, just understanding, pure and simple.

It was one of the things he liked best about Kayla. That, and her sexy body and cheeky smile. Right now there was a buzz in his body that made him eager to forget brunch and grab her hand to rush back to her house.

But he wouldn't, even though he had a shrewd feeling she'd be with him every step of the way. He wanted to get it right. Though exactly what that was, he couldn't be certain. He was interested in Kayla as a woman, as a friend, a lover, and was coming to care about her as someone special to look ahead with.

Interested? Turned on, hot, excited, more like. This morning the sky was more blue, the air clearer, his sense of purpose stronger. He had a life and suddenly he was enjoying it, and concerns about where this went with his boys had lessened. 'Come on. Let's get started on making the most of the rest of the day.'

Kayla laughed. 'Then we'll start on tomorrow.'

Tomorrow became two more days. Kayla hugged herself. Jamie was the *man*. They'd barely come up for air since the wedding, spending hours in bed here or at his house, watching movies snuggled up together on the couch, sharing meals and taking Shade for walks.

Last night reality had returned. Jamie had gone to work, and this morning she was at the ambulance station. She glanced around the room where the others on duty were quiet, eating breakfast or guzzling coffee, and on their phones, checking the internet, waiting for the first call-out while hoping it would be nothing too drastic. That's what she was thinking anyway. Something serious would bring her down to earth with a thud, and she so didn't want that.

Jamie was at home after knocking off at about six that morning. He'd called her a couple of times before she'd gone to bed last night just to talk some more. Like they hadn't said enough already. Every subject on the planet had been covered—except their burgeoning relationship. She hadn't wanted to raise it for fear of pouring cold water on her happiness.

What if Jamie suddenly decided he'd made a mistake and backed off? Or that he was only in it for the sex? What if he thought they were rushing things? Because they kind of were, and yet it seemed they'd been heading this way since they'd met on the mountainside months ago. And if that wasn't slow, what was?

Whenever the boys were mentioned, Jamie withdrew a little. What was that about? Didn't he think she'd fit in with them? He'd said they liked her and how good she was with them whenever they'd been together. He put them first, over everything, including his own happiness. She couldn't fault him for that, but surely he was allowed to have fun, and even another relationship? Surely he wasn't going to remain single because he was a father? That didn't make sense when he was such a loving man and had a lot to give.

'How was the wedding?' Becca asked from across the room.

'The best ever.' In more ways than one. 'Mallory and Josue cut a beautiful picture, and they're so happy.'

'Who's next?' Becca stuck her tongue in her cheek and winked at Kayla.

'Not me, for sure.' That was taking her newfound happiness too far. A relationship with Jamie, yes, but a wedding? *Why not?* She would never settle for less if she did fall in love again. A picture of a beautiful bouquet popped into her head. She'd swear Mallory had deliberately thrown it to her. She'd tried to give it back, but no such luck. It might be destiny waving at her.

Her phone lit up as a text came in.

Can't sleep. One half of bed's empty. Jamie xxx

Her heart softened.

You wouldn't be sleeping if it wasn't. xxx

Can't wait for the week to be over so we can get together.

She was working through to and on Saturday, and then, *Watch out, Jamie.*

Me too.

'We're on,' Becca called at the same time as the phone on Kayla's belt vibrated.

Reading the message, she grimaced. 'Eighty-five-year-old woman found on floor by bed, unconscious.' She shoved her own phone in her pocket. 'Let's go.' Being busy made the hours go past faster and brought Saturday and Jamie closer.

Jamie. She couldn't wait to hold him, have those arms around her. For the first time since returning to Queenstown the odd hours she worked were a pain. They didn't fit in with Jamie's shifts this week, and that was how it would always be. It was similar to being married to Dylan and her shifts not matching the long hours he'd put in. She was used to it, but that didn't mean she had to like it.

CHAPTER NINE

TWO WEEKS LATER it wasn't their shifts clashing that upset Kayla. It was because they'd finally got two days off at the same time, and Jamie was too busy to see her.

'I've got school enrolment to attend tomorrow, and then the boys have got a sports day to start the term off the day after. Sorry, there's not going to be much spare time at the moment.' Jamie sounded anything but sorry. More like this was how it would always be.

'I can come to watch them play sports,' she said.

'Maybe another time.'

She let it go. Arguing wouldn't win any points since he seemed determined about how this would play out. 'No problem.' But it was. There was a painful knocking in her chest. 'I'll see you later?'

'Why don't you join us for dinner tonight?'

Relief filled her, quietening the knocking. 'Love to. What shall I bring?'

'Yourself.'

'I like it. See you then.' Had she misread Jamie's reluctance about her going to the sports day with him? Could it be the boys' mother would be there and he didn't want any awkward questions? But if they were seeing each other, it wasn't to be a secret. She wouldn't stand for that. She couldn't imagine Jamie doing that either. Something else had to be worrying him. Not over her already? Her heart plummeted. Surely not.

Please, please, please.

Hang on, he'd said go round for dinner. She was over-thinking everything.

But when Jamie didn't kiss her when she got to his house, and made it clear she couldn't stay the night, it was hard not to wonder if she'd been right and he wasn't as keen as he'd appeared. 'Everything all right?' she asked when he returned to the kitchen after saying goodnight to Ryder and Callum.

'Why wouldn't it be?'

Leaning into him, she wound her arms around his waist, and rose up to kiss him. 'I've missed you.' So much she knew she loved him. He was a part of her now, always in her mind when she had decisions to make. It was Jamie who made waking up in the morning exciting and exhilarating.

His mouth covered hers and she fell into his kiss. Finally. It was as deep and full of passion as any kiss he'd given her. When they finally pulled apart, she was happy. 'That's better.'

'I've been wanting to do that since the moment you walked through the door,' Jamie admitted as he ran a finger over her cheek and started kissing her again. Suddenly he pulled back. 'Have to stop while I can.'

Her heart sank. 'You don't normally worry about stopping.'

Rubbing his chin, Jamie stepped back and sat on a stool, and reached for her hand. 'My boys aren't usually around when we get together.'

'So you don't want them barging in on us kissing, or more. I get that. But to be invisible isn't ideal. I am a part of your life now.'

Aren't I?

'I have to take this slowly, Kayla. If they get upset I'll call it quits and let you go.'

She stared at him for a long moment then pulled her hand free and sat down opposite him. Talk about blunt. Not what she'd hoped to hear. How well *did* she know him? 'Let's get this straight. I'm only a part of your life when the boys aren't around? When I get on well with them?'

His mouth flattened and his eyes dulled. 'You have to understand they come first.'

How could she not? It was plain as day. *And* he'd mentioned it often enough. 'I do, and wouldn't like you half as much if they didn't. I'm not going to hurt them, if that's what's worrying you.'

His sigh was sad. 'What if it doesn't work out between us? They've had more than enough to cope with in their short lives.'

'You're entitled to a life too.' She was all but begging. She wasn't walking away. She cared too much for him and wanted to share his life. Even some of it, if that's what it came to.

'Only when it doesn't affect my sons badly.'

'It doesn't have to. I get on with them and they don't seem to mind me being around. Not that we've done a lot together, but it's a start. You can have both them and me.'

'I want to, believe me.'

It hurt that he wasn't rushing to keep her with him and that wasn't only about being in his bed but everything they did.

Fight for him. Slowly, carefully, but don't give up already.

'Then we'll make it work. I don't expect to stay over when you have Callum and Ryder. Let them get used to me dropping in and out.' Was she getting ahead of herself? But the boys were always eager to see her and while Jamie hadn't said anything about her coming by often, his texts throughout the days when he wasn't being a dad at home told her he wanted more of her company. 'I don't want to lose what we've got, Jamie. You're special.'

He smiled.

At last. She relaxed. They would work this out.

'No one's said that to me for a long time.'

'Don't push it. I'm not going to repeat it just yet.'

'Damn.' He reached for her hand again, and tugged her off the stool to stand between his legs. 'You're pretty awesome yourself, Kayla Johnston.' Then he kissed her, slowly, mind-blowing with his sensitive touch.

It was hard not to leap onto his body and have her wicked way with him but they weren't alone.

Except four weeks later she was again struggling to understand where she stood with Jamie. For the two weeks Callum and Ryder were with Jamie, she hardly saw him. With her shifts not always lining up with Jamie's and what was going on in the boys' world, it was like doing a jigsaw wearing a blindfold. Jamie didn't seem to be making things easier. He always had something on when he wasn't working. Yet come the next two weeks when he was on his own, they were almost inseparable.

Now there was another fortnight to get through alone. At least Maisie was back in town, though it was hardly the same thing. After the amazing days and nights when she and Jamie had shared meals, bed, getting out on the lake in his runabout, to be suddenly alone at night and not have that sexy body to curl up against was doing her head—and heart—in. How could they go from full-on hot and sexy and sharing everything to quiet and withdrawn and no sex whatsoever and remain sane? She couldn't.

Worse, it hurt. Kayla was beginning to believe she was being used. Time to have it out. If he was going to break her heart then better to get it over with and she could go back to the busy, focused life she'd started on when she'd returned to Queenstown. Not that she'd got far with that idea what with the avalanche and Jamie interrupting her plans.

She drove to his house on a mission. Purposeful, ignoring the pendulum in her head asking, *What if he says go? What if he says sorry, please stay?* Only one way to find out and she was heading there to do exactly that. Not that she'd mentioned the L word. It was too soon to openly admit it, and she suspected it was not even on the horizon for Jamie. But what if he had no intention of ever settling into a permanent relationship that included the boys accepting her as part of the scene? That what they had was all about the sex and not much else? No. She refused to believe that. They connected so well.

'Where's Kayla? She likes sausages.' Ryder stabbed his plate with his fork.

'Yeah, when's Kayla going ride our skateboards again?' Callum added his two cents' worth.

Kayla, Kayla. Were the boys beginning to think she was letting them down? It was entirely his fault she wasn't here. Slowing things down until everyone was completely comfortable with her being in his life hadn't improved a thing and it had only made him more desperate to spend time with her.

Seems the boys are too.

So what was his problem? Afraid to take the next step?

Scared to get too involved and have his love thrown back in his face?

'Dad, where is she?'

'Working.'

'No, she's not. She's got tonight off. You're wrong.' Mr Know-It-All looked at him belligerently. 'I wrote it on the blackboard.'

'That's enough, Ryder. I've made a mistake, all right?' A big one involving a woman who had him in a state of amazement that he could even think of love again. A woman who had his kids writing down when next she'd be free to visit because they liked her so much. This was what he'd been hoping to avoid because he was afraid she might let them down.

More likely afraid to commit in case he was hurt again.

Starting over, trying to rebuild his confidence as well as the boys', trying to make them understand it wasn't anything to do with them or how they made their beds or brushed their teeth seemed too hard.

But what if it worked out for them all? Happy ever after? Did a relationship with Kayla have to go wrong? No avoiding how easily he'd fallen into loving being with her. They hit it off so well it was perfect. They liked similar food and being outdoors, shared a similar sense of humour. They had the same values about helping others and not hurting people. What could go amiss? Every damned thing. He'd loved Leanne, Leanne had loved him; they'd had a wonderful marriage. Where was all that now? He still didn't fully understand how Leanne had stopped loving him when little had changed in their lives, but she had. What if it happened again?

You'll never know if you don't take a chance.

'Kayla's here,' Dylan shouted, and jumped down from the table to race to open the front door. 'She's not working.'

'What? Are you sure?' Had she been reading his mind from afar, by any chance? Knew he was in a turmoil over her?

'Kayla, we're having sausages. Want one?'

'Best invitation I've had all day.'

Jamie sighed as her soft voice reached him, turning him to mush. How could he even be questioning himself about Kayla? He adored her. She did things to him he hadn't known for so long it was as though a drought had been overtaken by a flood of tenderness, excitement and hope. He wanted to believe in her, trust her with his heart, with his kids.

'It's your lucky day. I cooked too many.' He stood and hugged her. To hell with the boys. He kissed her on the lips, not fiercely, as he'd like, but just as longingly as he would if they were on their own.

She didn't reciprocate, remained impassive.

Warning bells started ringing. Something was wrong. Was she about to tell him they were over? Please, not that. He stepped back, pulled out a chair. 'Take a seat. Callum, get a plate and knife and fork for Kayla.'

She sucked a breath.

'You've already eaten?'

Easy, don't get uptight because you're fearful of what she might say. Wait and hear her out.

'No. I only dropped by to ask you something, and didn't think of the time. Sorry I've interrupted your dinner. I should've phoned.'

Since when did she have to do that? On the weeks he had the kids, that's when. 'Don't worry. It's great to see you. Really,' he added. It was. Whatever was putting that worried expression on her face, he was happy to see her, to have held and kissed her, however briefly. 'Like I said, there's plenty of food to spare. I got a bit carried away.' His mind had been on other things, mostly Kayla. She got to him in everything he did now.

'We got a new bottle of tomato sauce, Kayla,' Callum piped up. 'You can have plenty this time.'

She sat down. 'Sounds good to me. What's everyone been doing? How's school going this week?'

Jamie listened to the excited chatter from his boys, acknowledging how readily they'd accepted Kayla. They had right from the beginning, which cranked up his concern about being wary of her in their lives. She smiled as she listened to the boys talking over each other. A smile he looked for whenever he was with her, and hadn't received so far tonight. 'Here, get that into you.' He put the plate down and returned to his chair.

'Looks good.'

It was a basic meal, but the boys loved it, which saved a lot of arguments at the end of a busy day. Maybe not the greatest way to make sure they ate well, but anything that saved a lot of hassle was worth it. 'Careful or I'll cancel the food magazines I signed up for last week.'

'Trying to impress me, by any chance?'

'Absolutely.' Was it working? He wanted to rush the boys through dinner and into the shower so they'd go to bed and he could talk with Kayla, find out why she'd acted uncertain when she'd arrived. Instead he held onto his patience and enjoyed the moment. Like an ordinary family after a normal day at work or school. Normal. Family. Yeah, it felt good, despite Kayla's reticence. And his own.

'Can we have ice cream, Dad?' Callum asked, knowing full well it wasn't Friday night. 'Ple-ease.'

There wasn't a scrap of food left on either of the boys'

plates. He glanced at Kayla, saw amusement blinking back at him and caved. 'All right. Just this once,' he added, knowing they'd ask again tomorrow.

'You want some, Kayla? It's got jellybeans in it.'

'No thanks, guys.'

'What about me?' Jamie called after Callum as he headed out to the laundry and the freezer.

'You don't like it.'

'True.' He stood up to clear the table, reached for Kayla's plate. 'What've you been up to today?'

'Apart from dealing with a heart attack, a broken ankle and taking an elderly gentleman from the hospital back to the retirement home, not a lot.'

'A quiet day, in other words.' The heart attack victim would've made it or she'd be rattled. Unless that had been behind her quiet mood when she'd first arrived. 'You all right?'

'Fine.' Then Kayla looked directly at him. 'Can we talk when the boys are in bed?'

The alarm bells were back, tightening his gut, chilling his skin. Not fine at all, if that flattening of her sensual mouth meant anything, and he knew her well enough to accept it did. 'We'll have to wait a while. It's barely gone six.'

'No problem.'

Then why were her fingers digging into her thighs so hard? 'Kayla? What's up?'

'You've got more than me,' Ryder shouted.

'Boys, quieten down.' He crossed to the bench to sort out exact servings of ice cream, cursing under his breath. Holding out the plates, he told them, 'Take these to the other room and watch some TV quietly.'

'I didn't stop to think about what you'd be doing or

what time it was, sorry.' Kayla was rinsing dishes to place in the dishwasher.

His gut tightened some more. Kayla didn't do impulsive, unless there was a challenge involved. He shoved the ice cream into the freezer and banged the door shut.

A challenge?

'What's up?'

She inclined her head in the direction of the lounge. 'Later.'

Five minutes would be too long, let alone an hour that included showers, bedtime reading and lots of giggling. Plugging in the kettle, he made two cups of tea, all the time aware of Kayla watching him, winding him tighter than an elastic band stretched to its max. 'Come on. We'll sit on the deck.'

The sun was still strong, but the deck roof afforded some shade. Kayla sat on the top step leading down to the lawn that was long overdue a cut, and sipped her tea, staring at her feet. Looking vulnerable. Looking like all the fire had gone out of her. Like the Kayla he'd held after that traumatic accident where the woman's had heart stopped twice.

Suddenly Jamie's tension increased. Had he made her uncomfortable with his abruptness? He was only protecting himself, but he should've waited till she'd talked to him. If she was upset then he had to be patient and help her out. He wasn't used to standing back. If that didn't warn him how much he cared for her, then what would? He sat down beside her. 'Come on, spill.'

Her back straightened, her shoulders tightened as her head came up. 'You've told me Ryder and Callum must come first in anything you choose to do.'

He opened his mouth to reply.

Kayla shook her head. 'Let me finish.' She drew a

long breath, and as her lungs let go she continued, 'I understand, I really do. What I don't know is where I stand with you. I'm doing two weeks on, two off, my life revolving around the times you don't have the boys.' Her beautiful eyes were dark and serious. 'Am I being used?'

'No.' His heart banged hard. 'No,' he said, more quietly. 'Not at all.' He reached for her hand, trying to ignore the pounding under his ribs. She couldn't believe that. She mustn't.

She pulled away. 'You're sure? Because from where I'm sitting it looks like it. I can visit for a meal sometimes but don't get invited to sports days or to have a burger in town. Tonight's the first time you've even kissed me in front of the boys.'

What to say? She was right. He'd been deliberately keeping both sides of his life pretty much apart. Did he want to continue like that? Or was he ready to step up and meld it all together? 'I haven't been using you, Kayla. I admit to being cautious about getting too involved. Not only because of my kids but I'm afraid of being hurt again.'

'You think I'm not?' Those beautiful eyes locked onto his. 'I'm willing, ready, to take a chance with you, Jamie. I care for you, a lot.'

His heart expanded as love stole under his ribs.

'But if you don't feel the same about me then say so and I can get on with my life,' she added.

The warmth evaporated. She'd laid her feelings out for him to see, to decide what he wanted to do. He wanted her, all the time, in every way. Time to man up. Be honest. Lay his heart on the line. He opened his mouth, closed it again. This wasn't easy. It should be. Kayla wasn't going to make it any harder for him than he already did for himself. He adored her. He adored his boys.

Everyone had to be certain and feel safe. He had to try. But he had a feeling that trying wouldn't be enough. He had to commit or say goodbye.

'I see.' Kayla began to stand up.

Jumping to his feet, he took her hands in his. 'No, you don't. I want you in my life.' Hell, he hadn't said that to anyone since Leanne and it hurt because reality had shown him how wrong it could all go. This was like having a tooth pulled. He wanted Kayla to know how much he adored her, but saying it out loud? Hard to do. He squeezed her hands. Pulled her closer.

She tensed, leaned back. 'How much, Jamie? Fortnightly or all the time?'

There was no getting away with half-measures when Kayla was involved. Which was how it would've been with him too if not for his failed marriage. Did he want Kayla to walk away, never to come back? No. So was he ready to do this? He smiled, feeling good. She did that to him when she wasn't winding him up. 'How about all the time? See each other regularly every week and weekend and whenever?'

Her body sagged like all the air had evaporated out of her. 'Seriously?' A smile was finally starting, growing bigger by the second. 'Truly?'

'Yes, absolutely. We'll give it a go, see how everything works out.'

A flicker of doubt crossed her face. 'See how it works out? A trial run?'

'Sorry, that was blunt, but it's what I mean, yes.' Dropping her hands, he leaned back against the upright holding the roof above them. He had some say in what went on, and this was one time he wasn't backing down. He had to be certain their relationship would work well for the four of them before he committed one hundred percent. She must understand that. 'Makes sense to me. I'm not going through what I went through with Leanne ever again.'

'I am not Leanne. I'm Kayla.'

He held his breath. There was more to come. He saw it in her eyes, in the tightening of her body.

'I cannot "give it a go".' Her fingers flicked in the air between them to emphasis her words. 'For me it has to be all or nothing. Love's the whole deal, no part shares.'

'What if it turns out you can't handle being a stepmum or I don't like the way you care for Ryder and Callum?' His heart was breaking already.

'Then we'll work it out, talk about it. But it isn't all about them, Jamie. We're about us too. Our lives matter, our feelings for each other count more than anything otherwise we haven't got a chance. But a trial run? No thanks.'

The self-protective instincts began rising. 'You're not worried that your feelings of loss over Dylan won't taint our relationship? You won't be fearing you might hurt one of us if we get it wrong?' His fighting cap was firmly in place now. He wasn't giving up the idea of having Kayla in his life on a more permanent basis. But neither was he committing to for ever just yet.

'Of course the thought of anyone getting hurt worries me, but that's the nature of relationships. We all take risks. When I fell in love last time I never considered anything going wrong. Then life dealt a hideous blow, and I've carried the pain for a long time. Since I met you it's been ebbing away, leaving me happy and ready to start again. There are no guarantees, but I refuse to try out a relationship like taking home a dress to see if it is right for the occasion I have in mind.' Kayla leaned against the opposite post and regarded him. 'Jamie, I have fallen for you.'

Clang. That was his heart hitting his ribs. Kayla loved him? Was that what she was saying? Had he found what deep down he'd hoped would be his again one day? Bang, bang, went his heart. Yes, this could work out. It had to. He wanted this more than anything. Kayla was so special, he adored her with all his being. 'I care a lot for you too.' The L word was huge and stuck deep inside, not easily said, but he'd got close. 'I'm just asking for time. Time we can share as a couple and a family with the boys, taking it slowly.'

She nodded.

'Obviously there are a lot of things to talk through, such as which house to live in, though I'd prefer to stay in mine as the boys are settled.' Again he came back to his kids and what was right for them, ignoring what Kayla might like. Was he using the boys as an excuse because he was scared to commit? Was he really ready for a full-on relationship? Or did he want to continue living alone with no adult to discuss the day-to-day hassles with, to share a meal with, have fun with after all? The every-day things that couples shared and were more difficult when faced alone?

'Jamie?' Kayla was watching him with an intensity that warmed and worried him. 'You're not ready, are you?'

'Come on. I said we should give it a go and see if we are meant to be a couple. How more ready than that can I be?'

Her hair brushed her shoulders when she shook her head. 'I love you, Jamie, and for that I'd do anything to be with you. But I want the whole deal. Eventually marriage, maybe our own children—if possible.' Her voice wavered. Then she lifted her head higher. 'Definitely commitment. Not a "let's see how we go" approach, but a full-on, jumping-in, let's-do-it commitment. If you can't do that then it's best we call it quits now.'

The warmth chilled. Bumps rose on his skin, his heart was quiet and his mouth dry. He had no answer. He couldn't say, move in and marry me. It was far too soon. What if they argued all the time, or fell out over the kids, or she decided his job was too dangerous and asked him to quit, as Leanne had done? But she had mentioned more kids while knowing what his work involved. It was easy to feel they were good together when the pressures of everyday life weren't getting in the way. But he also knew how wrong even the best love could go, so he wasn't leaping in boots and all. 'I need more time.'

'I'm sorry, Jamie. I hoped we might've been on the same page, but guess I was wrong.' Stepping close, she stretched up and kissed him lightly on the mouth. 'Take care. I'll see you around.' Tears streaked her cheeks as she left, striding down the steps and along the path to the front of the house where her car was parked.

'Goodbye, Kayla,' he whispered around the lump blocking his throat. She loved him. No one had loved him for a long time. He wanted her back. Now. To share whatever life decided to throw at *them*. But his feet were stuck to the deck, unable to move. If he chased after her, he couldn't guarantee he'd give her what she wanted. And he wanted to be able to do that more than anything. If he weren't so scared.

CHAPTER TEN

'MAISIE, WHERE ARE YOU?' Kayla stared through the wind-screen at the crowds wandering through town. Couples walked hand in hand as they chatted and laughed, twisting her heart. Why hadn't she gone straight home from Jamie's? Because it was too damned lonely in her house, that's why.

'I'm heading home. Hang on. I'm pulling over,' Maisie said. 'Okay, what's up? You sound terrible.'

Nothing to what she felt. 'I just broke up with Jamie.' Was it a break-up when they hadn't really admitted to a relationship in the first place?

'Where are you?'

'In town.' She named the street she was parked on.

'Don't move. I'm coming in and we'll go for a drink. You can tell me everything.'

That's what good friends were all about. Kayla sighed and blew her nose. Damned tears wouldn't stop. She loved Jamie. And he didn't want her.

'That's not true,' Maisie said when Kayla told her everything as they sat in the bar with glasses of wine between them. 'You said he wanted to give it a go, that he cared about you. Sounds to me like he wants you.'

'You're saying I should go along with a trial run?'

Kayla stared at her friend. They were always honest with each other, sometimes too much, but tonight she'd have been happy with a hug and some agreement over taking a stand. 'That's not me, and you know it.'

'Hey, I'm merely pointing out Jamie obviously cares for you.'

'But not enough. I want to be a part of his life all the time but he doesn't seem to understand I'm serious and not intending to cause any problems, but apparently he's not a hundred percent certain we can make a go of a relationship.' Sipping her wine, Kayla remembered something else. 'I mentioned I'd like marriage and maybe kids one day. He never picked up on those.' She'd love kids of her own, and to have Jamie's would be amazing—if she could get pregnant and not miscarry.

Despite the grief Ryder and Callum had been through, it had never seriously crossed her mind that he mightn't want any more. Maybe it shouldn't surprise her, yet it did. He was a wonderful dad, and had a huge heart. Big enough for more children *and* her? She'd believed so enough to be prepared to take a chance on the hurt if she failed to become pregnant and see it through to holding their baby in her arms.

'It's not necessarily over. You've probably blindsided Jamie as much as he has you. Give him time to think everything through. He might come crawling up your drive to offer all you want and more.' Maisie looked sad, not hopeful, which didn't help. 'In the meantime, we'll get busy with shopping trips, and try to prise Mallory away from Josue's hip for a girls' weekend somewhere.'

'Something to distract me is definitely needed right now.' Or she'd go back to being a workaholic, filling in every hour to avoid thinking too much about what might've been. Maisie could say what she liked, but Jamie wouldn't come begging or try to put his case forward more forcefully. He was a man who made up his mind and stuck to it. So why couldn't he do that with them? Accept her love and let her into his heart? 'I need another wine.' She stood up. 'You?'

Maisie shook her head. 'Driving. We'll leave your car in town.'

Sinking back onto her stool, Kayla muttered, 'I'm being selfish. I'll drive home for the next wine. You want to join me? There's always a spare bed.' Two, in fact, since she had a three-bedroomed house all to herself. She'd invited Maisie to board with her when she returned to Queenstown, but Maisie was firmly ensconced in her brother's house. Damn it.

Feeling sorry for yourself?

Definitely. But she'd had her heart broken before, and this time didn't intend to fall into the doldrums quite so deeply.

'You really love him, don't you?' Maisie asked.

'It sneaked up on me. We've always had a connection, but it took a while to realise what I feel is love.' Silly, silly girl. She'd known there was every possibility of getting hurt and she'd taken the risk. 'When am I going to learn?' Long, lonely days loomed ahead. She could almost wish there was a search and rescue happening every day. Almost. But not even her hurting heart could really wish that on someone. At least Maisie was back in town, and Mallory did occasionally spend a day with them.

'Do we ever?' Maisie drained her glass. 'Come on.'

'Might as well.'

'Now you're being glum.'

Kayla followed, agreeing but unable to lift her spirits. 'Maybe I was too tough on Jamie. My way or no way.'

One well shaped black eyebrow rose as her friend nodded. 'There is that.'

'I was like that with Dylan sometimes.' He'd always taken it on the chin, sometimes giving in, sometimes not. A point in his favour. She'd never want a man to kowtow to her every wish. Today being an exception. Jamie in her life would be perfect. Couldn't he see how much she loved him and would do whatever it took to make it work for them? Except come second to all else. Was she wrong to be so adamant about what she wanted? Should she have given Jamie a chance? 'What have I done?'

'Stood up for yourself. Give yourself a break. I bet Jamie's going over everything too. Who knows what he might decide?'

I sure don't.

Kayla checked her phone. No messages. Not even a call-out from Search and Rescue to take her mind off everything.

The following four days off duty were long and slow. Her house had never been as clean and tidy as it was when she finally went back to work, and that was saying something. The windows gleamed, the oven looked as good as the day it had been installed. The lawns had been cut to within an inch of their lives, and not a weed showed in the gardens.

She rang Jamie once, only to be told he was on his way to a fire at Arrowtown and he'd call her later. He never did.

That told her where she stood. She didn't want to believe it. Pain flared harder than ever. She loved Jamie. They got on so well that none of this made sense. He'd said he wanted to spend more time with her, so why suddenly not talk to her? Was she struggling to deal with her determination to be together? She thought her call showed that the door was still open. But had he decided they were finished? Better to stop before they got in too deep and couldn't extricate themselves without hurting each other and the boys? Too late for her. She was aching head to toe with the love he'd pushed away.

On the second Saturday after their bust-up Kayla made up her mind to be proactive. Ryder was playing rugby at his school, so she'd go to the game. She missed the little guys almost as much as their dad. What if she had agreed to give it a try? They'd be sharing nights, having laughs and learning more about each other. But it would always be hanging in the back of her mind, what if Jamie decides to back off? Love was about commitment. Commitment got couples through the bad days, the hard decisions, the difficult moments. If they knew they could walk away from their relationship at any time, the chances of success were weakened.

When she'd fallen in love with Dylan there'd been no doubt about getting together. Neither of them could wait to share their lives. That's how it should be. But there hadn't been anyone else at risk. This time there was. Jamie always put Ryder and Callum first. She couldn't expect any different if he loved her. He hadn't mentioned love, though. Caring. Yes. A man of few words, it might take a bomb for him to utter the L word. He'd acted as though he loved her. Or had she been reading too much into his actions, his tenderness, his caring? Quite possibly, because she wanted it so badly.

Love had been missing for a long time. Her doubts of ever finding it again had overridden everything to the point she'd felt lonely, so when she'd admitted she loved

Jamie she'd expected the same in return. No hesitation, no worries, just acceptance.

She groaned. What an idiot. She'd been unfair. But he hadn't fought for her, hadn't said, 'Let's talk some more.' No, and neither had she. For someone who always fought for what she believed in she'd been hopelessly inadequate over her relationship with Jamie. What a shambles.

Parents lined the rugby field where two teams of young boys were running around, chasing the ball, with little idea of what they were supposed to do, Ryder in the midst of it all, a cheeky grin showing how much fun he was having.

Kayla watched for a while, happy to see him again. He was a character, pushed life to the full, and hated losing. A small version of his dad.

'Hi, Kayla. Why are you here?'

She looked down into Callum's upturned face and felt a knock in her chest. 'I thought I'd come and see how you guys are getting on.'

'Thought you didn't want us anymore.' He scowled.

Gulp. Is that what Jamie has told them? Please, not that.

'Of course I do. I miss you.'

'Might be best if you didn't say things like that,' came the deep voice she'd missed so much.

She spun around and stared at Jamie, her heart pounding hard. 'You don't like me being honest?'

'I don't want their hopes raised, then dashed.' Jamie stood tall and proud, but there were shadows in his eyes, like he hadn't slept much.

The intervening days since she'd walked away from him had made everything more difficult to understand. This need to defend herself wasn't how caring relationships worked. But, then, she wasn't in one, was she? 'You didn't return my call.' Where was the determination to see this family and hopefully clear the air a little that had brought her to the school field? Since when had she become so gutless? 'I remembered Ryder saying he had a game every Saturday morning, starting this week, so I thought I'd pop along and say hello.'

'I see.' But he didn't. It was obvious in the tightness of his face, the unrelenting straightness of his back, how his hands were jammed into the pockets of his jeans.

'I'm not using him as an excuse to see you. I miss you all, okay?'

'Dad, did you see that? Ryder got a try.' Callum was jumping up and down in front of them.

Jamie's head flipped sideways as he scanned the field for Ryder, whose teammates were leaping around and yelling happily. 'I missed it,' he growled.

'Dad!' Ryder was charging across towards his father. 'I got a try. I got a try.'

'Cool. Go, you. That's great.' Jamie high-fived his son. 'You rock, son.'

The whistle went, getting all the players' attention, and Ryder bounced back to join his team.

'First try ever.' Jamie watched him with love spilling out of his eyes.

'And you didn't see it.' Regret hovered between Kayla and Jamie. Because of her, Jamie had been distracted. 'I'm sorry.' It wasn't enough, but what else could she say? 'I really am.' She turned to walk away, go home and clean out the freezer or some such exciting activity.

A strong hand gripped her shoulder. 'Don't go, Kayla.'

Callum stood at his side, his worry staring up at them.

Hesitating, she waited. When Jamie said nothing more she turned to study the face she adored. She loved this man. She'd do anything to be with him. Anything except let him procrastinate over their relationship. 'I'll stay and watch the rest of the game because I told Callum that's why I'm here.'

'Good.'

She had no idea what was good. The fact she was staying for the game, or that she'd walk away at the end of it. He wasn't explaining 'Good' and she wasn't asking. Standing beside him, arms and hips not touching, she watched the kids running around, trying to get the ball off each other and often not knowing what to do when they did. A bit like her at the moment. 'How's your week been?'

Bloody lonely. Sleepless. Full of despair. 'Busy with the boys and work.' Normal, except it couldn't have been further from how Jamie's life had become since letting Kayla in. The feeling of having found something so special he was afraid to break it reared up in his face to prove that's exactly what he'd done. He'd torn apart what they'd had going between them. All because of the fear of facing being hurt again. What was he? A man or a puppy? An idiot or a careful parent? Using his sons to protect himself rather than the other way around?

Kayla said nothing. Though she appeared focused on the game, he didn't believe Ryder was getting all her attention. Tension held her hands hard against her thighs.

'We've got an S and R training day next weekend on Mount Aspiring. You coming?' They were bringing in a guy from Mount Cook to take the teams out for a day on the lower slopes.

Her head dipped abruptly. 'I'm planning on it.'

'The ten-day forecast isn't looking great. Heavy rain's expected.' Jamie sighed. Who gave a toss? What he really wanted to talk about was them, and ask how she was getting on, and if she missed him. 'What are you doing after the game?' Hold on. Why ask? Because he couldn't help himself. He'd missed Kayla so much nothing felt right any more.

'Might visit Mallory since Josue's working.' Her voice lacked enthusiasm, which was unusual when it came to her friends.

He ached to pull her into his arms, hold her close and tight, kiss the top of her head and beg her to give him another chance. Ready to go all out, then?

'Run faster, Ryder.' Callum was jumping up and down.

Jamie looked over the field and saw Ryder racing towards the goal line with all the other boys chasing him, including those in his team. 'Go, Ryder, go.'

Ryder looked around as though he'd heard him, and tripped, sprawled across the grass, letting the ball fly out of his grasp.

Wanting to rush across and make sure he hadn't hurt himself, Jamie held back, holding his breath. The kid wouldn't thank him for turning up like a crazed parent.

Kayla's shoulder nudged his arm gently. 'He's fine. Look how he's getting up and giving his friends cheek at the same time. He's tough.'

Warmth seeped in, pushing away the chill that had been settling over his heart. Kayla understood him so well. How could he not live his life with her? Not dive in and take all the knocks on his chin? Because for every wonderful moment there'd be plenty more knocks. His arm slipped around her shoulders, tucking her closer. 'I know.'

Kayla smiled. The moment Jamie put his arm around her all the sadness and loneliness fell away. She'd come home. They belonged together. No doubt. But where did that leave her? In limbo? Because nothing had changed. There was a conversation that needed to be had or she'd have to walk away again.

'Are you and the boys doing anything this afternoon?' Her heart was banging, her hands clenching, opening, clenching.

'We're heading over to Leanne's. Her mother's visiting and I always got on well with her. Still do. And I want to catch up.'

So why did he ask what I was up to?

'That's got to be good for everyone.' Kayla straightened away from Jamie and stared out over the field, not seeing anything except her hopes disappearing.

'The boys are staying on. It's Leanne's turn to have them.'

Meaning?

'We could have coffee when I get back.'

Shoving her hands in her pockets, she turned to look directly at him. 'We could. But why do I get the feeling you're not sure you want to?'

'I've missed you. I know I've made a mistake, but...'

'But?'

'Dad, the game's finished. We've got to go.' Ryder was running towards them. 'I want to see Grandma.'

Jamie flinched.

When he opened his mouth, Kayla nearly put her hands over her ears. Excuses weren't going to make her happy. He'd made his choice and it didn't include her. He couldn't integrate his family with her. Shaking her head, she turned and walked away. Again. Only this time she would not be turning up to watch a rugby game or phoning Jamie. It *was* over. She'd been slow to grasp how far over, but now she got it in spades. That hug had undone her wariness so she'd just have to dig deeper to put it back in place.

A distraction was required. A seven-point-two earthquake might go some way towards one. Or a blizzard closing all the roads and stranding people in the hills that she could go out to rescue.

When her phone rang three hours later guilt sneaked in. Had she brought this on? 'Zac, what's up?'

'Where are you? I think I just passed you on the road in Sunshine Bay.'

The speeding police car. 'You did.' She braked, pulled over.

'Caff's Road. Three-year-old girl backed over by vehicle in driveway. Can you come?'

She was already pulling out. 'On my way.'

The first person Kayla saw was Jamie. Then the little broken body on the gravel drive.

'Excuse me.' She pushed past people, dropped to her knees, ignoring the sharp stones digging in and reaching to feel the toddler's pulse in her pale neck. Beat, pause, beat, beat. Weak but real. It was only the start. There was a long way to go if she was to save this child. Blood from a wound above her eyes had stuck black curls to the girl's forehead. Her body lay sprawled at an impossible angle. 'Ambulance?'

'It's been called, but there's a hold-up due to an accident in town,' Zac informed her. 'That's why I called you.'

'She's breathing,' Jamie said. 'Barely, but she is.'

Kayla nodded. 'There's a thready pulse. You keep watching her chest movement.'

'No one's moved her,' Zac told her. 'Her name's Sian.'

'Sian, I'm Kayla, I'm going to help you, okay?' Of

course she wouldn't be heard but it was how Kayla did things and she wasn't changing that just because this kid was so badly injured she was unconscious and unlikely to be otherwise for a long while.

A woman was screaming at someone in the driveway. The mother? The driver of the vehicle that had hit the child? Kayla shuddered, shut the noise out.

'Zac, can you put the hospital on standby and tell them this is a stat one emergency?' Then Kayla focused on what she could do, not what wasn't available. Blood was pooling below the child's groin area and underneath, spreading across the concrete. 'A torn artery. She'll bleed out if we don't stop this. I need a towel or clothing. Now.'

Jamie had his shirt off before she'd finished and was folding it into a wad. 'Here.'

Pressing the wad in place, Kayla looked at Jamie. 'Hold it down hard. Don't worry about hurting her. We've got to slow that bleeding.'

'Onto it.' He took over while she checked the little girl's chest.

How was Sian breathing at all with the trauma done to her ribcage? 'Is there a tow bar on the vehicle?'

Zac again. 'Yes. I think it knocked her down then the ute went over her. The driver panicked and drove forward when he heard shouts.'

'She's lucky she wasn't pulled along,' Kayla muttered. She couldn't believe the child was alive. 'Where's that ambulance?' Would the rescue chopper be faster? She didn't know how long the lungs were going to hold out after the impact from that tow bar. She continued assessing the injuries. 'Two broken femurs, left arm appears fractured in more than one place, and as for internal injuries, who knows?'

'Breathing's slowing,' Jamie warned.

To hell with protocols. This kid's life was in danger. Kayla leaned in and carefully exhaled air into the girl's lungs through her mouth. Worried about moving the girl's head in case of spinal damage, she had to wait for the lungs to deflate, then breathed for the child again. And again. Time stood still.

'I hear sirens,' someone called.

She didn't stop, kept breathing, pausing, breathing for the child. When a paramedic appeared beside her, she said, 'Carl, we need oxygen, neck collar, spinal board and splints.' For starters. 'And tape to strap that wad in place before Jamie can release pressure on the bleed.'

Carl nodded. 'Jessie, you hear that?'

Jessie handed Carl the medical pack and went to get everything else.

With speed and absolute care, the little girl was slowly attached to monitors, her head held in place with the neck brace, and Kayla inserted an oxygen tube so that Jamie could immediately begin pumping the attached bag to keep her breathing. Carl taped down the wad holding back the bleeding. Finally they slid the spinal board underneath and placed her on the stretcher.

'I'll come with you,' Kayla told Carl.

'Good.' He didn't waste time talking, climbing into the ambulance to take the stretcher as Jamie and Kayla pushed it forward.

Kayla felt a warm hand touch her arm and then Jamie was gone. The door closed and the ambulance was rolling down the road towards town. That touch melted her, told her she wasn't alone after all. The man she loved had been there throughout the trauma of dealing with this seriously injured child and had still had a moment for her.

'Sian, hang in there,' Kayla muttered as she read the monitor and cursed the low heart rate. Please, please,

please. 'I do not want to do compressions on those smashed ribs.'

Josue and Sadie were waiting when Jessie backed them into the hospital bay.

And so was Jamie when Kayla walked out into the fresh air after filling the doctors in on all the details. Leaning against the wall in the same spot he had been the night they'd brought the German woman in after her car accident.

Like that night he called, 'You all right?'

She crossed over to him, but not straight into his arms. She wanted to, more than a hot shower, clean clothes and a painkiller for the headache pounding behind her eyes. But if she did, they were back to square one. Weren't they? 'Sort of. I'm shattered.'

'That's normal for you.'

'It never feels anything like normal at the time. I'm always terrified I'm going to lose my patient.'

'You were fantastic. I doubt Sian would've made it this far if you hadn't been there.' He brushed her hair off her face, then gripped her shoulders and looked into her eyes so deeply she couldn't feel the ground underneath her shoes. 'I'd trust you with my boys any day of the week. For everything.'

She stared, trying to read him and afraid to acknowledge what she was seeing because she wasn't exactly great at reading men. Not the men she cared so much for, anyway. 'It's what I do,' she said defiantly.

'I know. I've always known, but I've been afraid to accept it. I don't want them getting hurt, but you won't do that. Not intentionally, and I doubt in any other way.'

One tiny step and she'd have those arms she longed for wound around her, holding her near, supporting her shaking body. One tiny step and would she have the future she yearned for. Holding back wasn't easy but necessary. He was still only talking about his boys. Not himself. 'I won't deliberately hurt you either, Jamie. If I didn't believe that I wouldn't be here.' She was so close to falling in a heap at his feet that any release of the pressure from his hands and it would happen.

'I know that, too.' He brushed a kiss over her cheek. Not like last time. 'Come on, I'll drive you home. We can collect your car later.' Taking her elbow firmly, still supporting her faded stamina, he led her to his truck and opened the door.

'How did you come to be at the scene?' she asked.

'Leanne lives two houses down. We heard screams and I went out to see what was going on. She kept the boys inside, away from seeing anything.'

'Right.' Too tired to think what that might mean, she laid her head back and closed her eyes.

At her house he followed her inside and went down to the bathroom to turn on the shower. 'Get in and soak away the exhaustion and grime, Kayla.' His smile was soft yet serious. Filled with care and concern. 'I'll go put the jug on for a coffee.'

His clothes were as filthy as hers after holding down on Sian's injury.

'You need to clean up, too.' Kayla pulled her shirt off, undid her jeans zip.

He skimmed her cheek with a finger. 'You sure?'

'Are you?'

'Yes, sweetheart, I am. Nothing matters but us.'

Stepping out of her jeans, Kayla hopped into the shower and shoved her head under the water. She needed to be clean, to wash away the horror of the accident, and then she'd be ready for Jamie.

Joining her, he took the shampoo bottle and squeezed

some onto his palm, then began rubbing it through her hair, soaping her head, her face and down her neck. Tipping her head back for the water to rinse her hair, she closed her eyes and went with those hands. Down her arms, back to her shoulders and over her breasts, stopping to circle her nipples to bring them to throbbing peaks. Then his palms were soothing her stomach, her hips, thighs and then between her legs.

Suddenly nothing was slow and gentle but pulsing and hot. Her hands gripped his shoulders as she was lifted to place her legs around his waist, felt his need for her at her centre.

He was sliding into her, slowly, bringing with him a need so great it overwhelmed her. 'Take me, Jamie. Now.' Please.

He retreated, returned to be inside her. 'Oh, Kayla, love, I adore you.'

'Now, Jamie.' She'd start screaming if he didn't bring her to a peak *now*.

Hot, gripping sensations rocked her, took over all thought as he plunged into her and roared as his need spilled, bringing her to a climax along with his.

Afterwards they dried each other with thick towels and slipped into clean clothes.

'You should carry something dressier than a pair of orange overalls in your truck.' Kayla laughed as she sipped coffee on her deck overlooking town. It was easy to laugh, even when she had no idea what the future held. It just had to involve Jamie. Was she giving up on holding out for everything? He had just shown a little was better than nothing, but could she do a little for ever?

'Nothing wrong with these.' Jamie grinned. 'You can see me for miles.' Then his smile faded. 'I mean it, Kayla.

I love you more than anything. I've missed you too much these past couple of weeks.'

He'd said love. He loved her. 'I hear you.' But she wasn't sure what he was offering with his love. She waited, her hands rolling the mug back and forth, back and forth.

'I'd like a relationship with you. No what-ifs. No asking if I'm sure. Just leaping in and believing in each other.'

Her heart spluttered, started pounding. Really? Had he just said that? 'Yes,' she whispered.

Jamie hauled her into his arms and took her mouth with a kiss like no other. Her head was light. The sun shone brighter. But best of all Jamie was holding her like a piece of precious crystal, as though he never intended to let her go again.

Kayla kissed her man back with all the love swelling in her heart. She'd do anything for him. Anything. He was her second love, and she was going to hold onto him so tight they'd always be a part of each other's lives. Pulling her mouth away just enough to say, 'I love you,' she smiled. A smile filled with all the wonder and love that was her life.

EPILOGUE

HANDS IN POCKETS, Jamie watched Kayla as she sat in the autumn sun with a book in her hand. Her legs stretched the length of the outdoor sofa. Her hair was tucked back in a loose tie. There were shadows under her eyes and one finger kept scratching at the page she was staring at. There'd been no page turning for five minutes.

His heart squeezed with love. Kayla had turned his life around, putting him back on track for a happy future. He and the boys had moved into her house two months ago as it was more comfortable for the four of them than being cramped in his boxy one.

But now something was worrying the love of his life. There'd sometimes been a haunted look in her eyes over the past week that had twisted his gut. He thought he knew what the problem was but had been giving her space to tell him in her own time. Except a week was too long and they had to talk. Now. Kayla needed him, and he was here for her. His hand tightened around the contents of his pocket.

'Jamie.' She was watching him as she shifted so her feet were on the deck. 'I've something to tell you.'

Damn but they were so in sync at times it was scary. He sat down beside her and reached for her hand. 'I thought so.'

'I'm pregnant.' A hopeful smile appeared and for the first time in days her eyes were filled with sunshine. 'We're having a baby.'

A bubble of warmth swelled inside, filling him so much it hurt and he couldn't talk. He was going to be a father again. With Kayla. Her hand was soft in his as he lifted it and kissed her palm. 'I thought so,' he repeated.

'You guessed? Because I stopped having a wine with dinner?' Her smile widened, hitting him in the heart.

He loved this woman so much sometimes he had to pinch himself. Swallowing hard, he answered, 'Because you keep touching your stomach when you think I'm not looking, because you haven't slept properly for the past week, because I love you and know you.'

And because you've been tipping out your wine when I'm not looking.

He kissed her forehead. 'I love you.' They were in this together. A baby. *Yee-ha.* As long as the pregnancy went full term... He didn't want Kayla being hurt again.

'I should've told you straight away but...' Her hand clenched in his. 'I was scared, Jamie.'

'Of course you were. Do you know how far along we are?'

Her mouth lifted at one corner. 'Eleven weeks. I only ever made it to eight weeks before so this time's looking good.' She gasped. 'If I don't hex it by saying that.'

He hugged her tight. 'You won't.'

She sighed. 'I'm trying not to get too excited, just in case.' Touching his lips with her forefinger, she shook her head at him. 'I didn't notice I was late for the first month, and then it was as though I refused to believe what was happening the next month. This morning I toughened up and had an HCG. The doc says everything's looking good and there's no reason why I won't go full term.'

So that's why she hadn't been at home when he'd got

back from work. 'This is the best news. I'm loving it. Seriously. We are pregnant. I'm going to be a dad again.' And he'd thought things couldn't get any better since they'd moved in together.

'Isn't it wonderful? Oh, Jamie, I'm so excited. Now I've told you it's like I've put the past behind me totally. We *will* have this baby.' Tears streamed down her cheeks. 'It's amazing.'

Leaning in, Jamie kissed her, gently. 'Kayla Johnson, I love you to bits. Will you do me the honour of becoming Mrs Gordon?'

Her eyes widened and her smile grew. 'Yes, Jamie—oh, yes, please.' The tears were flowing faster. 'I love you.'

Taking the small red velvet covered box from his pocket, he opened the lid and held it out to Kayla. 'I had this made last week. I hope you like it.'

She stared at the ring made of gold with a dark sapphire set between two smaller diamonds sitting on white satin. 'It's perfect.' She raised her stunned gaze to him. 'How did you know?'

'Your mother showed me the photo of your grandmother's ring.' Apparently Kayla had been promised the ring as a child but it had been lost when her grandmother had gone into a rest home.

'Mum knew you were going to propose? And Dad?'

'I had to make sure they agreed.' He grinned. 'It's been hard not saying anything while I waited for the ring to be made.' He lifted it from the box and reached for Kayla's hand. 'I love you, Kayla. We are going to have a wonderful life together.'

He believed it, heart and soul. She made him happy, and strong, and ready for anything. He'd found love.

* * * * *

FALLING FOR THE BILLIONAIRE DOC

AMY RUTTAN

MILLS & BOON

For Christine and Sif,
for the inspiration and the name!

CHAPTER ONE

Freaking cold.

Dr. Henry Blake scowled up at the first few flakes of snow swirling around in the air. He hated the cold. He hated the fresh air, the woods and the windchill, and he scowled up at the cloud-covered sky, hoping he could melt every single last stupid snowflake that was falling down.

Why am I here again?

And then he distinctly remembered why he was back in Colorado in the bitter cold of February. He remembered why he had been dragged away from his warm, beautiful beachfront home in Los Angeles—to deal with a problem at his father's request.

He had been born in Aspen, Colorado. It was where his father was the governor and sat on the boards of many hospitals in the state. Even though it was Henry's birthplace, his family didn't spend much time here. His parents were elite and wealthy, and only came to Aspen when the powder was fresh so they could rub elbows with the rich and famous.

His parents preferred Denver, DC or New York City. Basically, wherever their powerful friends were, his parents weren't far behind.

Whereas he had always been left alone.

Alone in a large house in Denver.

Alone at boarding school for the holidays.

Alone and scared.

Henry didn't have many fond memories of Colorado.

Or the winter. He hated how coming back unpacked feelings he kept carefully locked away.

He had returned only because he sat on the board of Aspen Grace Memorial Hospital, one of the hospitals his father had invested a lot of money in.

And then there was the debt Henry owed to his father. One he was sure he could never really repay. One that left him beholden to the man who was biologically his father, but emotionally meant nothing to him.

Henry hated owing anyone anything, and he did care about the hospitals he was involved in.

Even if it necessitated being in Colorado and subjected to the winter he loathed so much.

His father had big plans for the future of Aspen Grace Memorial. But, apparently, there was a problem in going forward with tearing down the old and building the new.

And that problem was one Dr. Brown. Henry knew nothing about her although he had read a couple of articles she'd written in medical journals.

She was smart, a good surgeon, but very, very vocal about her displeasure with his father and the board of directors.

She was the reason he was back in Colorado. She'd been ignoring his calls and emails. Now he had to come and meet her face-to-face. Which annoyed him all the more.

More than the cold weather.

Henry jammed his hands into the pockets of his coat, trying to hunker down under his scarf as the wind shifted and blew a blast of snow straight into his face.

"You know, you should've dressed a bit better, Dr. Baker. This isn't LA."

Henry glared at his father's driver, who had pulled up to meet him at his parents' private hangar. While he was glad of the private plane and the ride, he couldn't help but be irritated by the reason for it.

You owe me, his father had snarled.

I owe you nothing, Henry had said. *Send someone else to deal with Dr. Brown.*

His father had glared at him. *Remember all those gambling debts? Remember how you walked away from medicine and almost ruined your career in Los Angeles, how we supported you after Michelle died and how we covered up all your indiscretions.*

A chill had run down his spine. *Yes.*

You owe me this. I saved your career. Sent you to the finest schools. You can deal with this problem. I can't do this with the election coming up.

Fine, but after I do this we're done. No more holding anything over my head.

Very well.

What would you have me do?

His father had shrugged. *Seduce her for all I care. Just shut it down.*

Henry had no plans to seduce Dr. Brown. Woo her maybe, charm her, but that was it.

And he hoped this one last favor would put an ending to owing his father.

To have it brought up every time he saw him.

Then Henry could be free.

Can you ever really be free?

"I won't be in the area long, and I have no plans for frolicking outside," Henry grumbled. "I have work waiting for me in Los Angeles. I only came to deal with Dr. Brown and get the demolition back on schedule."

His father's driver, Mike, laughed, and Henry had a sinking feeling in the pit of his stomach, which he ignored as he climbed into the back of his parents' luxury sedan, thankful for the heated seats.

Henry wasn't going to stay long. A week tops.

All he had to do was deal with Dr. Brown, listen to her issues and get everything back on track to build Aspen Grace Memorial into a cutting edge private medical facility. Then he could return to his beach house.

What's waiting for you there?

He shook the thought away. He needed to focus on the task at hand.

AGMH was run-down.

It was overcrowded and didn't serve the community. Tourists didn't feel safe using the hospital. They didn't like it.

The hospital board wasn't planning on doing away with the hospital completely. The board was going to build something better in its place.

Something that would bring in lots of money.

Only Dr. Brown didn't see it that way and she was protesting. Handing out flyers, stopping construction. Attending meetings at city hall to try to put a stop to it. It was slowing down the progress.

Henry really didn't care one way or another.

His father did, though.

So that's why he was here.

He owed his parents this. They had saved his life and reputation after Michelle died; however, after Henry dealt with this, he was done.

He'd sell his shares in the hospitals and cut ties with his parents.

He had spent far too many years trying to please them, hoping they'd love him, when it was clear they never would.

The only person who had ever loved him was Michelle and she was gone.

Henry sighed.

It was inevitable that his mother would soon come to see him, and no doubt she'd start harassing him about settling down and the family image. His parents hated his lifestyle of dating women in Los Angeles for short stints. It looked bad for their good family name.

The wholesome image his father promoted didn't seem exactly truthful when there was an unsettled son dating all the wrong kind of women.

If only the general public knew his real father.

His father was not a good family man.

His father was a charlatan.

Of course, the one time he had been serious with someone she hadn't come from the right family. She hadn't been good enough.

She'd been good enough for him, though, and he smiled as he thought about her.

She'd been gone for eight years, but the hole in his heart remained.

Michelle had been the first person to get through the walls he'd built as a child to protect his heart. The first person to truly love him, and he had adored her.

He had imagined a life, marriage, children with her, and in one tragic instance it had all been snatched away. He would never go through that pain again.

And he was tired of his parents throwing what they thought of as respectable women at him. All he wanted was to be left alone.

Was that too much to ask?

So now he was in Aspen to deal with Dr. Kiera Brown so that his father didn't have to, and with any luck this would be the end of it. The end of his father holding his indiscretions over his head.

Constantly reminding him how much he owed him.

How Henry wasn't good enough.

This was the last thing he would do for his father.

Henry knew, in his father's eyes, he'd never be that perfect son.

The one time he had come close to being that was Michelle. Only Michelle had thought he was worthy of love. Even that had gone spectacularly wrong when she had died following an accident. The only good thing in his life had been taken away eight years ago.

It still stung.

It still hurt after all this time.

Michelle had been his world. The only woman he had ever trusted. The only woman who hadn't wanted anything from him in return for his love.

She had loved Henry for himself. When Henry had been with her, he had forgotten all those sad, lonely years as a child.

She had given him hope.

Michelle had been his everything. Michelle and medicine. They had never failed him.

Medicine had made him happy at one time. Just like it had made Michelle happy, too, but in a way, in the end, medicine had failed Michelle.

And now Henry was jaded with life, with work.

He'd lost passion for everything.

He just wanted to be back in California and be left alone.

That's all he wanted.

He scowled the closer they got to town. The traffic

was backed up and the mountains surrounding the town were covered with skiers.

It was the height of the tourist season.

This wasn't the time of year he liked being in Aspen. He had a condo here he rarely visited. He'd come back maybe three times since he bought it, and that was in the summer. He often thought he should sell it, but he was glad he had it now. Hotels would be booked solid, they would be crowded and noisy, and there was no way he was staying at his parents' place.

He had enough bad memories of that house.

Is there any time of year you like to be in Colorado?

Michelle had loved Colorado. Though he hadn't understood why, if it had made her happy he would have stayed.

He'd met Michelle in Denver.

Why do you want to settle down in Colorado? he'd asked her. *Los Angeles is more exciting!*

You're from Colorado, she'd teased.

Exactly. He had smiled and kissed her. *Take it from me. There's nothing great about living in the mountains.*

I love the mountains. I grew up in Salt Lake City, Utah. I'm used to life elevated. Her blue eyes had sparkled. *Don't you think this would be a great place to raise a family?*

One day, he'd grumbled.

Exactly. She had wrapped her arms around him. *We'll both have thriving practices. We could stay here. I know you hate living in the shadow of your parents, but I love Colorado. We can live in Denver and take our kids skiing in Aspen, we'll stay at your parents' ski lodge and in the summer we can go back to Salt Lake City to see my family or even drive up to Yellowstone.*

He'd groaned. *I forgot you're an outdoorsy person.*

And you love me for it.

Michelle had been right. He *had* loved her for it. And it hurt his heart, even eight years later, when he thought of her. When he let those thoughts creep through into his mind. Of the life they could've had together. Maybe he would've liked Colorado more, Aspen more, if he had been with her.

If they'd had the family they planned on.

That had all been taken away from him.

Snatched cruelly.

He'd been back, but rarely.

And it was because he had let those thoughts creep into his head that he was so angry that he had been forced to come here and deal with this. At least he was almost free of his parents.

Mike turned down a street.

"Where are we going?" Henry asked.

"To the construction site," Mike responded.

"I was supposed to head to the hospital. That's where I was going to have my meeting with the heads of the departments and Dr. Brown."

"Dr. Brown is not at the hospital. I called ahead, Dr. Baker. She's at the construction site and she's protesting."

"She's protesting?"

Mike nodded. "I figured you wanted to speak with her first. In fact, I have instructions from your father to put an end to any kind of demonstration at the construction site. He doesn't want the police involved."

"Of course not," Henry grumbled to himself under his breath.

His father wouldn't want there to be a scene. His father abhorred the press unless it was good publicity.

A doctor campaigning at a new hospital site was not good publicity.

Of course, neither were his countless dates with Los

Angeles glitterati. Even though none of those dates were ever serious. The women wanted something from him and he from them. His father hated the tabloid shots of Henry. And just thinking of that, he smiled briefly to himself.

Mike pulled in close to the work site, boarded up for the winter but ready for construction in the spring. Henry was expecting to see more people with Dr. Brown because he knew there were others who didn't want AGMH to shut down. He was bracing himself for the worst and was taken aback when he didn't see a horde of protestors.

It was just one lone woman, bundled up against the cold, holding a sign that had a picture of his father's face with devil horns and dollar signs painted on it.

In glitter.

Portraying his father's greed.

She wasn't wrong. His father didn't value much; nor did his mother, which was something he had learned as a child being raised by servants and sent away to boarding school.

Henry tried to wipe the smile off his face, but it was hard not to laugh. It was kind of absurd—and admirable. He looked up and saw in the rearview mirror that Mike's eyes were twinkling with mirth, too.

"So this is Dr. Brown?" Henry asked.

"Yep." Mike nodded.

"I won't be long." Henry opened the door and pulled his coat tight as a blast of cold wind blew down from the mountain against him.

He slammed the door and Dr. Brown paused, but didn't drop her hold on the sign. The biting wind helped him to keep a straight face. So that was something.

"Dr. Brown?" he asked, stepping closer.

All he could see were two brilliant green eyes, staring back at him over a thick scarf that was wound around her face and under a knit beanie that was jammed on the top of her head.

"Yes?"

"I'm Dr. Baker. We were supposed to have a meeting at AGMH."

She rolled her eyes. "I don't need a meeting with the governor's son on my day off. I have more important things to do."

"What? Being the only one marching in the middle of a snowstorm campaigning against a new hospital?"

Those green eyes narrowed. "Exactly. Although, this is hardly a snowstorm."

"You do know that I sit on the board of directors for AGMH. I am technically your boss." He shivered against another blast of bitterly cold wind.

"Yes, but I'm not on call. I'm not on duty today, and the last time I checked it was my right to demonstrate wherever I want. So if you'll excuse me…" She hoisted the sign up further and continued her march.

She wasn't wrong, but he was annoyed just the same. This was not going to be easy.

"What're you hoping to accomplish?" he shouted over the wind.

She turned and looked back at him. "Are you willing to discuss terms?"

No.

That wasn't his position, but right now he wanted to get out of the cold and have a rational meeting. His father had made it clear he didn't want attention drawn to this situation. That's all he had to do. Get her to stop this, and he could go back to his life in Los Angeles.

What life?

"Sure," Henry agreed, lying through his teeth.

There was nothing really to discuss. He was going to tell her to end her foolish protest or find somewhere else to work. It was as simple as that.

Dr. Brown lowered her sign. "Fine. I'll go with you, and we can talk about this and see if we can come to some kind of resolution."

"I'm giving you a drive?" he questioned as she marched past him toward the car.

"I walked here. My house isn't far. We can go there if you'd like, but I figured you'd want to discuss things in the boardroom in the hospital. You know, exert power over your lackeys."

What was her problem?

And now he understood why Mike was laughing and why his father was in such a tizzy and hadn't wanted to deal with Dr. Brown himself.

Rock. Meet hard place.

"Fine," he said through gritted teeth. "We'll go to the hospital."

She nodded. "You know, you really should be wearing a thicker coat. This is winter, after all."

Henry clenched his fists.

Maybe this wasn't going to be easy at all. He climbed into the back of the car while Mike helped Dr. Brown wrestle her sign into the trunk and then held the door open for her as she slid in.

She was still wearing her hat and scarf.

"You have the heat cranked in here," she remarked.

"As you said. It's winter."

Dr. Brown pulled off her hat and a cascade of red hair tumbled out. He could hear the electric shock of static electricity, and some of her hair stood on end.

Then she unwound the scarf from around her face, and he was in absolute awe when he laid eyes on her.

Henry didn't know quite what he'd been expecting, but he knew it hadn't been someone so young. The Dr. Kiera Brown he'd been briefed on was not the person he thought she'd be.

He had expected a surgeon more around his father's age, given her lists of accomplishments. Not this gorgeous, vibrant woman sitting in front of him.

Not someone so beautiful.

There was a zing of something, a spark that warmed his blood, even in the bitter cold. Something he hadn't felt in a long time.

He'd been attracted to other women since Michelle, but it had been nothing like what he was feeling now. And that unnerved him.

"What?" she asked, noticing him staring at her.

"Your hair is standing on end." Which wasn't untrue. It was, and it was something he could focus on instead of her lips. Or instead of wondering how soft her hair was or how she tasted.

Pull yourself together.

She made a face and shrugged her shoulders. She pulled off her mitts and ran her slender fingers through her hair trying to tame it, but it just seemed to make it worse.

"So you're the governor's son," she said, pulling back her hair and tying it.

"And you're the thorn in my father's side," he remarked.

When Dr. Brown smiled, there was a glint of amusement in her eyes that Henry could only describe as mischievous. "I am, indeed."

He was in trouble.

Big trouble.

* * *

Kiera had known that Governor Baker was sending in his son to deal with her today, and she didn't care. That wasn't going to stop her from her mission.

The board of directors and shareholders of Aspen Grace Memorial Hospital were threatening to tear it down and replace it with an elite facility that would cater only to the wealthy who came to ski and frolic in a winter playground, which was all very well, but what about the rest of the people in Aspen?

Those who lived here year-round.

Those who couldn't afford the prices of the wealthy?

Lives were in jeopardy.

And she knew firsthand what a lack of medical care could do, especially when someone couldn't afford it.

Her best friend, Mandy, the only family she had in the world, had been working for a nonprofit organization as a nurse. She didn't have insurance, and when an accident left her paralyzed from the waist down all she could afford was an HMO who had botched her surgery. Kiera swore then and there that she would help those who couldn't afford proper medical care. Just like her late mother.

Her mother had been addicted to drugs and unable to get the help she needed, and Kiera didn't really remember her. Just snippets.

The only thing she recalled vividly was fear.

Her father, unable to cope with his own addiction had tried to be there for her, but more often than not she had been alone.

Scared.

Hungry.

Until one day her father had abandoned her in a diner in Colorado Springs.

Kiera swallowed the lump that had formed in her throat. She didn't want to think about her parents.

Or her father.

Or the fact she hoped he'd come back one day.

It wasn't logical.

What *was* logical was saving the hospital. She had to be strong. She couldn't get emotional in front of the governor's son.

She had to be strong. The clinic was all that mattered.

She might be a surgeon in the emergency department, but she gave as much spare time as she could to the free clinic that had started only because she had demanded it. She helped people like her parents and others that couldn't afford health care.

That made her happy.

It kept her busy.

Now, because of greedy bureaucrats, everything was threatened.

Aspen Grace Memorial Hospital was in danger and she was the only person trying to save it. She wasn't unfamiliar with fighting the good fight.

She'd done marches on Washington.

She'd stood up for the rights of people who were marginalized, as much as she could. And she'd taken a minor in social justice at college.

The biggest problem was getting more people on board with saving Aspen Grace Memorial, and it frustrated her. She didn't have the best people skills, and she had a hard time trusting, but she wasn't going to let that stop her.

The chief of surgery was on her side, to an extent, but she was the only one out there in her free time picketing, handing out flyers and attending planning meetings at

city hall. Yesterday, she'd been down in the dumps thinking that it wasn't working. Today she felt better now that
she was sitting next to Governor Baker's son.

She was getting noticed.

This was the traction she needed.

Do you think all this protesting is wise? Mandy had
asked, wheeling herself up to the dining room table where
Kiera was working on her sign.

*I think so. It's worth it. They want to shut down Aspen
Grace Memorial and build some expensive, private hospital. Only the wealthy tourists will be able to afford
medical care there.*

There are other hospitals, Mandy had stated gently.

*With the death of Aspen Grace Memorial comes the
death of the free clinic. None of the other hospitals have
our free clinic.*

Mandy had sighed. *I get that you're doing this for me.
You don't have to.*

It's not just for you.

Mandy's expression had softened. *Your mom?*

And your dad. She brushed a tear away. *It's not right.
He helped others and no one helped him. He couldn't
afford to keep up his practice and pay for his cancer
treatments.*

He never did tell me he was so sick, Mandy had said
sadly.

He didn't want to burden us.

I would've helped him, Mandy whispered.

So would I.

That had touched Kiera's nerve. It was guilt. Kiera had
been off working in Denver. At a hospital that had paid
her a lot of money. Growing up poor, growing up in the
system, the money had blinded her.

She didn't have so much time for Mandy or Wilfred back then. All that had mattered was work and money.

Mandy had been her only family and vice versa. Mandy had stayed in Aspen where they grew up, in her late father's home. She had worked as a nurse and was going to start work with Doctors Without Borders. Until the accident. Until the gunshot that had paralyzed her.

If Kiera had been there, she could've had Mandy sent to Denver or to a neurosurgeon who could've done a better job than the HMO did and maybe, just maybe, Mandy would be walking still. If she had been there, she would have paid for better care for Wilfred.

Kiera hadn't been there because she'd been greedy and working in Denver.

And for that, yeah, she felt guilt.

He didn't tell either of us, Mandy had said. *He was stubborn. Don't feel guilty. Although you never listen to me.*

Kiera had smiled and Mandy had taken her hand.

This isn't guilt, Kiera had said quickly. *This is the right thing to do.*

Kiera shook the memory from her head. It made her emotional. Again that pesky lump formed in her throat, and she was quick to swallow it down and get control of her emotions again.

You're strong. Remember that.

Mandy would be impressed that she'd gotten attention from the governor. Even though it actually wasn't Governor Baker himself, it was his son.

Still, it was something.

She'd gotten under the shareholders' skins.

The only thing she hadn't counted on was how handsome Dr. Baker actually was. She had imagined someone different. Like those rich stuffed-shirt bureaucrats she usually dealt with. It had taken her by surprise to see him standing there. Her heart had skipped a beat and her blood had heated.

He made her nervous.

He made her feel naked and exposed, which was unsettling. She didn't like attention. And she had a hard time with feelings of attraction.

She'd suffered enough broken hearts from people who had abandoned her in her life. She usually just locked those feelings away.

It was safer.

She was better off on her own.

Are you?

When Kiera glanced at him, he was looking at her, which sent a shiver, a zing of something down her spine.

He had dark brown eyes that seemed to see right through any kind of facade, and that was unnerving. He had perfectly coifed hair and he was incredibly tall. She pegged him at six foot three, minimum, and she was five foot nine. The way he looked at her made her sweaty and anxious.

Like when she stood out in a crowd. She always hated that. She preferred to stay out of the limelight. It was how she had learned to survive bouncing from place to place after her mother died and her dad had tried to stay clean and keep a job.

Only he never could.

She tried to blend in, be unseen so he wouldn't get angry at her. And when she was in the system, with other kids, she had remained quiet and hidden. It was easier.

At school and at work, she stayed in the background so people would never use her or hurt her. She knew how to survive.

The one time she had let someone in she'd fallen head over heels in love with Brent.

They had been colleagues and then something more.

She had never before let any man into her heart.

And then he had crushed it.

He had cheated on her and left her.

Abandoned her.

She'd learned her lesson then.

Never again.

Still, the way Dr. Henry Baker looked at her, like he saw her. He made her tremble with something she had never felt before.

Why are you thinking about how handsome he is? Get control of yourself.

Henry was the kind of guy she used to date before she found out that the men she typically dated didn't really care for the same things she did. The respectable kind of guy that would never fail you or abandon you didn't seem to exist.

She had thought dating men like Dr. Henry Baker, who were educated, would mean they would be interested in the same issues she was. She didn't want a man like her father, who had abandoned her and was only interested in partying.

She'd been sorely mistaken.

Men like Henry couldn't be trusted, either. Brent had taught her that.

When she had left her high-paying job for Aspen, she had expected Brent to follow her, take up the causes she was so passionate about. Instead, he took up with someone else. Someone younger.

Someone who had adored him and hung on to his every word.

It had hurt, and she had become disillusioned with

men, but she wasn't going to give up on helping others. Her foster father, the only decent man she had ever known, had taught her that.

Men like Dr. Henry Baker were usually embarrassed by her marches on Washington and her need to be involved in helping those less fortunate, but Kiera was undaunted, so she just stopped dating and focused her time on taking care of Mandy, Mandy's grumpy cat, Sif, and saving lives.

That's what gave her the ultimate fulfillment.

Did it?

Henry was all wrong for her. He'd be like Brent, not interested in the things she was. Only she couldn't remember having such a strong physical pull toward Brent.

She hated the way her body was reacting being around Henry.

She hated imagining what it would be like to run her hands through the dark brown curls that had just a touch of gray at the sides.

To nibble that strong jawline.

You just met him!

She shook the thoughts away. They'd just lead to trouble and she didn't want trouble.

Yes, you do.

It depended on the trouble and it had been some time since she had felt anything other than numbness. Kiera knew then and there she had to put some distance between her and Henry.

She had to focus.

"So, I'm looking forward to hearing what your father has to say about AGMH and the status of the free clinic. You're obviously here to negotiate."

His eyes narrowed. "No. I'm not here to negotiate."

"What?" she asked, annoyed. "You said that you were.

That's why I left the construction site. You wanted to talk to me about terms."

"This isn't some kind of union disagreement. You were alone out there."

"So? If you're not willing to discuss things with me, then you need to stop the car and I'll walk back." She picked up her beanie and jammed it on her head.

He rolled his eyes. "I do want to talk with you, Dr. Brown, but I'm not here to negotiate anything."

She'd heard enough. She was fuming and with the way her cheeks were suddenly hot, she knew they were bright red with anger. That always happened when she got mad. People might mistake it for humiliation, but, really, she was just furious.

"Mike, can you stop the car?" she asked. She knew the governor's personal driver well as he lived in Aspen, and whenever the governor was there, Mike wasn't far behind.

"Sure thing, Dr. Brown." Mike flipped on his turn signal to pull over.

"Mike, don't stop the car," Henry ordered.

"Mike, stop the car." Kiera glared at Henry.

"I have to stop the car, Dr. Baker. You don't live here, and I don't want to be on the bad side of the best surgeon in Aspen," Mike said. "I've got to listen to her."

Henry snorted. "Best surgeon?"

If she was a teapot or some kind of cartoon-like character, Kiera was pretty sure there would be steam shooting out of her ears.

Privileged much? Who did this guy think he was?

The car pulled over and she glared at Dr. Baker. "Thank you for the interesting ride, but I think I'll head back to continue what I was doing."

"No, wait." Henry rolled his eyes and reached out,

leaning over her and grabbing her hand to keep it from opening the door. His hand was strong and warm on her cold skin. His body, pressed against her, caused her heart to skip a beat. It caused a rush of something, and this time her cheeks heated for another reason. One she didn't find particularly comfortable.

"Why should I stay here? What's the point? You already told me you weren't interested in listening to me, so why shouldn't I go?"

Henry sighed and scowled. He ran his hand through his perfectly coifed brown curls and sighed again as if in resignation.

"Fine. How about I agree to listen to your reasons for not closing down Aspen Grace Memorial Hospital? Has anyone actually done that? Because from what I understand that's been mostly falling on deaf ears."

Drat.

He was right, of course. No one but the chief of surgery, Mandy and Sif the cat had listened to her, because no one would give her the time of day. She passed out flyers, attended meetings, but nobody seemed to get it.

Now she had a chance.

Dr. Henry Baker was a majority shareholder at AGMH. He was on the board of directors, though usually absent, *and* the governor's son.

She wouldn't get this opportunity again, and even though it seemed no one has been listening she must be making an impact. She was sure of that, because here Dr. Henry Baker was.

No matter how much he scoffed at her and didn't want to negotiate terms with her, he was offering the chance to at least listen to her.

"Okay," she said, pulling her hand back, wanting distance between her and Henry.

Henry moved away from her.

"Good."

"Is it okay to go?" Mike asked, glancing in the rear-view mirror.

"Yes," Henry said.

Kiera leaned back against the leather seats. Henry wasn't saying much, but he looked annoyed. She had a feeling he had thought this might be easier. He clearly hadn't been expecting someone like her, but honestly, she hadn't been expecting him either.

"Thank you for taking the time to listen to me, Dr. Baker. I appreciate it."

Henry rolled his eyes again, sighed and nodded curtly. "Well, it's not like I had a choice."

"You could've let me go back to my picketing."

"No, that's not a choice," he said drily. "I just hope this whole thing comes to a quick conclusion. I don't have much time, Dr. Brown."

She pressed her lips together, irritated that he had chided her as if she were a disobedient child.

So infuriatingly arrogant. Sexy, but arrogant.

What was coming over her? She'd never felt this kind of draw to a man before.

Kiera had never really experienced lust. Not even with Brent.

She had been attracted to Brent, but it wasn't like the spark of electricity she was feeling now.

She slid farther away from him, trying to distance herself physically from the pull of attraction.

"I hope so too, Dr. Baker, because, quite frankly, I don't have time for this, either, and neither do the people whose access to good, quality, affordable medicine you're threatening."

Mike snickered in the front seat and Henry scowled at him.

Kiera sat back against the seat and pulled off her woolen beanie, satisfied that she'd gotten in the last word. This time, at least, because she had a sinking suspicion that this wasn't over.

She imagined she had a fight ahead of her, but it was one she was willing to take on. Even though her boss and Mandy told her it was a battle she wasn't going to win, she was not easily swayed.

Dr. Henry Baker might seem scary and unapproachable to everyone else, but she wasn't everyone else and Aspen Grace Memorial Hospital was her home.

The home that she had to protect.

CHAPTER TWO

KIERA CLEANED HERSELF up in her office, and she thought it might be for the best to let Dr. Baker calm down. He hadn't said much to her since Mike had dropped them off at the hospital

Instead, he had made his way to the boardroom, and she had come straight here. It was good to put some distance between them.

For her own protection.

Plus, they hadn't exactly started off on good terms.

She knew he thought she'd be easy to deal with, when in fact it was the opposite.

Kiera knew exactly what happened when a new, flashier, private practice came into town. She'd heard all the promises before. How the free clinics or other charitable works would be kept open, but inevitably they never were.

They were always the first thing to get the chop.

Always.

And Kiera wasn't going to let that happen to AGMH.

There was a knock at the door, and she turned around to see Dr. Carr hovering in the doorway. He crossed his arms.

"What did you do?" he asked.

"What do you mean what did I do?" she asked innocently.

Dr. Richard Carr was her mentor. He had taught her everything she needed to know about being a surgeon. And when she'd decided to leave Denver and the private hospital she had worked at, Richard had been the first person to offer her a job.

He'd been the only one to encourage her in college because he was the only person she had trusted here. Dr. Carr was kind, and they usually agreed on most things. Except this. She knew they didn't see eye to eye on this.

Richard cocked an eyebrow and looked at her with disbelief as he came into her office and shut the door behind him.

"Dr. Baker is here. You know he's a majority shareholder in the hospital, right? And the son of the head of the board of directors."

"And Governor Baker's son. I get it. I know who he is."

"He has the power to fire you," Richard said, seriously. "So, I'm asking you, what did you do?"

"Nothing. I was protesting at the construction site—like I often do when I have a free moment—and he showed up. He was apparently under the impression that we were going to have a meeting at the hospital."

Richard sighed and crossed his arms. "Were you carrying around one of your signs?"

Kiera bit her lip, her cheeks flushing as she lifted up the sign she had so proudly made. It had been Mandy's idea to add glitter to the dollar-sign eyes.

Richard's eyes widened and he scrubbed a hand over his face. "Lord, have mercy."

"Richard, I wasn't on the actual property. Just the sidewalk around it, and last time I looked this was a free country."

He sighed. "It might be, but you're also a surgeon

at this hospital and you might have just screwed yourself over."

"He was prepared to talk to me," she said. "He was willing to hear me out."

Richard was surprised. "He was?"

"Yes. It's why I'm here. I've decided to be professional. No signs, no flyers. No ranting and raving. I can be a professional when I need to be."

A half smile tugged on the corner of Richard's lips. "Yes. I have seen this before."

"What made you think I was in trouble?"

"Dr. Baker is livid. He's pacing in the boardroom. I don't think I've ever seen the man so agitated. Not that I've seen much of him and definitely not since I was hired as chief."

Kiera found that odd. Usually a majority shareholder would take more interest in the hospital, but she knew from an internet search, when she had gotten back to her office, that Dr. Baker worked in a glitzy private clinic in Los Angeles and was something of a playboy.

Had a new, gorgeous, fake woman on his arm every week.

Usually, Hollywood elite.

He was privileged, and Kiera wasn't going to back down because Dr. Baker was throwing a hissy fit. Even if it cost her her job.

The thought scared her because then there would be no one to advocate for the free clinic. There would be no one willing to work it or give it so many hours. What would people do? She couldn't let them down.

It's not your sole responsibility.

Only she'd learned from the best. Mandy's dad, Dr. Wilfred Burke, had given help to those who couldn't afford it.

He'd given her so much.

"I promise to be on my best behavior, Richard."

Richard sighed and walked over to her. "You know I think of you as a daughter. I've known you since you were a struggling kid in college. Working odd jobs to pay to become a doctor. You were so selfless and so determined. You had it. You have it in you to be a great surgeon, and one of things I love about you is your determination to help others, but you can't do that if you're fired. Kiera, be smart about this. You're fighting for a great cause, but AGMH is falling apart at the seams. You know this and so do I. We're bleeding money, and the last thing the hospital needs is to piss off the majority shareholder."

Kiera sighed. "I know. I promise, Richard."

Richard nodded. "Well, good luck."

"Thanks."

Richard left, and Kiera took a deep breath to calm her nerves.

She could do this.

All she had ever wanted was to be a doctor. She wanted to help the less fortunate. She knew firsthand what it was like not to eat or have a roof over your head. Or to have parents too high to notice you.

Then to spend a year bouncing from group home to group home, waiting for family.

Miserable and scared.

She'd had no real family until the day she came to a foster home in Aspen. A widower, with a daughter her age.

Then she had had a family.

Then she had belonged.

Dr. Burke had been a good family physician, and he had helped those who couldn't afford care. His selflessness had inspired Kiera to become a surgeon and Mandy to be a nurse.

Mandy was her sister, her best friend.

She owed this to Mandy and to the memory of Dr. Burke. She had to be able to listen to what Dr. Baker had to say to her, just as he had been able to listen to her.

It had been a two-way street.

And they had been able to be professional.

With one last look in the mirror, she straightened her white lab coat, rolled her shoulders back and headed to the boardroom at the end of the hallway.

A ball of dread formed in the pit of her stomach and she felt nervous.

For the first time in a long time.

Don't let him bully you. You got this. You're strong. You've survived worse.

Kiera knocked.

"Come in." His voice was deep and set her on edge.

She opened the door, and at the end of the long, black polished table sat Henry Baker, his hands folded and his eyes staring directly at her. His mouth was pressed into a firm line, and suddenly that ball of dread, turned into a rock.

She felt like she was walking toward her own doom.

Don't let him spook you.

She had faced down scarier people than Dr. Baker. Of course, those other people had been patients, and they hadn't held the fate of her job in their hands.

They also hadn't affected the fate of the hospital.

That was the worrying bit.

Henry was wearing a dark, well-tailored suit, and now that he wasn't huddled down in his flimsy coat, she could clearly see how broad his chest was, and the color brought out the tan from the Californian sun.

Her pulse began to race, her palms sweaty, and she was annoyed that her body was reacting to him again. What was it about him that made her lose control? She didn't date doctors like him for a reason—she'd been burned by Brent. Lulled into thinking he'd cared for her when he was cheating and lying to her. She wasn't making that mistake again.

It was one reason she didn't date anyone. She didn't have time. She didn't trust.

"Shut the door if you will, Dr. Brown." His voice was deep, serious, and if she had been someone else it definitely would have scared her.

She closed the door and took a seat at the opposite end of the table, not waiting for his invitation, and folded her hands carefully on top of the table. She met his gaze and mustered every ounce of strength she had.

There was a glimmer of amusement in his dark eyes.

"Well, I'm interested in talking terms, Dr. Baker," she said, breaking the tension and silence that he was obviously going for. "I'm hoping we can make this quick. This is my day off, after all."

She knew the moment she said that, she'd made an error. That glimmer dwindled into a dark ember of annoyance.

But if she was going to go down, she was going to go down fighting.

Henry was trying not to see red. As an attending surgeon and a shareholder in other hospitals, he'd had to fire people before. He had reprimanded people. He had respect and he'd gained that respect from the way he handled himself in a boardroom.

He'd taken courses on it at his father's insistence when

he was younger. Yet, everything he'd learned didn't seem to have any effect on her.

Why wasn't this working? She was the most infuriating person ever.

Henry could feel his blood pressure rising, and there was a vein in his temple that was beginning to pulsate. He hoped she couldn't see it.

Dr. Kiera Brown unnerved him. She made him feel hot, and also irritated. It was an odd juxtaposition.

She made him want to pull out his hair and also take her in his arms.

She rattled his control.

And he didn't like that one bit.

Now that she was out of her bulky winter wear, professionally dressed and her red hair braided back, he could take it all in. A spattering of freckles across her cute button nose, pink full lips.

Even the cat's-eye glasses she wore complemented her. They were sexy.

She appeared to be professional. As he would expect from a member of staff of one of the hospitals he held shares in, she was a far cry from the woman he'd picked up earlier.

For a moment he forgot who she was.

Until she opened her mouth.

Then his head started to ache.

"I believe I'm the one who called this meeting, Dr. Brown, so I think I should be the one starting off the talk."

She nodded her head in deference. "Fine, but as I said, I have a lot of things to do."

"I thought you had a day off?" he asked.

Her green eyes narrowed. "Yes, but I have to get back

to what I was doing, and surprisingly I do have a life outside of this hospital."

"And I don't?" he asked.

She shrugged. "I don't know what you do in your free time. Frankly, that's not my business, just like what I do isn't yours."

He clenched his fist. "It does when your free time activities involve my hospital."

"Your hospital? With all due respect, Dr. Baker, I've never seen you step foot in Aspen Grace Memorial Hospital. Until now, that is."

He rubbed his temples and stood up. "Can we just get on with it? Why are you arguing with everything I say?"

"Are you going to fire me?" she asked bluntly.

Tempting. He kept that thought to himself. He wasn't allowed to fire her although, for her insubordination, he was sorely tempted to do just that. His father had made it clear that Dr. Brown was a valuable and well-liked surgeon both at Aspen Grace Memorial Hospital and in the town of Aspen.

His father didn't want his reelection to be tainted with firing such a well-known and well-liked surgeon because she was exercising her right to protest.

All his father wanted from Dr. Kiera Brown was to stop the picketing—of her own free will. Not because of the Bakers had persuaded her.

Seduce her for all I care, flitted through his mind.

The prospect had a certain appeal. Kiera was attractive, albeit infuriating.

No, he wouldn't stoop to that level.

Henry really didn't know how he was going to convince her to give up the campaign against the new hospital. And now questioned why he was even here and whether it might have been easier to ignore his father.

Except he couldn't.

He owed his father this and then he'd be free.

He'd no longer be beholden to him.

"No. I'm not going to fire you, Dr. Brown."

"Oh." Her eyes widened and she seemed shocked. She relaxed slightly. "Then why exactly am I here? I mean, you didn't seem quite eager to negotiate terms before."

"And I'm still not." Henry walked down to the end of the table where she sat and leaned over her. He got a whiff of her perfume. It smelled vanilla. It reminded him of a bakeshop.

One that was filled with sweet and sinful delicacies.

Get a hold of yourself.

"Look, tell me what you want. Tell me how I can get you to stop protesting against the new hospital and just do your job. Quietly."

Kiera leaned back and crossed her arms. "I'm doing my job."

"Protesting is not your job." Henry stood up and scrubbed his hand over his face. "Just tell me what I can do, Dr. Brown?"

"Keep the hospital open. It's that simple."

"It's not," he stated.

"Why?"

He sighed. There was no way he was getting into the complicated reason why he was here. He just wanted this dealt with so he could leave this all behind him.

"Henry, are you in here?"

A sense of dread traveled down his spine and curled into the pit of his stomach.

Oh, God. What was she doing here?

"Who's that?" Kiera whispered.

"My mother. Just play along and we'll get her out of here fast."

Kiera looked confused. "Play along? Okay?"

The door opened and his mother sashayed into the boardroom. She was dressed head to toe in designer clothes. It had been a while since he'd seen her. She came to California from time to time, but she never visited him.

He rarely wanted to make time for her. And the feeling was mutual. His mother was not the mothering type.

She only ever wanted to see him when it suited her.

Which was never.

He'd been disappointed enough by her absence in the past.

No one there to comfort him as a child.

She had never been there for any holiday or award he'd won growing up.

He had always been envious of his friends who had mothers who loved and embraced their children. Supported them and cheered them on.

Henry was lucky to get an air-kiss as a token of affection.

His mother was cold and selfish.

"Henry, I thought you'd be in here." She smiled brightly, and Henry walked over to give his mother a quick air-kiss.

"Mother, what're you doing here?" he asked in exasperation.

"I brought someone for you to meet," she whispered loudly. He was pretty sure that Kiera had heard.

"Mother, this is hardly the time and place…"

"Well, then when is the time and place? She's standing outside."

"You brought her here?" he asked under his breath.

"I can go and give you two privacy," Kiera chirped up.

Henry turned around and glared at her.

"I'm sorry, I don't believe we've met," his mother said frostily.

"No. We haven't," Kiera said brightly.

"Do you work here?" his mother asked.

Henry cringed. She wasn't tactful and had no boundaries.

His mother thought she was above everything and everyone else.

"Yes, I do."

His mother nodded and turned back to Henry. "Look, just come outside and meet this lovely woman. She's from a good family."

"Mother, I don't have time for this. Father sent me here to deal with the hospital."

"That can wait." She waved her hand dismissively.

"Mother, I promised Father I'd take care of this, so please let me."

"Honestly, you're acting like this is some kind of hardship. All I'm asking you to do is cooperate. If you choose the right girl and stop with your hedonistic lifestyle it would be so much better for your father's political career."

"That's the only reason you want me to get married?" Henry asked.

His mother's expression softened, which was unusual for her, but only briefly. "It's been eight years since Michelle and all that nastiness after her death—"

"Mother, don't," Henry snapped.

Why did he think anything was going to be different? Why did he think his parents would keep their promise? He should have just blown his father off, and then he wouldn't have to be here. Listening to his parents bring up his mistakes over and over again.

Now he was angry at himself for allowing them to manipulate him.

He wouldn't let his mother embarrass him. He refused to show any kind of emotion. The last time he did his parents had been horrified, so he kept it locked away. Now he was standing here trapped between the rock, which was his mother, and the hard place, Kiera.

Henry took a deep breath to calm his nerves.

How was he going to extricate himself?

Henry glanced back at Kiera, who was smiling, her arms crossed and her eyebrows raised as she watched the whole embarrassing situation unfold. It was mortifying. He was angry with his mother for doing this to him. They wanted him married to the perfect girl for his father's image... Fine, he'd give them that and then some.

"Well?" His mother asked. "Surely you can give me a few moments?"

"No, Mother, I can't. There's no need."

His mother looked confused. "What do you mean there's no need?"

His ears pressurized and his pulse raced. Thundering. He glanced back at Kiera and his vision went a bit blurry. His palms were sweaty.

"There's no need, because I'm engaged already, Mother."

"You're engaged? To whom?" his mother asked, shocked.

He blanked, glanced back at Kiera and took a step toward her.

"Kiera. I'm engaged to Dr. Kiera Brown. We're engaged. It's why I'm here in Colorado. We have to set a date."

CHAPTER THREE

KIERA COULDN'T ANSWER right away because she really didn't know what to say. When Dr. Baker had asked her to play along, she hadn't been expecting to play along with this.

His fiancée? What?

Kiera had to get out of that boardroom. So that's exactly what she did.

There was nothing to say. Let Dr. Baker try to figure out that particular problem on his own.

"Dr. Brown!"

Kiera stopped and waited for Dr. Baker to catch up to her. The last thing she needed was him shouting the ridiculous story he'd just fed his mother all over the hospital.

"Can I help you, darling?" she whispered under her breath.

Henry took her by the arm and led her into an empty exam room. When he shut the door, he let go of her arm and stood with his back to her.

"So when were you going to tell me that we're getting married?" Kiera teased.

"I'm sorry. I panicked." He ran his hand through his hair and turned around. "It seemed like the easy way out."

"The easy way out of what? We're strangers, Dr.

Baker, and I think it's safe to say that we don't particularly like each other too much."

Although, honestly, she really didn't know him enough to determine whether she liked him or not. It was what he stood for.

She refused to date or fake marry someone who was concerned about the almighty dollar first and humanity second. She was not going to be with a man like Brent.

She'd seen the pictures in the tabloids of Henry with a different woman each week.

No way.

No more Greedy Guses for her.

Who said he was greedy? You don't know him.

The anxiety rising in her since he'd told his mom they were engaged started to wane.

"Do you always have to be so flippant?" he asked, breaking her chain of thought.

"Sorry," she said, because she did feel for him, even though he had put himself into this situation.

He had also put her into it.

The difference was that she didn't have to take part. She didn't have to go along with his crazy lie.

"So what're you going to tell your mother?"

His eyes widened. "About what?"

"About what we've been talking about. You know, the whole *she's my fiancée* thing? What're you going to tell her now?"

"Nothing."

"Excuse me? What?" She was in shock again. Was she hearing him correctly? She felt like she was stuck in some weird television show where soon someone would jump out at her, tell her she was on camera and throw a pie in her face.

That's how surreal this felt.

"I'm not going to tell her anything different." He crossed his arms in defiance.

"You expect me to do it?"

"Do what?" he asked.

"Tell your mother you lied?"

"No."

She was confused. "What do you mean, no?"

Henry took a deep breath, looking as if he was in pain and rolling his shoulders. "Keep up this pretense and we can talk about what you want. We can talk about the free clinic and Aspen Grace Memorial Hospital."

Her heart skipped a beat. "Are you serious?"

"I can't make any promises, but if you go along with being my fiancée while I'm here in Aspen, then I will do what I can to make sure your concerns are heard and taken care of."

"So for the next twenty-four hours? You said something about heading back to California?"

"My trip is delayed. My father needs me here and I have a client consult now in Aspen. If, while I'm here, you agree to be my fiancée to keep my parents off my back, I'll see what I can do about your demands."

Something deep down inside of her told her to run, told her not to believe him because she'd been burned before by men like him. Men like her father and Brent. Men who used and abused and never made good on their promise.

Still, this wasn't real and she wouldn't be hurt. She had to remind herself of that.

For whatever reason, he wanted her to pretend to be his fiancée, and though she should say no, the prize was much too great to pass up on. He'd listen to her concerns, and he was willing to work with her. That was the crux of the matter.

And really, what would it cost her? All she had to do was pretend to be his fiancée for the small amount of time he was in Aspen. He wasn't cheating on her, or leaving her locked in some dingy hovel while he scored drugs.

Or leaving her alone at a truck stop diner in the middle of nowhere.

She shuddered as that long-repressed thought slipped into her mind.

She hated that it had come back. She didn't want to feel like the scared, vulnerable girl she used to be.

You still are.

And she shook that thought away.

Kiera was irritated that she had been put in this position.

"Can I think about it?" she asked.

His eyes widened and he looked annoyed. "You want to think about it?"

"Yeah, I do. I mean, an engagement is a big deal."

"You are the most infuriating woman I've ever met!"

"Then I'm going to have to pass." She moved to step past him, but he stood in her way.

"I'm offering you a chance to be heard, have your concerns listened to, and you have to think about it?"

"You're not promising me anything but listening to me. I need something more, and I really need to think about it."

Henry's eyes narrowed. "Fine."

"Thank you."

"Can I take you out to dinner tonight to discuss this further?" he asked.

The invitation caught her off guard. She couldn't remember the last time she had been on a date.

Wait, this wasn't a date.

Only she felt that anxious swirl in the pit of her stomach. Her mouth went dry and her palms were sweaty. All the classic biological signs of attraction.

It was infuriating.

Damn him.

Kiera was tempted to let him sweat it out, but she really did want what he was offering. She wanted her voice heard. She wanted to be listened to.

Lack of medical care for those who couldn't afford it would be devastating.

Mandy's father had taught both of them the power of compassion and medicine. Kiera wanted to help everyone, and the new private hospital would help only a select few.

"Sure. I would like to go out to dinner to discuss this further," she said, finally finding her voice.

Henry relaxed. "Great. Shall I pick you up at seven?"

"Seven is good. I live at two-five-six Green Lane. It's not far from here."

"Green Lane. Got it." He stepped to the side and opened the door for her.

"I look forward to discussing our arrangement further," Kiera said brightly as she moved past him.

He grunted in response.

This was a step in the right direction. Or was it?

She shook that thought away and left Dr. Henry Baker standing in the hall, scowling at her as she left.

Kiera wanted to get back home and fill Mandy in on everything, but as she walked away her pager went off.

There was a large trauma coming in, and they were calling in all available surgeons. Henry ran up beside her.

"What's wrong?" he asked, watching her glance at her pager.

"A trauma. They're calling for all available help to handle it."

"I can lend a hand. I am a surgeon," he offered.

Kiera nodded. "We can use it."

"Lead the way."

When they got down to the emergency room there was a flurry of activity as they tried to make space in the triage for the emergency cases that were expected in. Aspen Grace Memorial Hospital wasn't like other larger hospitals, and they didn't have interns or residents. They had a trauma center and good surgeons, but it meant that every available surgeon was being called in.

For the first time since Henry had arrived, Kiera was thankful he was here.

He was an extra set of hands, and this would give him the perfect opportunity to see that even though AGMH was small, it was mighty.

She got him a pair of scrubs, and they both quickly changed in the locker room.

Kiera handed Henry a yellow trauma gown and a pair of gloves.

Without her having to ask him, Henry tied her gown, and then he turned and she did the same for him, though he had to crouch slightly as he was taller than her. It struck her as odd, but also calming, which was a strange mixture, indeed.

She didn't have to tell him what to do. There was nothing awkward or weird about this.

It was like they both knew, instinctively, what the other needed. Like they had been working together for a long time.

Other than Dr. Carr, her mentor, there wasn't anyone else she worked with so well in the ER. Certainly not a doctor. She relied a lot on the amazing support staff. It was a bit unnerving, and her pulse was racing as she finished tying up his yellow trauma gown. Her cheeks heated. Why was something she did all the time making her feel this way?

All hot and bothered.

Her hands shook as she brushed the nape of his neck. She finished trying the knot and took a step back.

Trying to regain some control.

She pulled on her mask and slipped on her face shield.

"Do you know what the trauma is?" Henry asked, putting on his own face shield.

"Multi-vehicle collision. Apparently, there was a patch of black ice on one of the mountain passes," another doctor said.

Kiera winced. Black ice was the worst and, on a winding mountain pass road, a recipe for disaster. They stepped outside the ambulance bay doors. The cold wind bit her skin through the thin scrubs, but it wasn't long until they heard the first long, whiny wail of an ambulance siren heading toward them.

Her heart was racing, but it was just the adrenaline. It was her focus. Lives were at risk and she wanted to be here to save them.

The first ambulance stopped and the back doors opened as the paramedics began to lift the patient down out of the back.

"Patient is a forty-two-year-old female passenger and was ejected through the front window. GCS was three on the scene. BP is sixty over thirty. Suspected head injuries and possible internal bleeding," the paramedic said.

Kiera took over and helped the paramedics wheel the patient into a trauma bay. Henry was on the other side of the gurney. If there were as many injuries as she thought there would be on this patient, she was going to need all the help she could get. To her surprise she didn't need to inform Dr. Baker of what to do, despite his unfamiliarity with Aspen Grace Memorial's trauma room.

He just seemed to know where to go and what to do.

And that was exactly what she needed.

There was no time to explain.

Kiera palpated the abdomen and frowned when she found it was rigid and full.

"Her abdomen is distended. She has internal bleeding. We need to get her into the operating room. Stat."

"Lead the way, Dr. Brown," Henry said.

"Call down and have them prep operating room three," Kiera said to a nurse. "And I'll need a neuro consult."

"Yes, Dr. Brown."

Kiera continued setting up what she needed, to get the patient ready for the operating room. Right now, she and Henry had to get the patient into the operating room and try to stabilize her. She'd have a neurosurgeon in the operating room to monitor, and then once the internal bleeding was under control they could assess the head injury.

While the patient's pupils were still reactive, uncontrolled bleeding could kill her faster.

"You don't need to pull another neurosurgeon in here. I'm a neurosurgeon," Henry said.

"I thought you were a plastic surgeon?" Kiera asked.

"I'm both," Henry stated.

"Okay. Well, that's good to know. Let's get her to the operating room."

Henry nodded and wheeled the gurney out of the trauma room and toward the operating room, which was at the end of the hall from the emergency room. They handed off their patient to the operating room orderlies and made their way into the scrub room, changing out of their yellow trauma gowns and swapping for different scrub caps.

Kiera glanced over at Henry, who was scrubbing in beside her. She noticed how muscular his forearms were. She had a thing for muscular forearms, and peeking out under the sleeve of his scrubs was a tattoo. Her blood heated, and that flutter started in her stomach again.

She had been impressed by the way he had thrown himself into the fray of helping out with the trauma. He just seamlessly fit in. It was sexy as hell watching him work.

And she had a thing about tattoos. She couldn't see all of it, but his looked like the bottom of a tree, roots in particular. It was black and intricate and completely caught her attention. She hadn't taken him for the type of person who had tattoos. Of course, it had been hard to tell what type of person he was under the expensive designer suit.

"What?" Henry asked, noticing that she was staring at him.

"You have a tattoo."

Henry glanced down at his arm. "I do."

"I didn't peg you for the tattoo type."

A half smile tugged at the corner of his mouth. "What kind of person is that then?"

"I don't know." She smiled. "You know, that's the first time you've smiled since you got here. You have a nice smile."

The smile quickly disappeared, and he became serious again, as if he were bothered that she'd noticed he had a nice smile, which he did.

And she quite liked the tattoo, too.

What she didn't like was his moodiness. This hot and cold that he seemed to have. She had just met him, but she didn't know whether she was coming or going with him. One minute he was asking her to pretend to be his fiancée and the next minute he was all closed off and serious. It was driving her crazy.

"I think I should know about your tattoo—we are engaged after all."

Henry sighed and finished scrubbing, shaking the extra water off his hands. "We can talk about this at dinner."

Kiera chuckled to herself as he stepped into the operating room to get on his gloves and gown. She was looking forward to seeing how he worked and whether they would make a good team. She finished scrubbing in and stepped into the operating room.

Henry was operating on the opposite side of the table to Kiera as they repaired the internal damage that was caused by the car accident. The spleen was shredded and there was bleeding around the liver.

Henry kept an eye on the patient's blood pressure, but other than a head laceration, it appeared she was stable. Although, a CT scan would show if there was something that he would need to do.

Right now, they had to get the patient's internal bleeding under control.

As he stood across the table from Dr. Brown, from Kiera, he was impressed with her work. She might be infuriating, but he could see why Dr. Carr wanted to keep Dr. Brown around. She was talented.

So why was she wasting her time protesting the inevitable?

Aspen Grace Memorial Hospital would close.

Why was she wasting her surgical skills in a hospital that was small and falling apart when she could go to any hospital and save lives. Or, she could work in the new place his father and the board were planning to build.

Still, a part of him could see her point.

His father's new hospital wouldn't have an emergency room like this.

It would have trauma services, but only for those with insurance or the funds.

It wouldn't be an open emergency room.

It would only be open for the right price.

He didn't know if the woman they were operating on right now would have those financial means. If it were his father's hospital, she'd be turned away and that thought sobered him. At least, they could provide care like they were supposed to.

It made him resent his father's plans, because no one should be turned away.

He understood what Kiera was fighting for even though this wasn't his fight.

Helping those who couldn't pay their hospital bills was the reason this hospital was losing money. It was like the hospital was bleeding out.

"She lost a lot of blood."

Henry had stood there in disbelief. *"What're you talking about? When I left for Los Angeles she was fine and... she was working up the mountain..."*

Michelle's doctor had nodded slowly. *"The small town she was working in was remote. It was three hours away from the nearest trauma center. They only had a free clinic there and they couldn't handle it. Michelle's insurance wouldn't cover a helicopter ride and there was a storm. There was no way to get to her and we ran out of time."*

"I would've paid for it!" Henry had shouted. *"Why wasn't I contacted? She was my fiancée...she was a surgeon!"*

"I know, Henry. There was no time. If there had been a better hospital..."

"She would've had a chance?"

Sometimes all the money in the world couldn't save lives. So what did it matter?

It hadn't been able to save Michelle.

Aspen Grace Memorial Hospital was falling apart. The new hospital would bring more help to those who needed it.

Billing could take care of those who couldn't pay.

Billing was not his problem. Saving lives was his problem.

"Pressure is dropping," the anesthesiologist said, shaking thoughts of Michelle and the hospital's state of affairs from his mind.

"Having some more fluids. She has another bleeder somewhere," Kiera said.

Henry pulled on the retractor and spotted it. The bleeder on the splenic artery meant that the repair work was over. The spleen was beyond saving. "I think we should do a splenectomy. We have to cauterize the splenic artery."

Kiera cursed under her breath, her brow furrowed, eyes focused on her work. "You're right."

"I know."

Kiera glanced up at him quickly. There was a glint in her green eyes, but he couldn't tell whether it was annoyance or humor. Not with her mask on.

Maybe he'd find out what was going on in her mind if he got to know her better.

And that gave him pause, because he had no plans to get to know her. That's not what he was here for. He was here to do his job, and once that was done he could go back to Los Angeles, where it was sane.

Where it was safe.

He had no idea why that thought had crept into his head.

It was unwelcome.

He didn't want it. He didn't want to have that kind of thought.

They finished with the splenectomy and Henry scrubbed out next to Kiera. An awkward tension settled between them.

"So much for your day off," he said, trying to make conversation.

Silence had never bothered him before, but now he was uncomfortable and making small talk.

Which he found infuriating.

Brutally and blindingly infuriating.

"That's okay," Kiera sighed. "I love my job."

"You know, it's a bit weird without interns and residents here."

"Why?" she asked.

"You're a good surgeon. You should be teaching others."

Pink tinged her cheeks. "Well, there's no teaching program set up here."

"There should be. There could be if this new hospital was built."

Her eyes narrowed and her spine straightened. "Maybe if the money for the new hospital was put into Aspen Grace Memorial Hospital, then it could expand and build a teaching program."

"There's no reason to build on here," Henry said, his voice rising. "The new land..."

Kiera held up her hand. "Look, we can talk about this at dinner. I don't want to argue in the operating room."

"You still want to have dinner with me?" he asked, shocked. He had thought for sure that she would change her mind.

For one fraction of a second, he began to doubt his

rash plan to tell his mother he was engaged to Kiera, and his brain was trying to formulate how to get out of it.

Kiera smiled, sending a chill down his spine. As if this was far from over.

"Of course," she said sweetly. "We are engaged and have a lot of things to discuss."

"That we do," he said drily.

Kiera finished scrubbing out. "It'll be okay."

He cocked an eyebrow and smiled. "Somehow I don't think that it will."

She chuckled and dried her hands. "I'll see you at seven?"

Henry nodded, still a bit dumbfounded by everything that had happened since he'd gotten off the plane. He was missing Los Angeles, he was missing the sun. He was missing his work. No one bugged him there.

He wasn't annoyed when he was doing what he loved, when he was in his own space, in his own practice.

Kiera left and he finished scrubbing out.

It would have been easier to ignore his father and stay in his blissful bubble in Los Angeles.

Your blissful, lonely bubble.

Only he had almost ruined his life, his practice, everything when Michelle died.

His father had saved him and never let him forget it.

Henry sighed and grabbed paper towels to dry his hands. He quickly dried his hands and tossed the paper towels in the garbage. He was dreading tonight for a number of reasons.

Mostly though, he was dreading being alone with Kiera.

She drove him crazy, but she was feisty, beautiful and talented, and that was always a dangerous combination for him.

She was exactly the type of woman he liked.

Women like Kiera excited him.

They made him feel alive and he hadn't felt like that in a long time. It was a scary feeling. Kiera was the type of woman he had avoided for the last eight years because it was too dangerous for him.

He wasn't going to be hurt again.

He wasn't going to feel that pain, that gut-wrenching loneliness and the hole that Michelle's death had left in his heart.

So Kiera was dangerous for him.

She threatened his heart.

CHAPTER FOUR

KIERA OPENED THE door to the home she shared with Mandy. Though it was technically Mandy's home, Kiera had lived there since she was a young girl, when Dr. Burke had taken her in as his foster daughter.

"Kiera?" Mandy called out from the kitchen.

"Yeah. I'm home." Kiera shut the door as Mandy wheeled herself in from the kitchen.

"You were gone longer than I thought," Mandy said. "I was getting worried. There was an accident on the road, some black ice."

"I know." Kiera hung her coat up. "I got called into the operating room. I was helping with the trauma cases."

"Well, that explains it." Mandy relaxed, but for a brief moment Kiera could see an expression she knew so well. It was a mixture of relief and envy. Mandy missed her work. She missed helping others, taking care of the injured. It had always been Mandy's dream, but after the accident and her lengthy recuperation, her career had been ruined.

She could still be living out her dream.

And what about your dreams?

Kiera shook that thought away. She was living her dream—she was saving lives. She had had other dreams, like having a family. That felt frivolous now. Mandy and her father had taken care of her when she was young, lost and had no hope.

They had made her feel safe. They had made her feel loved.

They had given her a chance.

This was where she was supposed to be, so all those other dreams were just that. They were dreams. She couldn't trust anyone else with her heart enough to have that secret fantasy of marriage and babies.

The one time she had thought of having all that had been when she was with Brent. When Mandy had still been working and Dr. Burke was still alive. When her life had been perfect. Or she had thought it was. Everything fell apart soon after that.

Brent cheated on her. Mandy was shot, and Dr. Burke died with a ton of bills.

Mandy and AGMH were her life, her family now.

"Sorry I didn't call."

Mandy shrugged. "No worries, but I'm glad you weren't one of the injured. The roads out there were wicked."

"They're not too bad now. The salters have been out." Kiera sighed and made her way to the living room, sitting down on the sofa and leaning back.

There was a meow and an orange tabby jumped up beside her. Sif was Mandy's orange tabby but mixed with something. She had the grumpiest face. All smushed and grumpy like. Kiera always wondered what Sif was mixed with.

The devil most likely, but today was an angel.

That was something. She had dealt with one too many grumpy souls today.

At least Mandy's cat liked her today.

"So, you got called in from your day off?" Mandy asked, coming into the living room.

"I did, but I got pulled off the protest *long* before the accident happened."

Mandy cocked an eyebrow. "How come?"

"Don't sound so amazed."

"I am amazed. You're pretty focused, even somewhat crazed, when you're out there."

Kiera chuckled. "Thanks."

"It's the truth," Mandy teased. "On your days off you should be enjoying yourself. Living life."

"I am enjoying myself."

Mandy stared at her skeptically. "Uh-huh. Sure. So, who managed to tear you away from your mega fun day of protesting?"

Kiera sighed. "The governor's son and the majority shareholder."

Mandy's eyes widened. "Wow. They sent in the big guns, huh?"

"You know who I'm talking about?"

"I do. Dr. Henry Baker is one of the foremost neuro and plastic/ENT surgeons on the West Coast. He has shares in many hospitals, not all of them part of his father's vast empire."

"Vast empire?"

"The Bakers own a lot of Colorado. A lot."

"No wonder he's so arrogant," Kiera mumbled. "He's privileged."

Mandy chuckled. "You could say that, but he doesn't seem to run in the same circles as his parents. He rarely comes to Colorado. You must have made some kind of impression on the Bakers if they brought in Henry to deal with you."

"Well, I feel honored, I guess." Kiera paused. She

wanted to tell Mandy about the deal she and Henry had made, but also she didn't. It was clear that Henry was privileged—she knew that—but now she felt guilty for agreeing to Henry's crazy plot.

So he didn't want to be harassed by his parents for not getting married and continuing on the family dynasty.

That wasn't her problem.

Still, the temptation of what he was offering was hard to pass up. To save the free clinic, to save the hospital, the hospital she loved.

It was just a lie.

"What," Mandy asked, as if reading her thoughts.

"What?" Kiera's cheeks heated.

"There's something you're not telling me. I can read you like a book, Kiera. What happened today?"

"I was told to stop picketing." Which wasn't a complete lie, she had been.

"Did you get fired?" Mandy asked, worried.

"No. I didn't get fired. They wouldn't fire me for exercising my free will."

"Then what?"

"I'm going out to dinner in an hour with Dr. Baker."

Mandy's eyes widened and she smiled. "You're going on a date with the enemy?"

"I know," Kiera said drily.

"That's kind of fun," Mandy teased. "He's kind of handsome. Or at least he was the last time I saw him."

"He still is that." Her blood heated, and she didn't like that she was reacting to Henry. Sure, he was good-looking, but she'd met other good-looking men before and didn't know what it was about him that got under her skin so much.

What was different about him?

Why did he make her feel this way?

There was something about him that unnerved her. Like he could see through all her protective layers. He looked at her with a hunger that she was sure was reflected in her own eyes.

And she couldn't recall ever lusting for or being so attracted to someone like this.

What was also frustrating was he drove her absolutely crazy.

"So I guess I didn't need to save you spaghetti." Mandy headed back to the kitchen. The whole lower level of the older cottage-style home was open concept so that Mandy could get around easily.

It was accessible. Mandy's bedroom and bathroom were now in what used to be her father's office when he had his practice out of his home.

Kiera had the top floor, where there was a washroom and a large gabled room that she used to share with Mandy when they were younger.

Before Mandy's father died.

Before the accident.

When life had been simpler.

And Sif, the cat, just ruled the entire house.

"What're you going to wear?" Mandy asked from the kitchen.

"What do you mean what am I going to wear?"

"You can't wear what you're wearing. You're going out with a Baker," Mandy teased.

"So?" Kiera asked, puzzled.

"He's probably going to take you to one of the private restaurants in the resorts. One of those fancy restaurants up near the ski lifts or something."

"Ugh, I hope not."

"Come on, live a little. You said so yourself, you thought he was handsome."

"Why are you so invested in this?" Kiera asked.

"Because you never go out or have fun. You deserve to have fun. Sexy fun, even?" The last bit was said with hope.

"I can't stand him. He's trying to shut down my program. He's trying to shut down my hospital."

Mandy shot her a funny look. "So? Live a little. If I were you…"

"You're going to try to guilt me into dressing up, aren't you?"

Mandy smiled deviously. "Maybe. Is it working?"

"No." Kiera sighed. "Fine, I'll change."

"Do your makeup and hair. Wear heels."

"What is with you? Since when did you become my fairy godmother?"

"Oh, I quite like that title," Mandy teased as she scooped a large spoonful of spaghetti out of the pot and plopped it into a plastic container, making a squelching sound. "Besides, with you out of the house maybe Derek will come over."

"Derek? Our neighbor Derek?" Kiera asked, surprised.

Mandy smiled and a blush tinged her cheek. "He comes over from time to time when you're on a long shift."

"Oh. That's great." Kiera was surprised by that. Not that Mandy couldn't date or anything, but she had never seemed to be interested in doing so since the accident. She had never seemed to want to. All she had wanted to do was hang around with Kiera. Which was fine.

She wanted to take care of Mandy.

You deserve a life, too.

"When is he picking you up again?" Mandy asked, looking at the clock.

"Seven."

"You have an hour. You'd better get started. Dazzle him."

Kiera laughed, rolled her eyes and got up off the couch. Sif stared at her in disgust for leaving her and not continuing to pet her. Kiera was tired, and really all she wanted to do was curl up and go to sleep.

That was her life. Work, saving the hospital and sleep. Kind of pathetic.

She shook that thought away and headed upstairs. She walked into her room and opened her closet. It was kind of bare. And she could barely remember the last time she had gone on a date.

And then it came to her.

Brent.

He used to wine and dine her. The first man to do so. She thought he'd been the one. Her Prince Charming.

Boy, was she wrong.

When she'd told him her plans for Aspen, he'd told her his plans for someone else. Even then, she rarely dressed up for him.

"I don't have anything to wear," she shouted down the stairs. "Unless you let me go to dinner in scrubs?"

"No!" Mandy shouted. "You're not going to dinner in scrubs, or jeans or any kind of trouser. You're going to wear pantyhose, heels, makeup, and I'm going to do your hair. I'm going to live vicariously through you!"

Kiera smiled to herself. "Fine."

"I have a dress you can borrow. Have your shower, and then come down to my room and I'll help get you ready."

"Okay."

There was no point in arguing. She was invested in this project now.

Kiera had a quick shower and made her way back

downstairs to Mandy's room. Mandy had already pulled out a dress and laid it on the bed with a pair of heels. She was taken back by the unfamiliar garment. It was the most beautiful color of jade she'd ever seen.

It was silk and it shimmered in the light. It was a halter-style silk dress that would come just below her knees and looked formfitting, which made her nervous.

She didn't usually wear clothes like this.

Clothes like this exposed her, and she was too good at keeping herself hidden. She didn't like attention drawn to her unless she was protesting something worth fighting for. Any extra layer protected her. This dress left nothing to the imagination.

There was no hiding in this dress.

Hidden was safe, and she wanted that safety tonight.

It's why she liked scrubs. They weren't formfitting—everyone wore them. She blended in when she was at the hospital.

Funny for someone protesting all the time.

She shook that thought from her head. That was different.

This dress made her nervous. It was then she saw Henry's eyes in her mind. That gaze he gave her. The one that made her weak in the knees and flustered.

"Where did you get that?" Kiera asked, running her hand over the silken fabric.

"Well, it was actually for your birthday next month, but since you're going on a hot date, I thought you might like it now."

"You bought it for my birthday?" Kiera asked softly.

"I did." Mandy smiled sweetly. "You never go out, you never have fun and I saw it in the shop. It was made for you, and I wanted you to have it. I was going to take you out to one of those fancy places in town for your birthday anyways, but now you're going somewhere probably even more glamorous than where I was going to take you. No buts, you need to wear this."

Kiera sat down on Mandy's bed and threw her arms around her. "You're really the best friend a girl could ask for."

"I know. Also, you're damp, so you're wrecking my sweater and I have a date tonight, too."

Kiera laughed, trying to force back the tears that were threatening to spill. "Thank you."

"Go get dressed in my bathroom. I want to see this on you. That's the least you could do."

"I thought dressing up and letting you do my makeup was the least you could do?"

"Whatever, just do it," Mandy said.

"Fine." Kiera picked up the dress and went into Mandy's bathroom. She hung the dress on the back of the door and stared at it for a few minutes. She'd never had anything quite this nice before.

This was the kind of dress she'd always dreamed about when she was a young girl.

Daddy, can I have a dress? she'd asked, looking in the window of a store that had a pink frilly dress. She'd been able to see other girls trying it on with their mothers.

No, her father had snapped, his voice shaking, and she knew he was coming down off his high. *You're ungrateful.*

I'm not, Kiera had whispered.

You are, her father had yelled.

Tears had stung her eyes and she'd wiped them away.

And now here she was, holding a dream dress.

A lump formed in her throat.

Green was always her color.

She rarely wore it, though, because people noticed

her when she wore green. And she didn't like to be noticed that way.

When her dad had been on a bender or partying with his dealers and the unsavory crowd, it had been good to remain hidden.

The same thing in the foster homes.

It had been better to stay out of sight.

Was it?

And even though she didn't like to be seen, she got a secret thrill knowing Henry would see her in this dress.

Her palms were sweaty as she touched the dress and as she thought of her upcoming date. What was she doing? This wasn't smart. This was dangerous.

Henry decided to drive himself.

The roads were better, and he really didn't need Mike's sarcastic remarks tonight or him knowing about the deal with Dr. Brown. If Mike knew, he would tell his father and the whole plan would be blown.

The point of this was to get his parents off his back about getting married. And to annoy his father.

He knew that his father wanted to run for something more than governor one day, and having a single son who dated Hollywood starlets and was constantly in the gossip magazines didn't exactly look good for his father's political career. Henry's lifestyle didn't mesh with his father's political agenda.

Which was fine by him.

As soon as this was all dealt with his father would be off his back and he would have to deal with AGMH or Colorado again.

Would his father really release him from his debt?

That was something he hadn't worked out yet. He

didn't want to think that far ahead, although his brain was wired to do so.

Tonight he would deal with the here and now.

He'd worry about the details later, which was unlike him and why he didn't usually go into this kind of situation blindly. The more he thought about it, the more agitated he got. His palms were sweaty as he gripped the steering wheel and his jaw ached from grinding his teeth together.

You need to focus, Henry.

He was used to being alone. He preferred it. He was used to quiet.

He had to calm down or he'd never get through dinner.

He was still in shock that he had invited Kiera out.

Why? Had he forgotten she was his fiancée?

Henry smiled at that. What was he getting so worked up about? Maybe because he couldn't stop thinking about her?

In fact, he couldn't get her out of his head. After working with her in surgery, he could think of nothing else.

He couldn't stop thinking about her slender hands holding the scalpel, the way she operated with such grace and care. It had been a long time since he'd enjoyed operating with a surgeon he didn't know well.

Usually, he liked to work alone. Only then did he have control and control meant that he didn't have to rely on anyone else.

Which meant he wouldn't be disappointed or hurt.

Or angry because he'd been let down.

His practice focused mostly on plastics and ear nose and throat. That's why people in Los Angeles came to see him, because of his surgical prowess. His perfection. He didn't let his patients down.

It's why they paid him a lot of money.

Money that he didn't know what to do with other than invest it in hospitals.

He'd forgotten how much he liked working in trauma and on the general surgery aspect. The rush of saving a life rather than making someone beautiful.

He did save lives, though.

There were times he did surgeries to repair the effects of cancer. To help with the mental health and well-being of others, but in Los Angeles they were few and far between.

He'd forgotten how satisfying it was to save a life. To really get in there and help a patient out of danger.

That was what Michelle had liked most about medicine. That's why she had worked with first responders and flown into remote places—to save lives when time really was the essence. Michelle had helped so many people, but in the end...no one could save her.

No one had been there for her.

A lump formed in his throat and he shook the fleeting thoughts from his mind as he pulled up in front of Dr. Brown's house. Then it struck him that he remembered this place from when he was a young boy.

This used to be a doctor's office. A family practitioner.

Dr. Burke.

Dr. Burke had looked after Henry when he had broken his leg skiing. Henry had fond memories of the kind, widowed doctor and his two daughters. Though he had never talked to them, he remembered vividly them playing in the front yard, building snowmen.

He was seventeen and they had to have been about eight or nine years old. He had been jealous because they had looked like they were having fun and Henry had never been allowed as a kid to build a snowman or frolic like that in public.

Everything about his childhood had been regimented by his father's political career and his growing up had taken place in boarding schools and with nannies.

So he had envied Dr. Burke's daughters playing in the snow. So happy. One had brown hair, but it was the redheaded girl who had caught his attention because she was sitting up in a tree and pelting neighborhood boys with snowballs. Her red hair had been so bright against her tattered snowsuit.

It had caught his eye.

He'd laughed. And hoped that if he ever had kids, he'd give them a childhood like this—the one he hadn't got to have—and he would teach any daughter of his to defend herself against boys, too. To stick up for herself.

It's why he had always liked strong-willed women.

It then hit him who that redheaded hellion kid was.

No. It couldn't be. Perhaps she just lived in Dr. Burke's old place. Dr. Burke had died several years ago.

His pulse was racing as he stared up at the house again. He got out of the car and made his way up a wheelchair ramp that hadn't been there before. That's when he started to calm down. There had been no wheelchair ramp when Dr. Burke had been practicing.

Also, Kiera's name was Brown. Not Burke.

Henry took a deep breath and knocked on the door.

The door opened and he looked down shocked to see Mandy Burke, in a wheelchair.

"You must be Henry Baker? It's been a long time," Mandy said brightly. "I haven't seen you around these parts since you were a teenager."

"Mandy? Dr. Burke's daughter?"

Mandy smiled. "One and the same. Come on in."

"I thought this was Dr. Brown's house?" he asked, confused, stepping in and closing the door behind him.

"It is. She lives here. We grew up together."

"You grew up together? In this house?"

"Yes." Mandy cocked her head to one side. "You okay?"

"Just confused. Does your sister still live here?"

"Sister?" Mandy asked, confused. "I don't have a sister. All I have is Kiera."

His stomach sank like a rock as it hit him that the little girl he had thought so funny for taking on the neighborhood boys so long ago, the one with the red braids sitting up in that big tree, was Kiera.

It hit too close for comfort.

"I'll let Kiera know you're here," Mandy said. "Why don't you have a seat?"

"Okay." Henry sat down, a bit dazed, on the nearby couch, only to be met with a hiss and howl as a big orange cat jumped up and then took off like a shot as Mandy texted something on her phone.

"Don't mind Sif," Mandy said as she looked up from her phone. "She really hates strangers. Especially men."

"Great."

Sort of a fitting cat for Kiera.

It was then that Kiera came down the stairs. The first thing that he saw were her legs. Long, shapely legs that made him feel hot and bothered.

That was usually the first thing he noticed on a woman.

He couldn't help but think of those legs wrapped around him or running his hands over them.

Remember who this is. This is Dr. Brown, who you've made a deal with.

Only, he really didn't care.

She came down the rest of the stairs and he was stunned by her.

She took his breath away.

This wasn't the same woman he'd met all bundled up and marching with a sign.

But it was.

The color green suited her perfectly.

It brought out the green of her eyes, the coral color of her lips. And her eyes seemed to sparkle and dazzle in the light. Her red hair cascaded down over her bare shoulders, and he fought back the urge to run his hands through her hair.

He was absolutely speechless.

There was a pink blush to her cheeks as their gazes locked.

"I hope I'm not overdressed," she said, clearing her throat.

"You're not," he said, hoping that his voice didn't crack. "You look lovely."

The pink blush deepened. "Thank you."

"Shall we go?" he asked.

"Sure." She bent over and Mandy whispered something to her. There was a sparkle in Kiera's eye as she glanced back at him, a small smile on her face.

It made his heart skip a beat.

That look held some kind of promise, and he was fighting back the urge to find out what it would be like to kiss her. To have her smile for a different reason.

He wanted to know her secrets.

Focus.

Kiera grabbed her coat and he took it from her, helping her put it on. His fingers brushed the soft skin of her shoulders. He wanted to touch her more and he kicked himself for wanting that.

That's not why he was here.

This was supposed to be a business dinner.

He held open the door for her and she led the way down the ramp. He opened the door to his car and she carefully sat down, flashing him a bit more leg, which sent another zing of electricity through his body.

Damn. This was going to be harder than he'd thought. What had he gotten himself into?

He walked around the car and got into the driver's seat, trying to ignore that she was sitting right beside him. That they were alone.

Together.

Two strangers.

"No Mike tonight?" Kiera asked.

"No. I thought it should be just the two of us. You look very nice tonight, Dr. Brown."

"I think we'd better be on a first-name basis, don't you agree?" she asked.

"You're right."

"Although, I will admit it feels weird to call you Henry. We don't know each other."

He smiled as he drove away from the house. "I agree. Although, I do remember you now."

"What?"

"When I was a teenager Dr. Burke treated my broken leg. Most of his home, back then, had been a little clinic of sorts. My father liked Dr. Burke and had the housekeeper take me there. When I was there, I remember his two daughters playing in the snow. You were in a tree, throwing snowballs at a bunch of neighborhood boys."

She smiled. "Those boys were jerks."

He laughed. "I didn't know you were Dr. Burke's daughter."

"I'm not. Not really. I was adopted when I was ten. He's not my biological father."

"But he raised you."

"Yes." She smiled.

"Biology doesn't dictate family." And that was true. He had biological parents, but he didn't feel any real connection to them compared to some of the people they had hired to take care of them. He had had a teacher in medical school who took him under his wing and he felt more for that man than he did his own father.

His parents were always leaving him.

They hadn't raised him.

Others did.

He was more than ready to get this job over and done with so he could forget about his parents.

About his past.

He could move on.

Can you?

She smiled. "I always thought that, too."

"I was sorry to hear that he died. I was in California." He cleared his throat. "When did Mandy. I mean when..."

"She had an accident about eight years ago. Just after her father died," Kiera said, softly. "She had just graduated from nursing college, had no insurance and a horrible HMO who botched a very simple lumbar fusion. It paralyzed her."

"I'm sorry to hear that."

Kiera sighed. "I wasn't there. I should have been. Forget I said that."

"Said what?" He glanced at her briefly and she smiled at him.

"So where are we going tonight?"

"My parents are having a dinner. I was going to take you to a lovely, private restaurant, but my mother got word that we were going out and insisted we stop in for one of her charity dinners."

"What?" Kiera asked, clearly uncomfortable. "We are supposed to talk negotiation."

"Think of this as that. We do have to prove that you're my fiancée."

"I'm not able to handle the rich and famous of Aspen, although most of them don't even live here." Her voice rose and she was obviously upset. "We don't come from the same world."

"I believe we're both from Earth."

She chuckled. "Okay. Fine."

"We just have to make an appearance. Have a drink, dinner and then I'll take you home. Maybe if your cat doesn't attack me, we can talk about it at your place."

"My cat?" she asked.

"I sat on your cat," he said, annoyed.

She laughed. "Right, that's what Mandy said. You sent Sif into a tizzy."

"Sif?"

"Yes, but Sif isn't my cat. She's Mandy's cat. Sif does claim me."

"I thought it must be yours, seeing how it hated me and all," he teased, winking.

Kiera laughed. "No. Not my cat, but I will have to give her a treat later."

Henry rolled his eyes. "So, do we have a deal?"

"I'm still not comfortable with this."

"Well, think about it—most of the people at this fundraiser tonight are people who have power. Power to give money to hospitals, money to give to keep certain free clinics open or possibly stop hospitals from closing."

He looked at her again and could see the wheels were turning.

"Why are you taking me there? I thought your father wanted to stop me protesting?"

"And I have stopped that. He doesn't want you protesting in public, but I can't stop you from talking privately to investors and those who have money and political sway, can I? I mean, I might be your fiancée, but I'm not in control of you."

Kiera grinned and he couldn't help smiling. "I never thought I would say this, Dr. Brown, but right now you're my favorite person and I like the way you think."

CHAPTER FIVE

HENRY HAD LOST track of Kiera. Once he had told her she had free rein to talk to anyone she wanted at the fundraiser—provided she keep up the pretense of being his fiancée—she had taken off, and he had watched her as she worked a room.

She might like to hide, but when it came to Aspen Grace Memorial Hospital and that free clinic she was so determined to save, she came out of her shell instantly.

It was like all these people his parents were schmoozing were the neighborhood boys and she was in that tree just pelting them with snowballs.

He chuckled to himself as he took a sip of his champagne.

Also, he liked watching her from a distance. Admiring her. She lit up the room And in that dress, he couldn't tear his eyes off her. At least while she was schmoozing he couldn't be tempted to take her in his arms, because that's what he'd been struggling with all night as he watched her. She really was the most beautiful thing he'd seen in a long time.

He hated the fact that he was so attracted to her.

He had dated other women, beautiful women, but this was different. There was something about Kiera that drew him in. She was infuriating, smart, sexy.

She made his blood heat with lust, his pulse race with need.

She wasn't as shallow as the women he usually dated. She didn't want to use him. He was using her.

And he felt bad about that.

He was using her because being engaged to her would annoy his father the most. He might have to do this last thing for his father, but he was going to get some enjoyment out of it.

And that was picking someone who would irritate his father.

But that wasn't the only reason he had chosen her.

She was like a breath of fresh air.

She's not actually yours.

He had to keep reminding himself of that.

Henry tore his gaze away from Kiera, wandered past the crowds and headed toward a more quiet section of his parents' party. To a large floor-to-ceiling window that overlooked the mountains and the trees. He couldn't see the trees in darkness, but he could see the mountain lit up and people skiing.

Not long ago they had been saving someone's life. The road had been covered in black ice while the snow fell.

Now, it was like none of that had happened. It scared him how fast life moved on, that it carried on like everything was okay.

"There you are."

He turned when he heard Kiera approach. His pulse raced when he saw her. His gaze raked over her curves, because that dress didn't hide a thing and he liked what he saw.

"I thought you'd ditched me," she said.

"No. Parties like this aren't my jam. So I stay on the sidelines."

She cocked her head to one side. "You're always at Hollywood parties."

"Not by choice," he murmured. "Have you heard about the status of the patient we worked on? You didn't mention it when I picked you up."

"I have. She's stable and is expected to make a full recovery. That accident was bad, but it could've been worse. There were no fatalities."

"Good."

"Is something wrong?" Kiera asked.

"Nothing. I just hate these kind of parties."

"So why do you attend them then?" she asked.

He thought about it. "I don't know."

Although he did. In this instance it was a condition of his bail from his parents. These parties reminded him of his loneliness.

His parents preferred these types of gatherings to being with him.

"You want to go?"

He cocked an eyebrow. "Are you done working the crowd?"

"I am. See, the thing is, these parties aren't my thing either, but I don't look a gift opportunity in the mouth. I'm ready to leave, and hopefully we can finish our conversation. You know, the real reason you asked me out."

"I would like that." He set his champagne flute down on a table and held out his arm.

"I forgot to tell you something," she said, taking his arm.

"Oh?"

"You look really good in that tuxedo."

He chuckled, secretly pleased. "I'll take the compliment, Dr. Brown. I haven't had many from you since I arrived this morning."

Kiera was smiling, which he interpreted as a good sign.

He was more than ready to leave. And he wouldn't mind continuing their date in a more private location.

This is just a business arrangement. This is not real.

Suddenly he wished it was because he wanted her.

"Henry!"

He froze and grumbled as he heard his mother call him. He turned around, and his mother made her way through the crush of people.

"You two are leaving?" his mother asked, exasperated.

"We are, Mother. Kiera has work tomorrow and I have work to do for Father. Unless you have forgotten? We made an appearance like you requested," Henry said stiffly. He was annoyed his mother had interrupted his plans to escape unseen.

He didn't want her intruding on this. He was glad he didn't have to speak to his father, who was too busy wooing potential donors for his political career.

So, what else was new?

"Oh. Well, very well." His mother looked disappointed. "Do be careful getting home. I heard the roads up the mountain have gotten bad."

"We will." He gave his mother a perfunctory kiss on the cheek.

Henry's parents hadn't interacted with Kiera anyway. His mother had barely acknowledged her, but they had tolerated her here because she was a doctor and she was his fiancée. His parents saw Kiera as a political tool.

She looked good on paper.

Was he doing the same? His stomach knotted as that thought crossed his mind. He didn't like it, but it was the truth. He was using her. Kiera didn't know about his past or that he was here in Aspen because he owed his father.

And she didn't need to know.

This wasn't real.

It would be over soon enough.

Henry instinctively put his hand on the small of Kiera's back as he led her away from his mother, from his parents so-called friends.

He just wanted to leave. They got their coats and waited outside for the car to be brought around. Only once they were in the car and driving away from his parents' mountain lodge did he finally break the silence.

"I'm sorry for dragging you to that."

"It was fine," she said.

"You don't have to be nice about it." He glanced over at her.

She chuckled. "It really was okay. I did get to talk to a lot of powerful people and let them know what's happening with Aspen Grace Memorial Hospital."

"You think you swayed them?" he asked.

"I'm not sure whether I did or not, but at least I got to talk to them."

He was impressed with her. Her strength and the way she didn't seem bothered by it all. Why couldn't she have been this easy dealing with him earlier in the day?

"Also," she said. "I found they were easier to talk to when I mentioned that I was your fiancée. That they were talking to the future Mrs. Baker."

He smiled. "Don't you mean Dr. Baker?"

"Some of them weren't too open to the idea of calling me doctor, but that's sort of old-school. I'm the pretty wife," she teased, and he laughed with her.

"Well, that's not a lie."

"What's not?"

"The pretty part." And the moment he said it, he regretted it. It had slipped out. Not that he regretted saying she was pretty—that wasn't it at all—but that he had let her know, had admitted he found her attractive.

And he did find her attractive.

It's just that he couldn't have her. He didn't want to open his heart again. The risk of pain was too much for him to bear and the guilt of moving on with someone like Kiera, someone who reminded him of Michelle in spirit, was a big no-no.

That's why he dated the women he did.

He didn't date women who reminded him of Michelle.

Yet, here he was with Kiera.

They weren't dating, but he was pretending to be engaged to her.

"Thanks," she said, her voice rising a bit, and he knew that she was uncomfortable with his compliment.

An uneasy tension fell between them again. The only sound was his wiper blades, brushing the snow off his windshield. It made a horrible screeching sound, which just added an extra layer of tension.

"So, we haven't really gotten to talking about terms," she said, finally breaking the silence.

"Terms?"

"Yes. What will I get, Dr. Baker? Or more importantly what will you give to Aspen Grace Memorial Hospital?"

Kiera had not been expecting to be taken to a function like that. At first, she had been completely unsure about the idea because she was already uncomfortable wearing the dress, but then it had worked out well.

She wasn't sure if what she said was getting through to anyone at the party, but at least she was talking. At least she was getting her viewpoint across to those in power.

Talking about the hospital was easy.

What unnerved her was the way Henry had looked

at her. It had given her a thrill. It had made her pulse quicken, her blood heat, and when he had put his hand on the small of her back as they were leaving, it had felt right.

It had made her want him.

And she didn't like that one bit. She didn't have time for this.

She wasn't going to be hurt again.

By anyone.

She didn't want him to talk about how pretty she was, even though she enjoyed it. She wanted to talk about how handsome he was in his tuxedo because he really did look good. The tuxedo was well tailored and fit his body like a glove.

She couldn't help admiring the way he looked.

He looked good enough to eat.

Her cheeks heated as the thought crept into her mind. She couldn't think that way. She had to focus, and focusing on the hospital would do just that.

"What will I give to Aspen Grace Memorial Hospital?"

"Yes. I mean that was part of the deal, wasn't it? I pretend to be your fiancée to get your parents off your back, and you help me and my hospital. You have the power. You're a majority shareholder, you could convince the others to change plans."

"Changing plans isn't that easy," he said, and she could hear the exasperation in his voice. "Land has been bought."

"That free clinic gives quality medicine to those who won't be able to afford the private hospital. Surgeons donate their time there."

Henry sighed. "It's very noble."

"And a free clinic is not being considered for the new hospital, is it?" she asked.

Henry didn't say anything as he gripped the steering wheel tighter, his jaw clenched. She knew then it wasn't in the plans. The free clinic cost a lot. She was aware of that, but it was important. People died and were hurt because they couldn't afford proper care.

"It's not," he finally said. "Perhaps, if you can come up with another idea, I can persuade—"

"No. You promised me this if I pretended to be your fiancée. I'm coming to the conclusion that Aspen Grace Memorial Hospital can't be expanded. It's an old hospital."

His eyebrows raised. "So you're finally seeing that the hospital is old."

"You're right, but what I'm worried about is the people you'll alienate by opening this new hospital. People who rely on our free clinic. And that's my condition. That's why I've been protesting. I want people who can't afford to pay to be able to access health care."

"Okay."

"Okay?" she asked, shocked.

"Okay." She was pleased, but she didn't have long to relish her small victory as the car slowed down and they saw flares in the road.

"What is going on?" Henry said.

He pulled up beside a car that was on the side of the road. A man was waving his arms as they approached.

Henry rolled down the window. "Can I help?"

"Yes! Do you have a cell phone that works? I need someone to call an ambulance."

"We're doctors, what's wrong?" Henry asked, turning on his hazard lights.

"It's my wife. She's in labor and we slid off the road.

The baby is coming, the car is stuck and I don't know what to do. I don't know what to do!" The man was frantic, not that Kiera could blame him.

"You call the ambulance and I'll check on the patient," she said.

"You'll what?" Henry asked, but she didn't stay to listen as she climbed out of the car. The snow was coming down heavier. Even if Henry got hold of the ambulance, it would be too late. It would take the ambulance some time to get there and given that the man was frantic, Kiera would lay money on the fact that his wife was probably crowning.

Kiera climbed into the back seat of the car to see a woman, panting, her body covered in blankets.

"Hi, I'm Dr. Brown," she said. "Can I take a look?"

The woman nodded.

Kiera lifted the blanket and saw that the baby was indeed crowning. Yeah, the ambulance wasn't going to make it there in time.

"The ambulance is on the way. How can I help?" Henry asked.

"I need a first-aid kit, if you have it. I need some gloves or something. This baby is coming."

"I have a kit in the car." Henry disappeared.

"What's your name?" Kiera asked as she waited for Henry to come back.

"Miranda," the woman said. "Is my baby going to be okay?"

"Your baby is on the way."

"Here's the kit," Henry said. He opened it and helped her sanitize and put on gloves. She grabbed the extra blanket that was handed to her.

"Okay, Miranda when you feel that next contraction, I want you to push," Kiera said.

Miranda nodded, and Kiera could feel the contraction as she examined Miranda's belly to check on the baby.

Miranda began to push and Kiera watched, keeping her eyes on that baby.

"You're doing so well, Miranda," Kiera encouraged. "Keep going. Okay, now breathe."

The baby was coming fast, but everything looked good.

The next contraction came, and Kiera coached Miranda through it. The baby's shoulders were delivered. It took one more half push and the baby was born.

A little girl began to cry as Kiera worked. She couldn't cut the cord, because she didn't have any clamps. She could hear the ambulance siren. The paramedics could take care of that.

"It's a girl." Kiera tried to wrap the baby the best she could and handed the baby to Miranda as she waited for the placenta to be delivered, which came soon after. Once she checked it and wrapped it for the paramedics, she pulled off her gloves.

The paramedics arrived, and she watched as Henry dealt with them. She climbed out of the back of the car, slipping slightly on the snow. Henry's arms came around her to steady her.

"Good job," he whispered.

"Thanks. I'm glad we were able to help them." Henry's arms were still around her as the paramedics finished clamping and cutting the cord and then got Miranda and her little girl out of the back of the car.

"I've called a tow truck," Henry told Miranda's husband. "I'll wait here until they come. You go with your wife and new baby."

The frantic husband smiled in appreciation. Kiera was so thankful that they had been able to help. It was a simple birth and delivery, except that it was on the side of the road, in a snowstorm, in the dark and in the back of a car. Thankfully, there had been enough blankets in the car to keep the new parents and the new baby warm on the cold winter night.

"You acted fast," Henry said. "It's been a while since I've attended a birth."

"I wouldn't think that plastic surgeons would deal with many," she replied.

"They don't. I think the last time was when I was a resident. I'm glad you were with me. I'm not sure I could have been of help."

"I didn't do anything but catch and coach the patient," Kiera said.

"I'm still glad you were there," Henry said.

"Thanks."

The ambulance drove away and they locked the car. Kiera shivered in the cold. She sat back in Henry's car and it wasn't long before he joined her. They were stuck on the side of the road waiting for a tow truck.

The only sounds were the noise of the snow blowing around and covering the windshield and the clicking sound of the car's hazard lights.

"Well, this has been an exciting night," Henry stated.

"It has. I don't think I've ever been on such a crazy date in my life," Kiera teased.

Henry laughed. "No, that was unique."

He glanced at her and her heart skipped a beat. "You did look really pretty tonight."

"Thank you." Heat flooded her cheeks.

Her pulse was thundering in her ears as they sat there next to each other in the car. She shivered.

"Here." His arm slipped around her, pulling her close.

She knew she should push him away, but his arm felt nice and she stopped shivering.

And she couldn't remember the last time she'd felt something like that.

It felt good.

What was she doing?

She looked over at him. Her body was humming with anticipation. Her mouth was dry, and her breathing was fast as their gazes locked.

And before she could stop herself, she became swept up in something.

Something she didn't quite know how to control and something that she couldn't stop. And she wasn't completely sure that she wanted to stop it.

She knew it was wrong and shouldn't happen.

Kiera didn't know Henry, but in this moment she didn't want to stop the kiss from happening. His breath was hot on her neck, fanning her skin, making her aware of him. Every part of her tingled with something.

Her body was betraying her as it reacted to her enemy, to this man she didn't know and who wasn't the type of man she would ever think of going for.

This man was infuriating, privileged. He was everything she hated about this world. Yet, she didn't think he was what his parents were.

Kiera closed her eyes. She wanted him to kiss her, and her body trembled being so close to him, his strong arms around her. Her heart raced as she anticipated what it would be like to be kissed by him.

To have a kiss like this.

A forbidden kiss.

A sinful kiss. And though she should stop him, she couldn't.

His lips were gentle against hers. So many emotions

came bubbling to the surface as she sank into his kiss. Anger, guilt, lust.

Definitely lust.

That hot, heady need.

Kiera couldn't remember the last time she'd been kissed. And she certainly couldn't recall if she had ever been kissed like this before, or even if that kiss had been good, which made her think it wasn't.

Henry's kiss was all consuming.

Devouring.

She melted in his arms. She wanted him here, in the car, this man she had just met. The man who could either save everything she cared about or destroy it.

Henry's kiss made her feel like she was alive for the first time in a long time. Like she wasn't alone. Like she could have more, and that scared her.

For so long she had relied only on herself, something she'd learned at a young age. All she ever had to worry about was herself and Mandy.

And nothing else. But this kiss she was sharing with Henry made her feel safe.

What're you doing?

She pushed him away. "I can't, Henry. I'm sorry. I don't know what got into me."

"No, I'm sorry, too," he said breathlessly. "I don't know what got into me, either."

Kiera swallowed a lump in her throat, her heart still racing, her blood burning with an unquenched need.

Something she hadn't felt in such a long time.

Then they spotted flashing lights as the tow truck appeared through the heavy snow. Henry got out of the car, and the rush of cold air that blasted in calmed her down. She was able to regain some control over her emotions.

He came back to the car once the tow truck had the instructions.

"The driver said the roads are slick," Henry stated. "I'll get you home as soon as I can."

"Okay." She couldn't look at him. It was hard to look at him.

"I'm sorry for kissing you, Kiera. It won't happen again."

"Okay," she said, unsure that she didn't want that to happen again. She was relieved and disappointed at the same time, and it was a strange place to be in. "It'll be okay."

Henry nodded. "It will. I'll get you home and we can talk about this tomorrow. We can't let this affect our work."

"Sure. Sure. It won't." She straightened her shoulders. "It won't happen again."

Henry nodded and barely glanced at her as he drove back out onto the road.

It was a long, tense drive back to her place. The snow was still falling, and as he got out to help her up the slippery ramp to her house she hoped he didn't have a long drive to wherever he was staying.

"Are you headed back up to your parents' place?" she asked.

"No. The party will still be going for a while. I have a small condo in the new part of town. It's not far from where the new hospital is supposed to be built."

She nodded. "Just be careful."

"Thanks." He smiled. "Look, we have to work together. There will be meetings, and I will do what I can for Aspen Grace Memorial Hospital, as long as you do your part."

The reminder of why they had been at the party

tonight and of the deal they had worked out together brought her back to reality.

This was business.

Nothing more, and she'd been a fool to be swept up in such a trivial feeling like lust. This was a business arrangement, pure and simple.

She wasn't going to risk her heart on a chance.

She wasn't a fool.

She had walls for a reason. Walls were the things that had protected her for her whole life.

"I'll do my part. You needn't worry, Dr. Baker."

"Good night, Kiera," he said gently, and she thought she detected a hint of regret, but she pushed the thought away. She had to push him out of her mind.

There was no room for Henry.

And she had to remember that.

CHAPTER SIX

HENRY COULDN'T STOP thinking about Kiera and that kiss all night.

All he could focus on was how she had felt in his arms and how little space there was in the front of his car. How he had wanted to pull her closer to him. How he wished that they hadn't been on the side of the road waiting for a tow truck.

And how he wished that they weren't in the awkward situation of pretending to be engaged.

These were the thoughts that swirled around in his head all night.

He barely got any sleep.

He had several cold showers and went for a run on his treadmill. There was no change.

Nothing could get Kiera out of his mind.

When he'd been called to Colorado he had thought it would be an easy job. It would be no problem to shut down Dr. Brown's protest. He had foolishly thought this would be a simple thing to take care of.

Then he'd met Kiera and everything had changed in an instant.

He didn't know why he had kissed Kiera last night. It had been something he'd been fighting all night from the moment he had seen her come down the stairs in that stunning jade-colored dress. His blood heated as he thought of her in that dress.

Her long red hair tumbling down over her shoulders, the way her green eyes sparkled in the light. The pink tinge to her creamy cheeks.

The kiss flashed in his mind again.

You've got to get a hold of yourself.

He'd been doing okay all evening, resisting the urge at the party, but then he saw her climb into the back of a car and take control of a woman giving birth. She was smart and strong. Dedicated to her work, and that attracted him.

He wanted her.

Kiera was spectacular and he was overcome with an emotion, a need, that he hadn't felt in such a long time.

It scared him.

So, after tossing and turning all night, running on the treadmill and a couple of long, cold showers, he had got up as the sun was rising and had come to the hospital.

There was paperwork to do, paperwork he couldn't concentrate on. All he could think about was Kiera's lips. The taste of her. The softness of her hair as he ran his fingers through it.

Get a grip on yourself.

He dragged his hands through his hair.

He was tired of staring at the four walls of the boardroom. He needed air, and he needed to think. He usually had clarity when he was in the operating room, but he didn't have this option here.

He had no patients.

He was a surgeon with nothing to do. Normally, when he was plagued by indecision or a turmoil of emotions, he'd throw himself into his work, but that was impossible here.

So he was going a bit stir-crazy.

He needed air.

He needed to breathe.

Henry got up and opened the door of the boardroom, running smack-dab into Kiera.

"Dr. Brown!" he exclaimed. "I didn't expect to see you this morning."

"I was told you were here," she said. "And I think in public you should call me Kiera."

Henry laughed quietly. "Oh, and call you Dr. Brown in private?"

Pink tinged her cheeks, and she cocked one of her finely arched eyebrows. "Really? We're going to do this here?"

"What can I help you with?" he asked.

"Can I come in, or are we going to continue the conversation out in the hall."

Henry stepped to the side to let Kiera enter. He shut the door behind her and turned to face her.

"So to what do I owe the pleasure this morning?" Henry asked.

She held out a folder to him. "You wanted information about the free clinic. Here it is."

Henry took the folder. "Thanks."

Henry placed the folder beside the rest of his work. She glanced at the table, her eyes widening.

"You seem to have a lot of stuff piled up."

Henry shrugged. "It's not my favorite thing, but it's something I have to do while I'm here. As a shareholder, I have a few things I need to take care of, but I loathe it. I don't mind doing charting or operative reports, but business stuff isn't as exciting."

"Then why have shares in something that makes you do what you loathe the most?"

"Because it's a hospital and I want to support medicine. I just don't like the administrative work attached to it. I'd rather be practicing medicine than balancing a budget."

What he didn't tell her was that his father actually invested the money for him. He didn't mind that his money went to a hospital, but he didn't like the work attached to it. He didn't like the hold his father had on him and he didn't know why he kept jumping.

His father was never there for him. As soon as his father was satisfied, the protests were over, and AGMH was shut down, Henry would sell all those shares his father invested for him.

He was going to sever all ties.

He was done.

Kiera cocked her head to one side. "Why don't you come down and help in the emergency room today? You said you don't get to see many general surgeries in Los Angeles, and I know that Dr. Carr would gladly give you medical privileges."

It was tempting.

He'd rather be practicing medicine than doing paperwork.

"Okay, but I don't have scrubs."

"That's an excuse," she teased. "You were able to find scrubs yesterday just fine."

"Okay then. I guess I have no excuse. Take me to where the scrubs are and get me down to the emergency room."

"Is that like take me to your leader?"

Henry rolled his eyes. "Just show me where to go."

Kiera smiled. "Follow me then."

Henry followed her out of the boardroom. He was glad for the change of pace. He was glad he'd be doing his job, the thing he was passionate about. He'd be practicing, but he was nervous that he would be working with Kiera. Especially after what had happened last night.

Especially after the kiss that was still burned on his lips.

Maybe he should go back to the boardroom.

Still, the pull of working—not thinking about his father's or his own problems—and saving lives was a delicious distraction he couldn't get enough of.

He was calm when he was saving lives and helping others.

He could clear his head when he was in the operating room.

In the operating room he didn't think about Michelle, his parents or the loneliness that consumed him.

It was like breathing for him. It was calming. It came naturally.

It was his safety.

"You know," Kiera said, breaking into his thoughts as they walked through the halls. "We're going to have to tell Dr. Carr about our engagement. I mean, if we're going public and announcing to everyone we're engaged, we should let him know. He's not only the chief of surgery, but he's like a second father to me. Next to Dr. Burke, that is."

"How do you think he'll take that?"

"Take what?" Kiera asked.

"The announcement of our engagement. I mean, I don't know him all that well, but I assume he is aware of your protests at the new hospital site."

Kiera smiled. "I do know him well and, yes, he does know about my protests. He'll be hard to sell on the idea we're engaged. I've made it clear for years that I had no interest in ever getting married."

He was intrigued by that. "No interest?"

"No. None." Only there was something about the tone of her voice that didn't quite convince him she was telling the truth. She was putting up a wall, and he understood walls. He had his own.

"Maybe I should get you a ring, and then maybe he'll believe you really are my fiancée."

Kiera paused, not sure that she'd heard him correctly.

"Pardon?" she asked, trying not to show him how shocked she actually was.

"I said maybe I should get you a ring and make it more official. More real."

Kiera opened the door to the locker room where the extra scrubs were kept. She was stunned. Her palms were suddenly very sweaty and she wished she was anywhere but here.

A ring? Was he for real?

What would she do with it? She didn't want him buying her some frivolous thing to perpetuate a lie.

That made her nervous. She didn't want to wear it.

She didn't want him to buy her anything.

"I don't want it," she said, laughing nervously as she found her voice. "I think that's the most ridiculous thing I ever heard."

A smile tugged on the corner of his lips. Lips that she had become very familiar with last night and couldn't stop thinking about this morning.

And now she was in the locker room, pulling out a pair of scrubs for him, and he was offering to buy her a ring and seemingly enjoying her discomfort over the whole thing. Which infuriated her even more.

"You think this is funny, don't you?" she asked.

"I do. I never thought you would get so worked up over a piece of jewelry. It's kind of fun."

"Fun?" She grabbed a pair of scrubs and whipped them at his face. "I'm glad you think this is fun!"

"I have to get some enjoyment out of this."

Kiera rolled her eyes but smiled. "Fine."

Henry started unbuttoning his shirt, and all she could do was stare at him. It was bad enough that she had been up half the night thinking about being in his arms and that kiss. She had a bruise on her thigh from the stick shift.

She needed to get out of there.

Only she was frozen. She couldn't move.

She turned and looked away. This had not been her plan for this morning, although she was thankful for help in the emergency room. All she had been going to do was hand Henry the report on the free clinic and then distance herself from him, because that one kiss had gotten under her skin and through her defenses.

She was obsessed by the way it had seared her soul, burned her blood.

Made her yearn for something she was afraid to reach out and take because she'd been burned before.

Usually she could resist, but for some reason she couldn't resist Henry.

It rattled her.

And she didn't like to be rattled.

All she wanted to do was bury herself in work. If she kept busy in the emergency room and the operating room, she wouldn't have to see him until she collected herself. Until she stopped thinking about the kiss that had fired her blood and sizzled through her system all night long.

Work would help cleanse that. It would help her focus.

She could get clarity from saving lives.

It didn't matter that Dr. Henry Baker working with

her in the operating room and offering her a ring had not been on the agenda.

The whole idea was silly.

"You can look now, I'm changed," he teased. "Though, if you are my fiancée, you really shouldn't be embarrassed if I'm changing in front of you."

She glared at him. "You know what? I really like the grumpy, nonverbal, moody side of you, Dr. Baker."

He laughed. "And I kind of like getting under your skin a bit, Dr. Brown."

Kiera rolled her eyes. "Just follow me and try to stay out of my way today."

"I'll try, but you know if we're going to convince my parents that we're engaged, we're going to have to seem a bit friendlier toward one another."

"Don't I know it," she grumbled. She pushed the button to open the automatic double doors that led into the emergency room. Triage was busy, but it was mostly just people with minor ailments, and as soon as she saw that she frowned. "I wonder why they're not at the free clinic?"

"The free clinic was shut down," a nurse said, hearing her and passing by.

"What?" Kiera asked, shocked, spinning around to Henry.

He put up his hands. "I didn't shut it down."

"Then who did?" Kiera asked. "What's going on?"

"I shut it down," Dr. Carr said, coming over to them. "By an order from the chairman of the board."

Henry looked confused. "I am chairman of the board."

Richard nodded. "And yesterday you told me to shut it down."

"I didn't, though."

Kiera was having a hard time believing him, and she

didn't want to stand around discussing this. It was making her too angry.

"I have patients to see," she muttered, and walked away.

She couldn't look at him right now. She didn't want to look at him. She felt betrayed.

He had probably ordered it to shut down before they'd made their deal, but it still stung.

Henry followed after her.

"Kiera, I didn't order it to be shut down."

"I'm sure."

He frowned. "You don't believe me."

"Any reason why I *should* believe you? I don't know you."

He grabbed her arm. "You do. Remember?"

Kiera sighed. "You know what I meant."

Henry leaned forward. "I know that, but others don't—be careful."

She wanted to discuss it further, but the ambulance bay door opened and the paramedics wheeled in a patient.

"Twenty-three-year-old man. Third-degree burns over his face and his right arm."

Henry left and was instantly at the patient's side. Kiera followed as they wheeled the unconscious patient into a trauma room for workup.

"GCS in the field was a five. The patient has smoke inhalation. He was in a house fire," the paramedic said.

Kiera examined the man's nose and throat and saw evidence that smoke had infiltrated the lungs. "I need to intubate him."

Kiera grabbed a laryngoscope and visualized the cords as she grabbed the endotracheal tube and placed it down his throat.

A nurse used an Ambu bag to keep the patient breathing as Kiera listened with a stethoscope for breath sounds. She smiled, listening to the equal breath sounds. The patient was successfully intubated.

"These burns are bad. I'll wrap them and we'll treat the patient once he gets to the intensive care unit," Henry said.

Kiera nodded. She took some blood and sent it off to be tested for carbon monoxide.

She didn't say anything else to Henry. There was nothing much more to say though she couldn't get over the sick feeling in the pit of her stomach. Henry was quiet as he carefully cared for the patient's burns.

Once they were wrapped, they took the patient to the intensive care unit, got him registered and talked with the victim's family.

Now it would be a waiting game. The patient had high levels of carbon monoxide in his blood.

The hairs on his face and his nose were singed and when she was intubating him Kiera could see the smoke inhalation damage. He'd be in the intensive care unit until his lungs could heal.

"I'll change the dressings tomorrow," Henry said as he finished giving instructions to the intensive care nurses.

Aspen Grace Memorial Hospital didn't have a large intensive care unit, but they had a good one. Of course, they had a great free clinic, too.

"Do you think you forgot you ordered it closed?" Kiera asked.

"What?" Henry asked.

"The free clinic."

"I didn't have it shut down, Kiera. I didn't have time after I arrived."

"But Richard said the chairman of the board shut it down. You are chairman of the board."

"But I didn't do it," Henry snapped.

"Henry didn't, I did."

Kiera spun around and saw Governor Baker standing there.

Henry's spine stiffened. "Father."

CHAPTER SEVEN

"Do you mind telling me what's going on, Henry?" his father demanded as soon as they were behind closed doors. Kiera had returned to the emergency room because his father didn't want her to be part of the discussion.

"Do you mind telling me why I've been removed as chair?" Henry barked back.

"You're engaged to Dr. Brown—the person I sent you to stop from protesting. You're a liability to the project now."

"Hardly. Kiera has some good insights regarding the hospital. Insights that you and I don't have."

"You're a doctor. Are you telling me you don't have insight?"

"Not at this hospital. I suppose I've been rendered useless to you again."

His father rolled his eyes. "Please… She's using you. Can't you see that, Henry?"

Henry tried not to react to the kernel of truth his father was spouting. He'd been used before and he was not unfamiliar with it.

Yes, Kiera was agreeing to be his fiancée while he was in town, but he was using her, too.

Using her as a shield to annoy his father. Clearly, it was working.

He knew what was happening here.

The problem was that she was slipping past his walls, and he was afraid of being hurt.

He was also afraid of hurting her when this was over.

She's not into you. You won't hurt her.

Kiera was strong. She didn't need him, even if he needed her, and the thought spooked him because he had enjoyed being with her last night.

That kiss was something he wouldn't soon forget.

He liked being around her, and he resented his father for forcing him to put a stop on things.

"She's not right for you," his father said.

"I say she is."

And it gave him satisfaction he had chosen Kiera in the heat of the moment.

The woman his father apparently loathed.

Of course, his father hadn't liked Michelle much, either, because Michelle had been a strong woman, and that had driven his father crazy. His father detested strong women.

His father didn't want anyone defying him.

Which was all the more reason Henry was glad that it annoyed his father so much that he was engaged to Kiera.

And why he liked Kiera even more.

You're not really engaged to her, though.

And he had to remind himself of that.

Kiera wouldn't like him if she knew why he was here. That he had been sent to deal with her because of his past and the deal he had made with his father. She wouldn't like him if she knew that he planned to walk away from Aspen Grace Memorial Hospital and Colorado for good once this was over.

"What're you doing here, Father?" Henry asked. "You

pulled me from my work in Los Angeles, and now you swoop in to do my job for me?"

"I came here because I saw you were with Dr. Brown at our fundraiser and couldn't quite believe it when your mother told me you were engaged to her. To our enemy. The one thorn in our side, standing in the way of our new hospital."

"She's your enemy, not mine."

His father's eyes narrowed. "I thought you wanted me to forget about your indiscretions?"

"I do."

"This is not what I had in mind. You owe me, Henry."

"I'm working on it," Henry gritted out.

"How? You're engaged to the woman I asked you to stop! Did she blackmail you or something?"

"No. She's not like you."

His father grinned, but it wasn't a warm, happy grin. It was cold, calculating, the kind Henry was used to.

"Be careful, Henry. You have a task to do. Complete it."

"I will."

"I'm not convinced. Need I remind you that you're a majority shareholder in this hospital. Her blocking the new building threatens your investment, too." Which was true, but Henry didn't care as much as he had before.

"Kiera is prepared to discuss the new hospital if the free clinic stays open."

That had his father's attention. "The free clinic?"

Henry nodded. "Since I'm no longer the chairman, you'll find all the paperwork in the boardroom. Including a report on the free clinic. Now, if you don't mind, I have patients to attend to."

His father stepped in front of him. "Fine. I'll look at the report, but you and Kiera need to be seen."

"What're you talking about?" Henry asked, confused.

"It would help the board's reputation if you were seen out and about with Kiera. It would show our support for Aspen."

"I thought it angered you when I was in the papers in Los Angeles," he smirked.

"This is different."

"How?"

"She's a respected doctor in Aspen."

"You mean it would look good for your political career," Henry stated.

His father shrugged. "It couldn't hurt."

"No. That's not part of the deal."

"It is now since you bungled the original task. Get your picture taken with her. Announce your engagement. It'll look good, and then maybe we can consider the free clinic in the new hospital. Maybe."

Henry seethed.

All that mattered to his father was his political career. Why was he shocked about this?

He wasn't. He was angry that Kiera was involved because of him, because he had thought it would annoy his father the most. Now Kiera had been sucked into his father's agenda even more.

Kiera didn't deserve this, and neither did he.

"We're done talking about this."

"Henry, I invested those shares for you. Don't make me regret my generosity."

The threat sent a chill down his spine.

If he lost the shares, then he couldn't help Kiera and she wouldn't want to be around him. The only reason they were together was because he'd promised to help her. Their engagement was fake.

And if he couldn't, why would she stay with him?

What do you expect?

It shouldn't bother him, but it did.

He was angry.

Henry didn't respond and left the room. Frustrated.

He headed back to the emergency room, and though he should put some distance between Kiera and his uncontrolled emotions, he sought her out.

He hated losing control. Control kept the grief, the hurt, the loneliness at bay. Kiera was a balm to soothe his soul.

A balm that had a bit of a bite to it, but once you got past that burn, it was so good.

She finished up with a patient and walked over to the desk to input information. He crept up beside her, and she glanced up at him and raised her eyebrows.

"Whoa, that is some serious, dark, twisty energy coming off you."

"Want to go out?" he asked.

"What?" she asked, chuckling.

"Tonight. My place. Nothing fancy and I'll cook."

Her mouth dropped open and pink bloomed in her cheeks. "Okay...yeah. That sounds good."

"Good. I'll see you at seven. I'll text you the address."

And then he left the emergency room. He had to gain some clarity, some control of the emotions raging inside him.

And he had to make dinner, though he had no idea what.

He wasn't the best cook, and the last thing he needed was the papers proclaiming he'd poisoned his fiancée in some kind of scheme. He laughed at the paranoid thought.

You can do this.

And he could.

More importantly, he wanted to.

* * *

Kiera drove up to Henry's condo. He'd said it wasn't far from the main part of town, but it wasn't as close as she thought. She still had steep roads to negotiate and it was snowing, heavily, again.

His condo was in a newer part of town, a new alpine village. Another place for skiers to come and ski.

Another resort that catered to the elite.

The shops that lined the quaint little street were exclusive and unaffordable. Kiera parked her car in the village parking lot and walked up through the village that sat at the base of a ski lift. Henry's condo overlooked the mountain where all the happier skiers were enjoying a perfectly snowy night.

After she typed in his code and the entry door opened, she made her way to the elevator. The elevator took her to the sixth floor, which was the penthouse of this strange modern condo that looked so out of place in Aspen.

The elevator opened, and she was shocked as she walked straight into an open concept apartment that resembled a rustic ski chalet—with exposed wood beams, the floor-to-ceiling windows and a crackling fire put in the middle of a sunken living room.

Henry came out of the kitchen and her heart skipped a beat. She had thought he looked good in a power suit and tuxedo, but those outfits had nothing on seeing him in a pair of well-fitted jeans and a blue sweater.

The sweater was such a beautiful blue and brought out the color of his eyes. Made his brown eyes, deeper. Like mahogany. His hair was tousled and there were a few stray curls.

"You found it okay then." He took her coat.

"This place looks completely differently from the outside," she said, still stunned.

"It's why I like it."

"So this is your home away from Los Angeles?"

He nodded. "It is. I bought it a while ago, but rarely come here."

"You didn't want to stay at your parents'?"

"No," he said tightly, hanging up her coat.

"Well, I do like this place. It's open, but also warm and cozy."

Kiera followed him into the penthouse and down the steps of the sunken living room that was giving off a retro chalet vibe.

The fire felt good as she perched on the edge of his large sectional couch.

"Can I get you a glass of wine?" he asked.

"Yes. Thank you."

Henry headed into the kitchen area and Kiera relaxed.

"So, I'm intrigued about why you were so adamant in wanting to cook for me tonight," she said, trying to make conversation.

"Well, my father is convinced you're using me. And if we're going to continue with this ruse, I thought it best we got to know one another." He came back and handed her a glass of red wine.

"Is the wine to numb the pain?" she teased.

He smiled, a twinkle in his eyes. "Perhaps."

"Well, it's a good start."

She didn't like people, other than Mandy and Dr. Carr, to know too much about her. It was too painful. When she had let down her guard in the past, in particular as she had with Brent, she'd been hurt. People couldn't be trusted. They always left in the end, always disappointed you.

They were selfish for the most part.

Even she was selfish. She was only helping Henry out to get something from him.

And she didn't trust Henry; however, she was beginning to relax with him, and it was scary. She couldn't let him in. She just couldn't get hurt again.

"I'll go first. I'm forty," he said, breaking through her morose thoughts.

Kiera laughed. "I did know that tidbit."

"How?"

"I did research on you before you came to Aspen, and I'm sure your father's people have quite the dossier on me."

Henry chuckled. "Most likely, but I'm not privy to it. So you probably know more about me than I do about you."

"Okay, well what do you want to know?" Kiera hoped her voice didn't shake as she said that, because she really didn't like sharing personal information with anyone.

She hadn't had much privacy growing up and she liked to keep things close to her chest.

She didn't like to even remember her parents or her past. She didn't like reliving it. Those had been dark times. Wilfred and Mandy had made her life happy.

There was no need to think about the father who had abandoned her.

The person she had waited to come back for so long, and he never had.

She'd moved on.

Have you?

"Well, you said Dr. Burke raised you but isn't your father. Are you related to him?" Henry asked.

Kiera tried to swallow the wine caught in her throat.

"Wow, you really get to the heart of the matter."

"We're engaged, so I guess I should know about where you came from."

Kiera sighed. Her hands were shaking, her pulse was racing, and she felt sick.

"No, I'm not related to Wilfred Burke or Mandy."

"You seem nervous."

"I am." She set down the wineglass. "I don't... I don't think about it."

She trailed off as she thought about her past. Her mother had been so addicted to drugs that she'd died in an emergency room from an overdose, and her father had been unable to cope, either. He had left her in a dingy diner in Colorado Springs.

Kiera had sat there for hours, waiting for her dad to come back.

And he never had.

She'd probably be dead if she had stayed with her biological father. She would have started using. No one would have helped her, and she certainly wouldn't have become a doctor.

It had been the scariest moment of her life, but eventually she'd come to Aspen, and Dr. Burke and Mandy had taken her in.

"I'm not an orphan," she said quickly clearing her throat. "My mother died, but my father abandoned me at a roadside diner."

Henry's expression softened. "I'm sorry."

"Don't pity me," she said quickly. She hated the pity. There was no need for it. Not once Wilfred and Mandy became her family.

She was lucky really.

"This is me doing anything but."

Her heart skipped a beat. A flush of warmth spread through her. Usually people pitied her if they found out about her past, but she could tell that Henry didn't because he looked her in the eye and reached out to take her hand. It caused her to gasp slightly, shocked that he was reaching out to touch her instead of being uncomfortable with her past. She didn't pull away from the touch.

It made her feel safe.

Men she'd dated in the past had felt sorry for her once they knew about her past. She was not defined by her past. Only her present, but no one could see beyond her biological parents' tainted past.

It was another reason she didn't share anything about herself. She didn't trust anyone with her pain.

And she didn't want to let people in.

It was easier to stay single. To be alone.

Yet, here she was, engaged.

Not really engaged.

And she had to keep reminding herself of that. They were exchanging information in order to keep up the subterfuge.

"So that's my past. I was an abandoned kid who grew up in the system until a kindly widowed man with a daughter the same age as me took me in."

"How did Dr. Burke find you?" Henry asked.

"He became a foster parent. I was struggling in other homes and he chose me." She smiled as she thought of Wilfred. "I'll be eternally grateful. I was alone for so long."

"I can relate to that," Henry said, sliding close to her.

"I know that you can't. You had two parents."

"Two absent parents. I grew up in boarding schools and servants raised me."

"Similar, but not the same." Kiera took another sip of her wine.

"How do you mean?" he asked.

"You were still cared for."

"But not by my parents. They might not have physically abandoned me, but emotionally they did."

She melted because he understood her. He knew what it was like and tears welled up in her eyes. They were unwelcome. She didn't cry in front of anyone.

The only time she'd cried was when Wilfred died and she'd been with him after he passed.

He had told no one he was so sick, and Kiera hadn't made it in time to say goodbye, to thank him.

He had lain there. Calm. Peaceful. The nurses had told her what was wrong with him. They had told her about the cancer that had ravaged him. She had been allowed to be alone in the room with him. No longer was he in pain, and all she could do was drop to her knees and weep.

"I'm sorry," she whispered, her voice trembling as she tried to banish the memory from her mind so she didn't cry in front of him. "I guess we are the same in some ways."

"Well, this is kind of a bummer. How about something to eat? I made…something I'm not that sure of."

Kiera laughed, the sadness ebbing away. "Something that you're not sure of? That sounds appetizing."

"I wouldn't bet on it."

Kiera followed Henry into his kitchen. His kitchen was clean and looked like it had barely been used. It looked brand-new.

The kitchen at her place was used. Well used. Kiera could cook a few things, but Mandy did most of the cooking.

This kitchen looked like it just plopped itself out of a factory.

"Why do I smell plastic?" Kiera asked.

"What?" Henry opened the oven and she could see

a rotisserie chicken from a grocery store, still sitting in its plastic container. The plastic container was melting and dribbling down into some kind bubbly orange and green side dish.

She stifled a laugh. "You know that those chickens from the grocery store are actually cooked, right?"

"Yeah, well, it needed to be warmed." Henry grabbed his oven mitts, still with the price tag on them, and pulled out the melted plastic holding the destroyed chicken. And then pulled out another dish, a discolored, hardened casserole of some sort.

"What was that supposed to be?" she asked as she came to stand beside him and inspect the trauma more carefully. She was a trauma doctor, after all, and assessing the damage was part of her job.

And there was a lot of carnage here in this mystery side dish.

"It was supposed to be a sweet potato casserole."

"What's with the green?" she asked, wrinkling her nose and leaning over him.

"Spinach. I added spinach, I thought they might go well together. Apparently, I was wrong."

"You were so wrong. So, so very wrong."

"Well, I guess there goes my idea of cooking you dinner. The whole reason for inviting you here was to do that. Michelle always told me I was a terrible cook..." He trailed off and something changed.

He was no longer laughing. He walked away from the chicken and the sweet potato casserole.

"Who's Michelle?" she asked gently.

"I don't want to talk about it," he said quietly. "I didn't mean to mention her."

"Look, I told you about my past, tell me about Michelle, because obviously she is someone important. Someone a fiancée would know about?"

Henry ran his hands through his hair. "I don't talk about her, and I didn't..."

"I don't talk about my past," she said softly. "You didn't pity me, and I promise not to pity you."

She could tell it was difficult for him. It was something that stung him deeply.

Henry looked back at her. His eyes were dark, and all the mirth, relaxation and happiness that had been there a moment ago when they had been laughing over the chicken was gone.

It was replaced with pain.

"Michelle was my fiancée. She died."

"I'm sorry for your loss. How did she die? May I ask that?"

"She was a surgeon, as well. A trauma surgeon who worked with a search and rescue team. She really liked going into remote locations and saving lives. One day, she went in to help and there was an accident. She was in a remote spot and the small clinic there couldn't handle her injuries. So she succumbed to them. Even if she made it, I doubt she could've survived, now looking back. She might've had a chance, but who knows."

It was then that it hit her why he was in favor of building a bigger hospital, a better hospital. A larger emergency room, a bigger intensive care unit and a teaching program. When he looked at Aspen Grace Memorial Hospital he saw the sort of small hospital that couldn't save the woman he loved.

Her heart melted for him a bit.

It wasn't about money. It wasn't about making more money.

For Henry, it was something deep and personal.

And she understood that.

She wanted to save the free clinic because of what had happened to Mandy; Henry wanted to make sure that Aspen Grace Memorial Hospital was the best it could be.

"I'm sorry."

"Don't be." He scrubbed his hand over his face. "Well, now we know our deep, dark secrets. What do we do with this?"

Kiera sighed. "I don't know. We certainly can't eat dinner, because it's kind of horrific."

A smile quirked the corner of his lips. "Well, that's for sure."

"I still can't believe you tried to cook a cooked chicken."

"Shut up." The twinkle returned to his eyes. "Do you like pizza?"

"I could go for some pizza."

"There's a good place near the base of the mountain, by the main lodge. Would you like to take a walk there?"

"I would like that." And she would. She was enjoying her time with him.

"Let's go then."

Kiera followed Henry. He helped her with her coat, pulled on his jacket, and they took the elevator in silence down to street level.

It was snowing pretty heavily, but that wasn't stopping people from walking through the shops that lined the street. Although Kiera loathed these new mountain resorts and vacation time-shares that were built to cater to the elite, she did like the fact that they resembled perfect Christmas villages.

Except that it was February.

Still, it was nice to walk through the village. It was

snowing heavily and there was no wind. Just big, fat, fluffy snowflakes.

"I hate the snow," Henry grumbled.

"Why?"

"It's cold."

"You said you were born in Colorado. I mean your dad is governor currently and Colorado is his home state. I'd have thought you would be used to the cold."

"I've lived in Los Angeles for eight years. I've rarely come to Colorado since then, so I don't think I'm acclimatized to it. That, and I really never did like the cold." The cold reminded him of being alone. "Sure we had servants, but I was alone in a dreary house on top of a mountain. The wind scared me. So I've never been a fan of winter."

"I wasn't born here, but I don't mind the cold."

"Where were you born?" he asked.

"Helena," she teased. "So, nowhere with a warmer climate."

Henry opened the door to the pizza shop and a blast of warm air hit her in the face. The smell of actual, properly cooked food wafted toward her, making her stomach growl.

"We'll take care of that," he teased, obviously hearing her tummy rumble.

And her cheeks flushed, realizing he'd heard that.

"How about since you tried so hard and bought the wine, I buy dinner?"

"Deal."

Henry didn't like talking about Michelle, and he didn't know why he had opened up about it.

That was something he kept close to his heart. It was his pain to bear and he didn't want to share it with anyone else. It was something that he lived with, it reminded him to keep his heart in check.

That he couldn't put himself on the line like that.

He didn't know what it was about Kiera that brought it all out again. Maybe it was knowing her past, too, that made it easier. Kiera had got under his skin, from the moment she had climbed into the back of his father's car with that ridiculous protest sign.

When he thought of that sign, with his father's picture painted with devil horns, he chuckled.

He really didn't know what it was about Kiera, but he knew he liked being with her. She made him forget about a lot of things—he felt alive.

And he wasn't so alone. He laughed more. It had been a while since he had really laughed.

He hadn't realized how lonely he actually was.

Kiera slid into the booth across from him. "Pizza will be here soon."

"Good."

"It doesn't have plastic in it," she teased.

"That's always good."

"So, you must have a cook in Los Angeles."

"No, I just go out a lot or order in, that's if I'm at home. I spend a lot of time at my clinic. I work a lot."

"So do I."

"How does Mandy feel about that?" he asked.

"She gets lonely, but I love my work and… I learned from Dr. Burke, and he was always there for his patients. Working reminds me of him and I don't miss him as much. Besides, Mandy always encourages me to go out."

That struck a chord with him. He understood that.

Henry nodded. "So what kind of pizza did you order for us?"

"Well, for me I ordered just pepperoni, but for you, I added spinach."

Henry laughed with her.

It was good to laugh with her.

It was good not to be alone.

They finished the pizza and made their way back. Henry offered to walk her to her car. The snow was coming down harder. When they got closer to the parking lot, there were flashing lights.

"What's going on?" Kiera asked.

"I don't know."

It was the state troopers, and there was a roadblock up.

"Officer, is there a problem?" Henry asked.

"The road is shut down. There was an avalanche."

"We're doctors—was anyone injured?" Kiera asked.

"No, ma'am. The road is blocked, though, and we're asking everyone to stay put for now. It probably won't be clear until the morning. Do you have a place to stay? If not, the mountain lodge is setting up cots and a warming station."

"She has a place to stay. Thank you, Officer," Henry said.

He put his arm around Kiera and led her away from the parking lot.

"I guess I should find a place in the mountain lodge," she said.

"Why, when I have a perfectly good place?" he asked.

"Do you think that's wise?"

"Kiera, we're engaged. I think it's safe."

Kiera worried her bottom lip. "Okay. I guess you have a point."

"Come on. It'll be fine. We'll watch a movie and hunker down until the road is clear."

Kiera nodded, and they walked back to his place.

His pulse was racing. He only had one bed. He'd give that to Kiera and sleep on the couch, but for tonight, he was glad that Kiera was staying over.

He'd enjoyed his time with her.

And he was glad that, tonight, he wouldn't be alone.

CHAPTER EIGHT

"I SEE A huge problem here," Kiera said.

"The one bed thing?" Henry asked.

"Yes." She had her arms crossed and she was staring at the bed like it was on fire. Tonight had been lovely, and getting to know her better had made him want her more, but he had to resist.

This wasn't real.

His attraction might be, but their relationship wasn't.

Sharing a bed was out of the question.

"I don't expect to share a bed," he said quickly. "I want you to have the bed."

"Are you sure?"

"Yes. Of course, I may be the villain who swooped in, is threatening to shut down your hospital and has persuaded you to pose as my fiancée, but I am a gentleman first and foremost."

"And where will you sleep?"

"On the couch."

Kiera frowned. "That couch doesn't look comfortable at all."

"It's fine." He reached into a drawer and handed her one of his T-shirts and a pair of jogging pants. The jogging pants were probably going to be too big for her, but at least she wouldn't have to wear her jeans to bed and be uncomfortable.

And she wouldn't be sleeping naked or in her underwear, and he wouldn't have to think about that. Like he was thinking about it now.

Get a hold of yourself.

It was bad enough that he was thinking about her sleeping in his bed.

That she was spending the night.

So close.

He had to get a grip.

"You sleep here and I'll sleep out on the couch, and hopefully tomorrow morning the roads will be cleared and you can head back home."

"Okay. Thanks." She sounded nervous as she held his spare pair of jogging pants tight to her chest.

Henry nodded. "And I promise you that I won't try to cook you breakfast in the morning."

Kiera laughed, breaking the tension. "Okay, deal."

"Good night." He grabbed a pillow and a blanket from his closet, leaving Kiera alone in his bedroom. He shut the door.

He sighed and made his way to the couch. His condo was dark, and the only light filtering through was the light from the mountain through the heavy snow and the dwindling fire, since he'd turned the gas down low.

He stretched himself out on the couch and tried to get comfortable, but it was hard. His couch might be a sectional, but a sectional wasn't long enough in one direction for him to get comfortable, and he really didn't want to fold himself in half to get a good night's sleep.

Even if the couch were twenty feet long and twenty feet wide he was pretty sure that he wouldn't sleep well. Not when Kiera was so close. Her hand on his pillow.

Her scent on his sheets. He couldn't stop thinking about how nice it was to have her here.

To talk to someone.

He rolled over to try and get comfortable.

But when he closed his eyes, all he could think about was her in that jade dress and the kiss they'd shared in his car.

Just like he had done the night before. He had spent a restless night then and would now. It was the last sleepless night that had led to this moment, the result of making a rash decision and inviting her over for dinner. Now Kiera was sleeping in his bed, and he was here on the couch, and all he could think about was her.

You didn't plan the avalanche.

It didn't matter. She was here, invading his space.

Henry tried to turn on his side and couldn't. The couch was too narrow.

There was a creak behind him and he sat up.

"Kiera?" he asked.

She was standing in the dark, in his sweats and an oversize shirt, her hair braided over her shoulder. She looked even better than she had all dressed up.

"Yeah, I couldn't sleep, and I felt bad that I had your bed. I was going to see if you had any milk. Warm milk usually helps me fall asleep."

"I do have milk." He pulled back the blanket and got up.

"You don't have to get up. I can make warmed milk— in fact, I'd rather make it."

"I can't sleep. So why don't you make me a cup, too."

Kiera nodded and made her way into the kitchen. Henry sat down at the counter as Kiera pulled out a saucepan. She poured milk into the saucepan and started rooting through his bare cupboards.

"What're you looking for?" he asked. "The mugs are hanging up in front of you."

"I'm looking for cinnamon." She frowned. "You don't have any."

"I don't cook. Remember? The remnants of that casserole you called traumatic is in my trash can."

Kiera chuckled and pulled out a spoon to stir the milk. "Right. I forgot that you eat out."

"I was never taught the basic skills of cooking. Boarding school, servants and privilege, remember?"

"I remember. Well, why don't you come over here and I'll teach you how to stir some warm milk."

Henry got up and came up behind her. He could smell the lavender in her hair and it fired his senses though he resisted the urge to reach out and touch her as he stared down at the graceful curve of her neck.

"If you don't stir it often, it will burn."

"What?" he asked, shaking his head.

"The milk." She glanced up at him and there was a pink tinge to her cheeks. He was standing so close to her and all he could think about was kissing her.

He didn't really care about the milk or the hospital or the fact that his father was threatening to take away his shares. Shares he planned to sell anyway, and he'd give every red cent back to his father.

He didn't care that he had shared too much of himself today.

He didn't care about any of that.

All he could think about was the fact that Kiera was here. So close to him, wearing his clothes, and he could smell her hair.

"Stir the milk." He cleared his throat and took a step back "Right. Got it."

"If you had cinnamon, it would taste a heck of a lot

better," she said, turning off the stove and pulling down a mug so she could pour a cup for him.

He really didn't give a hoot about the milk right now. It was a distraction from the fact that he wanted to kiss her.

Henry took his mug and wandered away from the kitchen, back to the couch. He sat down with his drink, which really tasted like sawdust in his mouth.

Kiera came over and sat down on the far side of the couch, cupping her mug as she sipped at it.

"It really would be better with cinnamon," she said.

"I've never had warm milk before."

"We're going to have a conversation about warm milk?" she teased.

"No. I really don't want that. What I'd like is sleep."

"This couch looks great in here, but it's not exactly comfortable, is it?"

"I know. I'm getting old and I'm not used to sleeping on a couch anymore."

Kiera smiled at him. "Why don't you come and sleep in your bed?"

His pulse skipped a beat, and he wasn't sure he had heard her correctly. "What?"

"We'll share. We're adults. We can share a king-size bed, and you have enough pillows for a sufficient pillow wall."

Kiera couldn't believe she'd just invited Henry into bed. To share a bed with her because she couldn't get to sleep, even though she was incredibly tired. Henry had shared so much about himself.

He was just like her.

And she did feel so alone. She could feel her barriers slipping.

It was scary, but she was lonely on the other side of the high walls she'd built for herself.

She had been hoping he'd still be awake, and even though she should have just stayed in his room and tried to sleep, she couldn't. So she'd gotten up.

And as she was making the warm milk she was very aware of Henry standing close to her. She had also been very aware that she was sleeping in his bed.

Even though he had changed the sheets, she could smell him.

She could sense him. Everywhere.

All she'd been able to do was toss and turn, just like the previous night. Now she was wearing his clothes.

And more... She was sharing a drink with him and inviting him back to bed.

With her.

What had come over her?

What was wrong with her?

Ever since Henry had landed in Aspen and pulled her off her protest site, she'd been distracted.

She shouldn't have come here tonight.

She should've just stayed home.

Only she hadn't. She was here now, and she'd opened up to him and felt vulnerable and exposed. And now she was inviting him to share a bed.

She didn't know what she was thinking, but right now they were both tired, and there was a large bed they both could sleep on together.

"Let's go to bed." She set down her mug. "I'm pretty good at building pillow walls."

"Okay." He set down his mug and grabbed his blankets and his pillow.

Her heart was hammering in her chest like a jackhammer. It thundered between her ears, and she wondered if he could hear it, too.

She was nervous.

She'd dated men before, she'd slept with men before, but somehow this was different, and she couldn't figure out why.

It's just sharing a bed. That's all.

Kiera headed over to his bed to grab a few pillows, keeping one for her head as she set up a wall.

"You *are* good at pillow walls," Henry said as she walked around the bed and sat down on the opposite side of the wall.

"See, this can be done." Kiera pulled the blanket up. "We're adults. We can be civilized, and we can both get a good night's sleep."

Henry didn't respond, and when she peered over the pillow wall, she saw that he was lying on his back, his eyes closed, sleeping.

She smiled, watching him sleep in the darkness, just the light from outside casting shadows across his face. He looked kind of peaceful, this man who could be threatening her hospital, and her free clinic.

When she had heard that he was coming to Aspen, she had hated him. Hated the thought of him, but now that she had got to know him, it was different.

She understood him.

And that scared her. What if he abandoned her like her father had? Like Brent had?

What if Henry found someone else? Back in California it appeared he had multiple women and never for very long.

Brent had left her—what was stopping Henry from doing the same?

They were very similar, yet different. Her heart would break if Henry broke her trust. Of that she was certain.

This isn't real. You have nothing to be afraid of.

The problem was it felt real, and she secretly wanted it to be.

She relaxed against the pillow and tried not to think about the fact that he was so close to her, that he was within an arm's reach of her and that she was in his bed.

Kiera's eyes closed.

And she tried to sleep.

Kiera was vaguely aware of an arm around her and something curled up behind her. Something warm, and she didn't want to get out of bed. It was nice.

And then the realization hit her that she wasn't in her bed, because the thing that was curled up against her wasn't Sif the cat.

She opened one eye, saw Henry's arm wrapped around her and realized that he was spooning her. She slowly peered over her shoulder and saw that he was still sleeping and that the pillow wall was gone and spread out all over the floor. It felt so good to be wrapped up in his arms and she couldn't believe how soundly she had slept, but she had to get out of there.

Preferably before Henry woke up and it was all awkward.

She wanted to move, but she also didn't want to wake him up. She had to think of an easy way to slip out from under his arm without waking him, and she wasn't quite sure how she was going to do that.

Kiera started shimmying down under the blanket, trying to scoot under the crutch of his arm and the blankets to the end of the bed, where her plan was then to drop to the floor. As she slowly crept under the covers toward freedom at the end of the bed, she was thankful for the few Pilates classes she had taken.

What she hadn't counted on was the blankets and sheets still being tightly tucked in at the foot of the bed. And she hadn't thought there was a footboard on the bed frame, but there was and she was trapped, curled up in a ball at the end of the bed like some kind of freak.

"Um, Kiera?"

"Yeah?" she answered nervously.

Henry peeked under the blanket. "What're you doing?"

"Trying not to wake you up?" she offered.

He chuckled. "Mission accomplished."

"Ha-ha."

He disappeared and rolled away, and she clambered out from under the blankets that were now tangled around her legs.

He'd retreated to his side of the bed.

"So much for your pillow wall."

"Hey, my pillow walls are usually fantastic."

He smirked. "I have to say this was a first for me."

"What, pillow walls?"

"Usually I'm the one sneaking out of the bed in the mornings."

Heat flushed her cheeks at being caught, but there was a pang of jealousy there, too. The thought of him with someone else. Or multiple someones. And she was surprised over the little green-eyed monster that sprang up.

Why should she care?

This wasn't a real relationship.

She knew this about him. She knew the kind of women he usually dated.

"Good for you," she replied sarcastically. What she didn't tell him was that in the past she had been the one to sneak out of the bed when she slept with a man. The only differences were there hadn't been many men and it hadn't happened for a long time.

She didn't like sleeping over with her dates, but leaving in the morning gave her a chance to leave before they left her.

And with the way she had opened up to Henry, she was in full-on panic mode. She wanted to put some distance between him and herself.

She needed to get back to the hospital.

She had to remember why she was dating Henry, or rather why she was fake dating Henry. It was for the free clinic and those patients who needed her. And last night he'd made her forget all those things.

For one fraction of a second she had thought she was on a real date. She had forgotten what this was all about. It wasn't real.

And the only reason they had opened up and shared was to keep up the lie.

He was making her lose control, because she didn't share this stuff with anyone. Not even Mandy.

And that unnerved her. Since she needed to calm herself down and practicing medicine helped her, she needed to get out of there. She needed space.

"Where are you sneaking off to anyways?" he asked.

"I've got patients to check up on and some rounds," she said quickly. "So if the road is open I should get back to the hospital."

"Okay." He was lying there on his back, bare chested, so that she could see his finely sculpted chest and abs, his arm behind his head, looking devilishly sexy. The tattoo on his forearm was indeed a tree, but she tried not to stare at it or him, because if she focused too long on him, her stomach would start flipping with anticipation.

She stared at the sheets, instead, the nice Egyptian

cotton sheets, until she realized the bed was rumpled as if they had spent the night making love.

A zing of heat coursed through her.

When was the last time she had that kind of release?

It had been too long.

They hadn't, but the very thought of it made her body react. A rush of blood to her groin, her palms sweaty.

Great. Just great.

Yeah, she had to get out of there—and fast.

Kiera grabbed her clothes. "Thanks for dinner."

"You mean thanks for not actually poisoning you?" he teased, sitting up.

"Yeah. That. I'll get dressed and see myself out. Will I see you at the hospital later?"

Henry nodded. "Yes."

"Okay. Thanks again." She retreated from the bedroom to the guest bathroom down the hall.

She was quick about getting changed, cleaned up, and once she found her coat and purse she slipped out of the building and into the cold. Outside the snow was deep, but the plow had been by. All she had to do was scrape off her car and head back into town.

She'd get back to work and forget all about how good it had actually felt to wake up in Henry's arms. And how scared that made her feel.

She was lonely. She knew that, but she could deal with it. She knew how to be alone. She'd been alone most of her life.

She had learned to not rely on anyone.

Except Mandy, but even then, it was Mandy who relied on her.

Does she? She doesn't really need you as much as you need her.

And the fact she needed Mandy to combat her own

loneliness made her sad, but she was so afraid of being hurt again.

Of being left alone.

Of caring for someone and having it taken away.

It was a scary thing to think of, this thing called love. *Oh, God.*

Her heart began to race. She needed to get out of there. This couldn't be happening to her.

She wouldn't let it.

Henry checked on his burn patient in the intensive care unit. The patient was still intubated because the damage to his lungs was too great to try to wean him off the oxygen, but he was stable enough that Henry was able to work on the extensive burns.

He debrided the burns and dressed them again, a lengthy procedure, but he didn't mind. It was something he often assigned to residents or interns, but they didn't have those here at Aspen Grace Memorial Hospital, which was okay today. It kept his mind off the fact that he had curled up around Kiera. And the fact that he hadn't slept so soundly and so well in a very long time.

He hadn't realized until this morning how much he needed that kind of deep sleep. He had forgotten what it felt like to feel so safe and relaxed with someone. To know that he wasn't alone in the night.

He'd been a little freaked out to wake up and discover the pillow wall gone and Kiera in his arms, like it was the most natural thing in the world for his unconscious body to seek her out for comfort.

And that he liked it.

A lot.

And how he couldn't stop thinking about her bottom

pressed against him, the shape of her body and how it fitted so well against him.

He couldn't remember the last time he had slept like that.

Yes, you do. It was when Michelle was alive.

And he realized he hadn't slept that well in eight years. He'd been a zombie for eight years.

"Dr. Baker?"

He looked up from his work to see a nurse hovering in the door.

"Yes?" he asked, going back to his work.

"Your father is in the boardroom and would like to speak with you. He just called down."

Henry sighed, annoyed that his father was back in the hospital and intruding where he didn't belong. His father was obsessed with this new hospital, this new private clinic that his father felt would propel him to the pinnacle to his political career and gain him a lot of votes. And also make him the most money. His father had no real interest in medicine or saving lives. His father was not a doctor—he was a politician, and it all came down to money.

When Henry had been first tasked with coming here, he couldn't have cared less, but now things were different.

"Tell him that I will come and see him once I'm done with my patient."

"Yes, Dr. Baker."

The nurse disappeared and Henry went back to his work.

He knew his father wouldn't be happy that he hadn't jumped and gone to see him straight away, but Henry didn't care.

And his father could wait. His parents didn't care

about him. And it was about time he stopped caring for them and moved on with his own life.

All his father's plans for his ridiculously expensive, brand-new private hospital could wait. He really didn't have time for them today.

His father always expected him to jump when he wanted. Henry was not going to jump. Not this time. Even though his father saved him from his reckless life after Michelle died, he shouldn't have to owe his father for that.

No parent should ever blackmail their child.

Henry was tired of being embarrassed about it.

He was tired of hiding behind his mistakes.

Henry finished up his work. He checked the vitals of the patient, wrote up his orders and left the intensive care unit.

He didn't go to see his father; instead, he made his way down to the emerÁgency department to find Kiera. The emergency room was quiet. It wasn't full of sick people and he couldn't see Kiera anywhere.

"Have you seen Dr. Brown?" Henry asked a passing triage nurse.

"She's in the free clinic."

"The free clinic is open again?" he asked.

"Yes."

Henry left the emergency room and went through the doors into the free clinic. He spotted some of the hospital's nurse practitioners and Kiera was at the nurses station charting. She looked up and her cheeks flushed pink when their gazes met.

He smiled at her remembering how she'd felt snuggled up against him.

All warm and cuddly.

What has gotten into you?

"Good morning," he said, coming to stand by her.

"Good morning, I'm very glad the free clinic is open. I guess I have you to thank."

"Uh, yeah." Henry was glad the free clinic was open and that it made Kiera happy. He was shocked that his father had opened it up again. And now he was regretting not going to find out what had changed his father's mind.

"I have to check on a patient out of town and I wondered if you'd like to come with me?"

"Why are you going out of town?"

"It's for an elderly patient. She was one of Dr. Burke's and I've sort of been taking care of her. She's had a rash from her oral chemo, and I thought you might like to join me."

Henry should say no, because being alone with her probably wasn't wise.

He knew how he was feeling about her, but he didn't know how she felt and he really didn't want his heart broken.

Not that it would be her fault. She had made it clear this was simply a business arrangement.

It wasn't her fault he was falling for her.

So he shouldn't spent extra time alone with her, but he didn't want Kiera to go alone.

"I can come with you."

"Good. I was hoping you would, being a plastic surgeon. I thought you might know what to do for her skin irritation. I don't know any dermatologists."

He smiled. She was rambling. It was kind of cute.

"It's fine, Kiera. I can go with you. What time?"

"In three hours?"

He nodded. "Okay. I'll meet you out front in three hours."

"Sounds good." Kiera left to go back to her patients.

Henry took a deep breath. He knew his father would be waiting for him and he didn't care, even though he was curious to know what had caused his father to reopen the clinic. What kind of game was his father playing at?

Whatever it was, Henry didn't want to be involved in it.

Kiera had surprised herself by asking Henry to go with her to see Agnes, who lived two hours out of town and up a windy mountain road, but she had.

It's because he got the free clinic opened again.

Or at least that's what she was telling herself.

That she was so happy the free clinic was open, she had become delusional and invited him. That had to be it. It was a moment of complete weakness.

Liar.

That wasn't the reason. She enjoyed being around him. She had had fun last night. Just like she had had fun at the fundraiser. The night she wore the jade dress and he had kissed her in the car. That hot steamy kiss she still couldn't get out of her mind.

Kiera. You've got to stop this. He's not into you.

She wished he was.

It was nice being around Henry. And she couldn't remember the last time she had had so much fun. She couldn't remember the last time she actually wanted to be with someone again.

To spend time with someone who made her laugh. Someone who turned her on.

Someone who was smart, sexy and talented.

Kiera finished her rounds, changed out of her scrubs and packed what she needed to take for Agnes.

Once her car was loaded she pulled out of the staff parking lot and around to the front of the hospital. Henry had changed out of his scrubs and was dressed in jeans and a suede lambswool Sherpa coat.

Give him a pair of cowboy boots and a baseball cap and he'd fit right in with rural Colorado.

She pulled up and unlocked her door.

"Need a lift?" Kiera teased.

"Sure." Henry opened her back door and tossed his leather messenger bag in the back seat before climbing into the front seat next to her.

"If I didn't know any better, I'd think you were from Colorado."

He grinned at her. "Well, I am from Colorado, but I prefer California. It doesn't snow in California."

"I think it does in some parts of California."

"Not in my part of California. Not Los Angeles, not Huntington Beach, which is where I live."

"Fancy."

"It is. Quite fancy and peaceful." Henry grinned at her. "I love the beach."

"That sounds nice. Do you surf then, living so close to the water?"

"No. No time."

"Then why live at the beach?"

"It's the best, and the sounds of the waves help me sleep."

"Do you have problems sleeping?"

"I do. The sound of the water relaxes me. Sometimes," he said quietly.

"It must be hard for you to sleep in Aspen then. There's no ocean here."

"It is, but I forgot about hearing the wind through the trees, it's almost like waves sometimes. And also… Anyway, I slept well last night. Must've been the warm milk."

She glanced at him briefly. Her heart skipped a beat.

She had thought for a second he was going to say he'd slept well last night because of her, because that's how she felt, too.

She had slept so soundly with him beside her. She had been comfortable. She had felt safe. The only other time she'd felt as safe was the first night at Wilfred and Mandy's. Sharing a room with Mandy in a warm, dry, clean, quiet home had given her security.

"The milk would have been better with cinnamon," she said, trying to get her mind off him. Trying to forget his strong arms around her.

"You'll have to make it for me sometime again then, with the correct ingredients."

Kiera's cheeks heated and she turned her focus back on the road.

Maybe this was a bad idea, being alone with Henry for two hours.

At least Agnes would appreciate Henry. She was a feisty eighty-year-old woman who liked a good-looking man.

"So what kind of cancer does... Sorry, I don't know her name."

"Agnes."

"Agnes then. What kind of cancer does Agnes have and what is she taking for it?"

"Lung cancer with metastases to her brain and her bones, mostly her hips."

Henry made a face. "So she's on oral chemo?"

"Yes. She's had radiation for the brain mets. She's been this way for two years."

"Two years, and she's eighty and lives out in the country?" he asked, shocked.

"I know, right? She's pretty hard-core. She was one of Dr. Burke's favorite people."

"I look forward to meeting her."

"I can tell you, you'll make her day."

"Why is that?" he asked.

"She appreciates…" Kiera blushed and cleared her throat. "She likes a…"

"A nice piece of ass?" Henry teased.

Kiera laughed. "Yeah, I guess so."

"You guess so?"

"I haven't seen your…" She couldn't even finish that sentence with a straight face.

"Ass," he said quickly.

"Right. So I wouldn't know."

"Well, we have slept together, and we are engaged."

"A fake engagement," she reminded him. "Fake meaning, I don't see your ass and you don't see mine."

"Ever?" he teased.

Heat bloomed in her cheeks. "Right. Never. Ever."

Instantly she regretted what she had said. How had they gone from talking about their patient to discussing each other's posteriors? What she had to do pay attention to the road.

Nonetheless, she didn't mind talking about his bottom and wouldn't mind seeing it. It would be nice to spend more nights safe in his arms. To feel secure. To trust.

To love.

What has gotten into you?

Kiera kept her eyes on the road and watched for the turnoff to the windy road that headed up the mountain to where Agnes had a small log cabin and lived by subsistence and off-grid.

"Why does she live up here?" Henry asked as they hit a rut and were jostled back and forth.

"She farms, hunts. She likes living off-grid. She always has."

"I'm beginning to like this patient. She's hard-core and appreciates a fine-looking surgeon." He waggled his eyebrows as Kiera glanced at him.

"You know what? I think I liked you better when you were all moody and sullen."

"Thanks... I think."

She chuckled and they pulled up to Agnes's house. There was smoke rising from the stovepipe on the roof, which was always a good sign that Agnes was still alive and kicking.

As Kiera parked the car, the door opened and Agnes stood in the doorway.

"You made it, Doc Brown!" Agnes shouted. "And you've brought a friend!"

"I did. This is Dr. Baker."

Agnes eyed Henry. "Isn't he the governor's son?"

"I am," Henry replied.

"Well, you look fine. Your father is a tool." Agnes turned and headed back into her house. "Come on in."

Kiera laughed silently at Henry's shocked expression.

She might have been regretting her decision to bring him up here because she was scared about how she was feeling, but now she was glad he was there.

Agnes was going to make this trip fun.

So much fun, and for that the drive was completely worth it.

CHAPTER NINE

"SO? WHAT'S THE VERDICT?" Agnes asked as Kiera finished listening to her chest.

"You're still stable, but I really wish you'd move to town."

Agnes rolled her eyes. "Dr. Burke tried for ten years to get me off my mountain. A little cancer is not going to get me to move to town."

Henry gave Kiera an amused secret look.

"Agnes, I think you're in more pain than you're letting on," she said gently.

"I'm fine. I just have a rash that's annoying me. All over my chest." Agnes glanced at Henry and waggled her eyebrows suggestively. "You want to examine it for me?"

Kiera chuckled silently.

"I can take a look," Henry offered.

Agnes grinned. "So you're really not a politician then?"

"No, politics are only for my—what did you call him?—tool of a father?" Henry teased.

Agnes snorted. "I like him, Doc Brown. I like him. This is the kind of man you should marry!"

Kiera's mouth dropped open and all she could hear was a high-pitched buzz between her ears. An annoying hum, her nervous system trying to drown out the embarrassment of what was happening. What was Agnes insinuating? Had she heard something? Impossible—no one knew. She hadn't even told Mandy.

Warmth bloomed in her cheeks and she hoped she wasn't blushing.

"What?" Kiera asked, clearing her throat as she tried to regain control of her emotions.

"You should go after Dr. Baker here. He's older, hot, and you spend too much time marching for causes. You need to campaign for a piece of Dr. Baker."

"For important issues," Kiera replied.

"I know, Doc Brown, but you're young and you shouldn't be alone. What do you think of her, Dr. Baker?"

"She'll do." Henry grinned.

Kiera groaned inwardly and glared at Henry, who was trying not to laugh as his eyes twinkled.

"Well, I'm trying to get Dr. Brown to marry me. I mean she is my fiancée and all," Henry admitted.

Kiera snapped her mouth shut and glared at Henry, who was enjoying her discomfort.

"Well, that's wonderful, Doc Brown! Burke... Wilfred...your father, that is, would be so proud of you!" Agnes said.

"What're you talking about, Agnes?" Kiera asked.

"Wilfred wanted you and Mandy to be happy. That's all. You know he loved you, don't you?"

The mention of Dr. Burke's name and the association of Dr. Burke as her father struck a nerve with her. It made her emotional.

It was hard to breathe. Hard to swallow. She met Henry's gaze and the mirth was gone. And she knew he could see her pain.

He could see her grief and vulnerability again. She

knew how Dr. Burke felt about her. How she had loved him like a father.

How she grieved him still.

What she didn't like was losing control here in front of Henry and Agnes.

"How about I take care of that rash, Agnes?" Henry asked, changing the subject from Dr. Burke, for which she was grateful.

It was hard to think of Wilfred. He would've been happy to see her engaged, but would he have been so happy to learn it was a lie?

She thought it would have disappointed him.

It was a bit too much to bear.

She cleaned up her equipment while Henry examined Agnes. She smiled watching him with her. He was so kind and gentle. He had an excellent bedside manner.

He was charming, though it was no surprise since he dealt with a lot of high-profile, elite patients. Still, it was refreshing to see him extending the same courtesy to someone who couldn't pay his exorbitant fees.

"This cream and the dressing I just put on should be applied twice a day," Henry said. "If it worsens, can you call me and I'll come back to check?"

"I have a phone. I might be off the grid, but I have a phone." Agnes took the tube from Henry.

"I'll come back in a week anyway, Agnes," Kiera said, closing her bag. "You're doing well. Try not to overdo it."

"Thank you, Doc Brown and Doc Baker."

They slipped on their jackets and headed outside. It was dark, but the sky was clear. There were stars coming out against the inky black sky.

Kiera breathed in the cold air. It was cleansing.

"Thanks for coming with me tonight," she said, and it was true. She was glad he was here.

"Thanks for inviting me." He reached out and touched her face. The simple brush of his fingers against her cheeks sent a delicious shiver through her. A zing of need.

"Well, we should get back to Aspen." Kiera took a step back away from him, trembling, suddenly afraid.

"Right." He cleared his throat. "Right."

Kiera really wanted to kiss him, but she couldn't risk her heart. It was bad enough this whole thing was fake. She wasn't going to get hurt again. Even though she wanted to take the chance with him, to kiss him one more time, she couldn't.

She was terrified. How could she trust someone she didn't know? She couldn't get hurt again.

She wouldn't be left again.

She took risks all the time saving lives, but right here and now, she couldn't take this risk. She never wanted to take this risk again.

It hurt too much.

The drive back to Aspen was quiet. There wasn't much to say. Kiera was trying to focus on driving and not the turmoil of emotions racing through her. The desire that was consuming her.

She barely recognized herself.

She was losing control.

The wheel began to pull, and the car began to shudder. There was a loud pop and the car jolted.

"What's happening?" she shouted, gripping the wheel.

"I think you have a flat."

Kiera cursed under her breath and flicked on her hazards. As she did, her engine light came on and there was smoke. Her car sputtered, lurching forward.

"I think it's more than a flat," she murmured.

"I would say so," Henry remarked.

She managed to get over to the shoulder of the road. She was just thankful they were on the main road now, not on Agnes's treacherous, mountain road in the dark. And they weren't at a mountain pass. They were on a flat section of the road though still far out of town.

Once she got over to the side of the road, her car gave one last awful shudder and died.

It gave out with one last great heave.

"Time of death, twenty-one oh-two." Kiera leaned her head against the steering wheel and gently began to bang it.

"Hey, no banging the head against the steering wheel. This is a solvable problem."

She looked at him and picked up her cell phone to call a cab. The moment she touched it, it flicked off and the battery died. "Okay? My cell is dead because, apparently, I left it in the car on a cold night. How is yours?"

Henry pulled out his phone. "I have batteries, but no reception."

"Great."

"Well, we can't sit here. We have to get to a phone. This might be a main road, but I haven't seen any cars in a bit. However, about half a mile back I saw a restaurant and a motel. We could wait for help there."

"Let's go then."

As much as she didn't want to walk back to that rest stop, she didn't want to spend a bitterly cold night in her car on the side of the road, in the dark with Henry. The last time they had spent time at the side of the road in the dark waiting for a tow truck, they had shared a passionate kiss and she had let down her guard.

It had been a total moment of safety. Of letting go.

A moment of feeling she was free.

And she longed to feel that again.

Only it wasn't a smart idea to do that.

Not tonight, and not with her conflicted feelings. A small diner would be a perfect spot to sit up all night, drink bad coffee and keep warm.

And it was public.

Henry wouldn't try to make out with her in public.

Or would he?

They walked in silence along the side of the road, back toward that diner. Kiera shivered even though she had her winter coat on. The wind had picked up and was blowing down off the mountain. It sent a chill right down her spine and she couldn't wait for a cup of coffee.

"See, I was right," Henry muttered.

"Right about what?"

"California is so much better."

She chuckled through chattering teeth. "Right about now I would have to agree with you."

It was hard to walk along the side of the road, through slush and snow intermixed with chunks of ice. She had to concentrate on not falling over and keeping her footing so that she didn't stumble.

Half a mile, which wasn't that long of a distance, felt like it was all the way to Timbuktu. By the time they got to the diner, she was sweating from exertion and also chilled to the bone.

Henry pulled out his phone. "Still no bars."

"I'm sure the diner will have a phone that we can borrow." She opened the door and welcomed the blast of warm air.

"Grab a seat and I'll see if I can call a tow truck."

Kiera nodded and slid into a booth, trying to get warm again.

Henry made his way to the counter of the almost

empty diner and spoke with the waitress. She handed him her phone and Henry made a call.

As Kiera sat there and tried to warm up, she realized she was shaking for another reason.

She avoided places like this.

Honey, how long have you been here? the police officer had asked her gently.

Kiera had shied away. Her father didn't like police officers and had told her they weren't safe. *Dunno.*

Are you waiting for someone?

Daddy.

The police officer had nodded. *Where did he go?*

To the car. He left the money there. She'd brushed away a tear, wishing her father would come back.

Why don't you come with me?

I can't. Daddy could come back.

We'll let him know where to find you if he does.

You swear? Kiera had asked.

The police officer had nodded. *I swear.*

Her reverie was interrupted by a waitress.

"Coffee? You look like you need it," the waitress asked, interrupting the memory Kiera thought was long buried.

"That would be great. And one for my friend."

The waitress nodded and filled the two white mugs that were on the table. "The kitchen is closed, but we can do sandwiches if you're hungry?"

"I'm good for now, but thanks!"

The waitress nodded and walked away as Henry came and slid into the booth, still shivering. "The tow truck will take it into Aspen tomorrow morning and the only rental agency in this town is closed for the night."

"So, there's no way to get back to Aspen?" she asked.

She didn't want to stay here. She was uncomfortable. She hated diners.

"Not tonight. I even called Mike, but my father has him for the night. Mike said he can come tomorrow to get us."

Kiera groaned. "Great. Just how I wanted to spend my night, sitting up in a diner. Shivering."

"There is a motel right next door."

The suggestion caught her off guard. Her eyes widened and her heart hammered against her chest.

"What?"

"We're both wet and cold. We can hang our clothes up to dry in our rooms, have a shower and stay warm. And it's not a diner."

Henry was right. The last thing she needed to do was catch a cold. The smart thing was to cut her losses and try and get some sleep tonight. And Henry had said "rooms," although secretly she wouldn't mind sharing a room with him. Of course, since they had left Agnes's she'd been trying not to think about him.

Or kissing him.

Or the need he stirred in her. A motel wouldn't help one bit.

"Rooms, right?" she asked, quickly.

"Of course."

"Okay."

They finished their coffee, paid for some sandwiches and headed through the adjoining doors into the small motel that was attached to the diner.

The owner of the motel looked up from his paper. "How can I help you folks?"

"We were hoping you had a couple of rooms for the night?"

"I only have one room left," the motel manager said.

Kiera's heart started to race. "Only one room?"

"It has two beds," the owner said.

Even though she knew it would be a mistake, they really had no choice and she nodded to Henry, who looked just as worried as she did.

They were adults.

Nothing had to happen.

They could control themselves for one night.

"Okay. We'll take it." Henry paid the motel owner, and once the paperwork was filled out and the owner had handed them keys, they made their way back outside into the cold. Down to the end of the motel where they had the very last room.

As Henry put the key in the door, the sign flicked from Vacancy to No Vacancy.

"I've never seen that happen before."

"I'm sure you don't really stay at retro motels that were popular in the sixties."

"No. That's true." He opened the door and stepped in, flicking on the lights. Kiera followed him and she was relieved to see there were two beds.

The room was clean and completely outdated, but it was a warm and a safe place to be until morning.

She set her bag down on the bed closest to the door and Henry set down the sandwiches and his bag on the small dinette set. He locked the door and pulled the drapes so the streetlights wouldn't shine in on them.

"Do you want to shower first? A hot shower will warm you up faster. Then we can have our dinner." He wasn't looking at her as he peeled off his wet jacket and draped it over a chair.

"Yeah, that would be nice." She was hoping that her

voice wasn't shaking, revealing her anxiety about being alone with him in this room.

Not that *he* would do anything; it was herself she was nervous about.

She honestly didn't know why she was fighting it.

She was an adult.

She'd done this before and she wanted to again and with Henry.

You can't.

Only she really wanted to.

Her skin broke out in goose bumps, and she took off her wet jacket and placed it on the other chair.

"I'll be quick, so I don't use all the hot water."

Henry smiled briefly. "Great."

She nodded and felt her cheeks warm as she scurried to the bathroom. Once she was in there, she was able to lock the door and take a deep breath.

This was going to be a long night.

Henry heard the shower come on and he tried not to think about the fact that only a thin wall separated him from a very naked and wet Kiera. He had to pull himself together. This was not an ideal situation, that was for sure.

He'd rather be in his own room.

But would he really not think about her showering in his condo?

His blood was hot, his body wound tight because he wanted her, and he was holding himself back.

It had been a long time since he'd wanted someone like this.

This was probably a bad idea, but since they were stuck, he could resist for one night. He could make it through to morning.

Henry sat on the edge of his bed, waiting for his turn

in the shower. After that he was going to climb into his bed and tie himself down.

Because he was so tempted when it came to Kiera Brown.

So very tempted.

The shower stopped and his pulse was thundering in his ears as he watched the door open and Kiera slip out. A too-short towel was wrapped around her. She'd braided her damp, long red hair.

He kept his gaze focused on her legs as she scooted across the room, pulled back the covers and climbed into her bed, pulling the blankets up to her chin. She was shivering.

"Are you cold?"

"A bit. I didn't realize how much it had affected me," she said through chattering teeth.

Without thinking he left the safety of his own bed and came to sit down on her bed. She didn't move away from him. She just clutched her covers tighter, under her chin.

He reached back to his bed and pulled off the top cover. He wrapped it around behind her, pulling it around her. And then he pulled her close to him, holding her as she shivered. She was so close he could feel her breath on his neck and it sent a curl of desire through him.

He wanted to kiss her again, but when he had touched her face outside Agnes's place, she'd pulled away. Just like with the first kiss they'd shared in the car. She'd pulled away then, too. She didn't want him and that was fine.

Kiera gazed up at him, her mouth open and her green eyes sparkling in the dim light. He keenly remembered the feel of her lips and wanted to taste them again.

"Well," he said, breaking the silence that always seemed to come between them when they were close like this. "I think I'll go have a shower."

"Okay," she whispered, still shivering.

"You're so cold."

"I know. I can't get warm."

Henry glanced at the shower, but he couldn't leave her shivering like this. So instead he stood up and pulled off his shirt. Her eyes widened.

"What're you doing?"

"My clothes are wet and you're freezing. I'm going to climb into bed with you."

Kiera just nodded. She didn't argue with him, because he was pretty sure she knew the fastest way to regulate temperature was for him to take off his cold, damp clothes and cuddle up close to her.

And that's what he had to focus on.

He was just helping her stay warm. That was it.

He removed his wet socks and slipped off his jeans, keeping on his boxer briefs, so he wouldn't freak her out further. He grabbed the rest of the blankets from the bed and climbed in beside her.

Kiera didn't fight him or make a sarcastic comment. Instead, she snuggled up against him, her head resting against his chest as he held her in the double bed. And he realized she didn't have the towel on anymore and that it was her naked body pressed against him, holding him.

"Your heart is racing," she whispered, her head on his chest.

"Can you blame me?" he said, pulling her closer.

Her shivering stopped and she looked up at him. "No, because my heart is racing, too."

Henry touched her face. "You really are so beautiful."

Pink flushed in her cheeks and she worried her bottom lip. And all he could think about was how soft her lips were. How close she was.

How much he burned for her.

Wanted her.

Needed her.

"About that kiss…"

"We don't need to talk about that kiss." He wanted to do more than talk about that kiss. He wanted to relive it. Right here. Right now.

He yearned to taste her again. Over and over and never let her go.

He needed her out of his mind.

He wanted the lust out of his blood.

"I think we do."

"Why? It was a kiss. You made it very clear to me that you didn't want to kiss me, and that's okay."

"What do you mean?" she asked. "I wanted that kiss, Henry. I liked it."

His blood heated. "You pushed me away, and then tonight, when I touched you, you pulled away again."

Kiera sighed. "It's because I'm terrified. Henry, I've never wanted a man as much as I want you. You make me feel safe and that scares me."

"Wy does it scare you?"

"Because I can't trust you."

That made him pause. He wanted her to trust him.

"You're safe with me. I promise. I won't hurt you."

She reached up and touched his face and he closed his eyes, reveling in the sensation of her touch, the softness of her skin on his.

He grabbed her hand and instinctively kissed the pulse point of her wrist.

She was scared. So was he.

He'd been with other women since Michelle, but Kiera was the first woman who had made his blood burn with desire. She was the first since Michelle who made him want more.

And that scared him, too.

Kiera sighed as he stroked her arm, touching the bare skin he could.

He wanted her. He wanted to kiss her again. And he pulled her closer, touching her face, making her shiver as he touched her. Her breath coming quickly. He leaned in and drank in the scent of her skin.

Kissing her neck lightly as she sighed. Her blood racing through her neck, under his lips. The blankets that she'd been clutching to her so tightly fell away and he pulled her onto his lap, her long legs going around his waist as he trailed his kisses lower, his hands on her back.

"Henry," she whispered. "Kiss me. This time, I want you to kiss me."

He cupped her face with his hands and captured her lips with his. There was nothing more to say. He wanted her. He had wanted her from the first moment he'd laid eyes on her, when she'd pulled off her ridiculous woolen beanie and scarf after protesting outside.

He had wanted her every time she'd fought with him.

He had wanted her when she made her deal with him, when she came down the stairs in that jade dress.

Every day that he'd known her, he had wanted her.

And it was too much.

He prided himself on his control. Perfectionism, because when things were perfect he didn't have to feel anything.

He didn't want to feel.

He was numb, and it had been okay until Kiera had stumbled into his life.

His tight rein of control was slipping, and he didn't care. Not with her in his arms.

His tongue twining with hers.

He stopped himself, although it was so hard with her naked in bed with him.

"Kiera, I don't want… I don't ever want to hurt you."

And he meant it.

He cared for her. In this short amount of time she'd gotten through all his defenses like no one had done since Michelle.

"You won't," she whispered, her lips hovering over his, her delicate hands cupping his face. "You won't." And she kissed him again.

It was then he knew he was a lost man.

"Be with me tonight, Kiera. Be with me."

"I want that." She kissed him gently. "I want that. This doesn't have to mean anything. I just want to be with you. Feel you."

Henry couldn't argue except that for him it meant something. He took her in his arms, pulling her closer. Touching her like he wanted to.

Just as he had wanted to do when he'd first met her.

It was so good to feel again. It had been so long. He usually just went through the motions. This was different, something he hadn't felt in a long time.

A rush of feelings he couldn't even get a grasp on.

It was like being alive when he'd been dead before.

Awake.

It also felt like a dream, one he didn't want to wake up from.

They sank against the mattress together, kissing. He wanted to taste her, he wanted to be in this moment with her. Inside her. Claiming her.

He wanted Kiera to be his.

The realization jarred him, and he shook the thought from his head.

There was no need to think about this now, or that it scared him.

Right now, in this moment, all he needed was to feel.

Henry tipped her chin till she was looking up at him. Her cheeks were flushed, her lips were swollen from their shared kisses, and her green eyes sparkled in the dim light.

"You're beautiful." He kissed her again, his lips urgent as he pulled her flush with him. He didn't want an ounce of space between them.

He let his mouth tail down from her lips, down her neck and over her breasts, kissing each one of her pulse points.

Tasting all he could of her.

He was hungry.

"Henry, I want you so much," she murmured.

"I want you, too." And admitting that made him feel free. His life since Michelle had died had been about control.

Numbness.

Control so he didn't succumb to grief.

He didn't feel. There was no point to living.

With her in his arms and her wanting him, he felt free. Like something had sparked anew in him. He was alive.

"Do you have protection?" she asked.

"I do." And he was thankful he carried it with him always.

He shifted away, not wanting to leave the warmth of her embrace, to grab protection out of his leather messenger bag. He got what he needed and put it on. He returned to her and resumed kissing her all over, touching her, making her tremble under his touch.

She was hot and wet for him between her thighs.

"I want you," she panted, wrapping her legs around him, urging him to take her.

He was more than happy to oblige. Her pleas were all he needed as he settled between her legs and slowly entered her. Possessing her. She fit so tight around him.

Hot and warm.

It was almost more than he could take. She moved her hips, urging him deeper, to take her harder and faster.

She was so warm.

So tight.

He couldn't hold back as he moved in and out of her. Thrusting into her hot depths.

It was just the two of them, locked together, gazing into each other's eyes as they moved in sync. He ran his hands over her, reveling in the softness of her skin. He slipped his hand under her bottom, cupping her leg, holding her tight against him as he took her.

Just as she took him.

She wanted him as much as he wanted her.

It wasn't long before she squeezed him, gasping and crying out, her nails digging into his back as she came around him. It wasn't long before he followed.

Giving in to the pleasure.

He rolled over onto his back and she curled up against him, resting her head on his chest. Henry held her close, not wanting to let her go.

He had never thought it would be like this. He'd never thought he'd ever feel like this again.

When he was with her, he lost all control.

It frightened him, because he didn't know anything else besides control and grief.

It had been a long time since he'd felt anything close to love.

And that was terrifying.

CHAPTER TEN

KIERA DIDN'T KNOW when she fell asleep, but she slept soundly after making love with Henry. She'd been with other men, but nothing compared to this. Nothing had ever felt like this before.

She'd never before experienced this kind of pleasure with someone.

All consuming.

It had burned her blood until she'd erupted into a ball of flames, melting in his arms. At first, when he had taken her in his arms when she was cold, she had felt exposed and vulnerable, but he had made her feel safe.

And it just felt right.

She didn't feel afraid.

She felt she could be herself and she wasn't embarrassed. Kiera let herself go. She wanted him and she wasn't scared to tell him that. She'd wanted him from the first moment she saw him, and even though she was trying so hard to deny it she couldn't.

With his arms around her, she'd just let go.

She wanted to taste his lips.

She wanted to taste his passion.

She didn't regret her decision to give in last night, but now, in the light of day, she didn't know what she was feeling. She wanted to stay with him, but he didn't live in Aspen, and after the issues with the new hospital and Aspen Grace Memorial Hospital were taken care of, he was going to leave.

Henry had a practice, a home, a life in Los Angeles.

And Kiera was needed here in Aspen. She couldn't leave.

The last time she had been away, Mandy was hurt, and Wilfred had fought his cancer alone.

He'd died alone.

She couldn't leave.

Why? What is holding you here?

This was where her home was because this was where Mandy was. Mandy was her only family and vice versa. Keira couldn't leave her all alone.

Not after all Dr. Burke had done for her, all that Mandy had done to support her.

Where would her life be if Dr. Burke hadn't taken her in and raised her as his own? Kiera shuddered as she thought of that diner in Colorado Springs, of how alone she'd felt sitting there, watching at the window for her father to come back for her.

The flashing lights of the police cruiser, and going with the nice police officer to her first temporary foster home.

She remembered finally standing in front of Dr. Burke's house. She'd been scared, but his smile and the feel of his strong hand as he took her in and introduced her to Mandy had reassured her. That was when she had felt safe, she had felt at home. When Wilfred died and Brent left her for another woman she felt like that little abandoned girl again. Now, here with Henry, she felt the same safety and security. Still, she couldn't leave Aspen. She'd left once before and that had turned out bad. She couldn't leave again. This was the only place in her life that had ever been good. And any future with Henry was uncertain.

It was scary to even entertain the thought of leaving.

It was too great of a risk.

She couldn't leave Mandy behind. It hurt her heart to know that this fling with Henry was just that and it was temporary.

Soon he'd be gone and she'd feel...empty.

She owed it to Dr. Burke and Mandy to stay here.

Kiera sighed and got up as quietly as she could.

"You're disappearing on me again?" Henry asked groggily.

Kiera smiled and sat back down. "I didn't want to disturb you."

He reached out and touched her face. "Well, at least this time you have nowhere to go and I didn't find you struggling at the foot of the bed."

She laughed. "This is true."

He grinned lazily and pulled her back down onto the bed. "What's your rush?"

Kiera kissed him. "Mike is coming soon. I want to be ready."

Henry frowned and groaned. "Right."

"You sound so disappointed."

He scrubbed a hand over his face. "I'm sure Mike will tell me how angry my father is with me."

"Why would your father be angry with you? It was my car that broke down."

"Because my father wanted to meet with me yesterday. He summoned me when I was in the intensive care unit tending to our burn victim. Instead, I came down to the emergency room and we went to see Agnes."

"Oh." Kiera's stomach flip-flopped. "I wonder if it had to do with the hospital."

"Probably, but he opened the free clinic."

Kiera sat up straighter. "Yeah, but he still wants to close down Aspen Grace Memorial. He still wants to build a new hospital."

"Aspen Grace Memorial is outdated and falling apart. It would cost more to expand and fix what's broken than to build new."

She had a bad feeling. "I think you should have gone to see him."

Henry took her hand. "My father pulls this kind of stuff all the time. Expects me to be at his beck and call, and it's usually nothing."

"Why do you whatever he asks then?"

Henry sighed. "When Michelle died my life was a mess. I abandoned patients, almost lost my medical license because of it. I drank. I gambled. I was on a collision course to destroy my life. My father didn't want to ruin his career with a black sheep of a son, so he set me back on the right path. Hushed everything up, and I worked hard to sober up and save my career."

"Sounds like he cares."

Henry snorted. "Hardly."

"Someone who cares would help."

"He says I owe him. He brings up my past all the time to control me. Soon I'll be free though."

"What's that supposed to mean?" she asked, her stomach anxiously twisting.

"Nothing. Look, he wouldn't do anything drastic without one of the majority shareholders there. Don't worry."

"I thought you weren't the chairman anymore?"

"I'm not, but I still have shares and the right to vote."

"Right." She nodded, but something was wrong. Her insides were in knots and it just didn't feel right.

She didn't trust Governor Baker. Not for a second.

The man cared only about money, and she wouldn't put it past him to do something dubious. And now that she was learning how he treated his own son, it felt even more wrong.

Something was going on.

She worried that Henry was hiding more from her.

Kiera didn't doubt that he would do something underhanded, something sneaky. Henry had promised her that if she went along with his ruse he'd save the free clinic and see what he could do the rest, but what if Henry was like his father?

She didn't know him.

You're being paranoid. Henry is nothing like that.

She hated her sense of dread. Anxiety was eating away at her because she couldn't trust Henry not to hurt her. She couldn't trust anyone.

She was annoyed at herself for a fleeting second for entertaining something more with Henry. She had let go of the tight hold on her emotions and fallen into his arms.

"Are you okay, Kiera?" Henry asked.

"Fine." And she plastered on a fake smile. "I'm going to get dressed and ready for Mike to make an appearance."

"Good idea."

Kiera wrapped one of the tangled sheets around her body and scooted to the safety of the bathroom to get dressed.

She couldn't think clearly when she was in the same room as Henry. Having him naked in the bed, she was tempted to ignore the rational part of her that was telling her to be careful and not to trust him and instead listen to the part of her that craved his touch.

She cursed under her breath, unable to remember the last time she'd been so at war with herself.

Focus.

Kiera finished getting cleaned up and changed in the bathroom. As she left the bathroom Henry stood up, completely naked, and came over to her.

Her pulse was thundering in her ears as she stood there and stared at him. Her body thrummed with lust because, even though she was fighting her feelings, she was completely attracted to him.

Henry pulled her into his arms and kissed her again, pulling her flush against his hard body and giving her a kiss that made her melt.

Kiera didn't want to end the kiss, but she needed to if she was going to keep her sanity and her wits about her.

She pushed him away playfully. "You need to get ready."

He grinned, his eyes twinkling. "Fine."

She watched him head to the bathroom with his clothes. She closed her eyes, taking a deep breath.

She hoped she was wrong. She had to believe she was wrong about Henry. She was worrying too much, and she hated she couldn't let herself trust him.

She hated herself for being so afraid.

Something had changed about Kiera, and Henry couldn't quite put his finger on it. It worried him, especially after telling her about his past. About the mess he'd made of his life, but he was tired of hiding behind it. He was tired of being abandoned and it didn't bother him to tell Kiera. She was different from the women he dated in Los Angeles.

She was real.

Not vapid. Not shallow.

She was genuine, and that's what drew him.

For the first time, he wished that this wasn't a fake engagement. He liked being around her and he wanted her to come with him to California. He didn't want to leave her behind in Aspen when his time was up. He hadn't realized how lonely he was. Being with Kiera reminded him of what he'd been missing.

He just wasn't sure she felt the same or that she would leave.

You don't know unless you ask her.

That made him nervous and being nervous around her annoyed him. Kiera was getting under his skin, just like Michelle had, and he felt a pang of guilt for even contemplating moving on from Michelle's memory.

She's been gone eight years, and she'd want you to move on.

This was true, but was he ready to move on?

Henry sighed and finished up in the bathroom. When he left, Kiera had opened the drapes and was staring outside.

"Any sign of Mike?" he asked.

She glanced back. "No. Hopefully soon. I hope the tow truck gets my poor old car back to Aspen. Not that it's old."

"It will. Do you want Mike to take you back to your home or the hospital?"

"Home," Kiera said. "I have to check on Mandy. I'm sure she's worried sick."

"I called her from the diner and let her know."

Her eyes widened in surprise. "You did?"

"I didn't want her to worry, and I know you didn't want her to sit up all night."

She smiled sweetly. "Thank you. I meant to call her, but I forgot."

"My pleasure, and I'm sorry I forgot to mention it last night, too." He came up behind her and resisted the urge to wrap his arms around her and hold her. That's what he wanted to do, but he didn't.

He hadn't intended for last night to happen, but he was so glad that it had.

He had wanted it to happen.

A familiar car pulled into the parking lot.

"There's Mike," he said.

"I'll go return the key," Kiera said quickly, grabbing her stuff. "I'll see you in a few minutes."

"Okay."

Kiera slipped out of the motel room. Henry packed up the rest of his stuff and left the room. Mike parked the car and got out to open the back door for him.

"You're in hot water," Mike announced.

Henry rolled his eyes. "I'm forty. I don't really care if I'm in trouble with my father."

He was done. He didn't care if the whole world knew about his past.

He was tired of hiding.

He was tired of feeling he owed his father.

He was tired of hoping his father loved him, because his father never would and Henry had made mistakes. Mistakes he was ready to own.

"You might care about this." Mike took his messenger bag to put it in the trunk. "The board voted to have your shares revoked, back to your father. They appointed a new chair and the vote happened."

Henry's stomach sank like a rock. Right down to the soles of his feet. "What do you mean the vote happened?"

"They voted without you. The free clinic is gone. All emergency patients are being rerouted and Aspen Grace Memorial Hospital has been closed. They're not even going to build a replacement hospital. The new clinic is going to be for plastic surgery and other spa-like medical treatments. The entire staff have lost their jobs. Or they will when the hospital actually closes. Only the surgeons have been given severance packages."

"And this happened last night?"

"Your father was pretty angry that you didn't come and see him."

"How could he do that, though? He wouldn't do that, the press would be too bad."

"Yeah, but he didn't. Not really, because he appointed a new chairman of the board who made all the cuts. Someone who wasn't related to him. It doesn't look bad for him. He can spin it the right way since he's not the one who made the final decision. He might have been the executioner for Aspen Grace Memorial, but he didn't make the final blow."

Henry scrubbed a hand over his face. His blood was boiling and he glared at his phone, his stupid phone that couldn't even get reception.

How could his father do this?

Aspen Grace Memorial Hospital wasn't the only hospital in Aspen, but it was the foremost trauma center in the area. And the other hospital in Aspen couldn't employ that many people. So many people had lost their jobs. All for what? Because Henry hadn't jumped when his father called for him to come see him? Because he didn't announce his engagement or do what his father wanted and when?

Free clinics did cost a lot, but really he couldn't even give it a week?

What was the point of opening it for twenty-four hours? What was the point of sending him here?

Kiera was out of a job.

She's talented. She'd get another job somewhere else.

She could come to California with him. He would take her to California in a heartbeat.

"Don't say a word of this to Dr. Brown. I'll tell her myself."

Mike nodded. "I promise. I thought you'd want to know what you were walking into. Personally, I think it was a crummy thing to do all around."

Henry smiled at Mike. "It is."

Mike nodded in understanding as Kiera came out of the office.

"Hi, Mike," she said brightly.

"Good morning, Dr. Brown." Mike took her bags and put them in the trunk.

Henry opened the car door for her, and she climbed into the back. He followed and Mike shut their door before climbing into the front seat. The privacy barrier was up.

And Henry was glad for it.

He was reeling while he struggled to figure out what to say. It was going to crush her, and he felt like he'd betrayed her. He felt like he was some kind of villain who had seduced her and then crushed her dreams all in one swoop. He had meant to sell his shares and tell his father he was done, but his father had wrecked that.

He didn't know how to explain this now.

And he was so angry with his father.

Mike drove away from the motel. From that room where it had happened and where for a brief moment in time he got to be in her presence. It was just the two of them. Together.

Vulnerable.

There was no hospital, no past.

It was just them. Together.

They weren't enemies, they hadn't made a deal with one another.

He wanted to be back in that room, back her in arms. He just wanted her.

"Come to California with me."

Kiera's eyes widened in shock. "What?"

"I want you to come to California."

She chuckled. "I don't think so. What's gotten into you?"

"I don't know," he muttered, but he knew exactly what had gotten into him. What he didn't know was how to tell her the truth.

That he'd blown it.

He'd panicked and acted impulsively, and now he had Kiera on edge.

"The offer was sweet," she said, breaking the silence. "I can't leave Colorado."

"Because of your job?"

"Yes, but… Mandy is here. This is her home. I can't leave."

"Do you want to?"

"This is a very strange string of questions."

"Is it? We are engaged." He was trying to keep it light and having a hard time.

Kiera looked at him like he was crazy. "It's fake."

"Is it?" he asked, because he felt like what had happened between them wasn't fake.

A blush colored her cheeks. "I honestly don't know."

And it stung to hear her say that.

What were you expecting?

He didn't know.

"Right. You're right."

Her expression changed. "What's wrong? What's happened?"

Henry sighed. "So about that meeting I was supposed to go to yesterday."

"Right. The meeting. I remember."

"I thought it was my father just wanting me to do his bidding. Only…"

"Only?" Kiera asked. "Only what?"

"Only there was a vote and I was removed from voting."

"Removed? I don't understand," she asked.

"My father decided to be my proxy, since he bought my shares. He took over my shares and voted on the future of Aspen Grace Memorial Hospital."

"And?" Her voice was very quiet.

"Aspen Grace Memorial Hospital is going to be closed."

"And the free clinic?" she asked, her voice tight.

"It's gone."

"What?"

Mike pulled up in front of Kiera's home and parked.

"Kiera, it was shut down. And instead of a new hospital being built, they're going to be building a private clinic that focuses on plastic surgery and medical spa-like treatments."

"Plastic surgery?" There was an accusatory tone in her voice.

"Yes."

"Well, isn't that convenient."

"What?"

"You missed the vote and…" She shook her head. "What's happening to all the staff?"

"Laid off. Except the surgeons get a severance package."

"I see," she said calmly. She glanced out the window. "Kiera…"

"No. No. You broke your end of the bargain."

"I said I would see what I could do when we made

this deal. I wasn't there, and if I had been, I would have put a stop to it. I would've fought."

"Sure."

"Kiera, I was sent here to put a stop to your protesting."

Her blush deepened. "Well, you did that."

"No. I didn't. I was going to sell my shares, but to someone who saw the value in Aspen Grace Memorial Hospital. Someone who would stand up to my father and help. I wanted to be done with him."

Kiera didn't say anything.

"You don't believe me, do you?"

"Why should I?" Kiera asked. "It just seems too convenient."

"What do you mean?" he asked.

"Plastic surgery. Your specialty. So you're going to extend your practice here then? And selling shares? That seems noble enough, but why didn't you tell me this before?"

"What are you talking about?"

Now he was angry. He felt bad this had happened, but it wasn't his fault. Why couldn't she see that? He hadn't wanted this, and there was nothing convenient about this situation.

"You're a plastic surgeon. Your clients come here, all the elite do."

"So? I don't want to live in Colorado. I don't want to be here. My home is in California. I won't be working at this private clinic."

The way she reeled back, it was as if he had slapped her across the face, as if he'd hurt her, and that was the last thing he ever wanted to do. He would never want to hurt her. He had come here to deal with her; instead, he'd fallen in love.

"Is this why you asked me to move to California?" she asked, her voice catching. "Because you knew I would be fired?"

"I want you, Kiera."

She shook her head. "What we have isn't real."

And that hurt him. "So you only slept with me because of our deal?" He hated saying it, but he was hurt and had lost control.

He was angry with his father. He was mad at himself. All he wanted was her.

His heart ached because he was falling in love with Kiera. He'd known that since the first night they had spent together, with that ridiculous pillow wall between them. Apparently, though, he was the only one feeling these emotions. He'd put his heart on the line and she'd crushed it.

Why had he let her through his barriers?

Because you're lonely.

"How dare you insinuate that! You know that I can't leave Colorado."

"Why?"

"Because we're strangers, because what we have isn't real…"

"It was real enough last night, Kiera. Or did you feel anything?"

Because he wasn't sure. He had certainly felt something. Last night he'd come alive again, and he hadn't realized how long he'd been asleep. Henry was putting a lot on the line here and was scared at what he was doing, but he was learning that life was too short not take a risk. And after last night, he wanted to take that risk with Kiera.

He just wanted Kiera.

All of her. He wrestled with his guilt and his need for her.

He wanted her in California with him because he couldn't be here in Colorado. He couldn't be where Michelle had died, where his parents still lived. He couldn't live this life here. There were too many bad memories. He wanted to start somewhere new with her. It didn't have to be California.

They had both been through a lot of heartache and trauma here.

To move forward he wanted to put this state behind him and never look back.

He wanted to run away with Kiera.

He didn't want to leave her behind, because he felt what had happened to Aspen Grace Memorial Hospital was his fault. He was the one who had cost Kiera her job and he wanted to take care of her, even though she was capable of taking care of herself.

She worried her bottom lip and shook her head. "No. No. I can't leave Mandy. I can't leave Mandy."

"Mandy is a grown woman. You can leave her. She's just an excuse to hold you back from living."

"You know nothing of my life. Nothing," she snapped.

"I know that you're too afraid to leave. You're either feeling guilty because you weren't here when Dr. Burke died or you've been waiting for your father to come back. He won't come back, but, Kiera, you don't have anything tying you down now. You can come to California."

Tears slipped out of her eyes and rolled down her cheek. She brushed them away quickly.

"I can't come to California. You just don't want to be alone. You just feel bad for me. You were using me to get out of a deal with your father."

"That's not it at all."

"No. I can't leave Colorado."

"You're afraid," he snapped. "You're afraid to leave Mandy. Why are you so afraid?"

"Why are you so afraid to make Colorado work? You run from things, Henry. So no, I'm not coming to California with you. I won't run after someone who is always leaving. You broke your promise to me and now I have to leave. I have work to do and a clinic to save. Just stay away from me."

Kiera climbed out of the car and grabbed her bag from Mike.

Henry just sat there.

Angry with himself. Angry that she walked away, but also angry with his father.

Blindingly angry with his father.

Controlling his life again.

And it was going to stop.

CHAPTER ELEVEN

KIERA WAS STRUGGLING to fight back tears as she opened the door to the house. She slammed it shut and leaned against it, closing her eyes and shaking. She was distraught that Aspen Grace Memorial was shutting down, but she was angry with herself because she was more upset about the fact that she had turned down Henry's offer.

That she had said no to California and to him, because part of her wanted to go.

Only she couldn't leave Colorado. Maybe he was right. Maybe she was waiting still.

Maybe emotionally she'd never left that diner.

Mandy was here, but there was a part of her deep down that clung to Aspen and Colorado. She was waiting for her father to come back, even though he never would. Her mother was dead, her dad in prison and Wilfred, he was dead, too. No one was coming for her.

Still, she couldn't leave her family. She couldn't leave Mandy alone.

Loneliness hurt, and she wouldn't put Mandy through that kind of pain.

And that realization had hit too close to home.

She was angry with herself, but she could live with

herself if it meant she was taking care of Mandy, because it was Mandy who needed her.

Does she?

Mandy had Derek. How long would she really need her?

She was afraid.

Afraid of getting hurt.

Afraid of being alone.

"Kiera?" Mandy called out.

"I'm home."

Mandy wheeled out of her bedroom with Sif in her lap. "Oh, thank goodness, I was just about to call the state troopers. Especially when I was told your car had been seen being towed into the shop. I even called Agnes and she said you'd left."

"The car died on the way back and my cell was dead, but I thought Henry called you?"

Or did he lie about that, too?

He hadn't told her about his past or the fact his father had sent him here to deal with her. What if he'd just slept with her to distract her.

Well, it had worked.

"Henry called me, but I was still worried. I'm glad you're okay." Mandy cocked her head to one side. "Are you okay?"

Kiera broke down. "No. I'm not okay."

She made her way to the couch and sat down, and that's when the floodgates opened. She couldn't hold it back any longer. It just came out of her. Emotions she hadn't realized she'd been holding back, since Dr. Burke had died and since she'd been left alone in the diner. Emotions she had kept in check for so long because she never wanted to seem ungrateful for the second chance she'd been given when Wilfred took her into his home.

She realized she'd forgotten how to feel. She'd been so busy trying to be happy, to be grateful, that she wasn't really feeling.

"What happened?" Mandy asked gently.

"We were engaged. Henry and I."

Mandy's eyes widened. "Engaged?"

Kiera nodded. "It was fake. Or I thought it was."

"It's not?" Mandy asked, confused.

"We spent last night together."

"Oh!" Mandy smiled. "What's wrong with that then?"

"Henry wants me to go to California with him."

"Why don't you?"

"How can I leave?"

"How can you not? This is your chance at love. Take it."

"Love?" Kiera asked numbly.

"Isn't it? You spent last night together, and I saw the way you two looked at each other. It's pretty obvious," Mandy said.

"Yes. I think I'm in love with him."

"I know! It's great," Mandy said, smiling.

"No. It's not. The board shut down Aspen Grace Memorial Hospital. There was some kind of coup with the board and the shareholders. Henry didn't get a chance to vote. The hospital was shut down, and the free clinic is gone."

"What're they going to build in its place?"

"Some kind of private plastic surgery clinic. One that caters to the rich. Face-lifts and Botox. Peels. Who knows?"

"I see."

"I lost my job."

Sif leaped down from Mandy's lap and clambered up into hers. Kiera stroked the ginger cat lovingly. Sif's moods were usually erratic, but it seemed that Sif knew she shouldn't be a crazy banana pants right now.

That Kiera needed to pet her. It was nice.

"And Henry is going back to California, I take it?" Mandy asked. "Without you?"

Kiera nodded. "He wanted me to go with him. I said no."

"Why? I mean, I thought the whole engagement thing was fast and surprising, but…"

"It was a fake engagement. He told his parents we were engaged to get them off his back, and in exchange he was going to protect the clinic for me. Then the coup happened, and the clinic didn't survive the cut."

Mandy rubbed her temples. "Okay, so let me get this straight, you guys were fake engaged. So in essence you both were sort of using each other to get something, but then you fell in love with him and he fell in love with you, and now neither of you is happy."

"He doesn't love me."

"He invited you to California. I would say he cares about you."

Kiera shook her head. "He doesn't love me."

"Why? Because he didn't keep his end of the bargain?"

"No."

"Then what?"

"I'm afraid. What if…" Kiera trailed off, unable to finish the sentence.

"He cheats on you like Brent cheated on you?"

Kiera sighed. "Yes…"

"He won't."

"Still… I…"

"Then what? Why did you turn him down? Are you feeling guilty about the hospital and the clinic? Don't… Don't feel guilty about that. There are other good clinics around. You might have to leave Aspen, but there are other towns close by. You did a lot for this community. There's nothing to feel guilty about. Go with him."

"I can't."

"Because you said no?" Mandy asked. "I don't think he'll care if you change your mind."

"Mandy, how I can leave you?" Kiera brushed the tears away. "After all you and your dad did for me? How can I leave Colorado? I've never been able to leave Colorado."

"Yeah, because you're waiting for your family to come back? They're not coming back."

"I know that." A tear slid down her cheek. "I know that now. And how foolish is that of me? I've been sitting around here waiting for them to come back, feeling like that little girl in the diner when you and your father were my family."

"Exactly. He loved you." Mandy reached out and took her hand. "I'm always here. I won't leave you. Wherever we go, we're family."

"I loved him. And he left, too. I can't leave you. I left you once and…"

"You are not the reason for my accident. Don't you ever feel guilty about that. I've made my peace with what happened, and all the work you've done has been admirable, but I never asked that of you. Kiera, I'm fine. I'm okay."

"No. Mandy… I don't want you to be alone."

Mandy took Kiera's hand. "I'm not alone, Kiera. That's what I'm trying to say to you. Derek and I are getting married. He proposed and I accepted."

Kiera's mouth dropped open. "You're getting married?"

Mandy nodded. "Yes. I'm happy, Kiera. I love hav-

ing you here in my life, and you're welcome to stay for-
ever. You're my sister. I love you, but don't put your life
on hold anymore. Not for the family that abandoned you
and certainly not for me."

Kiera began to sob when the realization hit her that
she *had* been putting her life on hold. She did the things
she did because she was just *paused*. How long had she
been doing that?

Waiting for people to come back as an excuse to keep
everyone away.

And it hurt, because it was Mandy she clung to. She
was so alone, but with Henry she felt alive.

It was scary to feel. To be alive.

She'd spent so many years, just frozen. Waiting.

And she didn't know what for. Her biological parents
were never coming back. Dr. Burke was dead. Mandy
had Derek. Mandy had found love and was happy. Kiera
had no one, but she could if she would take a leap of faith.

Mandy didn't need her, and Kiera had been using
Mandy as an excuse because she was so afraid of opening her heart, of letting someone in, of losing someone
again. She was afraid of being left behind.

"I love you, Kiera. I will admit that I'll hate it if you
move to California, but I want you to be as happy as I am
with Derek, and if Henry Baker is that person for you,
you have to take the chance. Live your life!"

Kiera nodded. "I think I blew it with him."

Mandy smiled. "I doubt that very much. Go, find him.
Make things right."

Kiera pulled Mandy into a hug, holding her tight. "I
love you."

"I know. I love you, too. Go. Be happy, that's all our
dad wanted. He wanted you to be happy and he would
be proud of you for working and fighting so hard for the

free clinic, but he also knew what love was with my mom. And he wanted that for you. He wanted that for both of us. So, go claim it."

Kiera nodded. Sif jumped down off her lap and scampered away like a bat out of hell, which was Sif's usual behavior around Kiera.

"I'll be back."

Mandy nodded. "I want to hear all about it later."

Kiera grabbed her purse and headed out the door. She didn't have a car, but Aspen Grace Memorial Hospital wasn't far from her place. And she hoped that Henry had gone there first to confront his father.

She hoped that he wasn't getting on a plane for California.

At least, not without her.

"You closed the free clinic?" Henry shouted as he slammed the door of the boardroom behind him.

Henry's father looked up from the paperwork he was doing at the table. "It bled money. It made sense fiscally to do that. Maybe if you had been here to vote..."

"Voting by proxy takes into account what the absentee voter wants. You didn't take that into account."

"I thought I did," his father said.

"Don't give me that bullshit, Father. Your lackeys might eat that up, but I'm not one of your lackeys. Even though you want me to be."

His father's lips formed a thin line and Henry knew that he'd pissed him off.

Good.

He wanted to pick a fight with someone. He was crushed that Kiera had been so hurt and blamed him.

And Henry was angry with himself for putting himself out there only to be rejected. That his heart, was once more the object of pain.

He was furious that his father had sent him to Aspen and put him in this situation. And he was mad with himself for allowing it all these years.

His father would never change.

And he was tired of trying to please his parents for love they couldn't give.

He was done.

And he wanted to fight.

"Well, I'm sorry that I didn't understand your wishes, but Henry, you didn't seem to understand mine when I asked you to come to Aspen and deal with the Dr. Brown situation. Instead, you brought her to one of my fundraisers, where she spent the whole evening chatting up investors who were more than happy to invest in the free clinic. And then I find out you're engaged to her. And you couldn't even announce it like I asked. You had to sneak around."

Henry was confused. "So are you telling me that the free clinic has money?"

"Yes the free clinic has money, but that's not the point. The point is you were supposed to come into Aspen and you were supposed to stop her from her ridiculous protesting and shut the free clinic and the hospital down. You owe me this."

"I owe you nothing. You're just mad she ruined your plans."

His father's eyes narrowed. "A free clinic in the medical facility we have planned will attract the wrong kind of people."

Henry shook his head. "And your son getting married to someone like Dr. Brown sends the wrong message."

"I put up with Michelle because, at the very least,

she wasn't an abandoned child of drug addicts. Did Dr. Brown tell you that? Did she tell you that she was left at the side of the road at a diner. Her mother died of an overdose in a dingy Montana slum hospital and her father is serving time for selling drugs. She's the child of meth heads."

"She saves lives!" Henry shouted. "And those people may have biologically brought her into this world, but she is not their daughter. She's Dr. Wilfred Burke's daughter and he was a well-respected and well-liked physician in Aspen. Kiera is nothing like the people who gave birth to her. She's better than that. She's a healer. And so am I."

"You do face-lifts." His father rolled his eyes. "It's done. There's no changing the board now."

"It's not going to look so good to all those people who gave money to the free clinic now, is it?" Henry warned. "You're building a spa now instead of a hospital with a free clinic. That looks bad."

His father's back stiffened. "You wouldn't?"

"No. You're right. I wouldn't, but I can sever ties with you and Mother. How would that look to your potential voters? Won't they question why the beloved son of Governor Baker has cut ties with his family? Especially since you seem to spout off that family ties are so important and that we're all so close. Maybe your voters would like to know that you sent me off to boarding school and that you chased away the woman I fell in love with because she was abandoned as a child."

"You wouldn't." His father stood up. "You wouldn't dare do that to me. Not after all I've done for you!"

"What have you done for me? You paid for my education—well, I can pay that back. You put me on the boards of hospitals in Colorado, but I can see that it was to protect your own assets. I am thankful for you helping me out after Michelle died, but enough. I owe you nothing. I don't care if it ruins me. I'm done with you."

"You're done with me?" his father shouted. "You're ungrateful, after everything I've done."

"For what? The only thing I'm grateful for is that you taught me what kind of man I never want to become." Henry turned on his heel and left.

It felt good to tell his father off.

It was a relief to let that all go, even though he knew that it really wouldn't help. His father wouldn't change and Kiera wouldn't change her mind about him.

He'd put his heart on the line and it was broken again, but he'd taken away something. He'd been so afraid of opening his heart again because of what had happened with Michelle and how her death had almost killed him, but he was lonely, and Kiera had made him feel alive again.

So, even though he didn't have her, Henry felt like he had won.

He just wished that he could have Kiera, too.

He was still in love with her.

He loved her.

And he wanted to marry her, but he'd ruined that. From the moment he'd made a deal with her, he'd ruined that.

He pushed people away because he was so afraid of being alone.

And he had no one to blame but himself.

As he walked down the empty halls of Aspen Grace Memorial Hospital, he tried to shake Kiera from his mind, but he couldn't.

He needed to make things right.

He needed Kiera in his life. He wouldn't give up on her. He wouldn't abandon her.

Even if it meant he had to give up his practice and his beach house, he couldn't live without Kiera.

"Henry!"

He turned around to find his father calling him. "What?"

"Come back. Just please come back and let's talk about this more."

"What more is there to say, Father?"

"Just. Please," his father begged quietly.

Henry nodded and headed back into the boardroom.

"Fine," his father said.

"Fine what?" Henry asked.

"We'll put a free clinic into the new medical facility. It's won't be a hospital, but there will be a clinic. There's enough money to hire back some of the staff from Aspen Grace Memorial. We'll have an emergency free clinic available, and we can work with the other hospital in town for patients."

"You came up with that idea fast."

"It's what was suggested at the board meeting that you missed, but you're right. I turned it down and appointed someone as chairman who would vote the way I wanted."

"You performed a coup, Father. Don't sugarcoat it. I'm not a child."

His father nodded. "You can tell your fiancée that her clinic is saved, but Aspen Grace is in disrepair and it would cost too much to retrofit it and expand."

"I understand."

"I will make the calls to the appropriate staff. I just ask that you don't sever ties with us publicly. And don't sever the ties with your mother. In her own way she does care for you. It would... It would break her heart if you did that."

"I doubt that. She didn't have much time for me."

His father sighed. "That was my fault. She cares for you. She does. Please don't hurt her."

It touched Henry to hear his father talk so softly about his wife. It surprised Henry.

Maybe his father wasn't made of stone.

And Henry wasn't, either.

Henry nodded. "Thank you."

"You're welcome. I do care for you, Henry. I know we sent you off to boarding school, but that's…that's what I knew. It was how I was raised and… I'm sorry if I hurt you. I was wrong, but this is all I know how to give. I don't want you out of my life. I didn't want this to come to blows like this. I'm sorry for holding your mistakes over you."

Henry nodded. "And I hope that you understand that the way I am is all I can give right now to you, as well, but I am willing to try. You did the right thing here today, Father. You bit the bullet and it's a good thing. Keeping the clinic open is the right thing."

"I can't hire back Dr. Brown though."

"Why?" Henry asked.

"It would seem like nepotism in my election year. So I do apologize about that."

"Father, she's not really my fiancée. I persuaded her to pretend to be my fiancée to annoy you, and it worked."

His father smiled. "Is that so?"

"Well, I guess the apple doesn't fall too far from the tree, does it?"

"Then, offer her her job back. If you're not getting married to her, then please announce that so it doesn't look like nepotism."

"I will." Henry went to open the door.

"I do find it strange, though."

"What?" Henry asked, pausing with his hand on the door handle.

"I could've sworn that you two were in love. The way you two looked at each other during the fundraiser. The way I saw you look at her here in the halls of the hospital. And from what I saw in the papers when you two were at that small pizza place. I could've sworn that it was real."

"Papers," Henry asked, bewildered. This wasn't Los Angeles.

His father handed him one of the gossip tabloids that Henry was always featured in. And there it was. A picture of him and Kiera. They'd managed to snap pictures of him with a "mystery redhead," or so the headline teased.

He smiled at the picture and handed it back to his father.

"Well, it's not. I'll make sure she knows that her job is safe. Thank you."

His father nodded. "And I'll get your mother to lay off with the matchmaking. She just wants to see you happy. As do I."

Henry didn't say any more. He opened the door to the boardroom for a second time and left. His heart was aching.

He could've sworn that there were feelings between him and Kiera, but he'd been wrong.

And his heart was paying the price.

"Henry! Wait!"

He turned and saw Kiera standing at the end of the hallway. She looked out of breath, her hair was flyaway and her cheeks were bright red from the cold.

"Kiera, what are you doing here?" he said as he closed the gap. She was still trying to catch her breath.

"Sorry, the cold... I ran."

"I gather that," Henry said. "Why are you here?"

"I'm here for you."

* * *

Kiera's heart was racing and she couldn't believe what she was about to do. When she'd been with other men, when the relationship ended, she hadn't really cared.

Except for Brent.

She'd closed off her heart after Brent had broken it. She had gotten on with her life. She had had Mandy, but now she'd let Henry into her heart.

And when she thought he had betrayed her or used her, it had devastated her. Yet, he had asked her to go to California.

He had showed that he cared and she was so scared to move.

So scared to open her heart and take a chance.

Her pulse was racing. She had run all the way to Aspen Grace Memorial. Even though everything was mostly shut down, she still had a pass to the staff entrance and she'd gotten in. She'd just hoped that she wasn't too late and that Henry hadn't left.

And she wasn't too late.

He was still here.

She didn't know what to say.

"You're here for me?" he asked, confused.

She nodded and swallowed the hard lump that had formed in her throat, because she had never said what she was about to say to anyone, except Mandy.

She had never told Dr. Burke that she loved him.

She had never told anyone that she loved them. Not even Brent, because she'd told her parents that when she was small and they'd left her anyway.

It was a huge risk, but Kiera was tired of waiting.

She was tired of being alone.

Tired of waiting for a family that didn't exist. She had to make her own family and that family was Henry.

Henry was her family.

He drove her bonkers and she hated his father and everything his father represented, but she loved Henry.

He was her person.

And she wanted marriage, babies, everything with him. She wanted love, the hurt, the laughter, she wanted everything. She wanted everything she had secretly dreamed about.

He was her everything, and she had been almost stupid enough to let that slip through her fingers because she was a fool.

"I'm here for you." Tears stung her eyes. "This is hard for me to say."

"It's okay," he said gently. "You can tell me anything."

"Okay," she whispered. "Okay."

"You're shaking."

"I know." She smiled and reached up to touch his face, tears rolling down her cheeks. "I love you, Henry. Against every rational fiber in my being, I love you. You made me feel safe in a world where I have never felt safe. I've been using Mandy as a crutch, waiting for people who are never coming back. I've been wasting my life. Holding myself back. I love you."

He smiled at her tenderly. "I love you, too. And I'm sorry."

"For what? You tried to save the hospital. I know that's not your fault."

"No, I'm sorry for not telling you about my past and the debt I owed to my father. I was embarrassed by my mistakes. I still am, but they won't stop me. I don't want to leave you ever."

Her heart soared and tears slid down her cheeks. "I think I need you to kiss me."

"I want to do that, too, but I have something to tell you."

"Oh?"

"The free clinic has been saved. I told my father about us and I threatened to cut ties with him, which would ruin his political career, so he saved the free clinic."

"How?" Kiera asked, taking a step back. "It was bleeding money."

"That night at the fundraiser, you raised a lot more money than you know. The clinic is saved and it's yours if you want it. We can't offer jobs back to everyone who lost their jobs here at Aspen Grace Memorial, but we can hire back quite a few to run that emergency clinic."

"I'm so glad the clinic is saved, but I don't... I don't want it."

Henry raised an eyebrow. "What? I thought that's what you wanted? All this time, fighting with me tooth and nail. The awful signs you made."

Kiera laughed. "It's what I thought I wanted, but it was just something holding me here. I used it as a reason not to leave and not to live my life. You helped me come alive again, Henry. And, I don't want it. Mandy is getting married and moving on... I don't want to be held back. I love you and I want to be with you. And you love California. I've never been to California and I think I would like to go."

"What about Agnes, what about your patients?"

"Agnes will understand and Dr. Carr can take care of her. What I want is you. I want to live my life. Finally. I want to be with you."

She couldn't stop crying as the truth was revealed. She'd spent so much of her life trying to be controlled, trying not to let her emotions show, but it all just came spilling out of her.

"I love you, too, Kiera and I want you. I've held everyone at bay since Michelle died and I used her memory as a shield to keep myself from being hurt again, but then you showed up and got under all those defenses. I fought it as long as I could, but you brought me back to life, too, Kiera. I never thought for a second that you would be the one to bring me back to the land of the living, but you did. And, if you'll have me, I would like to turn our fake engagement into something real?"

"Yes." She smiled. "Yes. I would like that, too."

She threw her arms around him and Henry scooped her up, kissing her. He set her back down on her feet.

"So, I guess this time we can talk about a ring then?"

"A ring?" She laughed. "I don't need a ring."

"Oh, you need a ring now. And I'm not taking no for an answer."

"Should we tell your father it's for real this time?" Kiera asked.

Henry glanced back. "Later. How about we go take Mandy and her fiancé out for dinner? Let's celebrate with your family."

"That sounds like a plan, Dr. Baker. That sounds like a good plan indeed."

They walked out of the empty hospital hand in hand. Her heart was so full.

And for the first time since being a little girl, she felt like she was finally going home. The family she had longed for, for so long, had finally come to get her.

She was no longer incomplete, frozen and stuck in a holding pattern.

She was whole.

She was going to have a family and a real place to call home.

EPILOGUE

A year later, Huntington Beach, California

THERE WERE NO witnesses except for a justice of the peace who was standing beside him at the edge of the ocean and a small laptop sitting on a table that was connected to another laptop in Aspen, Colorado.

Mandy, Derek and Sif were crowded on the small laptop screen as Henry stood on the beach in the same suit he'd worn the day he met Kiera, exactly one year ago.

They hadn't wanted a big society type of wedding, even though that had been his mother's preference. Henry had been able to keep her at bay by promising her that she could throw a big society event when they headed back to Aspen next week.

One event. That's all Henry was going to give his parents. One photo opportunity. The rest of the time he planned to spend locked away in his Aspen condo with his new bride. This time, she wouldn't be shimmying out of the bed and there would definitely be no pillow walls between them.

It was just going to be the two of them, locked away for a good week.

There would be no work.

No traumas.

No medicine.

Just them.

Kiera walked down the stairs from his beach house. She was wearing a flowing white dress, and an ocean breeze caught it briefly. She laughed and held the dress down as she descended the steps and walked barefoot across the sand toward him.

His heart swelled with pride as he saw her.

Her red hair was braided back, but down, and golden strands shimmered in the bright California sun.

She was absolutely breathtaking.

Once they were in California, she had gotten a job as a trauma surgeon in the best hospital in Los Angeles, and for the last year they had been working hard.

After the ceremony, they were having a nice month-long vacation, and he was going to make the best of it.

She stood in front of him, smiling.

He took her hands.

"You sure about this?" she asked.

"Positive."

Kiera waved to Mandy and Derek on the screen.

The justice of the peace stepped forward.

"We're gathered here today to witness the union of Henry Terrance Baker and Kiera Micheline Brown. Do you, Henry Terrance, take Kiera Micheline to be your lawfully wedded wife?"

Henry smiled. "I do."

He pulled out a rose gold band that she had picked out from an antique shop in Venice Beach and slipped it on her slender finger.

"And do you, Kiera Micheline, take Henry Terrance to be your lawfully wedded husband?"

"I do." She pulled a simple platinum band out of her dress and slipped it on his finger.

"Then by the power invested in me by the state of California, I now pronounce you man and wife. You may kiss your bride."

Henry smiled, pulled Kiera in close and kissed her, like he'd been wanting to do as he'd counted down the days until they were locked away together in Aspen.

Kiera laughed and blushed.

Henry paid the justice of the peace, who handed them their certificate and then left them alone with their only wedding guests on the laptop.

"Congratulations, you two!" Mandy shouted. "We can't wait until you guys get here tomorrow."

"I'm excited to see you two, as well!" Kiera blew them a kiss and logged off.

Henry picked up the laptop and took his new bride's hands as they stood on the beach together.

"So where do we go for dinner?" he asked.

"I think I'd rather stay in."

He grinned lazily. "Well, you're going to have a whole month of staying in when we get to Aspen."

She cocked an eyebrow. "Is that a threat?"

"You can count on it," he teased, kissing her again. "It's just going to be the two of us on this honeymoon. We'll visit Mandy and Derek, and attend that one event for my mom, but the rest of the time, in our condo, it's just going to be you and me."

Kiera blushed and worried her bottom lip. "About it being the two of us…"

"What?"

"Remember that night a month ago? When we weren't on opposite shifts? That night in the hot tub?"

He grinned. "Yes. I remember that night quite well."

After two months of working opposite shifts, they had finally had a night together and he had taken full of advantage. He'd thought of that night quite often while waiting for their wedding day and monthlong honeymoon. So much so that he had had a hot tub installed at their place in Aspen.

He was going to surprise her with it.

"Well, it's not the two of us anymore."

It took him a moment to let that sink in. "What?"

"I'm pregnant. In about eight months, it's going to be the three of us."

"Are you serious?" he asked.

"Pretty sure. I did several tests because I was kind of shocked. I thought I had the flu, so I had a couple of different swabs while working in the emergency room."

Henry grinned and kissed her. "I'm so happy. We're going to have a baby."

Kiera grinned. "We are. So any kind of hot tub night you have planned in Aspen will have to wait."

"That's fine." He kissed her again and then reached down to touch her belly. "Hot tub time can wait. All I want is you…you two, and we can still have our honeymoon."

She blushed and wrapped her arms around his neck. "We most certainly can. I love you, Henry."

"I love you, too."

And he scooped her into his arms, carrying her up the stairs from the beach to their house to show her exactly what he had in mind for their honeymoon.

What he planned for the rest of their life.

* * * * *

COMING SOON!

We really hope you enjoyed reading this book.
If you're looking for more romance, be sure to
head to the shops when new books are
available on

Thursday 19th
August

MILLS & BOON

Coming next month

SECOND CHANCE WITH HER GUARDED GP
Kate Hardy

'In London, I never really got to see the sky properly,' he said. 'Out here, it's magical.' He turned her to face him. 'You make me feel magical, too, Gemma,' he said softly. 'And, right now, I really want to kiss you.'

'I want to kiss you, too,' she said.

He dipped his head and brushed his mouth against hers, and her lips tingled at the touch.

'Sweet, sweet Gemma,' he said softly, and kissed her again.

It felt as if fireworks were going off in her head. She'd never experienced anything like this before, and she wasn't sure if it made her feel more amazed or terrified.

When Oliver broke the kiss and pulled away slightly, she held his gaze. His pupils were huge, making his eyes seem almost black in the twilight.

She reached up to touch his mouth, and ran her forefinger along his bottom lip,

He nipped gently at her finger.

Suddenly, Gemma found breathing difficult.

'Gemma,' he said, his voice husky. 'I wasn't expecting this to happen.'

'Me neither,' she whispered. And this was crazy. She knew he was only here temporarily, and he'd probably go back to his life in London once his locum job here had finished and his twin had recovered from the transplant. Was she dating him purely because being a temporary colleague made him safe – she wouldn't be reckless enough to lose her heart to someone who wouldn't stick around? Or would it be like the misery of all those years ago when her parents had moved and left her behind?

'We ought to be heading back,' she said. Even though both of them knew there was no reason why they couldn't stand on the cliffs all evening, just kissing, the unexpected intensity of her feelings scared her.

Continue reading
SECOND CHANCE WITH HER GUARDED GP
Kate Hardy

Available next month
www.millsandboon.co.uk